CROSS *Linked*

CROSS LINKED SERIES BOOK 1

CROSS LINKED SERIES BOOK 1

RUSHELL ANN

CROSS LINKED SERIES

Cross Linked

Calm the Strom

All rights reserved. In accordance with the U.S. Copyright Act of 1976, the scanning, uploading, and electronic sharing of any part of this book with the permission of the publisher is unlawful piracy and theft of the author's intellectual property. Thank you for your support of the author's rights.
This book is a work of fiction. Names, characters, places, and incidents are the product of the author's imagination or are used fictitiously. Any resemblance to actual events, locales, or person, living or dead, is coincidental.

Copyright 2019 by Rushell Ann
Formatting by Red Umbrella Graphic Designs
Cover Art by Storm Cagle

To my dear niece Catherine:

Your enthusiastic attitude about my writing helped push me to finally finishing it. You walked through the first part of this story with me and helped edit it. Thank you for being as excited as I am about writing! One day you will see how beautiful your own art is and know that you shine like the brightest star in the sky!

Chapter One
Mysterious Friends

I still get queasy thinking about being with her, dead or not. I've had hopes she would call me to tell me she missed me, that she was sorry for the way she treated me and we could put all those bad memories in the past and bond like "normal" siblings. Normal? I'm still not sure what that is.

There was a time when we were little and Mom and Dad were still alive that Sam and I were inseparable, especially against the other kids in the coven. Samantha was my rock I followed without question until the time came for my magic to show itself (which it didn't) and her to realize that fitting in meant pushing me away. I had learned the supernatural community had a word for a human that had no magic, millies. The coven looked down on humans that had no special ability. Being called a millie was an insult and I was a millie. That was when I realized I had only myself to rely on, and how I mourned for my parents that had raised me to love strong and depend on family, but no more. Dead was dead, and I wouldn't be able to keep that hope for change.

Getting aboard a plane and flying isn't something that I was looking forward too, knowing where the plane would take me. I wish the old wives tails of witches flying on brooms were true because my stomach was rolling thinking about sitting so snug next to someone. I tried to avoid this when I booked my flight, but Ryan had insisted that our budget didn't warrant two seats, which I didn't understand since the tickets were paid by Sam's trust. I tried explaining myself but was cut off many times and told to just deal with it.

I'm taking deep breaths and trying to get as comfortable as I could, but I'm seriously considering coming up with some punishment for Ryan. Money hadn't ever been a problem for him as a commercial pilot especially with all the overtime he's been working lately. I have my own income from my part-time work at the nursery that I pretty much bank into savings. Money he won't allow me to touch because he insists he can take care of me. I stopped trying to argue my point on why I wanted to fly first class or buy two seats but he always wins so I gave up. This isn't a vacation, soaking up the sun on a warm sandy beach with a margarita in my hand. This is a funeral and bad memories. I wasn't drawn to violence much but sometimes I wanted to throat punch my husband.

"When the drink cart comes by get me an ice tea with three sugars but no straw. I hate how those little straws always fall out and splash you. Don't you hate that, dear?" my seat partner says to me.

I did mention I don't get along very well with strangers, didn't I?

"I'm sure you can order your drink when they get here." I smiled, trying hard to muster up my calm self, not that I'm mean to people but talking to strangers has always been difficult for me. I use to smile all the time and then I didn't. It had started when my folks died and got worse when I was kicked out of my coven.

"Oh no, dear, I'm channeling my soul mate. I felt him enter the plane after we were seated. Did you see that hunky man walk toward the back? I've had a few snippets of him over the years, but I've never been this close. This might be the time," she tells me as she lays her head back closing her eyes.

Seriously?

I have to learn to get along with others; I can't always judge a book by its cover. I couldn't tell where she descended from with her milk chocolate skin, braided midnight hair, bright clothes, and an accent I couldn't place.

"Soul mate, huh? No, I didn't happen to see your soul mate pass by, but if I get a chance I'll be sure to switch seats with him." This is going to be a long flight. Is my Karma that off?

It wouldn't be so bad if she didn't smell like nag champa, let alone having a handbag the size of my kitchen sink digging into my side.

"Did you hear that?" I asked the woman. I really need to get her name.

"Oh, and what did you hear, it wasn't my spirit guide was it? She always seems to flitter off when I need her. If you see her, you just let me know," the strange woman chimed as she continued to dig in her body bag.

I turned and looked at her, trying my hardest to see her as the bright, bubbly, older woman she was, but I was losing the battle with my attitude. Talking with her was helping my mind from thinking about memories best left buried. Do they serve alcohol on this flight?

Goddess I hope so.

I heard it again, a cat. I was certain and it was coming from her huge purse.

"Do you need me to get some tuna for the cat in your bag?" I inquired.

I was sure she wasn't allowed to have a cat in her purse, but I was not about to be the one who delayed the plane. Having the plane get off the runway was my top priority; my anxiety was on the rise. Soon I would be grabbing my carry-on and flying off the plane.

"Thank you, sweetheart, that's quite generous of you, but no. We just ate," she said with a straight face.

"I didn't catch your name dear, mine is Rosie Guerrero. But you can call me Rosie." She grinned at me and her smile met her eyes, which were these amazing burnished golden brown, ones like I had never seen. I really did need to adjust my attitude. I used to be a nice easygoing person, but years of cruel behavior from the coven had left me a little bitter.

"I'm Averill Beaumont, but you can call me Avery." I smiled at her, for once not annoyed by her presence.

That seemed to keep her quiet for a while anyway, long enough for me to try to relax and enjoy the view. Having a window seat was non-negotiable but made it almost impossible to get to the bathroom. I had better not have that drink I was drooling over; maybe sleep was on the agenda.

I'm not sure how long I was asleep for, but it wasn't long enough.

"Avery dear, the drink cart is coming. I'll order for you. You just go back to sleep." Rosie was practically jumping out of her seat with anticipation.

I sigh. "No Rosie, that's fine, wide awake now." Being sleep deprived is nothing new; nightmares have plagued me since I left Seattle, which has resulted in insomnia.

"What would you like?" The flight attendant grinned at me.

"I'd really like a Mountain Dew if you have it," I asked, knowing they didn't serve Dew.

"Sorry, we have coke products, but I do have a lime drink," she says as she searches through the drinks.

I closed my eyes and pictured an ice-cold mountain dew drink sliding down my parched throat. So much for our families supposed witchy powers. It might come in handy when I really wanted a Dew drink.

"I'll just take whatever lime drink you have, thanks." I opened my eyes, waiting for the drink.

As the flight attendant searched through her cart, I tried not thinking about the fact that I wouldn't be seeing my sister again. You always think you have the time to repair a relationship, call the person and apologize for whatever they thought you had done. This wasn't a fight between squabbling sisters. This was about not being good enough to be a part of a group that was my family, my coven.

I had been thinking about Samantha a lot over the past year. Wanting to pick up the phone and call, even offer to buy her and Aurora a plane ticket to come visit, but years of rejection from that community would always bring the phone back down with a bang. I didn't hold it against them that they were different, so why because I had not an ounce of power in my pinky finger was I the different "normal" one? Time had taught me to push all that back into the furthest recesses of my mind, proving easier to forget than to try to understand and deal with the pain in my heart that I had lost the only family I had left.

"Well, would you look at that? You are in luck today. I found a Mountain Dew. Not sure where it came from but it's all yours!" she tells me as she pours my drink.

I accepted the drink, thankful to whoever put that beloved item on this cart. It looked like my flight wouldn't be as disastrous as I thought.

The flight lasted almost six hours, which I slept off and on, and when I wasn't sleeping I was trying to read the book I brought. Miss Rosie had other ideas most of the time between telling me all about her spirit guide and trying to explain about her fascination with dream diagnosis. As talkative as she was, I started to listen to what she was telling me. Her knowledge on dreams was incredible; I might have to do some research on that one. My dreams since I turned eighteen have been bizarre to say the least.

"Rosie, what do you think about dreams involving wolves?"

This was the first time I had told anybody about my dreams; they just never made sense, and I didn't want anyone to think I was even stranger.

"Wolves you say? Well, I'd have to look in my books for reference, but I'd say that you need to be freed from something. Let me get back to you on that one. What do the wolves in your dream do?" She got out a small notebook and pen. She was really going to try to help me. For the first time in my life someone wanted to help me.

"It's not always the same dream, but there are several wolves, always the same ones and we're running through the woods. Sometimes we are playing and other times we are searching for something."

"So, in these dreams, are you with them or one of them?" Rosie asked.

"I think I'm one of them, though I'm not sure how I know that. When it's the dream where I'm one of the wolves I can't see myself."

"That's interesting. When you are with these other wolves do you feel anything specific?" Rosie inquired.

Should I tell her? "I…I feel–" I looked away from Rosie.

I felt a light touch on my hand. "Honey, listen to me. You can't be ashamed about your dreams or your feelings. Too many people hide from themselves. I won't judge you none, just tell me." Rosie smiled.

"I…I feel loved, a love I can't explain, but it feels like an all-encompassing love that transcends everything, like something is touching my soul. At times when I wake up, I cry uncontrollably because that feeling of love is gone and I want it back." Talking about this brings that tightness back in my chest and something else, guilt that I was married and dreaming about love.

"Now don't you worry about this, Rosie is going to help you figure this out. Give me your phone number and when I get home I'm going to do some research, and I'll get back to you. I have some friends that live out on a reservation and they have a few legends I need to ask about. How long are you going to be away from home?" Rosie wrote down my address and started talking but not to me, to her spirit guide. It's times like this that I would have thought of her as a coo-coo woman, but now I just think she is divine.

"I should only be a few days. My sister passed away, and I have to see to her funeral and bring my niece home with me." Telling Rosie this makes me feel bad that I haven't broken down yet over her death. Out of the two of us I was always the more emotional one.

"Oh Avery, I am sorry about your sister. It's good your niece is coming home with you. Misplacing a mother is always very hard, but she'll be fine with you for a while," Rosie stated.

Misplaced was such a strange word to use. I didn't have long to ponder that thought.

As Rosie continued to talk to her spirit guide, my mind started to wander back to the day I got the call about my sister. A costumer at the nursery had locked her keys in the car, and I had just managed to get the passenger door open–a trick I picked up from my grandpa–when my cell rang.

"Hello?" I answered the phone thinking it was Ryan calling from a layover.

"Yes, can I speak with Averill Sinclair?" When anyone called me by my maiden named it always sent a chill down my arms.

"This is Avery Sinclair, but its Beaumont now. How can I help you?"

"My name is Jeff Clett from Clett, Hammond, and Tyson. We're a law firm in Seattle, Washington. I'm sorry to call with this type of news, but your sister has passed away. She left instructions in her will that you were to become guardian of Aurora, her daughter. Her funeral will be a week from today. I hope that's enough time for you to get here. There are funds set aside to buy your plane ticket, so you let me know when you can get away and I'll make all the arrangements."

"Excuse me, Jeff, is that your name? Did you say that my sister is dead?" I boomed.

Who is this person, talking faster than a jackrabbit?

"Yes, my name is Jeff. Your sister hired us about a year ago and set up her will with instructions for us to call you if anything happened to her. I understand this must be a shock, but I have everything ready for you. Once you get into town, please call me and we can arrange a meeting. Your sister left a few things for you. Again, I'm sorry to have to be the one to tell you this. One of your sister's friends is staying at your sister's house with your niece. Do you need directions?"

"No...I...I'm sure she still lives in our parent's house if she's in Seattle. Thank you for calling. I will get back to you back when I know I can fly out." I had hung up and numbly opened the car door for the poor woman next to me. The woman was so thankful I was able to get her door open that she tried to pay me, but I turned her down. I had other things on my mind.

One thing that bothered me is I thought I would always just know when something extreme happened to Sam, just as we both felt it when our Mom and Dad had died. So it seemed strange that I hadn't had one of those feelings.

"Dear, are you okay?" Rosie asked as she softly touched my arm.

I turned to her and said, "Yes, yes, just thinking."

Just as I was about to explain to Rosie, the pilot came over the speakers and announced our decent into SeaTac Airport.

"Well, it looks like we have arrived. I'm so glad your husband didn't let you upgrade your ticket to first class or we would have never met and become great friends. I'm only stopping here for a few days and then it's back to New Mexico for me. I will call you when I gather up all the information I can." She held both my shoulders in her hands, squeezing. "Don't worry about anything, my spirit guide says things will work out, and she's never wrong," Rosie said and winked at me.

As we walked to the baggage claim I wondered how Rosie knew that I had wanted to upgrade my flight but before I could think more on that Rosie clapped and snapped my attention to her and away from my thoughts.

"Well dear, this is goodbye. For now, that is!" she gave me one last exuberant hug.

"Wait, Rosie, what about your soul mate?" I asked as I looked around for the man she had pointed out to me earlier.

"Oh, he's around here somewhere. I'm sure my trip won't be wasted!" And just like that she fluttered away with her long flowery skirt trailing behind her.

I just hugged a virtual stranger and that made me get a warm feeling in the depths of my chest. When was the last time I hugged someone? Physical contact became a foreign concept to me after my parents died, and besides what little intimate contact that Ryan displayed or had time for, my physical interactions with people was limited. I shook my head, clearing it out. I think this is a new friendship, if you can call it that, which might be very interesting. Making friends has always been more difficult for me, always feeling awkward not knowing the things to say in conversations, or more like what I'm thinking pops out of my mouth and most people don't appreciate that.

I retrieved my bag, made my way to through the busy airport, and managed to get a decent rental car for my uncomfortable drive to my childhood home while sitting in traffic. I don't miss Seattle's gridlock, that's for sure. One thing North Carolina has that Seattle doesn't is the sun. I do miss aspects of Seattle, like the culture and diversity, the way the city is always alive and moving, but I don't miss the gloomy days where you long for some sunshine.

My childhood home located in the Greenwood area of Seattle has a love-hate relationship with me. I always loved being so close to the lake where I would take frozen peas and feed the ducks. It was the one place I truly could be alone without the prying eyes of the coven.

As I pulled up to the house all those fears and hurt feelings surfaced right up through my chest. I leaned my head on the steering wheel and focused on taking deep breaths. In through the nose and out through the mouth. Isn't that what I'm supposed to do? Focus on something, anything. I could only assume the person watching over Aurora was Matilda, the head of the coven. I know, totally cliché. I had heard my folks once say that her birth name was something like Barbara, and she didn't feel it was "witchy" enough so she had it changed. To this day, I never thought of my parents as ignorant, but when it came to Matilda and her coven, they walked the line of ignoring Matilda's heavy handed behavior even if they felt it was wrong.

I mustered all the courage I could and got out of the car. I stood in front of a place that always brought two conflicting emotions, love and pain. All my childhood memories were here, every hug from my parents, every kiss to the forehead at night when they would tug me in after reading a story; to the pain of standing in my living room and being told that my mom and dad were dead. Once I walked up the wide cement stairs to the front door, all I could think about was Aurora. I hadn't seen her since she was a toddler running around in her diaper, calling me Airy. She was another reason I didn't want to leave the coven, but I was an outcast, and they would have killed me if I stayed. My Mom wasn't here anymore to protect me from this woman's hateful wrath, and either was Sam. I was thirteen when my parents died and Sam was my rock. In the beginning after our parents died Sam would stand up to Matilda. She wouldn't let her negative energy anywhere near me. As time went on and Sam threw herself into the magic world learning and growing as a witch, she left me behind. I can't say I blame her though; being part of a group has a secure feeling,

particularly having no parents around. I wasn't even sure if she knew about the death threats I received as a child.

As I was about to knock on the door it opened and a teenager I hardly recognized stood in front of me. Almost as tall as my five foot six frame with her white blond hair that hung halfway down her back. It was the eyes that made tears spring to the forefront, blue like the Hawaiian coast; sad eyes that wanted to be swallowed up.

"Hi, Auntie Avery," Aurora cried with a wobbly voice.

"Hi kiddo, it's been awhile." I started to reach for her, but she beat me to it. She threw herself at me and hugged me tight, shaking with sobs. I hadn't seen her since she was around three, but I made sure I sent letters and pictures of me so that Aurora would know she had family out in the world who loved her. She often wrote back, unbeknownst to her Mom.

"Oh Aurora, it's okay. It's going to be okay. Shh... Shhhh." I coo, holding her tight. "I'm here; we'll get through this together."

I heard someone clear there throat and I knew that immediately who it was as my body locked tight.

I stiffened my stance and tried to ignore it.

"Let's go sit down, Aurora; I want to get a good look at you." I pulled away from her with much reluctance and walked into the living room towards the sofa that sat under the large window facing the street.

Aurora turned towards the sound and standing with her hands on her hips, was the one woman I blamed most for my fractured family and the reason I hadn't seen my sister in close to ten years. I ignored my feelings and encouraged Aurora to sit down.

"Well well, if it isn't Avery. I never thought we would see you again. When you left, promising us you wouldn't return, we assumed that's what you meant," Matilda said with a brittle voice as she sashayed her way over to the chair opposite the couch.

Bitch.

"I would say that the circumstances surrounding the reason I came home would seem clear. I don't want to get into an argument with you Matilda, just leave it alone," I pleaded.

I turned toward Aurora. "Wow, you're almost all grown up! What are you fifteen or sixteen now?" I couldn't get over how much she looked like her Mom. Same face, same eyes. The white blond hair was the only thing I could see she must have gotten from her Dad whom I had never met and Sam wouldn't talk about.

"I'm almost sixteen, well half way there at the least. Auntie Avery, I'm so glad you're here. Mom's funeral is tomorrow, and I want you there with me. Say you'll come with me, please." She squeezed my hand, which meant she didn't want to be around Matilda any more than I did.

"Of course, I'll be there. What time is the funeral? I have an appointment with the lawyer later tomorrow afternoon," I asked both Aurora and Matilda.

"You are not welcome at a coven funeral, Avery," Matilda spat angrily.

"Matilda, please. My Mom would have…," Aurora started to say.

That pushed my buttons quick. I wasn't going to let this woman make my niece beg for anything. "Let me handle this, honey. I'm thirsty, could you see if you can find me some earl grey tea, two sugars, and some cream? Thanks, sweetheart." I nudged her with my hand to stand.

I stood and turned once Aurora was out of earshot.

How dare you speak to me like that? She was my sister, my family!" I pounded on my chest. "You people have taken everything from me. My father, my mother, and now my sister. I will come to the funeral, and you will keep your mouth shut around Aurora or so help me, Matilda–" I sat down taking as many deep breaths as I could without appearing to lose control. One thing Matilda didn't stand for was defiance.

"You are still the snot-nosed dud millie you were when you left. I tried to get your mother to give you up to a non-magic family, but she had it in her head that you were just a late bloomer. You can't threaten me," she said with a menacing look. "I would watch your step while you're here. You have no magic to defend yourself, and I would hate for Aurora to lose the last of her family." She started to point her finger at me. Finger pointing was how most magic was directed.

Before I could retort, Matilda went flying backwards and slammed down and into the chair.

"I have never been one to use magic against another witch, but you aren't acting the way my mother would have wanted you to. This is my Aunt, my family, the one I will be leaving with a few days from now. We both will be attending the funeral, and I don't want anyone from the coven speaking to Avery." Aurora walked into the living room and set my tea on the coffee table in front of me, smiling the whole time. Calm as can be.

I stared awe star stuck for a moment. It looked like my worries for Aurora weren't warranted, she had more of her Mom in her then I expected.

I patiently waited for Matilda to retort, but she wasn't saying anything, just glaring at us.

"Aurora, how come Matilda isn't moving or saying anything?" I asked as I peeked around Aurora to get a look at her. The spell didn't seem to affect her facial features because her eyes were squinting daggers at us. She wasn't the most attractive woman. Tall and lanky with a pointy nose and cheek bones. There didn't seem to be any softness in her at all. Her salt and pepper black hair was pulled into a tight bun at the back. Her clothing was the only thing that I ever like about Matilda. Today she was wearing a long cashmere sweater paired with a pair of black stretch pants with knee high boots.

Aurora waved her hands in the air. "Oh, well, that's a binding spell, which I must say hasn't worked that great before. I guess when you're mad it makes the spell a wee bit stronger." She chuckled. "Don't worry Auntie, I haven't hurt her, but she's going to be pissed when I let her go. Maybe we shouldn't go to the funeral; it's not as if they found a body. I would prefer to get my stuff packed and shipped. Besides we have to figure out how to ship Bella. She's not going to like to be caged; I bet I could give her some type of herb to keep her calm," Aurora mused.

Aurora just sat next to me, talking like nothing is wrong, while I stared at Matilda wondering what it was like and how it felt to put that woman in her place. I could tell Aurora was just trying to spare my feelings with the funeral, but I would let her have this one, as long as I didn't have to face those women.

"Auntie, are you listening to me?" Aurora snapped her fingers in my face.

"Oh, right, yes I am. Sorry, it's been awhile since I've seen magic used. It took me by surprise, I guess. Who is Bella?" I turned my attention back to Aurora.

"My husky. Mom got her for me two years ago for my birthday. She and I are inseparable, well, when she's not sleeping or chasing something. Please, say I can keep her, please? You won't even know I have her, I'll take full responsibility!" Aurora begged with a strangled voice.

She gave me those eyes, big round and hopeful. How can anyone refuse her? I know Ryan's allergic, but since he's gone so much I guess he'll have to accept it.

I smile.

"I wouldn't want to separate you from your Bella. How did your mother ever tell you no with those puppy dog eyes, geez! As far as the funeral goes, that is up to you. I have no desire to see all those people, but I'm here for you. I know you don't want to talk about it, but I need to know what happened to your mom. The lawyer didn't say how she died. If you don't want to talk about it…" I couldn't finish, just thinking about Sam was choking me up.

"Auntie, it's all right. Mom was in a house fire but they never found her remains. The fire chief said it burned too hot to identify anyone. Frankly, they were a little baffled at how hot the flame burned. One inspector even called it supernatural. The coven wanted to have a ceremony even though her body won't be there. I already tried to talk to them. Told them they needed to do a locator spell, but they wouldn't listen. After they refused, I did one myself. It didn't work. I didn't think it would, those spells are stronger with a whole coven," Aurora explained.

Aurora flicked her hand in Matilda's direction. "Matilda, I will release you, but you have to give me your word that you will leave my Auntie alone while we are here. Mom's wishes were for me to go with her and that's what I'm going to do." She waved her hand and Matilda shot out of the chair.

"How dare you use your magic against me? You will be punishment for this, I guarantee it." She pointed her finger from Aurora to me and spat, "I might not be able to stop you right now from taking Aurora, but she will come back to the coven one way or another."

As fast as she could, she left the house, slamming the front door just for effect. How the women of the coven allow her to lead is beyond me.

"You shouldn't provoke any of them, Aurora, some of those witches are extremely powerful. I seem to recall being punished many times. Just being around her gives me the creeps." I had to shake the chills out, the faster we could leave this area the better. I never trusted Matilda or any of her loyal whack-jobs.

"Whack-jobs, Auntie that's not very nice!" Aurora smiled at me.

"Did you...can you…? Did you just read my thoughts?" I asked her shaking my head in bewilderment.

"Your Mom could do that, but we all thought it was a fluke gift."

"I wasn't trying to, but you were practically screaming that word. I understand how you feel about Mom's coven, and I mostly agree, but being a witch isn't a bad thing, in my opinion," Aurora said with dejection.

"No, no, don't take it that way," I pleaded with her. I know I have bad feelings about magic, but this was my niece and I wouldn't have her feeling anything but love from me.

"There is history here you aren't aware of." I gave her hand a reassuring squeeze. "I wasn't treated well when I was in the coven after our parents died. I had to leave, it wasn't as if I had much of a choice, but I won't let you live with them. I know there are other covens; we can find one that doesn't treat each other poorly. And, Aurora, please try hard not to read my thoughts. It violates my privacy and well, it's just creepy!" I rubbed her shoulders wondering if I was ready for a teenager in my life.

Chapter Two
New Addition

"Is the dog going to howl like that the entire flight because I'm not sure, I might have to check with my supervisor?"

The guy behind the counter had picked up the phone obviously in distress; I guess he didn't know what to do with a screaming dog either.

"Aurora, please, do something. I don't want to miss our flight," I insisted. My palms started sweating; I could feel a panic attack approaching quickly. Other than flying, I haven't experienced this since I was a teenager myself. Just being back in this town has stirred up feelings that I would like to push back into their boxes where they belong.

I could hear Aurora saying something and then Bella just dropped.

"Oh, My Goddess. Is she okay?" I ran over to where she was in the kennel, fell to my knees, and threw open her kennel door. I stroked her and could feel her breathing.

“Maybe we should postpone, I don’t want her hurt. Aurora, are you listening to me?” I turned toward her.

“You told me to do something and I could tell if she didn’t stop barking I would have to take you to the hospital. She’s just sleeping. She will sleep until I lift the spell when we land. Mom taught me that one within Bella’s first week with us. Mom got upset with the barking and whining at night when we started kennel training her.” She smiled and started hauling me toward the terminal. I think I saw an eye roll in there somewhere.

“She won’t have any ill affects because of that spell, will she? Really, we can wait and see a vet about a doggie downer if we need to.” I kept looking back at the kennel as we walked away.

“I’ve done this before, she’s fine. I gave her passionflower mixed with some others herbs to help keep her calm, but I guess that didn’t work. Before Mom died she was teaching me alchemy, but I’m not very good at it yet. Will you trust me?” she asked me with retiring eyes.

How could I not with a face like that?

Okay, let’s just get going,” I said to Aurora as we walked to our terminal. I did trust her, but the use of magic had always made me uncomfortable since my experiences with it are connected to pain and humiliation.

Magic made me nervous.

After boarding and getting Aurora comfortable, I grabbed my iPod and zoned out to Sam Smith, that always seems to sooth my racing heart. I did hear Aurora make fun of my iPod asking why I didn’t have an iPhone. I ignored her and let the music lull me to calm thoughts.

Packing up the house didn't take long, with movers that seem to think anything can be thrown in with anything else, it made the packing go quickly. During the meeting with the lawyer I learned that Sam had invested money, left a trust for Aurora and had made me the executor of her estate. Aurora didn't want to sell her childhood home so we left it to a rental management firm to handle for us. The movers estimated that the furniture Aurora had decided she wanted to keep would arrive in Asheville, North Carolina, about a week after we did. At least we had a spare room for her.

Thinking about how Ryan was going to handle this change made me even more anxious. Ryan is type A personality—everything has its place and a teenager didn't fit into his life.

He and I are complete opposites but I've learned to be more like him to alleviate any discomfort. Clutter never seemed to bother me, but I learned quickly that order kept my husband a much happier person, even if he wasn't home often.

"You mean to make him happy no matter what makes you happy?" Aurora asked as she perused a magazine.

I took a deep breath. "Listen kid, that shit is going to get old really fast. First, my thoughts, unless I've expressed them to you, are mine and mine alone. Second, Ryan doesn't know my family history, or at least not about the witch part, so we need to keep that on the down low. That doesn't mean you can't practice, but nothing so open as to read his thoughts. That might make him really lose it.

"Auntie, no offense, but if you can't be who you are what are you doing with him?" Aurora asked me.

That was a good question, one I had been avoiding for these past five years. Hearing that question aimed at me and not from inside my own head made me gasp.

"He's… well, he's stable. He's worked for the same airline for years. He has a great sense of humor," I said as I thought about how I met Ryan, and the way I laughed through the entire first date, but there hadn't been much laughing lately. If I thought too hard about it, I couldn't think of the last time he laughed or made me laugh.

"What's his sense of humor going to be like when he finds out he married a witch?" Aurora put her ear buds in and closed her eyes.

Wait, what? No, she cannot tell Ryan I'm a witch, well, that my family is. I tried to bring up UFO's once and he made some silly comment that made me laugh, but it was clear he did not believe that extraterrestrial life existed, and that if it did it was evil. The way the conversation was shut down makes me think his mind isn't open to the supernatural. Aliens I might not be able to prove, but I knew for a fact that magic existed.

The rest of the flight was in silence since I slept almost the whole way. It wasn't that I didn't want to talk with Aurora about her mom, but the feelings I have about her are all so negative, and I don't think she would want to know how her mom pushed me to leave the coven, or the state for that matter. Maybe in time I can tell Aurora about her mom and our childhood, but not now. I have to adapt to having a teenager

I hardly know living in our home. I guess life was getting too boring for me with Ryan flying out all the time. Now to insert a teenage girl who just lost her mother, something I guess her and I can relate to since losing my mother and father at thirteen wasn't easy, aside from having a controlling sister who thought I should never have been born.

I can feel the damp grass squish beneath my feet; my vision a little blurry as I follow the sounds of howling coming from the dense forest in front of me. A light fog is sweeping low across the terrain, making it harder to see. Goose bumps travel from my neck to my hands, not from fear but anticipation of what I will find. It's dark but the moon light marks the path. I know I'm dreaming, but this dream is different. I wasn't alone; wolves have been guiding me. As I start to reach the barrier of the trees, a pain unlike anything I've ever felt rips through my body, bringing me to my knees with a scream that would wake the dead.

"Aunt Avery, wake up!" Aurora shakes me as I fly forward in my seat. I can't breathe, tears are flowing down my face as I realize I'm still on the plane and the pain was in my dream.

"Breathe, take deep breaths. Are you okay?" Aurora asks, with horror-filled eyes.

"I'm okay, it was just a dream. They've just never woke me like this before." I couldn't seem to open my eyes yet.

I felt a light touch on my shoulder.

"Miss, are you okay? Do you need anything?" The flight attendant rushed over.

Great, now I've attracted the attention of the flight attendants, how embarrassing.

"We're okay. Thanks for checking on us," I said with my hands over my face. The tears were still coming, just not as heavy.

"Did I… did I scream out loud?" Even though I knew the answer, I still had to ask.

"Yes, and I think the entire plane is awake now, but don't worry we're almost there. They already announced our landing has begun so no worries. Is your husband meeting us? How long have you and Ryan been married? Will there be enough room for Bella's kennel? Do you know when I'll start school, and what school I'll go to?" Aurora kept asking questions, not caring that I wasn't answering them; I was still trying to recover from my dream.

"I'm just glad you wanted me. I thought I was going to have to stay with Matilda and her old bitty crew," Aurora said with a smile.

When I regained some composure over my body and my emotions, I said giggling, "Wow, so full of questions." Giggling is a new thing for me, it sounded foreign coming from my mouth. Her questions helped me orient myself and get back to what we were about to do and not on the feelings that dream put in my heart.

"I asked my boss to swap cars with me, my jeep wouldn't fit Bella's kennel but her truck will have no problem. Ryan and I have been married for five years now. I haven't had a chance to check on your school yet, we have a few days anyway. Spring break just started for our county, and I want to get you settled in before we tackle that. Let's just get off this freaking plane and get some food, then we can worry about all the other stuff, okay?" I asked as I laid my head back.

I remembered every moment of that dream. Most of them leaving me with a feeling of loss.

"Cool, I'm excited to meet new people. Mom didn't like me mingling with millie kids so this will be exciting. I wonder if all the kids have accents. You don't seem to have a southern accent?" Aurora asked.

"You know you don't ever have to join another coven if you don't want to. That's your decision. We'll have to go over some rules about magic use, but we have time for that. As for your mom, she had to take over raising me after our parents died, and I know that put pressure on her. She wanted to make our parents proud, and I think she just might have lost sight of what's really important in this world."

"How come you never came to visit?" Aurora asked with no judgment.

"Can we table this discussion for another time, at least until we get you settled? It's a long story. I'm tired and need to decompress for a minute, but we will be spending lots of time together and all these questions will get answered, I promise." I patted her leg. They announced over the speakers that we had arrived in Asheville. As we gathered our bags and departed the plane I had a little hope in my heart that things were working out even in the face of a tragedy. We had to wait until they unloaded Bella and once we let her run around finding spots to pee we got her loaded up in the truck and off we went.

Ryan had another long flight so I didn't think we would see him until tomorrow.

Chapter Three
Sawtooth Pack

"I'm still not sure why we have to meet in Asheville, North Carolina. Could we be any more remote than this?" I watch my brother Jackson grab his third beer; looks like it's one of those nights.

"I know it's inconvenient, but the Peace Summit was voted on and this is what was decided. It's only a week and some of our pack needs a vacation. Just relax and enjoy the time away. We have a ton of acres to roam here without prying eyes." I pulled my laptop out and decided to get a little work done.

"Grayson, you ever meet the Alpha for the Cataloochee pack? The rumor is he's heavy handed and power hungry." Jackson asked, sitting across from me.

"I've heard those things too, but I'm leaving my opinion open for our meeting which isn't for a few days. I'm going to need you to get the rest of the pack coming in tonight settled in the cabin across the way. This cabin is the biggest; we'll use it for immediate family and pack meetings."

"What, you don't want Sasha in this cabin? I think there's an extra bedroom upstairs." Jackson smiled and leaned back in his chair. I'm not sure if he was staying out of my reach or not.

"Very funny, don't you dare mention this to her or I won't hear the end of it. The parents, you, your boys, and Tank are staying with me in this cabin, and I'm only allowing Tank to stay here because he and Sasha don't get along. Let's try to keep things mellow while we're here.

"If you look out the kitchen window you'll see the only house within miles is fairly close. I don't like being this close to millies, but this was the only thing available on such short notice." I stared at the yellow house that sat right down the hill at the back fence of the two cabins. Normally being this close to millies I didn't know put me on edge, but from the moment we pulled up to the cabins I felt at ease. Hopefully this is a sign that the time here with all the heads of the U.S. packs together will be smooth. Not likely, but I am an optimist.

Jackson and I both turned toward the road at the same time. With wolf hearing, we knew the rest of the pack was here before we could see them.

"Looks like the gang has arrived. I'll go help with luggage and direct the others to the second cabin. What's Mom cooking for dinner tonight? I think I saw a barbecue on the deck," Jackson asked. I laughed because I knew he hated to use the grill and Mom's cooking was always better than ours.

Most shifter packs don't have family members be the beta, the right hand to an Alpha, but I knew he was the best choice. He's level-headed and can back me up with his brute strength when needed. I trust him completely. No one in the pack has ever challenged him for his position, and I don't think that would ever happen. I might be the only one in this pack that could take down Jackson, which is why I'm alpha.

"I'll cook tonight. I saw a grocery store a few miles before the turn off. I'll have Mom make a list. It will be nice to get away from the chaos of everyone showing up. Let Mom know who's staying in this cabin with us, she'll keep Sasha in line." I shut down my computer and went out with Jackson to help Mom and Dad with their luggage.

A few hours later, after my interesting trip to the store and the many complaints by a few pack members, I had steaks sitting on the table next to the barbecue. I didn't have to buy as much as I normally do, but feeding a pack of hungry wolves on a regular basis makes for some strange looks at the store. At home in Idaho we have a butcher who is married to one of our pack members so it doesn't raise questions when we need an entire cow butchered for one single dinner. It helps that we have our own farm with live stock to supplement our horde. Forty steaks from the local grocery store seemed small to me, but several people asked me if I was throwing a party. I laughed a few times and just said, "Something like that." Trying to keep a low profile is important for our kind; to remain hidden from millie eyes. I never did like the term used for non-supernatural's.

I might just have to send different groups to the store. Small towns seemed to pay attention more, something to think on later.

I had just prepped the grill when our only neighbors seemed to have the same idea. A woman walked out the back door of her house, took the cover off her barbecue, and started prepping as well. She wasn't close enough she could see me clearly, but with my heightened senses I could see her just fine. Her work out clothes didn't hide her figure, which wasn't as toned as the woman I normally dated, but the curves were working on her just fine. Her brown hair was pulled back in a ponytail, and I could tell that it would hang to the middle of her back. She wasn't looking toward me so I wasn't sure what her eye color was.

What do I care what her eye color is? Grayson, get it together.

It had been too long since I'd meet that particular need; maybe it was time to squelch that thirst. A horny wolf isn't as level-headed.

"Are you grilling or ogling the neighbor, son?" My Mom Josie had snuck up behind me during my perusal of the woman.

I smiled down at her. "It's not my fault the back deck faces her back deck, and I don't think I was ogling her, I was just checking out my surroundings." I started placing the steaks on the grill.

"Doesn't being an empath ever get old, Mom?" I could tell that she was reading me.

"No, I like knowing how my family is feeling, especially when they decide not to share with me. Did I feel hope of a mate?" My Mom raised her eyebrow, the one that told me I was busted.

"Hope for a non-shifter as a mate, I don't think so. I don't want to add anymore headaches to this pack and having a millie as our butcher is about as much as I can take."

Just as my Mom was going to continue our conversation, the neighbor woman turn to look at me. Time stopped, or at least that's how it felt. I could see her gray eyes lock onto my blue ones and the pull was too strong. I tried to divert my eyes, but every time I tried I felt physically ill.

"Son, your steaks need to be turned." I heard my mom but couldn't seem to look away. She had a beauty that came pouring out of her eyes. "Grayson, what is going on? Are you feeling sick? Grayson?" Mom tried pulling on my arm, but I couldn't move.

The back door of the neighbor's house opened and out walked a man. He walked over to the woman and grabbed her arm, which seemed to break the connection. I shook my head to try to get my thoughts in order, and that's when Mom and I heard a scream rip out of the neighbor's mouth. A scream that gave me instant goose bumps.

I grabbed the deck railing and was almost over it when I was hauled back to the deck floor. "No, Grayson, you can't. That man will help her, let's just go back into the house," Mom said to me as she pulled me inside.

I couldn't respond, and it took Mom's entire strength to get me in through the front door. She might be older than me, but she's still a shifter and that comes with strength. I was stronger than she was, but I would never hurt my Mom no matter how bad I felt I needed to go to that woman.

"Grant, can you take over cooking the steaks, please, we have a problem?" My mother, smiled at her husband. Mom was a shifter and was strong, but she had a hard time talking and pushing me at the same time. My dad smiled and nodded.

"I'm on it. They won't be like Grayson's but they won't be burnt." Grant went out the front door and around the porch to the back deck.

"Let's just sit here a minute. I'll get you a cup of earl grey, and you just keep deep breathing," Mom said as she went about pulling down items for tea.

"Do you know what that was? I felt this pull, this whooshing in my head. When that woman screamed, I felt scared, Mom, like terrified. I don't think I've ever felt like this before. It's almost more powerful than my Alpha protective feeling." I had to walk over to the kitchen window so I could see onto her back porch. I need to know how she was.

"Cross-linked, Grayson, that's what that was, or I believe so," Mom shook her head, almost like she was perplexed by something.

"She seemed to be in pain when she was pulled away, that one I'm not sure about. When you meet your mate, you feel drawn to them, but nothing like what just happened. I'm not sure what that was, and I didn't feel any supernatural powers coming from her either. I would need to be closer to her to get a good vibe. This could be a cross-linked mating though." She smiled huge and patted my back. "Son, you should be happy. It's a great day that you've finally found her. Granted it would have been better if it weren't during such a tense time in the packs around the world. These supernatural eradicators are getting stronger." Mom was trying to comfort me, but I knew that was a farce. The woman across the way appeared to be with someone already, and even if she wasn't, she wasn't a shifter. No alpha in any of the packs had a millie for a mate.

I wasn't necessarily against a shifter and a human being a mated pair, I believe everyone should get to choose who they give their love too, but the discrimination is still strong. I don't want that headache. I've allowed it already in my pack; but I had never thought I would be stuck in this scenario. How would my pack feel about a millie as their alpha female? Would they accept her? How would she defend herself against a bunch of shifters? What will she think? Would she accept it, leave her family and everything she knows to be with a total stranger with a lunatic story of wolves and a 'special bond', or would she go running for the hills?

I had heard stories of these cross-linked mates, but that's all they were, stories. Millions of thoughts raced through my head I didn't even realized my mom was still talking. When I finally snapped back into reality, she was saying something about the Cataloochee Pack and work.

I stood up. I decided I needed to meet her, to explain things. I had this strong compulsion to be with her, nothing else mattered.

"Grayson… Grayson? Are you listening to me? Where are you going?" Mom grabbed my arm, but I hardly noticed. I was determined to meet her. My mate, I liked the sound of that.

I continued walking, smiling the whole time, almost to the deck when I got pushed over into the bookshelf. A giant pile of books fell onto my head. I stood up, pushing the books off. I looked over to my Mom, who was clearly the assailant.

"Well, okay, a simple, 'Hey Grayson, can we talk?' would've worked, but I guess this is fine too." I rubbed the back of my now slightly sore neck.

"Yes, that might've worked if you would've been listening! You had your head in the clouds. I sense strong emotions from you, your aura is almost blinding. What were you thinking about?" She gave me a puzzled look and crossed her arms over her chest. I was obviously not getting out of here without a thorough explanation.

"Well I… I mean I was just...I thought that...uh..." I looked around and grabbed the item nearest to me. "I thought our neighbor would like this book." I gave my award-winning, crooked smile, hoping to win her over so she'd let me leave.

She looked at me, down at the item in my hand and then back at me again. She raised her eyebrow. "That's a plant." I looked down, and sure enough, I was holding a plant.

"Oh right, that's what I meant. I thought she'd like this, erm, plant." Mom squinted her eyes, planted her feet, and poked my chest with her finger.

"I know how you're feeling, but you have to relax and get some food in your body," she said, and I could tell she meant business. My mom may be small, but she could put up a nasty fight, and I was not about to go there. I sighed. "Fine."

I sat down on the arm of the couch and ran my hand through my hair, trying to figure out what I wanted to say. She sat down across from me and tilted her head. It looks like we both needed a good explanation because I was just as confused as she was.

What was that? It was almost as if I was under a spell. My mind and body were working together, which is usually a good thing, until you lose control of it completely. Then it's just scary. I knew what I wanted, or I thought I did anyway. My mind was telling me to go to her, to release her from the pain in which she would be suffering without me; and my body just simply followed suit. When my Mom had pushed me into that bookshelf, I got my thoughts back and my body was mine again. I hadn't even realized I'd been moving. I started thinking about all the possibilities of me telling her all about pack life and what her life could be like amongst the wolves. The one thing I didn't think about was me. Did I even want a mate? Given the fact that she was a millie wasn't helping the situation either.

Before I knew it, my mind had gone into oblivion once again, and I was only snapped out of it by my Mom's, rather aggressive and persistent prodding.

"Let's have dinner, have a few beers, and then we'll all sit down and talk about what just happened. You need to approach this situation with a clear head. No good will come from you rushing over there and scaring those people. I know it's hard to stay focused, but I promise approaching this with delicate hands will make it easier in the end. Now, I'm going to go check on your father. We might end up with rocks if I don't." Mom patted my shoulder as she left me alone in the living room.

As I was going over everything in my mind, Jackson barreled through the front door. "Houston, we have a problem. Sasha and Tank are tearing up the other cabin. I hope you don't expect the security deposit back," Jackson said out of breath.

"Great, just what I needed. Christ, who invited Sasha to begin with?" I screwed up on this decision. I take a deep breath. "Let's go see whose neck I get to break." I got up and jogged after Jackson out the door. "What's the fight about this time?" I asked Jackson.

"I don't know, something about Spencer. Same old, same old." I could see an eye roll mixed in there.

"Again?" I wasn't surprised though. They fight over him a lot, for reasons I'm not sure about, Sasha and Tank have a very long and difficult relationship, if I'd even call it that. I guess I could say it's something of a 'love-hate' relationship, if you will. I still don't know why Tank even bothers to fight with her, it's pointless. Spencer isn't even his son, although none of us are too sure who his father is. It could be Tank, but the way they go at each other, it's hard to imagine Tank letting her get close to him.

As I climbed up the stairs of the cabin, I could hear destruction; great there goes a thousand buck deposit. I could hear Sasha screaming at Tank, something about him not being Spencer's dad, and he doesn't have the right to tell her how to raise him. Both sides were flinging profanities, maybe I need to send both of them home. No, I need Tank as back up at the summit meeting. Tank had been a pack enforcer for well over three hundred years. After the Eradication Day, not many wolves were older than a century. Tank is an elder, but you would never know it from his constant battle with Sasha and getting involved in her day-to-day decisions.

"Sasha, Tank, that's enough!" I yelled but held back any power as I walked through the front door. Neither one even acknowledged my presence.

"How would I even know if he's my son with you whoring yourself out to any male who shows you any kind of attention?" Tank was visibly pissed. Mom always said there can't be anger without love being there too.

"Whore...whore! Why you fucking—" Sasha didn't even finish her sentence, she jumped and phased as she launched herself at Tank. A mix of emotions flashed across her face before she finished her transition to wolf. Rage was clearly the strongest, but the one that shocked me the most was the brief flash of pain and regret. Although that only lasted a moment, anyone could tell that the relationship between these two was complicated.

With Tank's mammoth size, he easily overpowered Sasha even in human form, but Sasha's determination to overpower him was astounding. Maybe I should up Sasha's rank in the pack to enforcer. She seemed to be gaining the advantage in this situation. In the two minutes the fight lasted, they had managed to destroy a coffee table, two lamps, and somehow fling an object through the stained-glass picture window. That's going to cost me a pretty penny.

With all the power of an alpha, I threw the command for both to cease. “Enough!” I yelled and glared at them both. They both froze against their will. I kept it my power held back enough that they would be able to answer me but not move.

“What are you thinking? If you must fight, go in the woods away from human eyes and ears,” I flung my arms towards the broken window. “Do you realize that our neighbor, a human, is just a couple of yards away? How am I supposed to explain this?” I crossed my arms. I was furious. “We are here to meet with all the pack alpha’s to try and stop those that would chase us to extinction, and yet here I am, preventing you two from doing their job for them.”

“Well, he—” Sasha started, but couldn’t get any further because Tank interrupted. I watched him uncross his arms, his tan skin start to darken with emotion.

“Oh yes, lets blame all of this on me. It was your son running around like a mad dog outside where everyone could see. Do you honestly expect me to sit around and say nothing? What would we do if the millies saw a wolf running around outside? I’d imagine they’d call the police and probably have him killed or relocated. He’s six, what would he do, take a bus back? No, I don’t think so. I’d blame him for being irresponsible, but he’s just a pup. This is completely on you, if you were a better mother to him then—” A loud crack sounded from their direction, and then there was blood. Tank was holding his nose, which was dripping blood. His once white T-shirt was now sprinkled with color. He had a look of surprise mixed with fury.

Sasha grabbed Tank by the collar of his shirt and brought her face inches from his. I was just about to step in when Jackson grabbed my arm and gave me a look that meant I needed to let them work this one out themselves. I stepped back and watched just realizing that Jackson had showed up and I hadn't noticed. I had so much running through my mind and one of those things was how had Sasha broke free from my alpha hold? I pushed that out of my mind and watched and angry Sasha. Sasha was intimidating when she was angry.

"Don't you ever tell me that I'm a bad mother. Don't you ever tell me how to raise my child, and don't you ever undermine me. He is mine. Mine! Not yours or anybody else's, get that through your pea brain." She hadn't even blinked. She was giving him a glare full of nothing but hatred. "Stay away from me and my son, Tank."

"Gladly, but remember this. We are all part of this pack, and its each person's job to watch out for one another and intervene when necessary. As for Spencer, he doesn't have a man in his life..." Tank wanted to finish but one look from me cut him of midstream.

"Tank, you are staying in the larger cabin, please get your things and unpack. We'll be having dinner in fifteen minutes then a pack meeting to follow." I waited for Tank to leave before I ripped into Sasha.

"Jackson, can you please go locate Spencer and bring him to me. Also, please figure out what to do about the window." I didn't take my eyes off Sasha. She was a beauty with sun-kissed skin and chin-length, blond hair framing her heart shaped face. She was pretty average in height for a female wolf, around 5' 10", slim with a decent chest she always had to flaunt. She wore too much make up for my taste but most of the single males in our pack liked her, so it must work.

"Yes, alpha." Jackson left without a smart comment. Jackson knows when I'm in this mood it's best to do as asked.

"This wasn't my fault," Sasha started, but I put up a hand to stop her from talking.

"I'm done having this conversation with you. I don't care you and

Tank can't get along, but he's right about Spencer. You can't let him shift and run around an unfamiliar area. You had the option to leave him at home or not come yourself. I have never forced you to tell me who Spencer's dad is, and I hope you don't push me to in the future. Once the pack knows who the father is, things will change and I know you don't want that. Start parenting that child." I walked around, trying to right what they damaged. Damn, these wolves are expensive.

"He could be yours if you'd only let me in. I wanted him to be yours, but you push me away every time. Why?" Sasha walked toward me. I could smell her arousal and it didn't even phase me.

"Stop," I turned and growled at her. "One time Sasha, that's all we had and you know it wasn't even close to the time that Spencer was conceived. Your games don't work on me anymore. If you continue to cause problems while you're here I will send you home. Are we clear?" I stared at her. There was a time I had fallen for Sasha's good looks, but the manipulation she would use by sleeping with all the available men in our pack didn't do anything but make me ambivalent.

"Fine, but if you think you can get someone better than me you are sorely mistaken. You'll come around, they always do." With that said, Sasha took herself and her luggage to her room.

"Well, it's turning out to be an eventful day so far," I said aloud as I headed out of the cabin.

As I walked across the two properties, I could feel someone staring at me. I turned toward the human woman's house and saw her looking out the kitchen window. I couldn't understand my pull toward her, but I didn't have time to deal with it right now.

Chapter Four
Changes

I was watching him stalk from one cabin to the other through the kitchen window. His gate mesmerized me with long powerful strides and determination. He didn't seem like someone I would want to piss off. I could hear Ryan was still hounding me about what happened out on the deck. I wasn't sure how to explain it to him, that the pain wasn't so much of physical as it was emotional.

When we bought the house we were glad that the two cabins that flanked our back acre were vacation rentals. Our combined luck when it came to next-door neighbors had never been good, so not having constant neighbors helped with the feel of seclusion I had hoped for when searching for a house.

Asheville, a small mountain city, was the outlining area that drew me to this place. Farmland, rolling hills, mountain community with acres upon acres of pastureland; at one point we even had buffalo as neighbors in the fields beside our house. Watching the people at the two cabins, it seemed like they were having some sort of conflict. I hope that doesn't become a recurring theme, I like peace and quiet.

"Since you're feeling better after your episode ruined the grilling, I thought I'd let you know that I ordered pizza. I turned the grill off. Make sure you put the cover back on before you go to bed," Ryan said from behind me. I wasn't really listening as I watched the neighbor.

"Hello? Shit, Avery, what the hell is wrong with you?" Ryan snapped his fingers in front of my face.

"Pizza sounds great. Did you put olives on my half?" I asked as I continued to watch the neighbor storm between cabins.

"Olives on half? Fuck no, that shit is gross," he said as I turned toward him. I guess that meant we were having meat lovers. Which I don't mind, but I need something else, peppers, or olives. Ryan hated anything with color in his food and definitely not on his pizza. Dare a vegetable touch his meat.

"Have you seen the people staying at the cabins? I think they rented both cabins this time," I remarked trying to change the subject.

The cabins have a rustic feel with the wood exterior and beams exposed down to the non-stained faded siding. I could live in a cabin like that with a river or creek running through the property, no neighbors, just the house and wild wilderness. I had tried to get Ryan on board with a house like that when we started house shopping, but he kept saying that he didn't have time for repairs and he wanted something newer.

New isn't always better.

"I haven't really paid attention. So, Aurora seems to be adjusting fine. I just came from downstairs and her room is looking like the inside pages of a teen magazine. Did she ask you if she could put all that crap on the walls? You realize after she leaves we will have to paint, probably have to stucco too. I just don't understand why it couldn't have just stayed the way you had it decorated. It was simple, easy. She even used some thumbtacks. That means I'll have to putty later, didn't I tell you I didn't want any holes in the walls? Does she really need that stuff? She has one life size poster just inside her door and it scared the shit out of me at first. Aurora thought it was hilarious. Have you noticed how sometimes when you talk to her she is answering you before you finish your sentence? It's irritating." Ryan was picking up the mail and other items I had left lying around.

When he gets on a rant I stop listening.

I kept my eyes focused out the kitchen window, wanting to get another look at the gorgeous man across the way. Time to focus on my own relationship and not worry about what vacationers do to each other, I admonished myself.

I turned from the window and said, "I had posters like that when I was younger. She's trying to make her mark, have the room feel like it's her own space. She just lost her whole world. Try to have patience with her, please." I didn't even bring up the fact that Aurora was my only family and that she wouldn't be leaving unless she decided to go to college after high school.

I watched Ryan while he was reaching for his cell phone that started ringing from his back pocket. Waiting and knowing for confirmation that it was his work. He didn't seem to have any friends, but he sure did get massive amounts of phone calls. He never understood when I would tell him I was lonely, that I wanted to make some friends. When I start to make friends in the community, I could tell it bothered him, but I still didn't understand why.

I could tell by the way that he talked it was work. One of the down sides of his job is how much he's away from me. He usually works one week on and one week off, but they've had a shortage lately and he's been picking up flights that are out of town so he has to stay at hotels wherever the flights take him.

"So, where you off to now?" I asked flippantly. I hated to be angry, but I had only been home for a day and here he was again picking up overtime.

"Avery, don't. They need me, and I enjoy the overtime. Most people don't like their jobs, but I love mine. With all the extra shifts I'm picking up, we can take a real vacation. My mom has been asking when we can visit." He walked over and patted my shoulder. No hug like usual.

Ryan's mom, Liz, reminded me of Matilda and the other women in the coven. I knew from the first moment I met her that she didn't like me. I tried to be whom she wanted, but she always had to dig about my job, my education, my status in life or lack thereof. Ryan always seemed busy when we would visit her so that left me to deal with her by myself. I can hear her voice in my head, my hair was frumpy, and I should wear make-up. Anything she could do to put me down she did. Not once had Ryan ever stuck up for me. Can he blame me that I don't want to spend vacation with that viper?

"I understand, I'm sure a vacation is all we need. I appreciate everything you do. I still have another week off work so I can focus on helping Aurora settle in. Delphine said if I needed more time off I could take it," I said to him. I went over and hugged him, knowing that if I didn't it would start a fight between us about my lack of appreciation for all he does for me. He hugged me quickly and then went to go pack.

I walked to the door when I hear the bell ring.

Ryan didn't seem to mind Aurora's dog, but Bella did not seem to feel the same toward Ryan. If he is anywhere near her, growling would commence. He seemed to be ignoring her, but I have a feeling that won't last long. I made the decision that when Ryan's home, Bella needs to stay downstairs with Aurora. No need to poke the bear. Being a husky she has a lot of energy. Aurora goes jogging just about every day and takes Bella with her on a leash. It usually tires her down for the remainder of the day, but sometimes that doesn't even do the trick. We have been trying to keep Bella inside; we don't want her running up to the vacationers and bothering them.

"Get the dog, quick," I frantically said to know one, but it was too late, Bella swooped past the pizza delivery guy and down our front steps.

"I'll get her. Ryan," I yelled. "Can you come get the pizza and set everything up at the table, and I'll join you as soon as I have roped myself a frisky husky!" If I didn't get this dog under control I was worried Ryan would ask me to find her a new home, and Aurora would not be happy with that. I went for the back door, knowing she would be up the hill to chase the wild chickens. Some neighbors, not sure which ones, had free-range chickens. I'd seen them in our yard a few times. I just hope Bella doesn't decide to bring one home one of these days.

Yuck, dead feathered birds.

I love our piece of property, clear of trees so you can see the expansive mountain views, but it sits on a hill and there isn't much flat land. I climb through the fence that borders our property and start up the hill. I hope that the vacationers won't mind me walking about; you never know how someone will react. I had the owner call me one time because I had started a conversation with one of the vacationers when we first moved in, and I guess his wife didn't like that.

Bitchy woman.

I got to the road that runs in front of the cabins when I spotted Bella in the woods chasing something. Great, looks like my dinner will be cold by the time I get her rounded up.

"Bella, come here, girl. Let's go!" I hollered but she didn't even look my way. I didn't want to have to go stomping through the woods after a hyperactive dog.

"Can I help you with something?" A deep, guttural voice asked from my right. I squeaked and jumped a few feet in the air. Goose bumps raced down my arms. I didn't even hear him approach; it's as if he snuck up on me purposefully.

"No thanks, just trying to get a bad dog." I really don't want to have this conversation.

Ryan and I have both tried not to disturb the people who rent these cabins; this guy could offer to help then call the lady that rents them and complain. I don't want another nasty phone call, or an apology cheesecake. Last time the owner of that property called me I blasted her which ended up getting me a cheese cake with an apology note. The note was nice but the cheese cake was a nasty goopy mess that didn't even resemble a cheesecake? I would know, my ass loves cheesecake.

"Well, it looks like you could use some help. Your pizza's getting cold," he said to me. I could feel him getting closer.

I turned around and stared at him for a few seconds. I normally don't have a hard time talking to strangers, but this mountain of a man left me speechless for a few seconds.

"Okay, if you think you can help that would be great." Seeing him up close takes my breath away, this man was raw muscle from his shoulders down to his trim waste, which I could see since his shirt was snug. It should be illegal to wear shirts that tight. Is there a website 'tight shirts to show off your hot muscles'? While I was perusing his body, I got a glimpse of his eyes just briefly. He knew I was checking him out. I lowered my head to the ground, if I looked him in the eye I would probably cry from embarrassment.

I heard him chuckle.

"I'm pretty good with dogs. Give me a second." He jogged off into the woods. That gave me a great view of his behind.

I only got a glimpse of his face, but I'm sure it's the same guy that was out on the deck earlier. He's built like a Mack truck. He looks to be a few inches past six feet with black hair cropped short on the sides a little longer on top.

Mack, that's a great name for him.

A few minutes later, he comes walking back over to me with Bella trotting happily beside him.

"Have you been training her at all?" he asks me.

"She's my niece's. We've only had her here a few days. Well, actually, my niece has had her since she was a pup, but my sister died and Bella came with my niece, Aurora, so I don't really know if they trained the dog." I stopped talking, and realized I was babbling and telling the man information he probably didn't need to know, or care for that matter. I took a glance at his face and saw sincere pain for my loss.

"I'm so sorry for your loss. Were you close to your sister?" He reached out as if he was going to comfort me. I flinched, as his hand got closer. He stopped and lowered his hand.

He cleared his throat.

"The trick is to make sure she knows who the dominant is." He kept coming closer, and I kept taking steps backwards.

As I was backing up I tripped on loose gravel and my arms started pin wheeling. Just as his hand made contact with my arm, I felt a burning sensation down my arm through my hand. It hurt so bad my body gave up on standing. Mack caught me before I hit my knees on the gravel road.

"Hey, are you okay?" I kept my right hand clenched in a fist. The sharp pain was slowly fading, but the burning was slower to recede. I could hear him trying to sooth me, and Bella was licking my arm, but it took me a few minutes to get my mind to start working again. As soon as I came back to myself, I realized this guy was sitting on the ground with me in his lap, slowly rubbing circles on my back.

I leapt off his lap faster than I thought was possible and started backing away. "Tha... Thanks, so much, Mack, I'll um...try really hard to keep her in our yard, no need to call Georgia and mention this. Last time I had to endure a crappy store bought cherry cheese cake as her apology for yelling at me, which is a sin, buying crappy cheese cake, everyone knows you make cheese cakes by hand," I said as I turned tail and attempted to speed walk back down to our fence. I heard the guy tell Bella to stay with me and something about his name not being Mack. I thought I was the only one who talked to animals like they understood me.

I started jogging at one point, the need to get away from this situation driving me faster towards my house. I could hear him mumble about his mom's cheesecake but the blood in my ears was pounding so hard I couldn't really hear. My vision for that matter was getting dimmer.

Once I made it onto my porch I leaned against the side of the door jam and tried to get my bearings. The question that loudly popped into my head was how did he know we were having pizza? That thought hit me hard as I was walking in the back door. I guess he can see the road that runs in front of our house. I'm sure that's how he knew.

"Bella, no more going over there or I might make you into dog meat." I looked down at her, and she looked down to the ground with her ears lowered as if I punished her. Geez, no wonder this dog is hard to resist. Her clear blue eyes seem to pull you in and feel sorry for her. "Don't make me feel bad, you can't run all over the place. There are people around here who own guns and would rather shoot you than see one of their chickens killed. I know, kinda creepy, huh."

Well maybe I get to see that hunk again if she got loose. What am I talking about; I'm married. I have never been overly attracted to men. I'm not shy, more like I was so lost for so long that I didn't even think about relationships until I met Ryan.

I must be tired. With Ryan leaving so early in the morning, maybe we could call it an early night and have some alone time. Maybe that would take my mind off the new neighbors.

Without even noticing my extreme case of freak out, Ryan says, "Hey, so worked called again and they need me sooner than tomorrow so I'm going to load the car. Could you wrap up a few slices of pizza for me? Thanks."

Ryan walked away from me as soon as I came through the back door. I took a deep breath. A stranger who wants to help me and a husband who loves his job more than being at home with me. I went out and wrapped up his pizza and sat down with Aurora to delve into our dinner. I could tell that Aurora wanted to ask me something, but

I just shook my head at her. I think she understood or read my mind, either way, I excused myself and went to bed shortly after dinner and Ryan left.

I put on my ribbed tank top and cotton shorts, hoping that I could land in dream land. Sleeping alone is not new to me, but at least as a child I had our cat Lenny. A black and white beast of a Manx that no one messed with, but he was always gentle and cuddly with me. I remember my mom shaking her head when she'd come tuck me in, the cat would hiss and spit and claw anyone who touched him, except me. He died around the same time my folks did. Thinking about Lenny brought a desire for a cat, but I knew that wouldn't happen because Ryan was allergic. He seemed to be allergic to many things.

I hadn't set my alarm last night, knowing Ryan wouldn't be here and Aurora was settling in so I thought I would use this time to catch up on my sleep; if I decided to let myself. I heard some banging of pots and pans, and someone talking, maybe cursing a little. I rolled over to look at the time on the alarm clock. 7 o'clock in the morning is excessively early to wake up, especially when I didn't fall asleep until around 4 o'clock.

I guess it's time to wake up. I slept straight through without any bad dreams. I haven't felt this well rested in a long time even though it had only been a few hours. I had to pause for a second because I have been having nightmares since I was a kid. I couldn't remember the last time I woke up and hadn't remembered one. I hadn't heard from Rosie yet, maybe I should call her. Coffee first before I try to use my brainpan.

When I rounded the corner into the open living room and kitchen Aurora was singing and frolicking all around the kitchen island and it looked like she had my entire collection of dry baking ingredients sprawled out. Bella was sitting at her feet watching, and I'm sure waiting for something to drop, as she kept checking the ground for scraps.

"I made breakfast, hope that's okay. I didn't have the heart to wake you up. You seemed to be sleeping heavy. I don't think I've heard someone snore that loud," she said as she turned while flinging pancake batter across the cupboard fronts.

So who's cleaning that up?

"Coffee first, and I don't snore. I have to have at least one cup before talking commences," I grumbled to her as I went to grab a cup. I noticed she made herself a cup of coffee as well. Is she old enough for coffee, do I even care at this point?

Nope.

"Mom's been letting me drink coffee since I hit puberty, so no worries." She smiled over the rim of her cup.

I gave her the evil eye. "Thanks, I haven't slept that well in a long time. I appreciate the coffee and breakfast. Ryan doesn't cook, and when I'm here all alone I just don't have the heart to cook for one. I sometimes go to the local bakery, but my thighs and ass can't take it anymore. I might have a sweet tooth," I confessed and winked.

"We can totally go to the bakery, I love lattes and I want to check out job openings in the area. I only got a glimpse of downtown when we came through. I worked at a small coffee shop back home. I'd like to have my own money. My fabulous closet needs more friends, shoes, tanks; I have to stock up on my summer wear. It gets hot here, so I can have a plethora of flip flops." Aurora said in between shoving folded up pancakes in her mouth.

I had never seen someone eat plain pancakes before.

"Plus, Mom's life insurance trust says I get a thousand dollars a year for a clothes budget, so I'm ready to roll as soon as you're ready. I got a thousand bucks calling my name."

My life has changed in a huge way and coming to grips with it hasn't sunk in yet. School, clothes, dead sister. Be careful what you wish for, I remember thinking I was bored and needed some excitement in my life. Well I sure got that.

"You'll get used to it, just go with the flow. Mom use to tell me you were the easiest person to get along with. You were always smiling and loved with a fierce heart. Mom loved you very much, Auntie, don't ever think different." She smiles at me.

Thinking about my sister loving me shot a pain through my chest; I had to grab onto the counter to keep from crying out. I loved my sister with a devotion that probably seemed unnatural. I used to crawl in bed with her when I had a bad dream, which was often, and she always seemed to know when that was going to happen. She would lift the covers, welcoming me and tell me it would be okay.

When others in our community would pick on me she would stop them. That was when I was younger. Once I was labeled a dud, her feelings changed. They taught us that without your power you are just like humans and what good are they?

"When did you grow up, huh? I keep picturing you with jelly across your face. Calling me Ayee." I smiled and hugged her. She turned out to be an independent, bright, beautiful girl, and I couldn't be prouder of my sister at that moment.

I had better wear my yoga pants today. I had just finished reaching for the scrambled eggs when I noticed dark marks on my right palm. I stared at my hand, and it took a minute before my brain could comprehend what I was seeing. What looked like a tattoo was on the palm of my right hand. Thick lines made up the outline which looked like a wolf paw and inside each toe of the paw were symbols I recognized. These were symbols witches used to represent elements; water, fire, earth and air. I traced the design with my finger. It was beautiful.

"What the fuck is that?" I asked no one.

Aurora came around the island and went to grab my hand. We both saw a glimmer of electricity stream up and zap her hand. "Ouch, that hurt."

"There is a fucking tattoo on my palm." I was so speechless I didn't know what to say. I immediately knew that stranger touching me did this to me.

I looked at Aurora as her eyes got huge. I didn't like the look in her eyes, innately knowing it's one that didn't bold well for me.

"Auntie, I've seen this before. Well, not this exact drawing, but I've come across tattoos on palms that look similar. It was under the history section of one of our grimoires." She took a picture of my palm and told me she would do some research, then went downstairs to take a shower. She just walked away calm as could be. It seemed rational to freak out about this, but watching a teenager casually walk away made me think maybe I needed to let this one go for the time being. I turned my head when the downstairs door opened and Aurora popped her head out.

"I walked away because I could tell you were ready to freak out. Mom always taught me that you can't change what happened in the past, you can only change how you deal with the present moment. Sooo—" she waved her hands in the air in a dismissive motion—"I've already contacted a friend at the coven, and she's going to quietly check into the picture I sent her. She said it would take her a couple of days; she'll make sure to use the library when no one else is around for privacy. Now, I will leave you alone for a few, and you can come to grips that a strange man touched you and marked you." She blew me a kiss as she closed the door.

Who is this supposed teenager living in my home? It's like living with Grandmam again. She knew always how to direct a situation so that I wouldn't freak out. When Grandmam was head of our family she led with a smile, but people would scramble out of her way to do what she asked, well except Gramps. Aurora reminds me of her, and thank Goddess. What do I know about raising a teenager? I looked down at my hand and decided I would cover it until I could figure out how and what it was. I had a long sleeve shirt with a thumbhole that would cover the majority of it up.

I finished cleaning the kitchen, grabbed my purse, and walked out of the house in a fog. It didn't dawn on me until I turned the key in my car's ignition that Aurora was already in the passenger seat. I smiled and off we headed to downtown Asheville.

I was glad we were getting out of the house, we both needed a good distraction and coffee and pastries seemed like a good idea.

"It hurts the most when I'm lying in bed at night; she always tucked me in even as I grew older. If she couldn't be there when I feel asleep, as soon as she was home she would come kiss my forehead. I didn't always wake when she did that, but I woke up enough to know that she did it every night," Aurora said while watching downtown come into view through the jeep window.

I gripped the steering wheel until my fingers started to go numb. After I was pushed out of the coven, I didn't have anyone to talk to about my feelings and anytime I tried to bring up anything supernatural with Ryan he would shut the conversation down. I couldn't tell what this feeling was in my gut, was it jealousy? Jealousy over a child and the love her parent gave her? How pathetic is that.

I jerked right out of that thought and turned to Aurora. "I really need you to stay out of my head. I will try to talk to you about whatever I can, but reading me isn't going to fly with me," I clipped. I think I snapped like that because I felt a tingle in my head, almost like a bug walking on your arm.

"I can teach you to block me, if you want?" Aurora whispered.

I cringed when she asked me that because I could tell she heard what I thought and that brought guilt. "Sure, but I don't think it will do any good. Dud, remember," I said as I poked my own chest. "But give it your best shot," I told her as I pulled into the parking lot of Yummy Crummy Coffee the bakery, found a spot close to the door and turned the jeep off.

"Close your eyes and try to keep your mind blank. I want you to tell me when you feel anything," Aurora instructed.

I closed my eyes and tried to blank out my mind even with the noises and smells of the city surrounding us.

"I know you think you're a dud, but even so, I think you can feel when someone is reading you and stop them. Tell me the minute you feel anything," Aurora said.

It almost felt like a slight brush of a touch across my head, but so slight it was a brief tickle.

"You felt it, didn't you? That is what it feels like when someone is trying to read your thoughts. Now, I want you to stop me from doing that. Try thinking of a shield, or putting your hand up and swatting away the feeling. It comes natural to me, but I want you to try anyway. I'll give you a second then I'm going to try again."

As soon as I felt that touch, I put my hand up and it stopped. I kept one eye closed and peeked the other open.

"So, did I do it?" I asked.

Aurora laughed so hard I had to open my eyes all the way. My hand was right up in her face.

"I guess that's a way to do it, but it won't always be from so close by. I really think you aren't such a dud as you seem to think. If you didn't have any magic, Auntie, I don't think you could have stopped me." She turned around and hopped out of the jeep.

I pulled my hand back and followed. Huh, I didn't even feel my hand move.

"Hey Avery, it's been a few weeks. What kept you away so long?" Jason asked me as we made our way to the counter. His bakery is chic modern with a hippie flair. I didn't come for the decor though; he's one of the owners and makes the best caramel macchiato's in town.

"My niece is living with me now, and I had to take care of a few things. Plus, I just got my old jeans to fit again." I turn to Aurora with a smile. "Jason, I'd like you to meet my niece Aurora." I said as I noticed Jason's smile get even wider at her perusal. Jason was in his early twenties, but my niece was a beauty and it was hard to tell she was only sixteen.

"Hi Jason!" Aurora almost yelled. I can see she thought Jason was just as cute as I did.

"Hi Aurora, nice to meet you."

"She's looking for a job, if you have any openings. She'll be starting school next week, but maybe you need help after school or on the weekends," I told him as he handed me my drink.

"I'm sure we could find something for her. What can I get you to drink?" Jason asked her.

"How about a large mocha?" she asked while perusing the pastry case. All of us Sinclair's have a sweet tooth. "And that yummy chocolate chunk cookie," she told Jason.

"Sure thing, I'll bring it to you and an application." Jason winked as he turned to make Aurora's drink.

Aurora settled in at the table I always choose which has a direct line of sight to the front counter. I'm a people watcher.

I looked up when I saw Elise arguing with some guy in line. Elise was a gal I met when I would come to read and just relax. She works as a hairdresser in town; we've traded services in the past. I would get her screaming deals on plants from the nursery, and I would get high lights or a cut when I got courageous, and she always gave me a discount.

I didn't recognize the person she was talking to, but she seemed pissed off, and that was hard to do with Elise. She's was one of the most patient people I knew. I wasn't worried about her; she also was an instructor at the community center's monthly women's self-defense class she has drug me to on occasion.

I was well into latte heaven and Aurora was almost finished with her application when that same guy along with some other dude, came over and grabbed some chairs from a nearby table and proceeded to sit in between Aurora and I.

Well, I don't think so.

"I'm no photographer, but I can picture you and me together," sleaze number one said to Aurora. The same guy that had been bugging Elise. He had his arm around the back of Aurora's chair.

"Um, excuse me dude, but that's my niece. My sixteen-year-old niece. What, are you? Forty? That's disgusting," I hissed.

He ignored me, reached over, and ran his hand down the back of Aurora's hair.

Again, I don't think so.

"Did you sit in a pile of sugar? Cause you have a pretty sweet ass. An ass I'd like to get to know." He kept rubbing his slimy fingers over Aurora's arm.

Okay, now I don't have the patience of Jobe.

I snorted because that was some seriously stupid shit coming out of this guy's mouth. Before I could open my mouth, Aurora beat me to it.

"I'm lactose intolerant so please keep your cheesy pick-up lines away from me," she said straight to his face with not a smirk to be found.

I couldn't help it; I busted out laughing so hard I almost peed myself.

"You think this is funny, bitch?" jerk face asked.

His chair crashed to the floor, two of the legs had busted in the back and sent the guy flying. The guy got up, clearly angry, but not sure who to be angry at, looking between us and the broken chair.

I knew how the chair broke, and it looked like he might know how it broke too.

"You need to learn some manners, mutt," Aurora said to him as she crossed her arms on her chest.

Wait, I'm the adult, shouldn't I be the one to stick up for her? Maybe I need to pick up a book on parenting.

"Aurora, that's enough," I ordered. I turned to the guy who had picked up the chair.

"I'm trying to enjoy a coffee with my niece, and I would appreciate it if you left us alone." I gave him the high eyebrow.

"What, you witch bitches think you can make me look bad? I own this town!" he yelled. He went to reach for Aurora's arm, but I shot out of my chair and used both my hands to push him back with all I had. It didn't seem to do much but move him a few feet.

The whole coffee shop had stopped what they were doing and were watching with their mouths hanging open. I didn't blame them; I was just as shocked this situation had gotten so out of control.

"Looks like your dad never taught you any manners. That's a shame, like the world needs more assholes in it." I smiled but cocked my eyebrow at him. Here goes my attitude. I try so hard, but I can't keep my mouth closed when I most need to.

"I like a girl with a mouth like yours; it's good for other things too." He grabbed both my arms.

"Okay, Drake, let's just calm down." Jason came flying from behind the counter. "Avery didn't mean to be rude, she's just watching out for her family. Come back over to the counter, and I'll get you and

Stan a drink on the house. I just made some fresh blueberry scones. How does that sound?" he asked Drake.

"Yeah, Drake, take your smelly self away from us. I think I saw a doggie spa down the street," Aurora taunted.

I turned around and glared at her. Aurora, you aren't helping, I thought to her. I knew she could take care of herself with the help of her magic, but keeping magic a secret was still the law, and all I needed was the council coming after her.

Now I was a little scared, maybe this guy was pushed too far. I could feel the menace coming from him. I could have tried to be polite, but I hate it when people think they can push people around.

"Before you say another word, I would think about where you're at," came from behind me with that deep voice from last night. I turned around and there he stood. Goddess, he was a gorgeous man, and large.

"You have no authority here, Grayson, you're in my territory," Drake sneered.

Territory? Did Drake run part of this street like a gang or something?

"I might not have authority here, but you're in public." Grayson was staring at this guy like he could kill him, and I swear his eyes were glowing with a hint of burnt yellow.

Wait, what?

Like on clue, Grayson looked at me. "Are you okay?" he asked me. I watched his eyes change back to their sky blue.

"Grayson's a cool name," I beamed, staring into those sparkling eyes.

He smiled, snapping me out of my trance.

"Did I say that out loud?" I gulped.

"Yep," he said with a shit-eating grin on his face.

I noticed their attention was now focused on me.

Well, that just won't do.

"Well, it looks like it's time for us to get going. Thanks, Jason, here's Aurora's application. I'll call ya," I told Jason as I handed him the application, grabbed Aurora's arm and started to drag her out of the fray.

I did not want to be here if a fight broke out.

"Bitch, I am not done with you," Drake said.

That was all it took, Grayson's hand shot out and grabbed the dude by his throat. "I might not be from this area, but you'll do well to remember I am an alpha. You will leave her alone and any other women that comes into this bakery." He let go of Drake, but I noticed the guy Drake came with was ready for a fight, crouching on the balls of his feet. I had stopped walking when this started not sure if I should stay or go. My curiosity about this guy was peeked.

"My father will hear about this!" Drake yelled while he stalked towards the door. I watched Drake shake his head at Stan and then both guys hightailed it out the front door.

"Sorry about him, he's young and doesn't know when to quit," Grayson said as he visibly checked me from head to toe.

I decided I needed to introduce myself. "Hi, I'm Avery. Avery Sinclair, we kind of met last night," I stuck my hand out. He just looked at my out stretched hand as if he was trying to decide something. "Now who's being rude, it's just a hand. You put yours in mine and say it's nice to meet you." I frowned at him. That's how people introduce themselves, right?

"Sorry, just thinking about something. I'm Grayson Hayes." He held out his hand and we shook.

"See, that wasn't so… so…" I never finished what I was saying because the lights began to dim, and I felt a zing of electricity shoot down my right arm; that's about when the lights went out.

"Nope, not so hard, but now we're going to know each other a whole lot better. I should have listened to my mom and not followed you here. Jackson, could you help Aurora get their stuff? I'll meet you at the car," he said. Grayson scooped me up. I was semi-conscious of what was being said, but it was fading in and out.

"Auntie doesn't know about you guys, could you just put her in the jeep, and I'll wait till she wakes up? I'm not sure she's ready to know about your kind yet." Aurora said as she followed us out to the parking lot.

"This was going to happen eventually, might as well let her know about other supernaturals," Grayson said as he climbed into the back seat of the jeep with me in his arms.

Aurora got in the front seat and the guy that was with Grayson got in the driver's side of the jeep.

"I'm Aurora, by the way, Avery's niece. Thanks for driving. I don't have my license yet," she said as she buckled up.

"Hey." was all that the guy said as he buckled in and started up the jeep.

I could hear everything that was being said, but I couldn't open my eyes or move and eventually just drifted off.

When I did regain some level of consciousness, a burning pain on my right wrist brought me around enough to know I was lying in Grayson's lap in a vehicle. "My arm, the burning, it hurts," was all I could manage to say.

"I know it burns, it won't last much longer. Just keep your eyes closed. We'll be at your house in a few minutes." Grayson was staring at me with a look of sorrow. When he made contact with my arm, it seemed to dull the pain and I passed back out.

I woke up about three hours later in my bed. I felt hungover and couldn't remember anything except being at the bakery.

What happened after that? I swung my legs over the side of the bed and stood up. I fell back on the bed.

"Okay, so I should have sat a little longer. What happened to me?" I ask no one. After a few minutes of lying on my back with my legs dangling over the side, I was able to get up. I was still dressed in the jeans and long sleeve t-shirt I had on this morning, but on my right wrist was a leather band covering most of my palm and connected around my thumb as well. It was a soft, tan leather tooled piece with leather laces tying it together at the wrist. Beautiful was the only way to describe it.

I walked out into an eerily quiet family room. I started to panic and went from room to room looking for Aurora. After checking the whole house, I grabbed my phone to call Aurora when I realized I didn't have her number programmed into my phone. I'm going to have to fix that problem. I walked over to the kitchen window and spotted Aurora and some other people playing soccer in the neighbor's yard.

I didn't feel like being social with the vacationers so I opened the back door and called for Aurora. Once inside, Aurora went on about how nice the people staying in the cabin were. She hadn't mentioned anything about earlier this afternoon.

"Aurora? How did we get home today?" I asked her calmly.

"The neighbors, and once we got you home after you fainted they invited me to play soccer. I came in the house to check on you a few times, but you were sleeping so I took Bella back outside. The neighbors invited me to lunch, and we've been outside ever since. I didn't get to meet all of them because some were running errands, but I heard there are a couple of boys my age. Goddess, I hope they're cute. There don't seem to be any cute guys in this area and probably at school too and that would just suck."

Okay, that all sounded like it wasn't too bad, but why did I faint?

While I made dinner, Aurora told me I passed out at the bakery, and Grayson and Jackson brought us home. I was surprised, I'd never fainted a day in my life, well until now.

"Aurora, where did this leather band come from?" I asked, still a little foggy lifting my right arm to show her.

Instead of answering my question, she asked her own instead.

"Have you noticed anything strange with the vacationers?" Aurora asked me as she hopped up on the island barstool, totally avoiding answering my question.

"What do you mean by strange? Sometimes I can be strange, or so I've been told." I couldn't decide if I wanted to start tacos this late.

"Have you ever noticed when you're around other people with magic you get chills, almost like goose bumps?"

I dropped the package of meat on the floor. "What did you say?"

"You know, goose bumps. It happens to me every time I'm around another witch. Mom told me it was a way for us to know our own kind," she said with a straight face.

"So, you got those goose bumps when you were with the neighbors?" I asked.

Oh, please say no, please say no.

"Why don't you want to know that I got goose bumps? I thought you might be happy there were other witches in the area?" She frowned at me.

She was doing it again, reading my mind. "Aurora, you have to stop doing that. I hated it when your mom did it to me, and I don't like it any better when you do it. My thoughts are my own." I sighed.

"I'm sorry, really I am. You have to always be blocking, it takes practice. I know Mom said you were a dud, but I bet I could still help you."

Dud, I hate that word. Just one of the many that made me feel like I didn't belong. Goddess, I'm glad I moved away.

"Let's wait until after dinner then we can try. I do want to ask though, could you refrain from using that word? Just because someone doesn't possess magical abilities doesn't mean they deserve the negative label. Being normal has suited me just fine for thirty-two years. I don't possess any magic and frankly, I'm completely fine with that. I once thought lesser of myself because I was different, but I learned long ago that putting someone down because of their differences, is wrong and I don't want to hear anyone calling anyone names." I slammed the pan down.

"Hey, I didn't mean anything by it. Auntie, please don't be upset. I don't think any less of you or anyone else, that's not me. I was just repeating… I won't use that word anymore. Maybe sometime you could tell me about how it was growing up." She had come around the island and opened her arms. Wiggling her eyebrows, she gave me a wicked smile. "Common, Auntie, I know you want a hug."

I laughed and wrapped my arms around her tightly. She wanted

a hug, so I was going to give her a hug. I wasn't mad at her, I know my issues are mine and mine alone, and Aurora didn't mean any harm with a word that is widely used in the witch community.

"Agghhh... can't… breathe..." She started squirming around in my arms. Maybe I held on a little too tightly with her face buried in my chest as her arms were flailing a bit. I let go.

She took a deep breath of air and looked me up and down.

"Dang. I knew you were all about the whole lovey-dovey, touchy-feely gig, but that hug right there was a totally different story." She smirked. "You coulda' warned me before you tried to frickin' kill me! But hey, it's fine. I'll get you back one way or another." She walked slowly backwards toward the wall and slipped around the corner. I raised my eyebrows and chuckled. She's odd. Then all of a sudden, her head popped back around the corner. "Watch your back, Auntie," she said and winked at me.

I could hear her laughing as she went down the stairs to her bedroom. Yes, definitely odd.

I shook my head and finally made the decision that I wanted to make tacos, even though it was already ten to seven. I sang to myself quietly as I prepared dinner. I was chopping tomatoes when Bella came in and scared me. I jumped and let out a squeak, allowing the knife to slip cutting my pointer finger on my right hand.

I looked down and blood was dripping from my finger onto the cutting board. Ouch. I walked over to the sink to rinse my finger off and rolled up my sleeves so I wouldn't get them wet. I noticed that I still had that leather band around my wrist; it was pretty and I didn't want to get it wet so I untied the straps with my left hand and took it off.

Once I cleaned the blood off my wound, I grabbed a hand towel to keep pressure on it so it wouldn't continue to bleed. The towel brushed against the symbol on my palm and I had an impulse to touch it. I rubbed the design that circled my palm. It was a beautiful design, but where in the hell did it come from? I hoped Aurora's friend called back soon. There were ways to have the coven check your magical level, but the only coven I knew were not ones I would trust with that kind of magic use, not on my body. I went through that pain and torture when I was a kid and was not hip on repeating that anytime soon.

Chapter Five
Ketchum Pack

The Peace Summit started five years ago due to decrease in pack numbers and other issues interfering with keeping our existence secret.

With rivaling packs and the secrecy of our race, we had to meet to figure out who had been murdering our kind. Most humans don't know we exist. There are some that have integrated into our pack by marriage, but overall we keep our existence a secret. We don't know how the government would react to us, and until we do we keep to ourselves, but we do have to have a group mindset for our safety so we started getting all the alphas together once a year. We call it the alpha counsel. Each supernatural sector has their own counsel that rules each group, making and enforcing their own laws.

Each pack has their own way of ruling but for the majority have shifter bi-laws followed by all packs. This year the Cataloochee Pack was picked to host the event in Asheville, North Carolina. Maximus

Demarko is the pack alpha, and not one I'm looking forward to seeing again. He's about fifteen years older than my thirty-four years, and we never see eye to eye. He likes to rule with a heavy hand, and he treats his females like garbage, using them as he sees fit. How each pack treats their own isn't something I can get involved in, but of the twenty-six pack alphas across the U.S. I have a few that agree there needs to be change. Change is always slow and met with much resistance. A few of us have talked about having one alpha to manage all the packs for when things get out of hand and someone needs to step in. So far, that hasn't come to pass. There are always a few alphas' that don't want to be ruled; it goes against our nature to submit to anyone. However, the main reason the counsel is meeting this year is to address the hunters, and what we as a whole are going to do about them. Our numbers have been steadily declining and with birth rates lower than normal, the alphas' have concerns.

The hunters are a group of millies that feel any supernatural creature is an abomination in the eyes of God; well, their God. All supernatural worship some form of God or Goddesses, sometimes multiple Gods, but we don't hold any prejudices in our spiritual beliefs. We don't think non-magic users are below us, just different, as are we. One law that pertains to all supernaturals is that human life is precious in whatever form it comes in.

"I hate this. I know you say it's necessary but there are so many asshats in this room." Jackson and I had just walked into the conference room at the hotel owned by Maximus. Any alpha gets a little edgy when they are in unfamiliar territory. Our fight response runs high, and I could tell Jackson didn't like the power top off.

"Just keep your cool. Some of us have plans, but until they happen we have to all get along. I know it's difficult. Go see if you can find an itinerary. We might be stuck here, but I want to know how it's being scheduled. I want to get back to the cabin as soon as possible." I ran my fingers through my hair. Ever since I left Avery in her bed I couldn't settle down, not through physical activity or sleep.

"You mean you want to get back to see Avery. Man, I've never seen you this on edge. I might not be the one who has to keep my cool around here," Jackson said as he slapped me on the back. Jackson always loved a good drama in whatever form that came.

"Let's not talk about Avery here; I don't want anyone to know about her. It would put her more in danger, and we don't need that." I grimaced when I realized we were way to close to wolf ears.

Jackson just nodded and went in search of the program. I tried to get a head count to see if all the alphas were here, but it's hard to concentrate with that much power in one room. We usually schedule several breaks throughout the day just so that we can all get away from each other. Tempers tend to run high.

"I was wondering when you'd get here. You haven't returned my calls for the last few days." I turned around and saw a friend.

I smiled and reached out my hand. "Clay, sorry, man. I've had a few things to deal with since I got here. I know you wanted to get together before the summit started. How's your night looking? We could meet somewhere or you could come out to the cabins we're renting, see ma, have some dinner."

Clay Munger and I met when I had done some work in Washington State. He's the new alpha for the Tala Pack near Seattle. He's like me, he bid his time waiting for the right time to take over the pack and change the archaic ways. He's almost as tall as I am, probably around

6’2”, with long brown hair he keeps tied in a bun. On first meeting him, one would keep their distance because of the scare that runs from his eyebrow to his chin, but pack members see strength in battle wounds. He’s said to be a well-liked alpha.

“Sounds good. I’ll give you a call or you can text me directions. I’d like to meet some of your pack, and I hear your mom can cook a mean roast.” Clay winked at me.

“Yep, she keeps us well-fed,” I laughed as I patted my stomach. “I’ll text you directions. I’m glad you’re coming over. There’s something I want to discuss with you.” Clay raised his eyebrows at me.

I shook my head, and he understood it was private. It’s nice to have a few friends in this stuffy room. I grabbed a cup of coffee and made myself comfortable; most of the day was going to be about insignificant items such as how other packs aren’t supposed to travel onto other packs territory without asking permission. Unless a shifter is making problems for me, I let those few times it happens go. As I took a sip of the mediocre coffee, I noticed Jackson rubbing elbows with Clay’s beta. One of the many things Clay had done that didn’t sit well with older alphas was his choice of beta. Claire Swanson was the only female beta in the world. I didn’t have a problem with it, and if I had any females in my pack that were qualified for the job I’d have one too. Claire was used to the blatant disrespect that came with the job, but I still felt for both her and Clay. Jackson seemed to take a liking to her. He always did like the feisty ones. At least today won’t be boring for him.

As the day was winding down, and after many spontaneous breaks due to hot tempers, I was waiting by the exit for Jackson when I saw Max coming my way. This was the first time I’ve seen him since he came for a meeting in Idaho. I took a deep breath and tried to center myself.

"Grayson, it's been awhile. You were what, forth in the pack line. Impressive to go from wiping asses to leading a pack. I've always wondered how your old alpha didn't know how powerful you were." Maximus asked.

Maximus is a middle-aged, stout man with a full head of ginger hair and beard. His eyes were what you wouldn't expect from a red head, almost black they're so dark.

"I was surprised that you agreed to host this year's summit. You're not known for being generous or welcoming," I remarked.

Maximus had been prodding me for years. I'm still uncertain if it's because he can tell I'm stronger or if he wanted me to challenge him because he thinks he's stronger.

"Tax write off, or are you not familiar with business? Never claimed to be generous, all the alphas have to pay a fee to be here. Who do you think gets that money? Speaking of the city, I heard you met my son, Drake, yesterday. He mentioned you put your hands on him. It would be a shame to have to ban you from my city before the summit's over." Maximus stated.

"I'm not sure what Drake told you, but he was acting out of turn in a public place. I stepped in to make sure he behaved himself. Upsetting customers in a business you don't own is risky," I said as I scanned the room for Jackson.

He grabbed my arm, putting as much pressure as he could into his grip.

"Now hold on a second—my city, my business. He also mentioned you seemed to know the women he was talking to. If you have never been to my city how is it that you know people here? You wouldn't happen to be entering my territory without permission, would you?" His face was void of any emotions, which made it difficult to judge him. I wondered if he was trying to pick a fight, knowing if I entered his territory without permission would mean an immediate challenge.

"I meet people quickly, that's what happens when you have a nice personality. People actually want to talk to you." I could feel my inner wolf pacing, pushing to be let free.

"While you are in my city, you will treat all members of my pack with respect." Maximus demanded.

I nodded and shook myself from his grasp, abruptly turned and walked away, not typical for me, but I was done talking to him. I worried he would start asking more questions about Avery.

"Just watch who you push around here, Grayson. You might be an alpha, but you're not alpha of this pack, and I will step in if I have to. I heard you're staying at the Pine Valley cabins. Make sure to enjoy the view while you can." Max said loud enough so that most summit members would hear.

I wasn't sure what kind of threat that he was making, but it didn't bother me. From what I knew of Maximus he was more talk than action. He knew he wouldn't make it out of an alpha challenge with me.

When Jackson and I arrived back at the cabins, Mom had food ready and set out on the long dining table. I had texted Clay on the drive back, and he was on his way.

"Hey Mom, looks like we'll have another two for dinner tonight. Clay and his beta will be here shortly." I take a seat while I keep talking, "How did the day go? Anything I need to know?" She knew what I was talking about, but she just shook her head no and left it at that.

Clay and his beta Claire showed up we all sat down to eat Mom's famous pot roast. Conversation was easy and light with Jackson teasing Claire a few too many times.

After finishing dinner we all moved into the living room to get comfortable knowing this conversation wasn't going to be all pleasantries. I hadn't brought up the cross-linked mate subject yet. I had debated holding off, but I wanted to find out if Clay had any knowledge on the subject.

"As much as I love a home cooked meal, I have a feeling I'm not sitting here cause of my good looks." Clay pushed his hand through his hair and laughed.

"No, buddy, I got you beat in that department." Jackson licked his finger and rubbed it through his eyebrow. I hated to put a damper on what was turning into a hilarious beauty contest, but I needed advice and to update my pack as to what is going down. I would have done so over dinner but wolves tend to eat quickly.

"Yes, you both are the most handsome of us all. Now can we get down to fuckin' business?" I asked as I took a seat on the hearth and looked at Clay. "I invited you and Claire here because I wanted to find out if you had any information about cross-linked mates?" I blew out a huge breath that I hadn't known I was holding. Just saying took a huge weight off my shoulders.

You could hear the cabin wood creaking with the silence that was ringing through the living room. Everyone was staring at me with bewildered expressions on their faces.

"I'm sorry, did you say cross-linked mates? As in cross-linked mates of different supernatural communities?" Claire stated and Clay almost choked on the coffee Mom had handed out.

"Yep, that's what I said. It sounds like you've heard of it before. Because I could really use some advice on what to do," I said with a heavy sigh.

"Wow, so she's not a wolf?" Clay said.

"No, she's not, it would be a fuck of a lot easier if she were," I grunted.

I looked around the room and I couldn't read most of the expressions on the group's faces. Some looked shocked; some looked curious but most looked eager to hear more.

"So if she's not wolf then what is she? A millie?" Clay asked.

"We have a human in our pack, it was the first I'd heard of but he seems to be loyal to us so I haven't really given it much thought until now. There's more to it than that, she's… well she's..." I didn't get to finish.

"Oh, for heaven's sake!" My Mom looked at everyone with her chin out. "She's married, and she's a witch," she belted. Challenging anyone to speak up and say something. "It's really not that big of a deal."

"Not that big of a deal? She's married. I can't even tell her what's going on." I flung my hands up in frustration.

"Wait, did you say she's a witch?" Clay asked Josie.

"That's the whole point of cross-linked mate meaning, "Jackson murmured.

I gave Jackson a glare. I didn't need him pissing off another alpha.

My mom always the diplomat ignored Jackson. "She doesn't come off as a witch. Her niece is, but she doesn't have the supernatural flare that we all know each other by," I said.

"I'm not saying you wouldn't know your cross-linked mate, but what proof do you have that she is? Have you met her?" Claire piped up. Totally ignoring the witch question, like most of us wanted to.

This was what I didn't want to do, I didn't want to have to explain, it seemed too personal and hard to describe. To rip myself open in front my pack made me too vulnerable.

I held up my right palm for them to see. "This happened when I touched her hand two days ago. Our marks are matching." I lowered my hand.

Clay whistled. "Man, I wish I could help you, but I don't know anyone who has a cross-linked mate. I've heard stories, but nothing much." Clay shook his head.

"I might be able to help you," Claire spoke up.

"I'm all ears. If you think you know something." I couldn't help but notice the leering look Jackson gave Claire as she started talking.

"My grandfather was the alpha of a large Canadian pack, and I grew up with him telling stories at our monthly run. Sitting around the fires he told us of the cross-linked mates throughout all the paranormal communities," she explained.

"Are we really going to listen to her? She's not even from our pack. Cross-linking to other paranormals isn't possible or even conceivable." Sasha stood up her breathing was heavy.

"Sasha sit down, you will respect Clay and his beta. If you don't want to be involved in this meeting you're welcome to leave." I raised my eyebrows, waiting for an answer. She sat back down, not wanting to be put in her place any further.

"Claire, please go on. I would love to hear what your Grandfather told you," I said.

"My family comes from Europe with my grandfather being the

first generation of our pack to come to North America. He told us that shifters and other paranormals used to be cross-linked mates. He said that all paranormals, at one time, had worked together to protect themselves against humans. He spoke of a war that started between the shifters, vampires, witches, the fae, and other supernaturals. He didn't give much detail, but he did say that once the separation started, super groups weren't conceiving like they once had. The tattoo on your hand is similar to the one he used to draw in the sand to show us what it looked like. I know it sounds hard to believe, but my grandfather said he saw the tattoo and witnessed this for himself. He also warned that if the paranormals didn't reconcile we would eventually cease to exist. That to find our cross-linked mates we had to look outside of our packs, our covens, our clans."

"Are you saying that at one time a shifter would have been mated to say a vampire?" Jackson asked as he swished his almost gone beer.

"Actually, my grandfather said that his grandfather was cross-linked to a witch, but yes, all supernaturals were cross-linked including humans, hence the name cross-linked," Claire declared.

"Now I know your grandfather was crazy." Sasha got up to leave.

Claire took the few steps to stand in front of Sasha.

"I will let most things go, particularly from someone as low as you are in your pack, but I draw the line at disrespecting my grandfather. He was a much-respected alpha, and if he said he saw the mark then he did." She growled as she waited for Sasha to back down. You could see the flash in Sasha's eyes realizing she pissed off a girl who could kick her ass. Sasha bent her head to the side to show submission, grabbed her son's hand and then stalked out, slamming the front door.

Tank jumped up to go after her.

Yes, there relationship is more than it seemed.

"Don't, Tank, let her go. Sasha needs to grow up." I waved Tank to sit back down.

"I thought we were talking about Avery. She's not a witch, she's a human. So how is this symbol showing up on her?" Jackson asked.

"Well, don't you think mating with a human is still cross-linking?" Claire asked Jackson, who didn't respond and just stared blankly.

"I think it's time I go meet your mate, son, because I don't think Avery is purely human. Her niece showed a large flare, and she's a young witch. I asked her questions at lunch about her family and they are all witches brought up in the same coven, and Avery is not adopted." My mother stood up with a determined look on her face. Along with being a badass wolf, my mom could pick out a paranormal from across the room and tell you how much power they have.

Mom had flown out of the cabin and we all made small talk while we waited for her to return. The urge to go with her was so strong, but I fought that desire and continued to listen to the conversations around the room. It took my mom about twenty minutes before she showed back up. She had used the excuse that she needed to borrow a cup of sugar. I had laughed at her while asking her if that even worked anymore. Well, with the smile she had plastered on her face and the cup of sugar she carried, I guess that answered my question.

"Well, first off, I want to tell you son she's a fine woman. Second, it seems like your cross-linked mate is a witch," Mom stated and the room fell silent.

"She's a witch, are you sure?" I had to ask, this was the first I had ever heard of a wolf shifter and a witch being mates.

"Yes, her powers are weak, not used, but she is a witch. Along with her niece who just moved in. Her husband isn't home, and I'm not sure when he will be, but from what Aurora said today, her husband is a run of the mill human and doesn't know they are a line of powerful witches. She mentioned the Green Lake Coven, which is a very powerful coven." Mom went about putting the sugar away.

"Shit. So what do we do now?" Jackson still hadn't closed his mouth since Mom dropped the bomb.

"We do nothing except watch her. I have a feeling that if Max finds out about her, his interest might become a problem," I said as I took my beer into the kitchen. I could feel the muscles in my back starting to clench up. I craved my hot tub but would have to wait until we got home.

"Well, son, it's too late. I invited Avery and her family over for dinner tomorrow, six o'clock sharp," she said nonchalantly.

I stood up and shouted, "You what? You can't invite her over, Mom. I have a hard enough time staying away from her, but with her being so close I won't be able to control my wolf. How will that work with her husband sitting there? My wolf will not stand for that. How do you think she'll feel when I end up accidentally killing him," I threw my arms up in exacerbation.

"You and she are linked, son. The faster you realize that, the sooner you can accept it. Now, I'm going to bed. I've had enough for one night." She reached up on her tiptoes to give me a hug and kiss good night.

"Good night, Mom. Sleep well." I watched her and Dad walk up the stairs. As much as I wanted to be royally pissed at my mother, I knew she was just trying to help an impossible situation.

"She's married, Grayson?" I jumped at the voice. I had forgotten I hadn't dismissed the pack meeting so everyone was watching me.

"Yes, everyone, she's married and has her niece living with her. This goes for all of you, do not tell her anything. I don't even want her to know I share the same mark. No shifter talk, nothing. Jackson, go and tell Sasha about the dinner tomorrow and let her know that if she can't control herself or her son then she can just stay in for the night." I was cringing on the inside. Having dinner with someone who wasn't part of our pack just never happens. Wolf shifters tend to be boisterous and honest to a fault. Sometimes they acted like, well, animals. This wasn't how I pictured our first dinner. Tomorrow is going to be great. I can't wait. Ugh.

"Claire and I will keep our eyes and ears open tomorrow at the summit in case we hear anything. I'm sorry, man, to find a cross-linked mate and she's married. I'm glad I'm not in your shoes." Clay slapped me on the back as he and Claire slipped out.

How could I disagree with their assessment? How could I even get close to someone who's married? This will take some finesse for sure. As I was thinking this to myself, I realized everyone else had departed as well.

I needed some time to myself. I liked control and right now everything felt out of control. Maybe a good run would take some of this anxiety away.

Chapter Six
Anxiety

Lying in bed, I tried counting sheep, which by the way never works. So I tried placing myself at some random beach, relaxing in the sun. Nothing was working, sleep wasn't coming, and I had this feeling of unease. After having the older woman from the cabins come over and invite us to dinner for the following evening, I couldn't seem to settle down my nerves. I tried to quiet my mind. I went downstairs and worked out, then went out to my green house and watered and pruned my plants and even tried turning the TV on to a mindless reality show. Nope, none of it seemed to be working.

The woman who came over this evening seemed sweet. I just don't like getting to know neighbors that are only here on vacation. Having moved so much after I left Seattle I wasn't used to making any long-term friends. Since meeting Ryan, I have been able to make some friends in the area, but no friendships I wouldn't be willing to sacrifice if I had to move away. Part of that bothered me, even as a child I wasn't

able to make any lasting friendships because of the coven rules. I had once met a girl in my neighborhood, started to build a friendship but as soon as my sister had ousted me to our parents, they squashed that friendship. I had to go as far as telling the girl I couldn't be friends with her anymore. She didn't understand, and I couldn't explain it to her partly because it was against the coven bylaws but mostly because I didn't understand it myself. After that incident, none of the human kids in the neighborhood would play with me. I learned early on that being a loner was the way it was going to have to be.

Meeting Josie tonight had brought some of those lonely feelings to the surface because I had taken to her immediately, feeling at ease with her and asking question after question. Aurora never had a grandmother figure, so as soon as Josie had knocked on the back door she came flying up from downstairs ready to entertain. Offering her something to drink, acting as if she was family and not a complete stranger. Josie didn't seem to mind. In fact, she seemed rather taken with her as well. I wondered if she has any grandkids.

As I was trying to wind down, my cell rang. I knew who it was before I even looked at it. I'm really starting to hate Ryan's job.

"Hi." I said as a sigh whooshed out. I knew if he was calling this late it had to be because he was asked to take additional flights. His job seemed to be taking him from me more often than not.

"Is that anyway to greet your husband?" he asked with distain.

"It is when I know you're calling because they want you on some other flight. Its fine, Ryan, I know you're working hard. I just miss you, that's all." I was done getting mad about it. I was too tired to try to argue or reason with him.

"We are not having this conversation again, Avery. You knew what my job was, so stop being immature. I only have a few minutes to talk, and I hate it when you pout," he said. So instead of not seeing him this week, it would be at least two weeks before he was due home.

At the end of our conversation I had started to say, "I love you", but dead air was all there was. He had a tendency to hang up without as much as a good bye. I hung up and no longer had any desire to sleep. I'm not ambivalent as to what I expected to happen when I found out I was the legal guardian of my niece, but I thought maybe that would get Ryan to slow down and want to spend time with both of us. I had voiced my nervousness and concerns with him before she came to live with us, but he blew it off and said woman take care of children every day. "It's not that big of deal, Avery, she's practically grown." Ryan didn't know I was on birth control, or at least he didn't know I still take it.

When we were first dating I had brought up my insecurities with raising children, but he blew that off as well and said it was a natural thing, that I was making a bigger deal out of something humans have been doing for quite a long time. He even went as far as to go through my bathroom drawers until he found my pills and threw them away. On several occasions, I tried to express I wasn't ready yet. He was persistent, he would take me to dinner, a movie, something that would keep us occupied and the next morning I would find my pills gone. My older sister, if she were still alive and speaking to me, would have waited at my door for the next date with Ryan and told him to take a hike and not come back. Probably even would have put some sort of spell on him that would have him forget about me. She would have paced and lectured that I deserve better, that no man treats a woman like this, and on and on until I felt like the child who wasn't worth her

weight in this family. I know if I weren't so lonely I would have never married Ryan in the first place, but normal looked so good to me at the time. At least it felt normal, but what would I know about normal.

I felt caged and decided I should go for a walk. I looked out the window and noticed the brightness from the moons glow banking off the rocky ditch that illuminated the road. I thought about taking Bella with me as I felt we could try to bond since I hadn't spent much time with her. For a split second, pain shot through my chest thinking about Cosmos, my childhood cat and what they did to her. Cats, or a familiar, was considered paramount in a witches training. Ones cat would grow with you, sometimes helping you boost spells. The coven killed her right before I left. I found her hung in a tree in our back yard. I heard whispers Matilda had done it, but I never had proof.

I looked over at Bella, lying on her bed in front of the fire place, sleeping like she doesn't have a care in the world.

"Hey Bella girl, want to join me for a walk?" I asked her.

She sprang right up, ready to go. Glad someone was happy to see me, or it could be the wild rabbits on and around our property she was eager to chase. Bella chasing them made me realize how many rabbits we have living in our yard. I was always rooting for the bunnies when Bella would take off after them.

"I take that as a yes. Well, come on, I'll feel better having company." I talk to her as if she understands me. Hell, who knows if they can.

I pulled on my running shoes, grabbed Bella's harness, and decided these contraptions were definitely made by a man. Could anything be more complicated? Nope.

I love walking at night on the gravel road that runs in front of our house. The surrounding properties were mostly cow pastures with a few horses, but it's the darkness and the night's sounds when one world went to sleep with the sun another awakened with the moon and that intrigued me. I had taken walks most nights since moving to North Carolina, and it became a game to search for the owl that loudly made itself known. Living outside of town helped keep me calm. When I spend too much time in the city my anxiety grows, nature always seemed to keep me serene.

Our walk down the four mile road didn't take as long as I had imagined. Bella didn't seem interested in the smells all around but stayed as a sentry attached to my side. I didn't think too hard on this until I felt her stop on a dime, freeze and let out a low, menacing growl that stopped me even before I felt the leash resist my forward movement. At least she's on a leash and can't run off. Goose bumps fluttered across my skin, my arm went straight to Bella's back where I felt her hackles rise. I tried soothing her, but she sensed something that I didn't. I think my niece bringing her dog might be working out; hopefully she can scare whatever is lurking in the bushes away from us.

"Calm down, it's just you me and some noisy insects. And maybe a sleeping snake or two." I hadn't seen a snake, but I've met people in passing who had and that was enough to know I didn't want to come across one, poisonous or not. The bugs are definitely bigger and louder in North Carolina, especially the cicadas. With the moon's glow I could see at least twenty feet down the road, but the shadows made it hard to tell. Bella's growl got worse and I was staring at a particular shadow that looked like it was slowly moving out of the bush toward the side of the road.

"Maybe it wasn't such a good idea to bring you. Don't tell me that you're scared of cows, cause they are known to get out and roam down the street. Let's head home." I start back toward my driveway, which wasn't too far, but she's planted solid behind me.

"Bella, let's go. This way." I tug once more on her leash. Nope, she's not moving, but her growling is getting more intense. My fight or flight mode was in full swing, my muscle started tensing and my breathing became faster. Maybe it's time to run.

"Now you're starting to freak me out. Bella, come." I patted my leg. Just when I was about to grab her collar I slide my gaze at the bush line. A pair of silver eyes starred back at me. I could see a hint of white teeth. Could be a coyote, but I've never seen one this close to my house.

"Bella, come now!" I yanked on her leash, but she wasn't budging.

I'm trying to remember what they say about two dogs that get into a fight. Are you supposed to pull yours back or drop the leash and let them go at it? Even though she isn't my dog, I like having her around. Not to mention the fact that Aurora would be devastated if anything happened to her dog. It was times like these that I wished I wasn't a dud with magic.

"Okay, unknown creature, whatever you are. My harmless dog and I are going to stay out of your way." I force Bella to turn around, and I start to drag her away. It's taking every ounce of will power I have not to look back. If I look back and the coyote is following us, I might just scream like a little girl, and I don't think that would help our cause. Don't they say don't run, or that an animal can sense your fear? Well, I'm oozing 'freak out' pheromones all over the place. My heartbeat is so loud in my head I can't hear anything else and my pits are drenched with sweat.

I'm hoping that if we make it past the tree line of our property we should be okay. We made it just past the trees when the growling got closer. I kept walking though I couldn't help but glance back. My one bad encounter with a dog came flooding back to me.

A neighborhood dog had tormented me for months as I walked past his house on my way to school, always pulling on his chain wanting to take a piece out of me. I started to cross the street, having a feeling that the chain wouldn't hold. I had tried compassion for the dog, considering the possibilities that maybe it was mistreated and that if I tried to be nice it might befriend me. When that didn't work, I had resorted to walking on the other side of the street trying to not give the dog anything to notice. Until one day that didn't work. Its chain had snapped, and it charged me like a raging bull. If it hadn't been for a neighbor sweeping his walkway I would have been mauled by that dog.

It seems I'm out of neighbors with brooms.

As I start to drag Bella, the coyote (which is the biggest one I've ever seen) came running full speed right for us. I dropped Bella's leash on pure instinct just as Bella leapt and met the coyote mid-flight, right in the path that would have taken me out. I stood stock still for about ten seconds, trying to comprehend two dogs were fighting, and not to just fighting, viciously ripping each other apart. Bella's scream launched me into fight mode. As soon as I realized that Bella wasn't faring well I looked over into the ditch and ran for a stick before I turned and begin my attack, swinging as hard as I could. Right after the blow landed on the coyote I was knocked into the ditch by Bella. I rolled ass over end a few times. I started to right myself when I felt the coyote rip into my arm. My closest neighbor a mile away could probably hear my scream. I struggled with the beast for a few seconds, thinking the whole time I was going to die. I reached with my left arm and dug my fingers into the dirt tearing my nails up, grabbed a handful of whatever I could and chucked it behind me, knowing that that wasn't going to save me. The feel of teeth vanished, and I heard a scuffle then a yelp. I tried to move my neck but the pain was so great I just laid there praying that Bella was all right. After what felt like forever, another animal screamed and then nothing. It was quiet again.

I felt a touch on my shoulder and tried to turn my head, and then a familiar soothing voice was talking to me.

"Just lay there for a second. It's going to be okay. I'm going to look at your arm first then I'm going to pick you up. Do you think you can handle that?" Grayson said as he stroked my neck.

I couldn't answer him, I just nodded. I guess I might not have broom-wielding neighbors, but I have a nice soothingly voiced neighbor who saved my ass from utter annihilation.

"Bella, please check on Bella..." was all I could push out. The pain in my arm was turning to a burning fiery feeling that brought on lightheadedness. The way I had fallen must have pulled some muscles because I struggled to even lift my head.

"I'm going to take you first. I've got someone coming for your dog," Grayson responded. He rolled me over carefully, and I tried to make out his face, but I was in so much pain my eyes refused to open. Being in that much pain makes focusing, let alone thinking even one coherent thought, almost impossible.

"You have to take Bella first," I said on a moan.

Grayson growled, "Your mutt can wait; I'm more worried about you. Your arm is bleeding and I don't know how bad it is yet."

He tried to push his arms under my body. He was going to take care of me first. Not going to happen.

"If you pick me up, I will struggle and hurt myself. Please, you don't understand. That dog is all my niece has left of my sister. Aurora won't recover if her dog dies, please..." I couldn't finish the sentence as a sob was closing my throat.

"Okay, okay. I'll look after Bella, but I need to rip this shirt you're wearing to take care of the bleeding first. You're welcome to try to fight me, but you won't like the outcome," Grayson retorted.

Before I could answer, he had started ripping my shirt from bottom to top. I didn't know you could rip a shirt like that. If I was alert enough I might have been more freaked that I'm lying in the dirt in only my bra, but at least it was my lacey black one I forced myself to buy. I didn't even care he was ruining my shirt instead of his own.

It hurt a little when he wrapped my arm, wrist to elbow, but I was finally able to see Bella lying in the ditch next to me, her chest rising and falling. She was alive and that was all I was worried about.

When my gaze fell onto Grayson, I realized why he was using my shirt instead of his own—he wasn't wearing a shirt, or any clothes for that matter. I watched him pick up Bella with such care, whispering softly to her that it was going to be okay. I knew from one look that this man cared, and he cared about many things. I didn't have much time to contemplate this when all of a sudden we were swarmed with people.

He started barking orders and everyone moved with quick precision, as if they had dealt with situations just like this all the time. I counted four people I didn't recognize moving around, deferring to him like he was a general and they were his soldiers, very bizarre.

"Jackson, get Avery and take her to the big cabin. I'm going to take Bella to Sasha's. Mom, I want you to call a vet and get him out here," Grayson said.

The older woman placed her hand on his forearm. "Grayson, son, is this wise? Isn't this because of Sasha?"

"Dad, you take Tank and find Sasha, take her to the cabin, and sit on her!" Grayson barked.

He was walking toward me with Bella.

"Son, I think…" his dad started to say.

"I don't care what you have to do to keep her in check, literally sit on her ass for all I care. She'll be lucky I don't rip her neck out for this," Grayson boomed again. He was clearly pissed.

I wasn't used to his kind of presence and as soon as he came closer, I yelped.

He took a deep breath and sighed, "Jackson, please carry Avery to the big cabin." He turned around and walked toward the two cabins behind my home.

One of the guys came and softly picked me up. He looked familiar, maybe he was with Grayson at the coffee shop. I had no choice but to put my arm around his neck, carefully laying my other one across my stomach; even that hurt. A man who was too gorgeous for his own good had never carried me in his arms before.

"Hi Avery, I'm Jackson. Most people just call me Jack, but you can call me whatever you like." He walked me to the larger cabin behind my home. They had to walk across my property to get to the cabins.

"Wait, wait, my niece. Can you just please take me to my house? My niece is home alone, and if she wakes up she might get scared. If you take me home, she can help me." I looked into Jackson's eyes and boy did he have lovely eyes. The green was a mossy color with a reddish brown exploding from the middle. I hadn't ever seen green eyes quite like it. I think he said something to me, but I didn't hear one word.

“I’m sorry, what did you say?” I shook my head to come back to the present.

“I said that as soon as I have you settled I will go sit and watch your house. If your niece wakes up I’ll bring her to you, don’t worry. Grayson will not be happy with me if I left you alone. And his mood isn’t going to improve anytime soon, so let’s just get situated and then we’ll deal with the rest. Okay?” he asked.

“Okay,” I breathed.

This man could talk to me about anything, and I would listen. Wow, I need to get a grip. One soothing man, one smooth talker, and I was putty. I guess shock makes you go all goo-goo over sexy men.

We had just made it to the door. I had kept my eyes closed because I was starting to feel nauseas when I felt myself being set on my feet and then turned and swept into the warm chest and arms of my soothing Grayson. “I’ve got her, Jack.” As I wound my arm around his neck, I was able to see him from the porch light we were approaching.

Oh, boy, am I in trouble.

“If you could go make rounds at her house and make sure her niece is safe, I’ll wait for the doctor,” Grayson told Jack.

“You got it, boss. Just yell if you need me,” Jackson said and off he ran at high speed. I wonder if he runs marathons?

I didn’t know what to say so I just took everything in that was happening. I had seen the cabins previously when the owner had given me a tour years ago, so I knew they had that country cottage, warm vibe.

“Thank you for saving me. I’ve never encountered a coyote before. I didn’t know they would attack like that. How does Bella look? Do you think she will live? Please, tell me she will live," I pleaded with him.

"She'll live. She might be down for a while, and she's definitely beat up, but she'll live." He laid me on the couch in front of the fire, pulled a throw blanket from the back of the couch, and draped it over me. He placed several more logs on the fire, and I couldn't help but close my eyes with the warmth.

"Hey, don't go to sleep. The doc should be here in a minute. I want you awake," Grayson said as he was tapping my cheek. I opened my eyes to stare at him. I wanted to tell him that I don't think dog bites mean you can't sleep, but I wasn't going to argue with that grumpy face.

To defuse his mood I ventured, "Hi, I'm Avery, and you're Grayson?" I asked with a week smile.

He chuckled.

"We've met a few times," he smiled.

After I was done talking, he took a deep breath through his nose, and you could see his control slip back into place. The energy this guy radiated is off the charts. As I was trying to think of something to say, the door to the cabin opened, and I looked over the end of the couch and watched the older woman who had come over earlier in the evening walk through with towels in her arms and a bright smile.

"Grayson, why don't you get some water boiling and make Avery some tea. Would you like some tea, dear?" she asked me as she set the towels on the chair.

"Sure, tea would be fine."

I watched Grayson leave the living room and make his way into the kitchen. I was trying to ignore the burning in my arm as I sat up a bit and started to take off the shirt that was soaked through with blood.

The woman put her hand on mine and said, "Oh, let's not take that off just yet. The doc should only be a few more minutes. I had him check out your dog first, she seemed to be in worse shape than you. I know I introduced myself earlier today but I wasn't sure if you knew I was Grayson's Mom." She ripped the towels with her hands into strips and laid them over the end of the couch. Again with the flimsy material ripping like it was made out of paper. Was I just not working my upper body enough?

"I don't need help right now, I'm not dying. I would prefer that the vet work on Bella," I snapped out as Grayson walked back into the living room. "I'm so sorry, really I didn't mean that, it's just that Bella was given to my niece by my sister and my sister died recently. Aurora loves her dog," I said to both Grayson and his mother.

"Honey, my husband is with Bella and I assure you she is good hands. He has treated many wounded animals in his days. I married that man for a reason," she said as she started to get up and relieve Grayson of the tea he made. "Here, drink some of this. You must be in shock, your color's not great, but tea will help."

I accepted the tea from her, not tasting the flavor, but within a couple of minutes the fog that had unknowingly surrounded my brain lifted a wee bit. Maybe I was in shock, though I wouldn't know what that felt like. Everyone seemed so calm. My heart rate was decreasing, and I could take a deep breath again.

"Is the coyote dead?" I asked wondering if we needed to call animal control.

Josie pulled up a chair right next to the couch I was laying on. She grabbed my hand and patted it. "Honey, don't you worry about that,

we took care of it. You just relax and drink your tea. I can imagine that whatever calm you have gained will be gone once we have to mess with your wound," Josie said with a frown.

"I'm just concerned we left a wounded animal out there. They can be unpredictable. What if other coyotes come from its pack? What if it's suffering? Maybe we should call animal control." I sat there drinking my tea, wondering how my day turned out so horrible. What I couldn't stop thinking about was Aurora. If she heard any of the noise the dogs made. Her being a young witch without direction can be dangerous, especially if they feel threatened.

"Avery, you need to stop worrying. My other son is watching over Aurora. He has two sons about her age. He won't let anything happen to her, I promise," she said with a reassuring smile. Josie had brought a button up shirt with the sleeves cut off and with great care she helped me put it on.

Grayson came and stood behind the chair his mom was sitting in. "Hey Mom, could you go check on everyone for me. That would be a huge help. I don't want to leave Avery until the doc gets here. I've never met this doctor and I'd be more comfortable staying here with Avery," he said as he squeezed his mom's shoulder.

"Sure, son. I'll be back." She waved to me as she left.

"Sorry about my mom, she tends to hover and coddle," he said as he took her seat. "I know she dreamed of having a girl but ended up with two rough and rowdy boys, so she tends to mother quite a bit," Grayson said with such love. Here was a man who truly loved and adored his mother.

"It's okay... I lost my mom at a young age, and I miss it. She seems too young to be your mother," I said as I starred at this handsome man.

His thick eyebrows naturally arched which made me think he was constantly curious.

"We have good genes in our family," he said with a smile.

"Thank you for saving me. I don't think I would have survived that attack if you hadn't shown up," I said as I looked out the windows. I couldn't get myself to meet his eyes. Men didn't intimidate me, at least not until now. Ryan might not back down and usually gets his way, but I could always meet his eyes.

He reached over and lifted my chin. "I'm glad I was there, and you are here, so let's not dwell on what could have been. The past is that, in the past." He smirked.

"I guess it just seems like I need rescuing, between just now and at the bakery today. Really, my life is never this exciting, or life threatening. I'm actually boring," I giggled as I finally looked up and met his eyes. His eyes are more extraordinary than Jackson's, the lightest golden amber ringed his eye then a dark brown ring and then the golden color again. It made his eyes look like they glowed.

"Wait, weren't your eyes…" I started to say when he looked away from me and when he turned back they were back to the sky blue from earlier.

"Life is meant to be exciting, so I don't mind. Plus, excitement is overrated, there are many days I wish my life was boring," he said just as he looked away from me with a tilt of his head, as if he had heard something. I listened but didn't hear anything except the crickets. Living out in the country I got used to the quiet. Grayson gave off a calm energy that put me at ease. I got the sense he was a man who could just sit on the front porch, with a beer of course, and watch the beauty around him.

We sat for a few minutes, not saying anything, I normally don't mind quiet but I felt like there were things to be said, but I had no idea what.

Just when I was trying to think of something to say to break the silence a knock came at the door. Two loud rasps, loud enough I squeaked and my tea spilt down the front of my blanket. Like this was helping.

Grayson got up to answer the door, but before he walked away he looked at me and said, "I won't leave you while you're treated, so don't worry."

I didn't think I had been worried about that, but when he said it this tightness in my chest I didn't know was there released so rapidly it came out in a whoosh of breath.

"Okay," I told him with a small smile.

Grayson opened the door and stood in front of whoever was on the other side. I couldn't hear what they were saying, but I could tell that it made Grayson nervous to let someone he didn't know look at my arm. His back was ridged and his posture said 'not welcome'. Grayson stepped aside as a small man with wire rim glasses smiled at me.

"Hi, I'm Dr. Leman. I hear you have an arm that needs looking after," he said as he ignored Grayson, walked over, and sat in the chair Grayson had vacated.

I held up my right arm. "Yeah, a coyote tried to take it for its dinner. I think I might need stitches." I grimaced.

"Well, let's take a look, shall we?" He wasn't an old man, only a wee bit older than Grayson and I. I would say maybe late forties, early fifties. His brown hair was short, but I could see a hint of gray at his temples. It was his eyes that made me relax. They were a warm brown, and he had wrinkles around them, which told me that he smiles a lot.

"Ow, ow... okay, that hurts!" I yelp at him as I tried to pull my arm back.

"Grayson, I need you to hold her for me, the shirt seems to have stuck to the wound. Pulling this off is going to hurt," he warned.

"Hey Doc." Grayson squatted down next to my head and stared with his intense amber glowing eyes at the doctor. "How about you give her something for the pain first. I'm not a doctor but that seems like the first thing you might do."

I could tell he was losing his patience, and I wanted to get this over with.

"I need to see the wound before I decide how to proceed. Plus, I don't know what this young woman might be allergic to," he told Grayson firmly.

I swear I heard Grayson growling, the rumbling was vibrating the couch. I looked at Dr. Leman and decided just to get this moving. "Here, I'll take it off," I told him. I grabbed one end of the shirt, and as fast as I could wound it off my arm. As the last piece pulled off, I blew out a breath that I had held because that hurt like a bitch. I was trying to be strong and not show how badly it hurt.

"See that wasn't so bad," I told Grayson. As I looked up at him, he was looking at my arm and frowning. I decided to get it over with and look at it myself, which was a huge mistake.

From my elbow almost all the way to my wrist, I was flayed open to the bone in a half circle. When I had pulled the bandage off it pulled the flap back and I could see veins, muscle, tissue, and bone. I could see my arm bone.

"Oh my Goddess, oh, my Goddess, oh my Goddess," I cried as

I started to breath faster and faster which caused the wound to pump blood faster. The room started to spin.

"You need to calm down, Miss, you're increasing your heart rate and that is going to make it more difficult to stitch you up," he told me as he started to put on gloves.

"Grayson, I need to go to the hospital. This is bad, and we have to call an ambulance...like now!" My voice was raising.

"And the pain, I think I might die. Is that possible, could you die from pain?" I screamed.

"If you don't give her something to calm her down, I'm going to get my heart rate going and then you're going to be the one in pain, Doctor. Where the fuck did you go to medical school?" Grayson was now standing and ready to pounce on this guy.

"Okay, okay, I'll give her something, hold on. I told Clay I wasn't an E.R. doctor. I don't handle traumas like this, most of my patients are the elderly," he said as he filled a syringe with some sort of chemical. I watched as he looked for a vein in my good arm. I'm not sure how long it took, maybe 10 seconds and I was out.

Chapter Seven
Sawtooth Pack

After the idiot doctor gave Avery something that put her under I had made a decision. I squeezed his shoulder hard enough to bruise and said, "Okay, you're done. Put a real bandage back on her arm and leave. If you're that incompetent, I don't trust you to sew her arm up. She needs a trauma doctor, and you sure as hell aren't one," I sternly scolded him. I was already pulling my phone out of my back pocket. If I called Leroy, he could be here in a few hours, and talking to him would help me not hurt this fucker.

"That's not necessary, I can sew up her arm. There doesn't seem to be any other damage," he said as he was looking over her wound.

"Stop! Put a fucking bandage on her arm," I hissed at him just as Leroy was answering his phone.

"Alpha, everything okay? I didn't expect to hear from you," Leroy asked concerned.

I glared at the pissant as he slowly put a bandage on her arm.

"No, everything is not fine. I need you. How fast can you get here?" I boomed at him while watching the doctor finish up.

"I'm off today, but I'm supposed to be on call for the next week. Is one of the pack hurt?" Leroy asked confused.

"Hold on a sec," I told him. I didn't want to talk about the pack in front of this guy. I waited for him to gather his things and leave.

"No, not... yes one of the pack, look I'm not getting into this over the phone. This is pack business, and it comes first, above your job at the hospital. I need you, and you need to make it here within the next few hours," I was getting impatient. Leroy will just have to make do, I'm sure his other patients can go a day or two without him.

"Christ, Grayson, Teri is ready to pop. Who is going to make sure this birth goes smooth if I'm not here? She can't go to the hospital," Leroy pleaded. It struck me with unease to hear that the confident Dr. Leroy wasn't so confident in this birth.

"Haven't you done hundreds of births? What's going on? Isn't Teri's husband's nephew, Christian, studying under you? How long until Teri gives birth? A week? Because I only need you a day at most. I wouldn't ask if it wasn't important." I was ready to make it an order which couldn't be ignored.

I knew that Avery didn't seem to have much damage below the flesh, but I also knew that if you have any Tom, Dick, or Harry sewing you up, it could turn bumpy and bunched when healed. I'd seen people that almost couldn't work their muscles the way they had once done because of a botch sewing job.

"Christian can handle a lot, but not surgery, not yet. I'll leave on the next flight." Leroy took a deep breath. "I'm just nervous, but I can be back in time as long as what I'm doing is simple. It's her first birth.

We might need to think about getting another doctor in our pack. We're growing too much for me to handle everyone myself. It will take years for Christian to be at my level, and he might decide pack life isn't where he wants to do his practice," he confessed.

"I know, and I want Teri to have her mind at ease, but you'll only be gone a day at most. Use our pack plane. We flew commercial here so it's open for you. That way you can get back right away. I'll have Dad come pick you up. You won't be here more than a few hours. I can't tell how bad it is, but it seems to have gone to the bone. I tried to let a local doctor do the work, but he didn't give her anything for pain. I wanted to rip his throat out. Just get here, I need you Leroy," I admitted.

"Okay, sounds like you're hanging on by a string. I'll be there with my medical kit, and we don't even have to go into who I'm actually treating til' I get there," he said before he hung up.

Leroy had the making of an alpha, but his deep heart made the hard choices almost impossible for him, so he hangs back and treats those he can and tries to stay out of pack politics. We were lucky to have him join our pack almost fifteen years ago. His pack in the southwest had broken down after their alpha had died, and he traveled around looking for a new permanent home, which he found with us.

Jackson had walked in during my conversation with Leroy. "Man, you sent the doctor away? Why?" he asked me as he walked over to check on Avery.

"That guy was an idiot. I didn't want him to touch her. It's bad, Jack, the wound goes to the bone. Has Sasha said anything? I asked him.

"Sasha hasn't said a word, Mom, Dad, and Tank are with her.

She's going to have to be punished for this, but I think we should send her back home and deal with it later. Tank's pretty wired." Jackson ran his hand over his face. "This whole thing is messed up," he told me.

"When Leroy leaves tomorrow he can take Sasha and Spencer with him. I'm done dealing with her; we have too many other problems to deal with. She needs to learn to put the pack first, not her own desires or whims. I want Leroy to do a blood test on Spencer and then test every pack member she's slept with. That boy needs a male figure in his life, I'm done letting this go. Everyone has his or her own job in the pack, we all have been trying to help when we can, but he needs a constant male. I'm leaving you in charge of this, Jackson. I need to focus on my new mate and how to keep us all safe," I ranted as I paced in front of the fireplace."

"Okay, one thing at a time. Let's get Avery fixed up and find out what is going on with you two. Why don't you go lay down, and I'll watch over her until Leroy gets in. You need to have your wits about you tomorrow. I have a feeling this shit is going to come to a head, and I don't need you tired and cranky." Jackson came over to me and put his hand on my shoulder.

I relaxed at once. As soon as Jackson had said those words it solidified why I chose him as my second.

"Thanks, brother, but I think I'll stay awake. Why don't you go make sure Sasha and Spencer are packed? Tell Tank he can bunk in Sasha's cabin with your two boys, and let Mom and Dad know that they can come back and go to bed, but Dad needs to pick Leroy up from the airport. It will be hours before Leroy gets here."

Before Jackson can fully turn away, I stop him with a hand on his shoulder. "Thanks, I couldn't have a better second, or a better brother," I said to him, and I meant it.

As Jackson was heading to the front door there came a light tap. Jackson grabbed the handle and whipped the door open.

"Is my Aunt here? She's not in the house." Jackson stepped back so Aurora could come in, and Aurora didn't waste any time. She spied her Aunt right away and ran over to her.

I realized I hadn't asked Jackson why he wasn't watching Avery's niece but I didn't get a chance.

"Why is she unconscious? What happened to her arm? I knew something wasn't right. I woke up, and knew she wasn't okay. Should we take her to the hospital?" Aurora fired question after question at both of us. She immediately put her hands on her aunt's temples and closed her eyes. Avery started to thrash around but didn't wake up.

I flew across the room and went to grab Aurora. I had been around her when we brought Avery home and she seemed reasonable, but I didn't like her making her aunt agitated. Before I could touch Aurora's arm, one of her hands went up, stopping my forward movement.

Jackson knowing I wouldn't have stopped my progress on my own volition went into action. He didn't come close to us, but he positioned himself behind Aurora with his hands lifted up and palms out. "Now just calm down, both of you. A coyote attacked your aunt and Bella defended her, but your aunt got hurt in the fight. A doctor was here and gave her pain medicine, that's why she unconscious. Our personal doctor is on his way from Idaho. Now, I'm not sure what you were doing to your aunt, but Grayson doesn't like it. It's best if you not do that again. I just came from the other cabin, and the vet showed up and is treating your dog. She seems to be okay, but needs a few stitches, like your aunt," Jackson said soothingly while watching me.

I tried to talk and couldn't do that either. I was frozen in place, not a feeling any alpha would like. My aggression was contained but not for long.

"You keep trying to push past my hold, if you continue I will make it worse. Us witches don't like to be manhandled, especially by mutts who think they can take what doesn't belong to them," she said as she glared at me.

That did it for me. A teenage witch was not going to hold an alpha immobile, not on my watch. With every ounce of power I had from being alpha I pushed and grabbed her by her arm, not enough to bruise but to show I was serious.

Aurora gasped.

"Listen here, little witch. Your aunt was hurt, and I helped her. I'm still helping her, and you would do well to not call anyone a mutt. I'm not sure what you did to me, but I can tell you I didn't like it, and it won't be happening again. I'm the alpha in this pack, and you will show me respect, specifically in my home," I told her while I was still holding her arm.

I could feel her gathering her power, and her lips were moving but no words came out. I maneuvered her back and stood between her and Avery. I looked toward Jackson, wondering how to handle the girl who had grown a large pair of balls in a room with two wolf shifters.

"Aurora, if you lay one hand on anyone in this room I won't be happy. Please, Aurora, I'm okay," Avery suddenly mumbled as she put a hand on my arm. I moved my hand to her and linked my fingers through hers. I turned and smiled at her. She seemed to be back under which made me feel better. I didn't know much about this woman, injured and fragile, but I felt so protective of her I wouldn't let even her niece get too close.

I was about to tell Aurora that she needed to go sit down so we could all talk when the cabin door opened and in walked my mom and dad. Mom always has a way of showing up at the perfect time.

"Oh good, Aurora dear, I'm glad you're here. Let's get some hot cocoa. Goddess knows I need one. It's been one event filled day. After the huge power rush my son pushed out, I think everyone's nerves are shot," Mom exclaimed to the room as she swooped in and took Aurora into the kitchen with her.

The cabin had an open floor plan, but she was far enough away that I could relax. I could still hear my mom talk to Aurora. She was telling her how not to act around alpha wolves, and how she could get the same result if she just followed a few rules. I stopped listening because she had taught us boys the same rules. I knew she had it under control.

"Son, I hate to say it, but Sasha needs to go home. Tank is having one hell of a time trying to keep her calm," Dad told me as he sat down next to the fireplace.

"Jackson was just coming over to relieve you, but then Aurora showed up. Leroy's on his way. I'll need you to pick him up at the airport. When he's done here, he'll be taking Sasha and Spencer back with him," I told him, but looked back down to Avery who had fallen asleep again.

I took the seat next to Avery. Mom brought Aurora over to sit opposite from Dad at the fireplace.

"So, Aurora, we know you're a witch, and you know we're wolf shifters. Care to tell me how your aunt isn't a witch, and how she doesn't know about other supernatural communities?" I turned to her and asked. I could tell Aurora had reservation with talking about her Aunt.

She pulled her shoulders back and took a deep breath.

"My aunt is a witch, but I think her powers are either not as strong as most witches or they haven't fully manifested yet. I'm not sure, but I know other witches when I'm around them, and I can't feel anything from her. I heard rumors she left the coven because she was exiled," Aurora told me.

"Oh my," my mom whispered.

"My grandparents were killed in a car accident when my mom and Avery were young. If she had had the training I did she would have known all about you guys and other supernaturals. Our coven leader who took over once my grandmother was killed didn't believe in letting Aunt Avery learn alongside my mom. She banned her from all magic teachings or gatherings. My Mom said that having a dud in a community almost never happens. Aunt Avery was ostracized from a young age, at least that's how my mom talked about it," Aurora admitted to us.

I couldn't imagine being treated like that by my own family. I didn't know what to say, but I could feel the rage growing for what had been done to her.

"That is terrible, that should have never happened to your aunt. Children and family are precious no matter who they are or what they can or cannot do. We mean your aunt no harm, we just want to help. Right, Grayson?" Mom gave me the look. I knew that look, the look said follow me without question. A look I had not yet in my entire life went against. The title “Alpha” doesn’t carry any weight with my Mom, and that’s okay.

“Of course, we only want to help. Our doctor will be here in a few hours. Why doesn’t everyone get some sleep. I’ll watch over Avery,” I announced to the room. I needed a little piece of quiet before Leroy arrived.

“I brought her phone, her husband might call. He’s a pilot and is traveling, not sure where.” Aurora walked over and handed it to me. “Personally, I wouldn’t call him. He’ll just blame her for walking my dog so late at night, but it’s your call. I’m going to check on my dog and then head home.” She waved to us as she walked out the door, calling out a good night.

I turned to my mom. “Should we have someone go watch her? Or should she take my room here? What do you think?” I asked her.

Dealing with the pack was one thing, but there aren’t many pack members who couldn’t handle themselves.

She waved me off. “You must not know much about witches, honey. That young lady can take better care of herself then most werewolves I know,” she told me as she kissed me on the cheek before she grabbed Dad and headed upstairs to their room.

I stared at the cell phone in my hand. Just thinking the words ‘her husband’ made my whole body shiver. No, I don’t think I’ll be calling her ‘husband’ to explain what happened. Dealing with getting her healed was all I could do at this point.

“Christ, Grayson, you need to get a handle on this,” Jackson’s voice drags me out of my reverie. “I’ve been sitting here, and you didn’t even notice. We need you on your game tomorrow. We have to convince the counsel that Hunters are a problem. You are a respected alpha at that conference, please get some rest. I'll stay awake, just sleep in the chair if you can't leave her side, but please rest," Jackson pleaded with me.

I agreed, and chose the wing back chair next to the couch. I could kick my feet out and get a few winks of shuteye. She won't wake without me knowing about it. My concern for Avery was blocking my wolf senses, and that's a vulnerability I wasn't willing to admit to. I don't think Jackson has ever seen me unraveled enough to drop my guard like this, and frankly neither had I.

Chapter Eight
Crazy Town

I woke up with a burning on my right arm. I laid there and listened to the room trying to center myself and take in my surroundings. I knew someone was sleeping somewhere close to me because I could hear heavy breathing. It took my mind a minute to recall where I was. The coyote attack, my arm, and Bella being hurt was all gradually coming back to me.

I slowly opened my eyes and sitting there in a chair next to me was Grayson. His arms crossed and hands tucked under his armpits. His ankles crossed at his feet. He looked so peaceful sleeping there. I looked around for Aurora, remembering I had awakened at one point and knew she was here, but it was all still so fuzzy.

I laid here, letting the atmosphere of the house flow through me. It's something I had been doing since I was a child but never told anyone about. I didn't do this often because I could get over loaded with a bunch of mixed feelings, most of which weren't my own. The

house was asleep.

A thought popped into my head, and I looked over at the coffee table to see my cell. I should probably call Ryan, but he never reacts well when I don't follow the scheduled call time; if he even answers. I'll just wait; there isn't much to tell him anyway. Other than the fact that my arm was a coyote's meal. I tried to sit up with my bad arm to see what time it was, and an intense sharp pain made me flop back down. Yeah that hurts!

After a few minutes of deep breathing and allowing the pain to decrease I was able to sit up cradling my right arm. I was able to stand and take in more of my surroundings, no danger, just a farmhouse cabin, with a fire smoldering in the stone-faced fireplace. I needed to find the bathroom. I spied a throw blanket on my way and quietly tucked Grayson in and proceeded to find the bathroom down a hall.

I managed to make it to the bathroom and with the use of only one hand wiggle my yoga pants down. It looks like I won't be doing any plant work for a while. Thankfully, Delphine could run the nursery by herself, but I would miss the money. Ryan tried talking me out of working all together, but I didn't like the idea of someone taking care of me. It took a while after we married for Ryan to finally realize that this was something I wasn't budging on. I did compromise and went part-time, but when Ryan started to work more so did I. I just didn't mention it to him, and since he believed he should pay for everything, I had started putting my money away. So for the first time in my life I had a decent savings account. I had realized early on that Ryan's money was Ryan's. It didn't bother me, but I had to have money of my own I didn't have to give a detail report about where that money went. I had kept my account separate from Ryan. If his money was his, mine would be mine.

Getting my pants back up was more taxing, and I was starting to feel some throbbing in my arm when I grabbed the glass knob to exit the bathroom. Voices were talking right outside the door.

"Is she a prisoner or someone we're helping?" a voice I didn't recognize whispered.

What?

"I'm just waiting to make sure she doesn't need help, you'll understand when you see her arm, Leroy," Grayson muttered.

Oh, my Goddess. Was Grayson waiting in the hall thinking I was seriously going to ask him to help me pull up my pants?

Not happening.

"So, who is this mystery woman that has you pulling me from a high-risk pack pregnancy?" the voice asked sternly.

"She's my cross-linked mate, and she's a witch to boot," he said with a sad undertone.

"I knew this pack would be exciting. I saw how you handled the last alpha, I knew you would lead the wolves in the right direction. Shaking life up a little bit, are we?" The man called Leroy laughed.

Did he just say wolves, witches, and something about a pack? Like as in werewolf packs? There can't be; I would know, wouldn't I? That had been one of my first questions as a child, what other magical beings were on the earth with us? I was always ignored, but it didn't stop me from asking.

"Well, you might want to help her open the door because I think your new mate is an eavesdropper." Leroy chuckled as he walked away.

I panicked and flung the door open, coming face to chest with Grayson.

"I wasn't purposely trying to listen, it's just that, well, when I…," I began to explain.

Grayson put his finger to my lips. "It's okay, we were having a conversation right outside the door. If it was top secret, I think we could have found a better hiding place." Grayson smiled down at me.

Seeing this man smile brought a blinding smile from me. It had a feeling he didn't get a chance to relax and smile often enough.

He grabbed my left hand and pulled me into the living room. "We need Leroy back home, so let's get this over with," he said to me and deposited me on the couch.

Leroy had a doctor's black bag with him which he placed with plop on top of the coffee table right in front of me. "I'm Leroy McCormick, the doctor of this bunch. If you'll let me, I'd like to take a look at your arm and see if we can get this taken care of?" he asked as he held out his hand.

Most doctors made me nervous, mostly because they had the bedside manner of a gnat, and thought they were the smartest in the room. This man had a calming presence about him. He was almost as tall as Grayson, but he had a copper colored goat tee that matched a full shaggy head of hair.

"Sure, the other doctor put a bandage on it. He was a nice guy but a little dense if you ask me," I told Leroy matter of fact.

"Well, I will try not to be too dense, Miss…?" he asked as he started to undo the bandage.

"I'm Avery, Avery Sinclair. Well, actually, Beaumont, Sinclair is my maiden name," I was babbling again. "It's nice to meet you, Leroy," I told him as I observed a glow coming from under the bandage where his hand was. My arm felt like it was bathing in a cool water bath with bubbles tickling along the top.

When he finished unwrapping the bandage, I noted it didn't look as bad as it had hours ago. "With a wound this large, I would have suspected more damage on the inside," he tells me as he inspects my arm. I also noticed when I woke up that my arm didn't hurt as much as it did before I passed out.

Leroy pulled out some vials and needles after he put on gloves. He explained he was giving me a local anesthetic, but I stopped listening. My mind wandered to the conversation I heard while in the bathroom.

"So, what? Grayson you're a werewolf and you're a fairy, Doc?" I asked the two of them, trying to wrap my brain around all that was happening; deep breathing through my nose.

"No," Grayson bellowed.

"Sort of," came softly from Leroy.

"So, one of you is and the other isn't? I always thought witches weren't the only supernaturals, but no one confirmed it until today." I looked at Grayson; he didn't seem to be happy with my question.

"The fae exist, but I've never come across one," Grayson tells me as he's eyeing Leroy.

"Well, today you get the pleasure right along with Grayson to meet your first fae." Leroy bows as best he can while sitting. "Half-fae actually, but fae none the less," he adds.

"How did you know," Grayson asked me.

"I saw my arm hours ago, right after the damage, and it was much worse than it is now. I noticed the purple glowing, and well I could tell it was some sort of healing magic. I might not be a witch with powers, but I can recognize magic used like that," I said as I looked between Grayson and Leroy. The tension level in the room started to rise and it made me squirm.

"Grayson, you need to go take a walk. Having Avery moving while I'm stitching isn't the best idea," he calmly tells Grayson.

"I'm staying right here until your done and for you to explain why we have a half-fae living in our pack and I was never told," Grayson forced out through clenched teeth.

Well, shit, like I want to be the cause of strife in a family. I made a mess of my own family, I certainly didn't want to mess with someone else's. I started to do my meditative deep-breathing—in through my nose, slow deep, out through my mouth. I closed my eyes so I could focus solely on my breathing. After several minutes, I felt Leroy's touch on my arm loosen and Grayson release a long breath.

"Perks of being an empathic witch, I see," Leroy says to me with a smile.

"Nope, not a witch," I said with a singsong voice, looking right into Leroy's eyes, which only made him smile deeply at me.

I felt Grayson move closer to me to watch my arm get sewed up. "Could we please focus on her arm before we talk. Even if you healed her some, it's still wide open and needs your attention. Stop smiling and do your job," he said almost on a whisper. With my good arm, I put my hand on his shin. He seemed to be angry, and I didn't want him to be.

"He won't thank you if he finds out you're doing it on purpose," Leroy said to me but was watching the stitches he was putting in my arm. I felt Grayson stiffen under my hand, and knew I was still making this situation worse, so I let go of his leg.

"I'm not sure what you think I can do, or who I am, but I have no powers. I'm not part of a coven, they kicked me out. So, whatever you think I'm doing, you're mistaken," I told Leroy and Grayson.

"Mmhmm," was all that came out of Leroy's mouth, and it was a good thing because I could feel the tension rising in the room again.

What is he talking about me being an empath witch? Not that I knew much about witches, I knew there were different kinds of witches. Each one having a different affinity for things, but I would like to think I would know if I had some supernatural ability, wouldn't I?

Leroy finished my stitches, which took some time because of the amount needed, and then he put an ointment on it and a bandage. The pain meds he gave me must be good shit because I wasn't feeling any pain at all.

"Don't get this wet, so wrap it up with plastic bags when you bathe. I'll write you a prescription for pain meds and an antibiotic, but most important is to keep this dry and clean. I'll leave you some directions before I go," he instructed me as he put away his supplies and went into the kitchen to throw away what he used.

Before Leroy left, I saw him and Grayson talk in the kitchen. Grayson seemed pissed, while Leroy only smiled as he walked out the door. Having been the cause of most of the problems in my own family I stayed away from confrontation as much as possible.

I wanted to talk to Grayson about werewolves, but I didn't know what to say. I knew nothing of their kind and felt shy about asking.

"Go ahead and ask, I can see you want to know. I know I would." He came and sat at my feet on the couch. He splayed is arms along the back of the cushions and rested his right ankle on his left knee. He seemed too genuine in his openness.

"You knew I was a witch, or that my niece is one. How?" I asked him. It just came flying out before I thought about it. I had a million questions, and I'm not sure that one is the first I wanted to know but that's what popped out.

"All supernaturals have energy, a hum that can't be mistaken for a human. We have a different frequency, for a lack of a better word, than humans, actually most groups have their own signature vibration," he explained softly.

I didn't know how to proceed. This was new territory for me; in my life, no one had answers to any of my questions relating to all things supernatural. He could tell I was tongue-tied and saved me.

"Have you never felt anything from being around your niece opposed to others? Being out in public and you come across someone that makes you comfortable or more comfortable than usual?" he asked me.

"I really don't think I have that ability, or any ability. My family comes from a long line of witches, but that knowledge is all I have. Further knowledge was kept from me for the safety of the coven," I told him.

I could have sworn I heard him say, "fuckin' paranoid witches," under his breath.

"Okay, we are going to have to treat this as if you were a pup in our pack. Let's not overload you with a bunch of information right now. You've had a traumatic couple of days. You need rest and I have few prescriptions to fill. Plus, I have to take care of things with my pack, and I have the Summit to attend later," he finished telling me before he stood, taking my good hand and pulling me up.

His hand felt warm.

"Wait, one more question. So, um, do you like turn furry and howl at the moon?" I asked straight-faced.

Grayson took a deep breath.

"Yes Avery, I turn furry and sometimes I howl, but not necessarily at the full moon. We have two forms, half and full. I can do both but it's mostly full which appears like most North American wolves would look with a variety of colors and much bigger," he said as he walked me to the cabin door.

I started to think about his words and froze rock solid, halting his progress to the door.

"Oh, shit!" I whispered.

Grayson spun so fast I almost fell over. He had a worried look on his face.

"One of your pack members attacked me," I stated calmly.

He stared at me for what felt like minutes, before he rearranged the look on his face. "Yes, I'm sorry to admit that's true, however, I will guarantee it won't happen again. The person who did this is flying home with Leroy when he leaves, which he probably has already."

"Who was it?" I asked.

He didn't say anything but his lips were pursed."I deserve to know," I demanded.

"Sasha," he said with remorse.

"She could have killed me or Bella, are werewolves dangerous?" I asked now with my shoulders pushed back a little, my head held a little higher.

"Are humans dangerous, Avery? The fear your coven instilled in you is a fear you need to keep front and center always. Supernatural beings are like any human, they can be unpredictable, cunning, fierce, and deadly accurate with a fast to react nature. Keep those words with you, and you'll do okay, but walk into a situation with a being that has more power than you and for you to not be understanding of that power, well let's just say you wouldn't make it long in one of our communities. Stop over thinking everything like a pup and just know I know what's best," he explained.

I have to be okay with this new bestowed fact just because he says so wasn't sitting right with me.

Oh, I do not think so!

I snapped out, "You will step away from me and stay there. I'm going home, and if I so much as see a mutt (a word I heard Grayson calling Bella) in my yard I will not hesitate to use my shotgun. I am one of "those" humans." I flung my hand from him as he was went back a few steps. I opened the door with my good hand, slammed the door, and fumed all the way to the back door of my house.

Dismiss me; make me think I am not worthy. Not that he said those things, but I'd seen this alpha attitude in my coven, and I'll be damned if I ever let people treat me like that again; or had I been allowing my husband to treat me like that?

CHAPTER NINE
PROGRESS

I stood there staring at the door for a minute, trying to understand how that went sideways.

"Oh honey, I thought I taught you better than that," I heard my mom say as she headed into the kitchen. She'd always been a light sleeper and again with her uncanny ability to know when someone needed her. Whenever something seemed to weigh on me she would have a comforting ear, and apparently advice I'm going to hear over my glass of scotch; two fingers.

I sat at the kitchen table and really took in the artisanship of the table. Two types of wood inlaid on the surface. The legs were lion's feet.

"Christ, I've managed to be a healthy man without needing my mom's advice on my love life thus far," I sulked.

"Honey, as much as I love and admire my first born. I would like to take a cast iron upside your head," Mom said as she took a deep breath. "You are ignorant to humans as she is to supernatural. Did you hear what her niece said to us? She was an outcast; she was nothing to them but a liability. She has had to be it all for herself with no family to fall back on. She wasn't brought up with a pack, or a coven, or a clan," Mom softly told me.

I thought she was waiting for me to say something.

"Grayson, you can't tell the woman that she's as ignorant as a pup. How would that make you feel? Help her navigate this new world while supporting her. Be the alpha I know you are, but remember that she isn't one of the pack yet and doesn't know anything about us. Also, son, what do you really know about witches?" And with that she took her tea, patting me on the shoulder, and left me to my scotch. I imagine she went to track down my dad.

I had a lot to think about, but I needed to eat before dealing with the Summit. I set about making myself something, seeing as my mom hadn't wanted to do that for me. Guess she really didn't like how I handled Avery. I agreed with her on that. That wasn't one of my finer moments.

I checked in with Jackson on my way out and made sure he got Sasha and her son on their way with Leroy and to have him check in with Avery about Bella's health. She would make it, but Sasha had done a number on her. That is one tough husky, going up against a wolf shifter. We are ten times stronger and faster than a domestic dog or wolf in the wild. She was lucky she wasn't killed, or I'm lucky she wasn't killed. I don't think I would stand a chance to build a relationship with

Avery if I let her niece's dog die.

"I got this Grayson, go deal with our biggest threat. Make them listen," Jackson told me. This was why he was my second; I could trust he would handle things while I was away and support me behind the scenes.

It had been hours sitting here listening to these alphas do the circle jerk about how to handle the deaths and disappearances of pack members all over North America. A few alphas had flown over from Europe, but most didn't want to get involved with North American problems. The True Hunters—what we had so named them since we didn't know who they are—were so secretive no one knew of a location. Our intel wasn't much but a few rumors, a few sightings, but we had yet to catch one so we were going about this blind. We knew they had activity in the Bayou area of Louisiana, but other than that, nothing. We needed an insider, someone to infiltrate the group, but they had ways of detecting supernaturals that still stumped us.

I felt like banging my head against the wall. I was sitting next to Alistair, an alpha from the southwest. He hadn't said much during the past few days, but I could tell by his grunts that he was getting tired of these meetings with no progress.

Alistair leaned toward me and said, "The problem is that we aren't uniting our communities. The wolves keep to themselves, we need to get all supernaturals together to see what we can accomplish. We need a supernatural that is undetectable." As soon as he said this, Avery popped into my mind. Here was a witch who didn't have the flare supernaturals have; she went undetected in our world.

Maybe there were more like her. "Alistair, you're on to something." And with that I stood up and walked to the podium that faced the group.

"This isn't getting us anywhere; we're all talking in circles. I vote we have one alpha represent us, and we seek out the other supernatural communities to form a counsel, one where we can gather all information and stop these murders. We are all targets of these allusive hunters, and I believe we need to band together. Our history states that we were all united at one time, and that's where we need to be again if we truly want change. We want our families safe. Do they feel safe now?" I asked the group.

"What are you saying, Grayson? That one of the alphas will be above the rest?" Maximus asked with a sneer.

"If you learned your history you'd know there was a hyper alpha. An alpha that made sure all alphas followed the rules we set for ourselves to keep us safe," I told Maximus.

I turned back to the rest of the groups and waited for them to respond. I was almost certain I would get the votes on this to pass. I had heard chatter that everyone was frustrated and we needed some guidance.

"I second this motion," came from Alistair.

As the minutes ticked by more alphas agreed. "Now we need to vote on a representative. That person needs to be our liaison with all the supernatural groups," I told the group. I was getting ready to give my opinion on how to pick a specific alpha when someone yelled out "How about you, Grayson?"

Now, wait a minute.

I shook my head. "I didn't say it had to be me, voting needs to take place," I started to say but stopped when I noticed Alistair was walking up to the podium. This couldn't be good."I think we should all vote right now," Alistair told the group.

"Let's not be hasty. We could make up a ballot and vote tomorrow," Max spoke from his spot in the middle of the room, where he was starting to rise from his seat.

"Since we have Grayson on the table already, let's just vote now. We're all here, which means we could wrap this up today and all get back to our packs. All for Grayson being our ambassador, say aye," Alistair asked after he said his own aye.

The entire summit said aye at the same time, all except Max.

"Now all those in favor of Maximus being our first councilman, say aye," Alistair asked the group.

A few ayes, but it was clear they all wanted me to be the one to take on this nationwide problem.

Well shit.

"It's settled, Grayson is our new ambassador for the North American wolves. He will appoint who he sees fit to help him and who to add to the new counsel with votes from all of us. This also means that with what he has to do to find the other communities and the expense that this will incur, all the North American packs will be funding an account specifically for this. With as many packs as there are it won't be much from each pack," Alistair continued to talk to the group and I thought maybe they chose wrong. With all the details he was throwing out there, wouldn't it be best if he lead this new path for the North American werewolves?

After all of the specifics were outlined, I followed Alistair out of the room to get some refreshments.

"I know you mean well, but why didn't you just throw your own hat in the ring?" I asked him.

"I thought about it, but I'm not as well-known as you are. You have a thriving construction business that caters to the supernatural community and the humans with a variety of contacts. You are a people person if a wolf ever was. You know how to smooth over most situations, when most alphas would tear someone's head off. In addition to this, we need the most powerful wolf we can get. I'm not doing this just for you. I intend to ask for the next position to you on the council. I can handle all of the computer stuff, and the electronic side of things. Before the end of this summit I'm putting a vote to be the next councilman," Alistair told me as he poured his coffee.

"So, you just didn't want to have to travel." I laughed.

"There's that. I detest flying, and you'll be doing it a lot. I heard you have your pilot license and own a plane," he finished like that was the end of it.

I was getting ready to explain that I did have a business to attend to when a group swarmed him and started asking questions. No one was asking me anything, which was fine by me. Small talk really isn't one of my strong suits, and Alistair decided I was the one to put this council together then he could sooth all the ruffled furs. I was starting to realize that I just wasn't prepared to take on such a large endeavor with a mate sitting out there unprotected. I still had to handle getting my pack and my new mate back to Idaho.

Still married.

Still not with me.

Listening to Alistair explain how this council would work, the ins and outs of it all, I realized again that him letting all the packs know that they all would be contributing to this endeavor at least made me feel better. Fueling a plane even if it was a small one was not cheap.

That got me thinking about Avery. What my mom said was true. What did I really know about witches? Avery's niece seems to be well-versed; it was a good place to start. I texted Mom and asked her to run over and get Aurora's number. After she textxed it to me I commenced working on learning anything and everything about witches.

Chapter Ten
Witches, werewolves, Vampires, oh my!

It took a while for my anger to wear off. My arm hurt and the sling that Jackson brought over was cumbersome, but Jackson had told me that Leroy thought it would help keep my arm immobile so that I don't pop the stitches. There wasn't much I could do to take my mind off that bossy wolf. The bossy wolf that helped me track down my niece's dog, the one that saved me from that wretched man at the bakery, and the one who saved me and got someone to patch up my arm last night. Oh, and he slept in a wing back chair next to the couch I slept great on, watching out for me. As all those thoughts rattled around in my head and the day progressed I found it harder and harder to remember why I was mad at him.

In all that happened last night I had completely forgotten about the tattoo that mysteriously appeared on my palm. The design was beautiful, but something supernatural was going on and there was no other explanation for it.

I felt like I needed to be more freaked out about what was happening, but I think growing up in a coven had at least made it so this wasn't so bizarre as much as it was fascinating.

I was drinking another cup of coffee, as if the last two helped with my anxiety. My nerves were amped up and my thoughts wouldn't shut down. Part of me wanted to pack up Aurora and start completely over somewhere else. Another part of me wanted to shove all that was happing into a little box and cram it deep in my mind where I couldn't find it again. One very small part of me was willing to see how these things progressed.

It popped into my awareness that ever since I ran into that handsome vacationer things have started happening that have never happened to me before. First I was going to decline to go to dinner, but the only way to figure out what's going on was to be in the wolf's den.

With that put aside, knowing dinner with the big bad wolf was going to be fascinating, I decided to switch to hot cocoa and sit down with a juicy romance book I had started last week. Maybe take a few catnaps; it was still hours away until dinner and Aurora had already checked in with me to let me know she was spending the day at the smaller cabin with her dog. I was so relieved to hear she was going to be okay, aside from some grave battle wounds. That made me look down at my arm, I'll have a nasty scar to remember it by as well.

Hours later I still hadn't heard from Ryan, but that wasn't what worried me. Sometimes he got busy and wouldn't call for days. What worried me was that I was going over to the large cabin behind my house for dinner with a family of werewolves. What if the food to eat doesn't satisfy them? I laughed and thought of my red, hooded, pea coat. I think I needed to pull it out of my closet.

Standing in front of my opened coat closet I contemplated my coat choices. Maybe red invoked anger and I should go with black.

"Let's get a hustle on, Auntie, are you going to stand there looking into the closet hoping it will have life's answers, or are you going to pick one? Let's head over for dinner. I'm starved," Aurora said to me as I turned and gave her my best adult glare.

I grabbed my red coat and decided I'm not sure I liked teenagers. As I was finishing buttoning and loving the tingle this jacket gave me, I saw Aurora had the biggest Tupperware that I owned stuffed full with chocolate chip cookies.

Kiss up much?

"I heard that," Aurora said as she waited for me at the bottom of the stairs, waiting to trek across the property to the large cabin. Looking up at the cabins brought me comfort. When I knew the cabins were vacant, I would come sit on the hill and watch the sunrise in the mornings, drinking my coffee and contemplating life.

As we approached the deck, I started to think maybe we should turn around, but Josie was waiting on the porch with a huge smile on her face. She was different from Ryan's mom, who would have a scowl on her face anytime she saw me. Josie was on the shorter side and didn't look a day over forty. She had a few strands of gray in her auburn hair, but she didn't look old enough to be a mother. She has a hippie vibe to her with her torn jeans and peasant style blouse.

"Oh, look, cookies. How wonderful, let me take those from you, dear. I'm afraid they won't last but a few minutes. My group sure has a sweet tooth," she said as she smiled at us, motioning to us with her hand to follow her in.

Who doesn't have a sweet tooth?

How could anyone who has a sweet tooth look like the bunch of werewolves in front of me? The room was packed with animal magnetism from the young to the old. Not one of them looked out of shape. Not one. I noticed they moved the living room furniture around to make room for two long tables. I tried counting heads but everyone was moving around.

"Do I have something on my face?" I asked the room, while trying to figure out why everyone was just staring.

Everyone just kept staring and my anxiety kept rising which in turn made the air in the room start to get heavier. The air felt like cement in my lungs. I started to breathe faster; my palms were getting sweaty and my vision was narrowing, which only made my anxiety kick up a thousand percent. It felt like weight was crushing my chest.

I started backing up toward the door, my vision fading as goose bumps broke out across my skin. I looked for Grayson but didn't see him. I knew I had to leave, my fight or flight response was kicking in, and who knows how these werewolves were going to react.

"Auntie, it's okay," I heard Aurora whisper softly, but it didn't matter. I couldn't be here, I had to get away.

I thought I heard Josie tell Aurora not to interfere, but I did hear her tell someone to get her son and do it quick. That was it, I was done.

Done, done, done. If I didn't leave right now I wouldn't be able to breathe.

I turned, flung opened the door, and shot out and down the porch

stairs faster than I've ever run in my life. I had just made it to the bottom when two arms engulfed me.

"It's okay. Shh. no one is going to hurt you. You're safe," I heard his voice and my breathing started to slow, my vision started to return, and the pain in my chest was relaxing.

"This is my mistake. Too many people, too soon," Grayson softly cooed into my ear.

He turned me around and picked me up. Cradling me in his arms, he walked back up the stairs, and sat us both in a porch swing. He had my face tucked into his neck and was stroking my back, neither of us saying a word. I didn't know what to say. I had freaked out and ran out, making myself look like a fool.

"No one is going to think anything bad about you. Let's just sit here for a few more minutes, then we'll talk about it," Grayson whispered.

"Are you a mind reading werewolf?" I asked.

He chuckled. "No, but I can imagine what you might be thinking."

I raised my head a little. "This isn't funny."

"No, it's not, but just because we're werewolves doesn't mean we can read minds," Grayson stated with a soft smile.

"Well, some witches can read minds, so how was I supposed to know?" I huffed.

"Really?" Grayson asked.

"You make it sound like witches can only do spells and potions."

"To be honest, I thought only vampires could read minds," Grayson admitted.

"Huh, so the almighty alpha doesn't know everything."

Grayson just stared at me. He probably thought I was a freak of nature.

That's when a thought hit me. "Wait, there's vampires on earth?" I strangled out.

We sat there for a good ten minutes, and I actually started to fall asleep, which should have freaked me. I was real close to dreamland when the screen door opened, and I realized that I was a married woman sitting on a strange guy's lap all snuggled cozy. I flew off his lap as if it was on fire, tried quickly to straighten my clothes and not look guilty.

It was Aurora with the most devious smile on her face. "Just wanted to let you know that dinner's on the table, and we're all waiting until you two decide we can dig in." She giggled as and slipped back inside.

"So, are you good to go and meet a few members of my pack? No one will hurt you, I can promise you that. We are just like humans, well, except we aren't, but you get what I'm saying?" he asked me almost nervously.

"Yeah, I get what you're saying. I think I'll be alright. Honestly I don't know where that came from. I haven't had one of those in years. Maybe it was because of the attack last night. Did you ever find out why I was attacked?" I asked.

"Okay, slow down. We just got you calm. Let's take this one step at a time. We'll go in, introduce you both, and then eat. How does that sound?"

"Okay, I can do that." I tried to smile at him.

The introduction wasn't terrible, everyone seemed nice enough. No one made me feel bad, and I noticed no one starred at me again. I met both Grayson's parents, Josie and Grant, and his brother Jackson, his two sons Tyler and Trace, and Tank who looked just like his name.

Aside from my inquisitive niece who couldn't stop talking and finishing people's sentences, I actually had a great time. The few members of Grayson's pack seemed like normal down to earth people as long as I didn't think about fur and large teeth. Aurora seemed taken with Jackson's eldest son, Trace, who seemed to ignore her.

We were just finishing dinner when someone knocked on the door. Josie excused herself from the table to answer it while her husband Grant brought everyone coffee and carrot cake. Josie hadn't been joking when she said the cookies—which were near four dozen—had been eaten before I came back from my anxiety attack.

"That's my favorite, thank you." I gleamed to Grant when he plunked a huge piece in front of me.

"We aim to please, Avery," Grant said then proceeded to pass out the rest of the dessert. Baking werewolves, who would have thought?

I looked around and noticed that everyone focused on the door and not the super moist, delicious cake. Idiots.

"Aurora, if you're not going to eat yours then I am," I told her as I reached to grab it.

"Uh, Auntie, I think cake time is over," she said with a scared look on her face.

"Cake time isn't over until the last crumb is gone," I said with a full mouth. I did not care how un-lady like it made me look. This shit is the bomb! Do you think anyone would mind if I licked my plate?

The vibe in the room suddenly became hyper alert. Everyone had pushed away from the table to stand. I was the only one eating heaven on a plate, well, actually three plates of cake.

"Okay, if anyone leaves their piece of cake alone I'm not responsible for its disappearance," I belted and started laughing whiling keeping my eyes on everyone's lonely cake.

Jackson came around the table and pulled my chair out and grabbed my arm, gently yet firm, and moved me behind him away from the front door.

"Why are you all that protective of your cake?" I asked him. Jackson didn't answer, just kept staring straight ahead. I knew the vibes in the room had changed but I wanted to ignore it and keep eating the cake. Who could blame me. I didn't want to deal with anymore drama.

Okay, maybe I should pay more attention, something's not right.

Grayson came through the front door with a guy I had never seen before, but you could tell just by looking at him that he was not a good one. He reminded me of a mobster. He was wearing a nice tailored blue suit if it wasn't for the shiny metallic shirt and tie. He reeked of power and money and wanted everyone to know it.

"Avery, I'd like you to meet Maximus Demarko. He's the resident alpha of the Cataloochee Pack," Grayson said to me but was looking at his brother.

I snorted then waved

"Uh, hi. Nice to meet you Mr. Demarko." What else was I supposed to say?

Maximus started to walk toward me while Jackson was backing me up.

"It's just Max, Avery. And it's a pleasure to meet you," he said with a thin, lingering tone.

We all just stood and no one was saying anything.

I attempted to make my way around Jackson, saying, "Dinner was nice, and dessert was the bomb. Well, it was awesome to me meet ya'll, but I have to get my niece home. I'll just see you all later." I told the room. It seemed like the party was over. I frowned down at my third slice of half-finished piece of cake, thinking I needed to learn how to bake.

"Unfortunately, that won't be happening. I have a few questions for you and your niece." He waved his hand toward my niece. Okay, now I was starting to get mad and my calm happy mood was shifting and it was shifting fast. Once I was on that train, it usually ended up in a derailment.

"I'm not sure what you need to know about my family, and I but I'm not what you are. We'll just be leaving, thank you very much," I snapped.

"You have broken pack law. You will sit your ass down and answer my questions," Max said to me, and he looked like he meant it. I almost thought I felt a wave of something in the air when he demanded we sit down. I blew it off and glared at him.

"Max, I will allow you to ask your questions but if you talk to Avery like that again we're going to have problems" Grayson ordered. He took up a position between Max and his brother, hopefully to back Aurora and I.

"There's enough room over here by the fireplace. If anyone wants more coffee, let me know," Josie announced to everybody.

When everyone else started to congregate in the living room, I decided I should too. I took the wing back chair that was farthest away from Max. I was hoping Grayson's pack would have my back, and I let out a huge rush of air when Grayson and Aurora flanked my sides. If all else fails, I knew Aurora had enough control over her magic to get us out of here.

"Let's get on with it," Grayson growled in frustration.

"It's come to my attention that we have two witches living in my territory, and they haven't made themselves known or asked for permission to live here," he aimed his accusation at me.

No one said anything, so I guess I have to answer these questions myself.

"First off, I'm not a witch, and my niece just came to live with me a few days ago," I calmly told Max.

"So, you are claiming you're not a witch, but you're your niece is?" Max asked me.

I was getting ready to answer because I didn't really understand what the big deal was.

"My aunt is not part of the supernatural community; she doesn't understand why you're even asking her this. I'll let you know that I already emailed your pack and let them know who I am, and that I'm not a practicing witch within a coven. I contacted the coven in your territory and submitted my application. I left Seattle and came to live with my aunt a week ago." She was scrolling on her phone for a second before she looked up. "Here, I just pulled up the email that I sent to your pack IT guy on my phone." Aurora rose from her seat and tried to hand her phone to Max.

Max waved off her phone, I'm sure because he knew she had done what she was trying to show him.

There are protocols for witches living in wolf pack territory? That didn't make any sense.

"My niece has to get permission to live in a free country?" I asked Max, placing air quotes around permission.

A hand landed on my left shoulder with slight pressure. Grayson cut off Max before he could answer my question. “Not every pack has the same rules, and not all alphas are the same. I don’t require other supernaturals to announce themselves in my territory unless they are directly on pack land,” Grayson explained to me.

“We’re not in your territory, Grayson, and we’re not talking about your pack or pack land. These two witches have settled in my territory,” Max explained.

“I followed your protocol for moving here, and my aunt didn’t need to because she’s considered a dud in the witch community, so that voids the law you think she broke,” Aurora stated with her arms crossed. Aurora seemed to know what she was talking about so I didn’t interrupt.

“You might have followed the rules, but your aunt was born of witches, therefore that makes her a witch.” Max looked back to me as if I could say anything.

No one said much because really what could anyone say. I was born of two witch parents so he’s right, even if I didn’t have any power.

“Okay, so what would you like me to do? I could email your pack, or I bet Grayson could find me some paper and I could submit my request directly to you?” I asked.

“We have several options and the good news is that I get to pick.” Max smile at me.

That didn’t sound good, but really what was the worst he could do, tie me up and whip me?

As if.

Aurora leaned down me and whispered, “Actually, Auntie, that’s exactly what he could do.”

I flew out of my chair and stepped forward pointing my finger at him, my temper having caught the best of me. "If you think you or anyone dare lay a hand on me—" I didn't get to finish because a pounding was coming from the front door.

Not again!

Now who's here?

I'm not sure what caused me to stand up to this man, a man who exuded scary.

Josie excused herself again like a good host to answer the door. She came walking back into the living room with two men and a woman roughly the same as age Grayson and I. I immediately noticed the woman because she was almost as big as the men; beautiful didn't describe her. She was oozing fierce sexual energy right up with the danger that leaked from her vibrant blue eyes. I wasn't sure if I should be afraid of her or kiss her, if that was my thing.

"Max, I'd like to introduce you to Kalon. He just arrived in your territory so we can kill two birds with one stone," The burly man said and winked at me.

"You brought a vampire into my territory without my permission?" Max asked.

"What is with you and the word permission? What? Are you king and no one told me?" I asked.

I was done with this pompous ass.

Grayson squeezed my shoulder again, not enough to hurt but enough that I understood I was not helping.

"Max, let's not do anything rash. Let Kalon tell us what he has to say and then you can make your decision about Avery's punishment," Grayson proclaimed.

He said it as if I could be punished, like that was an option.

This dude really did have an ego problem. As I was thinking about what I would do to Max if I did have powers, the vampire was approaching me.

"A feisty witch is a fun witch," Kalon purred. Yes, it sounded like a purr.

He was close to what I pictured when I thought of vampires. He was tall and lean, not very bulky, with angular features. His jaw was pointed and he had a cleft in his chin that made me want to reach out and put my thumb in it. He wasn't anywhere nearly as hot as Grayson was, but I'm sure some women found him irresistible, especially those almond-shaped, ocean blue eyes.

I almost lifted my hand to touch him but was worried he might bite me?

"You can if you want. I won't bite." He smiled.

I let out a breath and rolled my eyes. "Not another mind reader. This is exhausting. Can I just go home now?" I asked no one. My arm was starting to burn, my head was hurting from all this activity, and I wasn't sure I wanted to handle any more drama. Going from boring to constant excitement was wearing me out.

Kalon looked around the room, I assumed he was looking for another vampire since I had mentioned another mind reader. He looked back at me and raised an eyebrow. I shook my head hoping he would understand that I wasn't going to elaborate.

"I brought Kalon here because he has information about cross-linked mates, and I had a feeling he could help with some confusion," Burley guy announced.

"Cross-linked mates? I thought I was in trouble because I'm an undocumented alien?" I told him.

"How delightful, a funny witch." Kalon snorted.

"All right. I can see we're not making progress. One thing at a time. First, we've cleared up Aurora's issue. Next is Avery…," Grayson started to say.

"Who is a witch in my territory, which makes her my problem and not yours Grayson," Max said.

"Actually, Avery belongs to Grayson through their link. Once that link was established no other has a right to her," Kalon said as he accepted a cup of coffee from Josie and took a sip.

"Linked? What foolishness are you trying to get everyone to buy?" Max blustered.

I looked at Grayson who was staring at me with a sad look on his face.

"I'm not sure what you all are going on about, but I'm married, and I don't belong to anyone," I told him, and only him.

"Clay, I have to thank you for calling me and bringing me to the best drama I've seen in a decade," Kalon said while he glided over to the fireplace and took up a front and center position.

Yes, glided.

I could tell he thought this was amusing.

"What are cross-linked mates and what gives you story-time power?" Max asked Kalon.

Kalon set his coffee cup on the mantel, rolled up his long sleeve to expose his right palm. He held it up for all to see. I tried to understand the design I was looking at but couldn't place it. It didn't look anything like the mark on my palm.

"Although it might not look exactly the same as Avery and

Grayson's, as each cross-linked pair gets their own unique design just for the two of them, it's still a cross-linked mate mark," Kalon told us.

He gave us a minute to absorb that bit and started in on the rest of his sad tale. "I met my mate several hundred years ago in Ireland. She was a local healer who had been traveling to a village when she came across my near lifeless body in the woods. I had been mortally wounded, I was going to die. It took a while, but she was able to nurse me back to health with herbs and the power of the mark we shared. When I finally woke up, I immediately felt a connection to her and we both shared this mark. I had heard of cross-linked mates through my travels but had never met one. She was in the dark as to what I was. She's human, a pure human with no supernatural abilities. I won't get into the rest of my story as it doesn't have anything to do with why I'm here today, but I will say that cross-linked mates are our version of soul mates. The kind many don't find. The one person who shares a part of your soul, a soul that just melts into yours. It's a true and rare gift." Kalon finished with picking up his coffee cup and giving Grayson and I a salute.

"What the hell does all that crap you just spewed have to do with a witch breaking my pack laws? Nothing! She will face judgment, and I don't care what tattoo she has on her hand. You want me to believe you mated with a mere human? You might have gotten your jollies off with the human whore, but the supernatural can't reproduce with human scum," Max growled at Kalon.

I didn't know any vampires, but I could tell this vampire didn't like Max talking bad about his mate. He moved so fast I didn't see it. One second he was standing crossed legged, drinking his coffee without a care, and the next he had Max by the throat shoved up against the far wall, choking the life out of him.

"Wolf, I am an old vampire. One who has patience that would make Mother Teresa look like the devil, but you, you are pissing me off. My mate had no match in grace, love, and compassion on this earth, and it's only because of her that I haven't ripped your throat out. Disrespect me if you will, but not her," Kalon spat at Max.

I didn't think Max was a match for a vampire, but I wouldn't want to test that theory, and thankfully, Grayson didn't want to either.

He swiftly moved to Kalon and put his hand on his shoulder. "This is not the way to help Avery. Max is not like most alphas, but all supernatural communities have them. He's not worth it," he said softly. I held my breath, waiting to see if someone was going to die in front of me.

He dropped Max like a hot potato and glided back to his perch in front of the fireplace.

"Before you start a war with the vampire community, let's get Avery out of the way. Kalon is right about the link. Avery and I share a mark. All I know is what I've heard from Clay's second and now from Kalon who has a mark similar to ours. As alpha of my own pack, I claim Avery as mine. You cannot touch her or punish her. What she thinks to be true is what she thought. If she has magic she doesn't know how to use it," Grayson firmly told Max.

He's claiming me, like a puppy from the pound.

"You forget yourself, Grayson, this is my territory, and she doesn't have my permission to be in it. I smell no mating mark, which makes her unclaimed." Grayson growled at the last statement.

"Fine, if you say I can't punish her, fine, but she can't stay." Max

straightened his shirt, and I could see his ego peeking out again. For a minute, when Kalon had him helpless and pinned to the wall, I could see a vulnerable side to him, that maybe he regretted being an ass.

I guess not.

"Can't stay. Buddy, my husband and I bought that house over there." I pointed in the direction of my home. "You can't just kick us out. This is still America." I told him.

"Your husband can stay, but you are a witch who doesn't belong to the local coven, and you're not registered. This is how it works. I can make you leave whether you like it or not. You have a week to be out, you and your niece. I'm revoking her rights to be in my territory too," Max said as he pointed at Aurora then left as quickly as he came.

I turned to Grayson, my mouth hanging open in confusion, ran up to him, and grabbed his shirt. He didn't try to stop me from pulling on him, but he put his hands on my upper arms holding me but not forcefully.

"What just happened? Did that fucking piece of shit just tell me I have to leave my house? I can't believe this is happening!" I said in agitation. The seriousness of what just transpired started to really sink in. I kept pulling on Grayson's shirt.

"Why didn't you stop him, why didn't you do something?" I yelled and pounded on Grayson's chest. I heard a couple of gasps, but I didn't care. As I saw it, this was Grayson's fault. The feeling of not belonging slammed into my chest. I had never dealt with my abandonment issues, and here it was happening all over again.

Grayson took a deep breath. "It'll be okay. I'll figure something out. We have a week, which is generous," he looked at me as if he believed he could make this better.

"Are we even going to talk about this cross-linked bullshit everyone is spewing? Why do I have a tattoo on my palm that matches yours?" I asked him. Grayson's brows drew together.

"What Kalon is saying is true." He released my arms and started pacing, running his fingers through his hair. "I know it sounds crazy and hard to believe, but you come from a family of witches, powerful ones from what I'm being told. There being cross-linked mates out in the world can't be too hard of a leap of faith," he said as he turned to me.

"Leap of faith? You want me to buy into this when I'm married. I can't talk about this right now. What am I supposed to tell my husband? Oh, sorry Ryan but I can't live in the house you bought, and we can't be together because I'm from a family of witches and am being kicked me out of this state because I've somehow broke some egotistical wolf shifter laws? In addition, I have a soul mate I just found. Are you into a three way? How do you think that's going to go over?" I asked him, eyes bulging and my hands placed dramatically on my hips. I think in my ranting I totally forgot about everyone else in the room.

I heard growling coming from the pacing man and decided I might have pushed a little too far.

"There will never be a 'three way' as you put it," Grayson boomed as he held my gaze with his glowing gold eyes. Was that the wolf behind the man staring at me?

Clay changed the subject. "I have a feeling Max did this because Grayson was voted to speak for all wolves with the other supernatural communities, and he's throwing a little tantrum."

"It doesn't matter why he did it. He's still is making us leave. I'm a married woman so all this is a moot anyway. My husband doesn't know about supernaturals and I want it to stay that way. I'm not sure how he would react, and I don't want to find out," I told everyone.

"Little witch, if your husband is a good man, why would he care if you're a witch? That is what you should be asking yourself," Kalon singsonged with his eyes on me.

I decided to ignore Kalon and his vampire wisdom.

"Can he really make us leave?" I asked Grayson.

He nodded. "Every alpha has their own territory laws, as do most groups of supers. I could make it so you could stay, but that would mean challenging Max for his position, and I can't have two territories that far apart from each other," Grayson told me.

"Challenge him? What do you mean by that?" I asked.

"Fight to see who's stronger, sometimes the winner lets the opponent live, other times it's to the death," Grayson explained.

"What? To the death? Oh, hell no, I'm not having you put your life on the line for me," I stated.

"Well, I'm glad you care about my life." Grayson chuckled. "But I'm alpha, and I decide when and who I challenge." He smiled.

No one said much for a few minutes. My mind was reeling with questions. I was going to have to tell Ryan about my family, about Aurora. My whole body shivered.

"Auntie." Aurora came up to me and put her hand on my arm. "I don't think that's such a great idea."

I frowned at her.

"I know you hate it when I read your mind, but you can't tell him. Something's not right about him. I've tried reading him, and I can't.

I've never come across someone, more importantly a human, I'm unable to read. My intuition flares up around him," she told me softly.

"Maybe he's just someone you can't read. I'm sure there are people out there just like him," I told her.

"I don't mean to interrupt, but I couldn't help but overhear what you two were discussing. First, I want to say I've never come across a witch who can read minds. That's a vampire trait, but a bigger question is why she can't read him. I've never come across a human I can't read either. Maybe another supernatural, especially a witch, but they are trained to block and have magic to use. A human...," he shook his head. "They don't possess that power, human is human."

"No offense, but my niece not being able to read my husband's mind doesn't bother me in the least. It's an annoying trait I hate," I told him.

"That might be the case, but I think you should take her warning. If he can block your niece then something is not right. Maybe he is supernatural, and you don't know it," Kalon said.

"He's not," Aurora and Josie said in unison.

"Kalon, I need a favor. I need you to go to your council and ask about killings that have been happening. We call them True Hunters, but we don't know their actual names. I've been chosen to meet with all the heads of the super communities and find out what I can," Grayson explained.

"I will, and I'll let you know who to contact. It might take me a few weeks. I've been a nomad for a while and haven't dealt with vampire politics in some time," Kalon responded but kept starring at Aurora. "I might have some other questions to ask the council as well.

I didn't like the way Kalon was watching Aurora. "We're getting off the subject here. I can't talk about this right now, I need time to think about things, and Delphine called and asked me to work tomorrow. I've missed so much time I'm not sure I still have a job," I told no one and everyone. "Thanks so much for dinner. Even though it seems I got more than just dinner out of this," I nodded to Josie as Aurora and I went to grab our coats.

Grayson met me at the door. "Rest tonight. We'll talk tomorrow. I have one more day at the summit, and then I'll be free. We can come up with a plan. Please, don't worry. I won't let anything happen to you." Grayson grabbed my coat off the hook by the front door and helped me put it on. It was a sweet gesture I hadn't experienced before.

I have never had anyone help me with my coat, and honestly, it made me choke up a little.

"Thanks," I said, but couldn't look at him. I walked out the front door and hoped Aurora followed.

Chapter Eleven
The Prickly Wild

I was thankful I was able to get away from my life and focus on work. Trying to wrap my head around all that had transpired in just a few days would start the headache cycle all over again. I thought the best thing to do was go home, get some sleep, and hope that working through my day in the dirt would help clear things up. Since my grandfather first introduced me to plants I found that it helped center me. Plus, I wasn't sure if Delphine would give me more time off.

Delphine La Croix was one of the first people I met when I first moved to Asheville. I worked odd jobs in towns, from barista at coffee bars to waitressing at any diner that was hiring. I even, on occasion, would work under the table for local locksmiths; a trade my grandfather felt duty bound to pass on.

My grandpa, Isaiah Sinclair, had been a locksmith his entire life and snuck lessons whenever I was able spend time with him. My Dad didn't think his girls needed to know how to open any lock, but my grandpa would just say with a wink, “He’s not the boss of me.”

Delphine had come into the diner I had been working at for a week. My savings were running out, and I had planned to look for another job, but because the pay was so bad, I worked doubles everyday leaving no time for job searching.

From the minute I served Delphine she had openly chatted about the nursery, The Prickly Wild, that she owned and right before she left her money on the table for her breakfast, she let me know that she was hiring a full-time assistant and handed me her business card. I giggled when I realized she was exactly like the name she gave her nursery. I remember taking a huge breath and realizing that what I needed had just landed right in my lap. Thank the Goddess for this small favor. If I had to deal with butt smacks from the slimy manager one more day I might not be held responsible for what I did.

I went to the nursery the next day before my shift started at the diner and found Delphine to be a quiet and firm, yet very comforting presence. She showed me around The Prickly Wild, which was the biggest nursery I had ever been to. She had one other employee who had been with her for many decades, but he wasn’t around when I was there. She explained she needed someone to do anything and everything it took to run this place and that it was working independently and having enough forward thought to make decisions without constant supervision. She had just described me to a T. I told her that I knew some about plants, but that I would love to learn and any reading material I needed to pick up, with her suggestion, I could do. I was so nervous that she wouldn’t give me the job that I almost started to cry.

I had been in Asheville for a few weeks and had not found a place to live that I could afford. When I got the recommendation to move to

Asheville from a customer at a coffee stand I worked at, I hadn't done the research that I normally do when I chose my next destination. I usually made sure that the cost of living was low enough that I could support myself with a mediocre job and housing wasn't outrageous, like it was with most places. What I learned quickly is that as beautiful a place as it was to live, finding a job that you could sustain even the essentials was almost impossible.

When Delphine told me my pay was more than what I had been making, and she had a studio for rent onsite at the nursery, I could have passed out. She hired me on the spot and said that if I called the dinner and gave notice she would be very disappointed in me. She might have even said something about calling the health board because of rodents. I shivered, asked her where to put my purse and jacket then spent the day digging in dirt, lifting heavy pots from here to there. I realized by the time my first day was done, that this was a great way to stay in shape. Delphine even gave me a hiring bonus of a hundred dollars to get me by until my first paycheck came in.

The studio was above a barn on her property. I loved it. The smell left a little to be desired, but with my pay increase, I could afford to go buy some candles and at least cover the smell.

Delphine had watched out for me from the first time we met, and I hated to go down to part-time after I met Ryan. Delphine just shook her head and agreed, but I could tell she didn't like it much. With the death of my sister, Delphine had told me to take as much time as I needed. I should take more, but with what just transpired I couldn't take another minute being that close to those wolves.

Aurora had said she was spending the day at the small cabin, helping her pup recuperate. Which was fine, I didn't need her in my head today anyway. I couldn't even keep up with my thoughts.

I parked next to the greenhouse and walked toward the back where I knew I'd find Delphine. She was a creature of habit, that's for sure.

"If you've come to work, great. If you've come to tell me you quit, I don't accept. I have a ton of work that's backed up since you've been gone, and I need your help," she grunted as she moved pallet after pallet around the room. This woman was a powerhouse of energy and strength. She worked circles around me.

"Delphine, I am here to work, but I have to tell you something," I said to her. I opened my mouth to tell her everything, but closed it when I realized that I did come here to work and not think about my life problems. I could absorb myself in plants. She hadn't mentioned my sling holding my arm that seemed to be healing at a rapid rate. I almost didn't wear the sling today but thought I would give it some more time to heal.

She didn't respond so I went into her make shift office to find out what had come in with her last shipment and start setting up displays. There was a bell attached to the door of her greenhouse so if someone came in I would hear it and go search out the customer. Delphine liked it that way, she tended to be a little rough around the edges for most costumers' likening; although I didn't mind, I wanted the customers to come back.

While working at The Prickly Wild, I have been learning about different plants used for medicinal purposes. Delphine called herself a green witch, but never expanded on what that meant. I assumed she meant a hippie who loved the earth, but knowing I came from a line of magical witches I did think she could be one, but I'd never seen her use any kind of magic to speak of.

I was also in charge of answering the phone when it would ring, which wasn't often.

To help me break out of my thoughts the phone rang.

"Thank you for calling The Prickly Wild. How can I help you?" I asked the caller.

"Put Delphine on," someone barked.

I put the phone down and jogged to the back of the greenhouse and told Delphine she had a phone call. I hadn't finished marking off today's deliveries, so I happened to be in the office when she came to take the call.

"Yep," she said into the receiver.

"Okay," she said again, followed by a few huhs and hums. She ended the call saying, "What do you think?"

"This is why I'm a solitary witch," Delphine said as she slammed the phone down.

"Is everything all right?" I asked quietly, knowing the chances of her sharing were slim to none.

"No, Avery, everything is not all right. I now have to ship a ton of shit, and buy property I haven't seen, and my world just got really busy. I hate busy," she said to me with her hands on her hips.

"Okay, I didn't understand half of what you said, but isn't busy good when you're selling goods?" I asked her.

"You probably should have started the conversation this morning with, 'Oh by the way, I'm the mate to an alpha wolf and I'm in some dip shit'," she glared at me.

"The local coven called?" I asked, but already knew the answer. I had a feeling Delphine was a witch, but I didn't ask, and she didn't offer, so I assumed she didn't want to talk about it.

"Why didn't you request residency when you moved here?" she asked me.

"I didn't know I was supposed to," I admitted to her. I put up my hand when she gave me the how could you not know look.

"I know what you're thinking. Honestly, I didn't know. I was raised in a coven but kept out of all supernatural knowledge, I barely know about witches," I confided in her. It felt good to be able to tell her about my former life. I felt like keeping it from her was lying to her.

"When I started your herb training I noticed you were lacking in knowledge, but you should have told me about your past. Have I ever given you any reason to doubt how I feel about you?" she asked. It was clear I had hurt her feelings.

"I'm sorry I hurt you. I was rejected by my coven, my family years ago. When I started moving around, I thought it best to be normal, just be the human I am. I was always afraid of what witches would think knowing I'm a dud. I had a feeling you were a witch, but I also knew you didn't belong to the local coven so I let things lie," I admitted.

"You're right. I don't belong to the local coven. I've had my use of them in the past, but to find a great coven where you don't have to put up with political bullshit is hard. When I moved here I felt them out and didn't want to be a part of that, but I registered so the alpha in this territory wouldn't blow a gasket. I can't believe you didn't know." She sighed. "Why did your coven throw you out? You are certainly not a dud. Who is the brain-dead leader you have running things in your old coven?" she asked me.

Delphine waved her hands in the air and blew out a breath before she continued, "Actually, I don't want to know, that would just add to my to-do list. Well, now that we have that out of the way; let's deal with your pile of shit. You didn't register and now you have to leave the area. Where does this alpha of yours live?" she asked me.

I just stared at her for a minute.

She snapped her fingers in front of my face. "Listen up, girly, you need to snap out of this. Keep up, make plans, and put them into action. Stop being stuck in the past. That's where it is, in the past. Can't change it, so why dwell," Delphine said.

"I think his pack is in Idaho, the Sawtooth Pack. I don't know what city or anything. Too much has happened in the last few days for me to even know where to begin." I plunked myself down in the office chair and put my head down on the desk. The headache was starting again.

"Okay, first things first. I want you to look in the computer files and find my real estate agent. Give him notice that we will be out by the end of the week, and I want this place sold. Call movers and get them here and packing by tomorrow. The plants have to be the last to leave. Today's Monday, so I want the plants moved on Friday. Look up Sawtooth in the address book and find me Leroy's number. He's the local healer in that area," she kept mumbling to herself all the stuff she needed to do. It sounded like she was preparing to move, leaving the area.

"Um, Delphine, what's happening? Are you closing your business? I don't understand," I asked quietly.

"Of course, I'm closing up shop. I can't be your green witch advisor and teacher from across the U.S. The Goddess spoke to me days before I met you and told me where to go and who to seek out once I did. I'll admit that she hasn't talked to me since, but I know you're part of my destiny, Avery, so get moving, we have tons to do."

"What?" I screeched.

My green witch advisor and teacher?

Did she just say the Goddess talked to her?

Well crap.

"I don't have time to for this. Do as I asked," Delphine said as she left the office.

I didn't want to be staring at the door with a stupid look on my face if she came back in because that would just send her through the roof. So I started on the tasks she asked me to do. The last thing was bringing her Leroy's number before I grabbed my stuff to leave for the day, but I had to ask.

"How do you know Leroy is part of Grayson's pack?" I asked her.

She was watering the hanging baskets when she looked at me. With no emotions on her face she stated, "I didn't know Grayson was the alpha of Leroy's pack, but I know where Leroy lives because he's my mate," and went back to watering.

Okay, now I'm completely lost and confused. That wasn't what I had expected her to say. Since I had known her, she didn't date. She was alone unless she had customers or was working with her employee. I had asked her one time why she didn't have a boyfriend. She looked right at me and said, "What the hell would I do with a man," and kept working. I assumed she was either gay or just fed up with men. Which I couldn't blame her; most men were dumber than a box of rocks.

I could tell I wouldn't get much more out of Delphine today, maybe I could work on getting her to open up to me tomorrow.

Chapter Twelve
Rosie doesn't it again!

I stopped at the Fish Shack on the way home to get Aurora and I something to eat, and let's not forget Bella. I wonder what they've been feeding her? That was something new, worrying about feeding someone other than me. I hope Aurora likes fish, because that's what I was in the mood for. Greasy fish and chips with extra tarter. Yum.

I didn't hear Aurora in the house when I came through the door, but I set up our food on the island in the kitchen and texted her. She texted back right away that she was on her way. I still hadn't heard from Ryan, which wasn't abnormal but it still felt like something was off.

I knew if I called Ryan and told him about the injury, he would probably come home, but I wasn't sure I wanted Ryan in the mix with Grayson and his pack of unpredictable wolves. Plus I had no idea how to tell him about this mate mark.

My phone rang and brought me out of my thoughts.

"Hello?" I asked.

"Avery, I'm so glad you answered," said a female voice I recognized immediately. I took a deep breath, more out of relief than anything.

"Rosie, I'm so glad you called," I told her.

"You'll be relieved once I tell you that my spirit guide has been chatting my ear off. I started researching your dreams, but my guide wouldn't let me finish. I know about the wolf attack, and I know about your cross-linked mate. But what you don't know, and I hate to tell you that you are in danger, extreme danger," she said with remorse.

"I'm okay. My wound is healing quickly. I met several wolves last night, and they all seemed rather nice, not real talkative, but nice," I told her.

Rosie started talking, but I could tell it wasn't to me. I just listened and focused on being patient. When she first started talking about spirit guides, I wasn't real interested, but now with everything going on I'm hoping her spirit guide has some insights.

"Avery, I need you to listen to me. I need you in Idaho in five days, no later. If you stay—" She took a deep breath—"if you stay past the five days you will die." She finished the sentence blowing out a deep breath.

"Die, as in dead? How would I be in danger?" I asked her.

"I don't know. I've been arguing with my spirit guide for days, but she's not talking to me about this anymore. I'll keep trying, but I need you to believe me and keep yourself safe. I know where the Sawtooth pack, is and I'll see you there in a week or so. I have to go, but we'll speak soon. Bye, dear," she said as she hung up. Leaving me with more questions than answers.

This was one of the reasons I wasn't sure about this new friendship, it seemed one-sided, or two-sided, her and her spirit guide.

I wasn't done asking about my death.

This was not what I needed.

Could an alpha kill someone who was in his or her territory without permission? How was I going to explain everything to Ryan? He's a human who won't understand. I had to put my thoughts on hold when Aurora came blowing into the dining room with a guest at her side.

"Thanks for dinner, Auntie, is their enough for Trace to eat with us?" she asked me as she took a seat next to me. I gave her the look, even though I'm sure she could read my thoughts.

"Sure, I always get extra, never know when the midnight munchies might hit," I said as I got up and grabbed an extra plate.

"I appreciate this. My dad's on cooking duty tonight, and I try to eat other places on those nights," Trace said with a grin.

With that grin I could totally tell why Aurora was infatuated with this kid.

"I'm sure it's not that bad." I laughed.

"He's not a terrible cook, but the basics are all he knows. He over cooks any meat, and by that, I mean someone once broke their tooth," Trace said and started to grab some fish and French fries.

"In that case, it's best to feed you. We don't need any more emergencies." I finished dishing up myself once both kids had their fill. Someone once told me you never want a hungry teenager living in your house if you cherish your sanity.

As we ate, I listened to Aurora and Trace talk about popular music, TV shows, and other things I eventually couldn't hear anymore because I was thinking about my own life and what the next few days held for Aurora and me.

Rosie's warning had me worried. I had never been involved with magical warnings, but I do know they can happen. A seer had contacted my mom before her and Dad's death and warned them. I didn't know what it all entailed, but I remember them having a discussion about it, and they couldn't agree on what to do. I guess they picked the wrong choice because it wasn't but a week later they both were dead. I hadn't thought about magical warnings, but now that I had one of my own I couldn't stop thinking about them.

My arm was starting to itch, so Aurora helped me clean and change the bandages after dinner, she also reminded me to take my antibiotics which I did. Trace said he would take Bella the leftovers, leaving us alone together.

"Remember I told you about Rosie from the plane ride?" I asked Aurora.

"Yeah, the high-energy lady that had snuck her cat onto the plane inside her purse. What about her?" Aurora looked up from just putting the last piece of tape on my arm.

"Well, she called right before you got here with bad news." I took the supplies and put them back in the bathroom with Aurora following me.

"She sounds like a spiritual witch, Auntie, especially if she talks to spirits. Not all witches can do that. From my studies, I gathered they are never wrong. Maybe you should listen to her. Plus, the spirit world doesn't get involved with the living world unless it's important for a mass of the population," Aurora said as she sat on my bed.

"She says I need to be in Idaho in five days, which means I can't stay any longer than two days. That means we would have to pack up and go. But where?" I motioned with my arm between the two of us.

"Trace said that we could go with his pack, back to Grayson's territory," Aurora said with a tentative smile.

"You're acting like this isn't a big deal. I'm being forced from my home. I know you have to adapt too, but I've been running my whole life. I finally found a quiet, safe place," I said with frustration.

"Quiet doesn't equal safe, and I can't think of anywhere we'd be safer than with a pack of people who can change into wolves," Aurora quietly added.

I looked at her, and the amount of courage this kid had in her pinkie finger I couldn't seem to muster up for myself. I was scared and that fear was starting to make me freeze.

"I don't know why Mom treated you the way she did, and I'm not going to defend her, but I will say Mom told me that when life gets tough we stick to together and trust each other. Do you trust me?" Aurora asked me.

Did I trust this teenager to know what's best for me, a grown woman?

"I've never had anyone who earned my trust more until I met you. I do trust you. If anything, you showed me that you were willing to stick up for me when the coven you grew up with wanted to hurt me. You see evil, so yes, I do trust you. I just need time to come around. All the signs are there that something's not right in Denmark. So yeah, I think going with the pack might be our safest bet. I just don't know what to do about Ryan?" I said to her and to myself.

"Well, I can tell you that I don't see you two together much longer.

I don't want to talk bad about your husband, but I see a separation of the minds in your future," and with that comment she left my room.

What do people see that I didn't in Ryan? He might not be the most emotionally available person, but he's never physically hurt me.

Aurora popped back in through my door and made one final statement before bed. "There are many ways to hurt people without being physical. You should know that better than anyone," Aurora said as she slipped out of my doorway and was gone.

I knew people could hurt others without using their hands; the coven was a prime example. Being ostracized can hurt just as much as a fist. Not that they didn't physically torture me too. Let's not think about those memories.

I lit a few candles and lay in bed, trying to calm my thoughts. The first image that popped into my frantic brain was the conversation I overheard from the bathroom when Grayson was talking to his pack doctor Leroy. He had called me his mate. Now everyone's talking about us being cross-linked mates, soul mates. It was hard to convince myself a cross-linked mate wasn't possible when I came from a family of magic wielding people. But then again, I did just figure out that there's more than one kind of supernatural being in the world after all these years. Lighting candles with a flick of the hand, or brewing a potion to make someone tell the truth are possible, so why wouldn't a soul mate be possible?

I stared at the candle on my bedside table and flicked my hand at it, hoping it would light. If I'm being kicked out of my home and my life because I'm a witch I'd better get something out of it. I closed my eyes and tried to focus on the candle, pushing my energy toward it. I opened my eyes and nothing was different. The candle's ghost flame danced along like it was laughing at me. I grabbed the comforter and rolled over; I didn't want to look at the candle, which represented the defective side of me.

Little did I know that every candle in my house and every house within a twenty-five-mile radius lit at the same time a few minutes after I fell asleep.

Chapter Thirteen
Distant relative? Lie much!

The phone ringing interrupting my perfect dream. I was right in the middle of sitting down at a table loaded with cupcakes, swirls of creamy frosting dotted with different colors of sprinkles. I had a tall glass of milk and was just about to bite into my first one.

"You better be important because I was about to be in chocolate heaven," I mumbled sleepily into the phone.

"Why haven't you called me?" I heard a familiar voice bark.

I sat up and opened my eyes, realizing I was finally talking to Ryan. I've wanted to talk to him, ask him to make this all go away, but now that I have him on the phone, what the hell do I tell him?

"I'm sorry I haven't called, but it's been super busy around here. I didn't get a chance," I told him.

"Busy? How busy can you be?" Ryan asked. I could tell he was starting to get upset.

"Well, I've got a teenager to take care of, and I work. Delphine

needed me this week," I told him.

"That's why I didn't want you working. As soon as Aurora's moved in you stopped calling me. You used to call me once a day and leave a message if I was busy. I look forward to hearing your voice once I'm able to retrieve it," Ryan whined.

"I like my job. I would actually like a full-time job. And Aurora just lost her mother and needs to feel the support." I take a calming breath. "Look, I don't want to fight with you, it's too early," I told him, pulling my phone away from my face to check the time.

6:30 am.

Who is up this early?

"Well, I don't want you picking up any shifts this weekend because I'm off Friday through Sunday. I want you and I to take a drive down to Mom's," Ryan said.

Shit, here we go.

"Ryan, I can't go with you to your Mom's this weekend." I was trying to stall to figure out a lie. I hate lying. "Our distant aunt tracked us down. She's very old and ill. She doesn't have any children of her own, and she needs someone to come take care of her for a while. Aurora is too young to do it alone, so I'm taking her with me. She can homeschool until our aunt is better." The lie just flew out of my mouth. I stunned even myself with how flawless it sounded, and all that came out of my tired mind with no coffee to fuel it.

"Why can't Aurora go live with this aunt?" Ryan asked.

"Did you just hear me? Our aunt is old and sick; she needs help. I can't ask a teenager to do it by herself. She's sixteen, not twenty-six," I scolded him.

"I've never heard you talk about an aunt before. Where does this

Aunt live?" he asked me.

Don't tell him where you're going.

"Avery, are you still there?" Ryan asked.

My silence probably made him think the call dropped. Our house was so far into the mountains I was rarely able to talk on the phone without dropping a call. I swore I heard a voice tell me not to tell Ryan where we were really going. It made goose bumps instantly appear on my arms.

"I'm here. She lives in central Oregon somewhere. I didn't get the specifics on the phone, but she's texting with Aurora. She needs us there by Thursday, so I won't see you when you get in on Friday. We'll take the dog, so no worries about I'll call you and let you know more when we get there," I told him hoping this ended the questions. With no coffee, my brain wasn't firing as fast as it could be.

"Fine, if you must go, go. But I don't want this to be a long-term thing. I'm sure she can be put into one of those places for old people who are retired. You're not a nurse." He sighed in annoyance. "Look, I have to go, but I expect a phone call from you daily," Ryan said and then hung up.

No, I love you. No, how are you. I was starting to think that I'd made the right decision about not telling him what was going on with the attack, the alpha kicking us out of his territory, and definitely not about the cross-linked mate business.

Maybe Aurora was on to something with him.

"I'm right!" Aurora yelled from the kitchen.

"Stop reading my mind!" I yelled back.

I threw back the covers and decided I had so much to do in the next few days I might as well get started. I was also wondering why Aurora

was up so early.

I had just filled my coffee cup and was putting in my dash of vanilla coffee creamer when Aurora spoke. “How are we going to move all my stuff and your stuff and not have Mr. Tight Pants getting into a tizzy?”

“Mr. Tight Pants?” I asked her. She didn’t answer, and I wasn’t surprised.

I was getting ready to answer when someone knocked on our back door right next to the kitchen island. It startled me enough I spilled my coffee down the front of my razor back tank top.

“Fuck!” I spat.

“I’ll get it. Here, use this to clean up.” Aurora handed me a dishtowel.

I realized it was pointless; I was just going to have to change shirts when in walked Grayson with his brother Jackson.

Walking in with a look of concentration was Grayson, followed by Jackson, who was sporting a look of happiness.

“Did we catch you at a bad time?” Grayson asked me, eyeing my wet tank top.

“Not if interrupting my first cup of coffee is important,” I told him as I filled my coffee again.

“Aunt Avery is a little cranky before her third cup of coffee. Maybe you guys should come back in a bit.” She smiled at them.

“I’m not cranky. I’m... fine, I’m a little cranky. It’s no one’s fault but yours. Every time I’m around you—” I waved my arms toward Grayson— “my life gets more and more complicated. I’m running out of energy to deal with it.” I glared at all three of them. “At least let me finish my first cup of coffee and then hit me with whatever you have up your sleeve,” I said.

Grayson kept opening his mouth and closing it. I raised my eyebrow at him.

"Auntie, you're scaring the big bad wolf so much that he's speechless," Aurora said to me. That got Grayson to raise one of his eyebrows at her.

"Tell me about it," I said to Grayson.

"This is my first encounter with teenagers, and I don't know what to do with them," I said to Jackson.

"Well, I think that Aurora needs to go see her dog. She's starting to get restless, but won't let anyone close. She needs a walk. Do you mind?" Jackson asked Aurora.

"Yeah, I'll go handle her. You can talk my aunt here into packing up everything we need. I have a feeling we will never be allowed back once all this goes down," Aurora said to Grayson and Jackson and off she went.

I took a deep breath, closed my eyes, and asked the Goddess for patience not to duck tape that kid's mouth shut.

"I find the more you keep a teenager busy the less frustration you'll feel," Jackson offered.

"Would you two like some coffee?" I asked. I guess I should be hospitable, or at least act like I was raised right.

"That would be great, thanks," Jackson said and Grayson just nodded his head.

I poured them both cups and got my creamer out, but they both waved it off. I guess I'm alone in my creamer addiction.

It was quiet for a few minutes, which was fine by me. I needed those quiet times to shore up my defenses, not that I had much I could argue with them on. I had a wolf pack alpha telling me I had to move, a bizarre tattoo on my palm, and another alpha telling me I was his one true mate. Oh, and let's not forget that Rosie called and said my life was in danger.

"I can see the tension in your posture. We aren't here to kidnap you. We're here to help you," Grayson said after he took a sip of his black coffee. Who drinks their coffee with no cream or sugar? I did notice that Jackson had put a dash of sugar in his.

"I don't feel like I'm being kidnapped, I feel like I'm being strong armed into leaving my home. I had to lie to my husband and make up a sick relative on the fly. I don't like lying," I told them both.

Grayson looked like there was something he wanted to say, but was interrupted by his phone ringing.

"Yeah?" he answered.

"Huh, okay. Thanks," he told whoever was on the other end and hung up.

"Avery, do you know a Rosie?" Grayson asked me.

I just stared at him while he stared at me with that knowing look in his eye. "I do know a Rosie who talks to spirits. And who is off my Christmas list." I glared at Grayson.

Grayson put his hands up. "Hey, she called us. But what she did say had me and my pack very concerned for your safety," he told me.

"I have to go into work today. My boss, Delphine, seems to be moving to your neck of the woods too, and I have a ton to do for her," I explained.

"I could get my boys to help pack you and your niece's items while you're out today. Just tell us what you want, and we'll get it loaded up. We went and got a truck this morning. We're ready when you are." Jackson smiled at me.

“Wow, you guys aren’t messing around. You rented a truck?” I asked Grayson.

He shrugged his shoulders. “I know this is hard for you, but being an alpha and knowing what kind of man Max is, I’m not ready to push him,” he said to me.

I was getting ready to address the whole cross-linked mate issue, but he beat me to it. “Let’s not worry about this yet.” And he pointed to his tattoo. “Let’s get you moved and safe. One thing at a time. Jackson and his sons are going to drive the truck. I’ll drive with you, Aurora, and Bella. It might take us a few days to make it back home, so pack what you need for the trip. I’m sorry you had to lie to your—Ryan. But I think it’s best you don’t involve a millie in this. It will just cause problems.

“Millie?” I asked.

“It’s not derogatory; it means ‘run of the mill’ just a saying someone came up with. I can see and feel you getting defensive, which is curious in itself because you’re a witch,” Grayson said to me.

“You all keep saying that, but I don’t have powers like the rest of my family. That’s why I was pushed out of the coven,” I said to him.

“So it was your niece who lit all the candles in both cabins last night?” Grayson asked.

“What?” I asked in shock.

“Yeah, I was up late last night, and all the candles in the house lit at the same time. I checked with Jackson, and he said the same about the small cabin. Unless your niece was messing around it had to be you. I know you don’t think you have magical abilities, but I have seen several things you’ve done that prove you do. Remember when you got mad at me and shoved me back? You didn’t touch me when you did that. And I won't even talk about the fact that you can control the emotions of others when you try," he said while looking down at his coffee cup.

I too just kept my gaze on the rim of my coffee cup. Part of my, a huge part, knew he was speaking the truth. He seemed not to want to push too much. Almost like he was giving me time to catch up to him.

"Do you think the mark that we share might have something to do with my magic showing up?" I asked him. I looked up and he was looking at me with hope in his eyes. He didn't say anything but did give me a shrug. We stood in my kitchen silently drinking coffee for a few minutes.

"Okay, looks like it's time for me to go grab the boys and the truck. Avery, leave a list of stuff you want brought with you and the boys and I'll get started" Jackson asked me.

I sucked in a huge breath startled. I hadn't realized Jackson was still in the kitchen.

I looked at Grayson and he was trying to hide a smile behind his coffee cup.

"This is all happening so fast I'm a little overwhelmed," I admitted.

"I'll take some of that off your shoulders if you let me," he stated softly.

Letting someone else help me with my problems wasn't something I was used to. I had been taking care of myself for so long it felt weird giving up that control.

"Okay, I'll go pack a bag for myself, and I'll text Aurora to let her know to pack her stuff. I'll leave a list on the island of what I want put in the moving truck. Most of the furniture in the house is Ryan's, but Aurora might want most of her stuff in her room," I told Grayson.

"Why is most of the furniture Ryan's? Did you not come into the relationship with belongings?" he asked with a frown.

"I didn't. I traveled a bunch before I settled here. I didn't like to haul stuff, so I rented places that were furnished. My jeep and a few bags make for easy travel. And now it will make it seem less like I up and left my husband for no apparent reason," I confessed.

I seemed to be confessing quite a bit to Grayson.

"That must have been hard, not having a place to call home. People to lean on. I've always lived in a pack and grew up with many mom's and dad's. We all look out for one another," Grayson said to me.

"Must have been nice," I sneered and then realized Grayson hasn't done one thing to me, and yet here I was, taking out my problems on him.

"I'm sorry, that wasn't nice. I get green with envy sometimes, and it's not pretty. I'm glad you grew up with family supporting you. It should be that way for everybody." He nodded his understanding and rinsed out his coffee mug and put it in the dishwasher. As I finished my coffee I decided that I needed to lead in the future with love on my heart. I finished my coffee, washed it out and got to work packing my clothes and a few other belongings. I didn't think Ryan would notice, he isn't home much anyway. I did leave a note for Jackson's boys all my plants needed to be brought to the nursery so that I could take those with me. I had worked hard on all the plants in my house, and they would die if left here. Ryan wasn't a nurturer.

Delphine was quiet when I showed up and had a list of chores for me to do, which was fine. I'd been talked to enough today. I was just finishing up a phone call with a mover when my cell beeped. I looked at it was a text from Grayson.

G: I'm outside with your houseplants

Me: I'll be right there

That was one thing I didn't have to do. I had almost the entire nursery arranged and ready for loading. I still thought it was strange that Delphine was following me, but I don't think she was only coming for me. Her mate Leroy was there. I hadn't been around him long, but I could tell he was a soul in waiting. The way he talked to Grayson, like he knew about love and could write a book or two about it, made me think Delphine was going back to have a look at her past. I didn't understand going back, after you are pushed away, why would you ever look back? It made me wonder who pushed who away?

I had made a promise to myself that I was never looking back. I never returned to a place I had lived, never made lasting friendships. No pain.

I guess Grayson must have been here a while because he had tracked down a pallet and had all my house plants loaded on it. I love a man who takes action without hand holding.

"Thanks, that saved me some work," I said with a smile.

"Anything to get you to smile like that." He winked at me.

I lost part of my smile. "Yeah, there hasn't been much to smile about at lately," I said.

Grayson didn't lose his smile. "Well, we'll just have to fix that, won't we."

He was easy to be around. He made me feel comfortable without even trying and that made me pause. Being around people had always been work; with Grayson it was natural.

"So, Jackson has the truck being loaded. I think they're almost done. The Summit is over so I have time. How about you introduce me to Delphine and put me to work. Many hands make less work," he said.

I introduced Delphine to Grayson. When she shook his hand, she tilted her head to the side exposing her neck. What was that? A wolf thing? It seemed strange since Delphine wasn't part of Grayson's pack, but I had too much on my mind to try to figure out pack politics.

It took most of the day, helping the drivers load up all our inventory, but a workout was exactly what I needed. Thankfully, my arm hadn't hurt much today. I hadn't seen Grayson much, but I knew he was helping to pack up the nursery.

"Avery, let me look at your arm." Delphine's voice startled me. "I think I have some herbs that can speed up the healing and help with scarring." Delphine took me back to her office.

I had on a long sleeve shirt with a sports bra underneath, so I just took off my shirt. Delphine unwrapped the bandage that Aurora had put on last night. I was worried the bandage would be stuck to the healing scab, but it seemed to come right off.

"What if the plants don't make it in the move?" I asked her. I had been thinking about this all day.

As she was working on my arm, she answered me.

"I doubt some of them will, but I can't just leave them here, so might as well try. I did well enough last year that if I lose most of my inventory it won't hit the pocket book too hard," she said.

Running her finger along my arm, she continues, "I guess you didn't get as hurt as I thought you did," Delphine said.

I snapped my vision to my arm, and she was right. There was a faint white line where the gaping wound was supposed to be, but it was closed up like it had happened years ago.

That couldn't be right.

"Something's not right. My arm was torn open all the way to the bone two days ago," I told her as I ran my other hand down my arm. There was a faint line that showed where my arm was torn open, but it looked as insignificant as a cat scratch.

"Looks like the linked marks are working properly, that's a bonus," she said to me as she put her supplies away in the bin that was sitting by the door. We had just a few things left in her office to load up and her nursery was done. It looked different empty, cold even.

"What do you mean the linked mark is working? The mark on my hand is what healed me? Like..." I didn't finish.

"Like magic," Delphine smiled and walked out.

I was getting tired of short, sweet answers from the people in my life. But this time I smiled too, because magic was awesome when it was used properly.

Chapter Fourteen
Road Trip

I was used to being on the road, even though I hadn't had to do it in almost five years. Eating fast food, living out of a bag became my routine. But having company on the road isn't the same as being alone. I liked it, except I had four churlish wolves and a mind reading teenage witch that all wanted different foods, didn't like the beds in the motels we picked, and the list goes on, not including having to make sure Aurora's dog got potty breaks. I think all people who want to have children should be around teenagers for a month; I bet half decide they like the "no kid" life.

Jackson and his two sons were on the trip with us, driving the moving truck, the rest of Grayson's family had flown back to Idaho. I had insisted on driving at first, then realized that if Grayson drove I could nap when I wanted to. He smiled but didn't say anything. I was done, I wanted to sleep through this entire trip. I practically threw him the keys, grabbed my blanket and pillow, and was out before anyone could blink. Before I drifted off to dream land I did hear Grayson ask Aurora if I was always able to fall asleep so fast. Aurora said she thought I had a hard time sleeping but that lately she thought I had stopped having nightmares and seemed to sleep through the nights. She also mentioned that empaths tend to be drained faster than most as they tend to absorb from high energy people like herself, or take on negative energy. They started discussing empathic witches, but I was sleep before they said anything that could freak me out.

I got lucky for the first two days of our trip, whenever I would call Ryan it went straight to voicemail, so I knew he had his phone off. It made me feel better I didn't have to continue a lie, just tell him we were doing okay and to tell him that I would call again the next day. The weird part was he didn't return any of my calls or text me that he got my messages. That part wasn't like Ryan. This whole mess wasn't normal so I decided not to take on problems that might not be real. I'm sure Ryan was just busy and would contact me when he could.

I think by the third day I had finally irritated my traveling group. With Jackson driving the moving truck, pulling off the interstate wasn't as easy. I had picked up a map of tourist sites at one of the gas stations we stopped at and had highlighted things I wanted to see. I even influenced Grayson to change his travel route so that I could see and take pictures of things I found interesting. In fact, I made everybody take pictures with the biggest ball of yarn, the biggest frying pan. The best was the biggest dairy cow in history. We took quite the detour for that one, but I didn't care. I wanted a picture with a humungous cow. Who wouldn't?

All six of us were standing on the side of the road next to the fenced in cow.

"How do you expect to get a picture with the cow, Avery? It's in the far end of the pasture. Isn't it enough that we drove out into the middle of nowhere to see it?" Grayson grunted.

With my hands on my hips, I demanded, "I expect you four boys to go into that pasture and bring it over. You are wolves, are you not?"

Grayson bugged his eyes out at me. "You want us to change into wolves and, what, herd it over here? We aren't herding dogs, Avery. We are wolves. You do know what those are, don't you?" Grayson was getting a wee bit upset.

"Yes, Grayson, I do know what wolves are. One tried to rip my arm off several days ago." I gave him the death stare. I hated to use what one of his pack did to me against him, but I really wanted a picture with that cow, and my brand-new blinding white converse shoes weren't getting dirty to do it.

"You owe me," Grayson said before he went over and grabbed his brother and nephews. Trace and Tyler were all over catching a cow.

All four guys gathered around and I could only assume that they were talking strategy until they each started to undress.

Wait, hold on!

"Um, you can't get naked! What if someone sees you?" I yelled. That didn't stop them. They were doing all of this with the big moving van blocking them from the road, so it really wasn't an issue, but I didn't want to see any naked bodies.

I covered my eyes and reached in front of Aurora and covered hers too.

"Auntie, you're ruining all the fun," she whined.

"Your mom would kill me if she knew I was letting you watch naked boys and men undress. Let me have a little adult supervision. It makes me feel like I'm doing something my sister would approve of," I pleaded with her. She didn't say anything but let me keep her eyes covered. I didn't know how long it took to change into wolf form, but it couldn't have been more than a couple of minutes when I heard a bark. I looked up and on the other side of the fence were four gigantic wolves. Two large wolves and two smaller ones, all different colors. I could tell which one Grayson was because he was staring right at me with those yellow. His coat had a reddish tone across his back and his belly and legs were cream. The one distinct mark I noticed was the mask of dark-red color he had around his face. He was a beautiful wolf. He yapped once more and off they flew through the pasture to herd me a big cow.

I guess that's my queue to get my camera ready.

As soon as I realized what I had asked them to do I felt bad. They did seem to enjoy themselves though, mud flying everywhere, chasing each other until it was time to focus on the cow. As soon as they got it moving, and boy did it move, I started thinking maybe this wasn't such a good idea.

The cow was moving a steady clip toward Aurora and I. We had gotten on top of the fence so we could take a quick picture, but the cow didn't seem like it was going to stop. Its eyes were huge with fear, and it was gaining speed.

"Um, Aurora, I think we need to get down," I stammered. I scrambled back down the fence but Aurora was still sitting there.

"Aurora, move it!" I commanded.

"I'm stuck!" she screamed. I could see she was trying to fling her leg over the fence but something was caught. I climbed up and was trying to figure out where she was stuck. I heard frantic barking, and I looked up.

This was not going to happen. I closed my eyes and pulled with all I had on Aurora's torso. I heard the fabric tear as we tumble to the ground. I kept waiting for the cow to trample us, but it never happened. My eyes were tightly shut, my body covering Aurora's, knowing the damage the cow could do when it trampled us, but I didn't hear any noise.

"Um, Auntie, I think you need to realize you have power. Look what you did to the cow." Aurora swept my hair out of my eyes, and I looked up toward the top of the fence.

There, suspended in a leaping motion was the biggest dairy cow I had ever seen. She was breathing but not moving. The fear was still prevalent when you looked in her eyes.

"I did that?" I asked Aurora as we both stood and started wiping dirt off our pants.

"Yeah, I think it's like the binding spell I put on Matilda, but you did it on a moving target which is much harder to do. Even I'm not that advanced." She looked at the cow in awe.

As Aurora and I were admiring the mid-flight, motionless cow, the boys had gone back over the fence and changed.

"Okay, ladies, I think we've had our quota of near death experiences. Get your butts over that fence, and let's get this picture. I'm suddenly in the mood for a big juicy burger," Grayson said as he helped us both over the fence.

Trace took the picture and made sure that it didn't show the cows feet not touching the ground. That wouldn't have looked strange at all. Aurora and the boys helped the cow get unstuck because I had no idea how to do that, or how I did it in the first place. I had tried but nothing happened. I waved my hands; I concentrated really hard, but nothing. Aurora had laughed the whole time until Grayson lost his patience and growled while prowling toward me saying, "You better release that cow before I get to you or their will be a consequence.

"What?" I squeaked as I backed up away from him.

"Avery," he growled still coming at me with a determined look. I didn't want to know what my consequence would be and the fear of not knowing caused the cow to slowly lower to the ground but I didn't noticed because I had a chest in my face. Grayson's arms came around me and he said quietly, "I would never hurt you. Well maybe a spankin' here or there," he smiled.

Once the cow situation was fixed, we all piled back into the vehicles and off we went. I was feeling seriously guilty about my decision to take that cow picture. I let an hour go by before I had to atone for my mistake, I just couldn't stand it.

"Guys, I'm so sorry I asked you to do that. It wasn't my best idea. I had no idea that would happen." I hung my head with shame.

Both Aurora and Grayson busted up laughing; it wasn't until I yelled "hey" that they tried to reign in their composure.

"Babe, I haven't had that much fun since high school and a bunch of us broke into our rival school and set all the frogs' free from the science lab, put talcum powder in the football team's pants, and put cling wrap on all the toilets," Grayson admitted.

"You did all that in high school? You seem so responsible now," I said.

"We were a bunch of teenage wolves with extra testosterone who needed a good outlet. It was pranks or fighting, and we couldn't draw the kind of attention that fighting brings to our pack," he said.

I could understand needing to release all that energy, but then a thought hit me.

I turned in my seat and looked at Aurora, "You better not do any of those things. You'd be in big trouble." I glared at her.

Aurora raised her hands. "How did what happened become my fault?" She smiled innocently.

"I've learned by being around my nephews that we don't talk about everything they can't do. Let's focus on what they can do. If you give a teenager something they can't do, they will do it in spite of you. Trust me," Grayson said.

"You're probably right. I'm not very good at being a parental figure. I'll take that into advisement. I know the cow wasn't a smart idea, but it means a lot you went along with it," I said as I put my hand on his arm.

"I saw that smile many times today, so I'll keep doing what I gotta' do to keep it there." Grayson patted my hand.

Someone so concerned with my happiness, it was a foreign concept to me. Thinking about Grayson and his pursuit of my happiness made my mark start to feel warm.

What the heck?

I didn't get a chance to think about it when my phone rang. I wasn't one of those people who walked around with their phones stuck to their face so I had to dig in my purse to find it. I didn't look at the screen, I just answered.

"Hello," I answered.

"I'd like to know why you had to take all of Aurora's furniture to visit a sick relative?" Ryan asked through clenched teeth. I didn't hear Ryan this angry very often, so it threw me off.

"Ryan?" I asked.

"Who else would it be?" he demanded.

Shit. I wasn't very good at lying on the fly, so I just spewed what was at the top of my head.

"Well, our sick aunt only one extra bed. I didn't want to have to sleep on the floor, so we brought Aurora's stuff. She has an extra room, but not the furniture," I explained. I thought it sounded legit.

"And does that explain why every piece of clothing you own is gone, including all the house plants?" he asked.

Oh, well, this one might be harder to explain.

"With your schedule all of the plants would be dead within a week, and I've spent years growing them since babies, so I dropped them at the nursery. And my clothes, well I don't have a ton of clothes, and I wasn't sure what the weather would be like," I said while nodding, thinking that was a great explanation.

"What's going on?" Ryan asked quietly.

Okay, what to do? Continue my lie and damn my soul to hell, or fess up, and hope he'll totally understand.

"Auntie," Aurora pleaded from the back seat.

I pulled the phone away from my face, hit the mute button, and turned toward the back of the jeep where Aurora was sitting.

"If you think he isn't going to know something fishy, you are out of your mind. He is smart," she told me.

She's right and I didn't know how to handle this situation.

"I don't lie because I have a shit fit when people lie to me. I don't believe lying is necessary, and I'm really bad at it." I probably shouldn't talk to Aurora like she's an adult, but I need her to understand where I'm coming from.

She didn't say anything before Grayson decided to enter our conversation. "First, I think leaving Ryan on hold is causing suspicion, and second I think you need to keep him in the dark for as long as possible. When Rosie called me she explained the threat wasn't from the supernatural. I don't know what that means, but I feel exposed out here and would feel better if you at least waited until we're back on pack land. I can control it better, and I'm pretty sure Satan would not want you in his territory." Grayson chuckled at the last comment.

Okay, he made a good point.

I quickly took Ryan off mute and realized Grayson was right. Leaving him on mute wasn't such a good idea.

"Ryan? Can you hear me? Hello?" I asked through a rushed voice.

"I'm here," he said quietly.

"Aurora and I are still driving and the reception is spotty. I'll call you when we are settled in a room for the night. Nothing's going on but wanting to take care of family," I told him.

He didn't answer for a minute and I had to ask twice if he was there.

"Okay. I'll talk to you later." And he hung up.

We always used to say we loved each other before we got off the phone. I hated lying to him, but my gut instincts were with Aurora and Grayson. I couldn't tell him just yet what was going on. I at least owed him an in-person conversation. I didn't even want to try to explain the mark on my palm, let alone that I had magic powers.

That started a whole slew of thoughts racing through my head about my powers. What Grayson said about the candles went right in line with what I had been trying to do that night with the candle at my bedside. Why, after all these years, would my powers finally be emerging?

Late bloomer?

"Auntie, I think you should try to sleep," Aurora encouraged me.

"I'm not sleepy," I told her.

Grayson put his hand on my knee. "Aurora and I can't breathe because your tension is filling up the inside of the jeep. I'm so tense I might break your steering wheel," he said.

"You better not break my jeep. I love this jeep," I glared at him.

"So why don't you turn on some music and relax?" he asked.

I was about to respond when he squeezed my knee and smiled at me.

"Okay," I said and put on some pop, which always relaxes me, propped my pillow on the passenger window, and went off to dream land. Sleep was something I dreaded anymore and that felt so nice that I slipped off to sleep.

We ended up stopping at a hotel on our third night in a small town in Colorado that had a heated in-door pool and hot tub. Aurora decided to swim. I had brought my suit just because you never leave home without it, and I soaked in the tub attempting to ease the tension from the drive. Sitting in a car was starting to hurt my rear end and making me stiff. Soaking was doing the trick of making me forget that a part of my body hurt, plus my arm was mostly healed so that was a bonus.

"Can I join you?" I heard asked.

I had my eyes closed and my head back so when I opened my eyes I saw Grayson standing there in midnight blue swim trunks. You could tell with the tight t-shirts and relaxed fit Levis he wore that he was a very fit man. But with the no shirt and bare legs I found out there wasn't a single piece of him that wasn't honed to its full potential.

Oh, my Goddess!

"Sure, it's a communal hot tub. No sign that says you have to ask." I replied flippantly.

He just smiled and climbed in beside me. Even being surly to this guy wasn't making him go away.

I decided to close my eyes and lay my head back, trying to ignore there was a gorgeous hunk of a man sitting next to me, but it was hard when his leg kept brushing against mine. The first time it happened, I was startled and jerked.

"Sorry," I heard him whisper.

I ignored that because it wasn't like he was sitting that close, but I felt drawn to him and couldn't pull myself to slide to the other side.

"It's okay. I'm a little uncomfortable, but I'll get over it," I told him with closed eyes.

He didn't say anything.

I listened to Aurora making friends at the pool, laughing and giggling like teenagers are supposed to do. I smiled. I might not be a great parental figure, but she was laughing and being a kid which made me happy.

"She's a good kid," Grayson threw out there.

"Yeah, she is. She's nothing like her mom. Well, at least not the version of her I remember. Before our folks died she was more relaxed. She didn't care that I couldn't do magic, in fact she would try and protect me when it came time to do things with the coven. It got her into trouble a time or two, and I hated that she put herself out there for me, but I knew she loved me then," I said still with closed eyes.

"I've talked with your niece about covens and the witch communities, and from what she's told me I don't think all covens treat their own the way that yours treated you," Grayson said.

"You're probably right. I don't know much about covens. After I left mine I didn't want anything to do with magic, covens, witches or…" I started to tell him.

"Or people," he quietly finished for me.

"Yeah," I whispered.

"Just so you know. This cross-linked stuff is just as hard for me as it is for you," Grayson said.

I peeked an eye open and Grayson had slide down and had his eyes closed and head resting on the edge of the tub.

I didn't say anything because what could I say. He was right. He didn't ask to be shackled to me anymore than I asked to be thrown into him. Maybe I needed to not be so wound tight around him, he didn't deserve my anger. If anything, Grayson has been helping me since the first time he met me.

We soaked in the tub for a while, before we both decided it was excessively hot and got out.

We all agreed to meet up for dinner at a diner across the street from the motel.

"This is the best chicken fried steak ever." I declared to the table.

I couldn't help it, it was the bomb. The plate was humongous and covered in deep fried yumminess, sides of mashed potatoes and country gravy. Another one of my ultimate favorites. I looked around and everyone was smiling at me. What? Didn't they like what they picked?

"Auntie, you're a nut." Aurora smirked.

I just smiled and shrugged my shoulders.

I couldn't fight her on that.

I was halfway through my mashers when Aurora's phone rang.

"Yeah," Aurora answered it.

I watched her and wondered what friend from back home was calling her when the smile on her face fell, and she started to look freaked out.

"Okay, thanks Trixie. Let me know if he comes by again and text me his number," she said and hung up the phone.

"Who came by?" I asked. Even though I could tell all four of the wolf boys had that question.

"Um, well, it was…," Aurora looked down at her half-eaten burger.

"Spit it out," I told her, not interested in my food anymore.

She looked up and right into my eyes. "I guess my dad is looking for me," she stated, picked her burger up, and continued to eat.

"I can see why that would be upsetting, but you don't have to worry about it. He can't find you if you don't want him to," I told her.

She just stared at me while chewing her food.

"Um Mom might have forgotten to mention something to you about my dad. I'm going to tell you, but I don't want you to freak out," she advised me.

"Okay," I said.

"Well, so remember when Kalon wondered why someone in the room could read minds, and he was the only vampire in the room?" she asked me.

"Yeah?" I said slowly. I think I knew where this was going.

I nodded.

"My dad's a vampire," she said and grabbed her coke sucking down half the glass.

I guess everyone was surprised because all four boys started choking on their drink and food.

"What?" I screeched.

"You drink blood?" I asked calmly because frankly that was the first thing that popped into my head.

Aurora giggled. "No, but I do have vampire traits. Like the reading of minds," Aurora told us.

"Apparently, Grandpa Isaiah was half vampire and half witch, too," she also imparted on us.

"Nope, that is not true. He would have told me," I said with confidence.

She just shook her head and continued to eat like what she told me didn't rock my world.

Grayson was sitting next to me and put his hand on my thigh. "Avery, we didn't know about the cross-linked mates either, don't feel left out. You also left the coven at a very young age. You probably would know more about your family if you hadn't," he said.

"So, this is my fault?" I asked him.

"Uncle Gray, that's a loaded question. I wouldn't step on that land mind," Trace told his Uncle Grayson.

Grayson completely ignored his teenage nephew. "None of this is anyone's fault. These are just facts; things that have happened that can't be undone. No reason to start blaming anyone. Let's just take the information and move on," he said with a grin as he squeezing my thigh at the same time. His touch seemed to calm me down.

"Okay," I said because what else could I say. My niece was part vampire, which if I really thought about it was cool.

"Thanks. I think it's pretty cool too. If we hadn't had to flee the area I would have liked to talk to Kalon. He's the first vampire I've ever met," she finished.

"Aurora, please stop reading your aunt's mind. I know she doesn't like it. And I can tell you if you do it to me I really won't like it," Grayson said and he wasn't grinning anymore.

"Well, you don't have anything to worry about. The barrier around your mind is strong. I have been trying since I met you to get through and I can't," she told him with a pout.

"That's because he's alpha, it comes with the job," Jackson jumped into the conversation.

I looked across the table at Jackson. "What do you mean it comes with the job?" I asked.

"Well, all supernaturals have magic. Grayson has more. It's where his alpha power comes from," Jackson informed me.

There was so much I didn't know.

"What's your pack like?" I turned and asked Grayson.

"A pain in my ass," he said matter-of-factly as he picked up his burger. As I watched him eat I realized I should have ordered a burger. It looked really good.

At that thought, I had a burger right in my face.

"Take a bite," Grayson said.

I just stared at the burger then him. "That's okay, it's your burger," I told him and waved my hand as to shoo him away.

"What's mine is yours, plus I would really like a bite of yours," he smiled.

Ryan would never share off his plate with me, he would say 'it's rude', so I got used to just eating what I ordered. There was something intimate about sharing food.

His burger did look really yummy, so I caved. I leaned over, closed

my eyes, and took a huge bite. The thick beef with the mayonnaise and mustard mixed with the crisp tomato and lettuce exploded on my tongue. I couldn't help myself, I moaned.

"Oh, my Goddess. This is really good," I said through a mouth full of deliciousness.

I continued to chew my bite, wishing I had a burger of my own. When I was done, I opened my eyes and noticed everyone was staring at me.

"What?" I asked incredulously.

"Here, you keep that half; I got the other," Grayson said as he put the half on my plate.

"Maybe you're part wolf after all," Trace said and he and Jackson laughed.

"I wonder if this is part of the mating mark? They start to take on the characteristics of their partner," Aurora stated.

I frowned at Aurora. "It was just a good burger, nothing to get excited about, folks," I told her and the rest of the group.

"What do you love more, beef or vegetables?" Aurora asked me.

"Well I do like meat, but I prefer vegetables. Though, I don't see how me loving his burger means I'm taking on more of a wolf appetite," I told the group.

No one said anything, but they all had smiles on their faces. So, I took my eyes off them and looked at our table. Everyone had one plate of food while I had several. Along with my chicken fried steak and mashed potatoes with gravy, I also had a side of sausage links, bacon, and pancakes.

"You normally eat this much?" Grayson asked me.

"It must be the road trip hungers," I said, but I had a feeling this wasn't normal. I usually ate three to four smaller meals in a day. If I ate too much in one sitting I would feel sick. I had consumed almost everything I ordered, and I still felt hungry.

Whatever.

I ignored everyone and finished my food. So I was a little bit hungrier than usual, not a problem. I still wasn't buying into soul mate legends making my appetite increase. I had heard of pregnant women eating more, but they were eating for two.

Once we finished, we got back on the road. Grayson had told us we still had another day of travel before we'd reach pack land. I was ready to be out of the jeep. I loved my jeep, but this was the longest trip I had been on in years, and my legs were getting cramped.

I looked behind me and Aurora was asleep in the back seat with Bella when Grayson starting telling me all about his childhood and what his parents were like. I listened because you could hear in Grayson's voice how much he cared for and admired his folks. He talked about how much he and his brother would get into trouble. They sounded like mini devils.

Through all the stories he was sharing one thing stood out above all, Grayson and his brother were as close as brothers could be. I envied that, but I was happy that he had that.

"Tell me about your sister," Grayson asked me gently.

"We used to be close, until we weren't," I stated. My voice was tense, my words were short and clipped. I hated talking about the past.

"What were you two like when you were close?" Grayson asked.

"Sam, but she preferred to be called Samantha was my best friend and protector. The first house I remember only had two bedrooms, so Sam and I had bunk beds, but I slept mostly with her. I got scared at night laying in the dark. She would pretend to be annoyed that I asked to sleep with her, but she would always welcome me. She even sang me to sleep sometimes." I took a deep breath. "I forgot about the singing, she had such a beautiful voice. Like an angel," I said softly.

"Sometimes life has a way of getting in the way and it causes people to lose their way. It sounds like she was a good person. She just got pressured into the choices she made," Grayson said to me.

"Yes, but she made those choices," I blurted out. I was obviously still holding onto those emotions. Maybe when I'm not fighting for my life I could really focus on letting go of those hurt feelings.

"Everyone makes mistakes, but the best thing about being human or a supernatural human is you can start over once you make them, learn from your mistakes and grow," Grayson said.

"She's dead, that's one place you can't fix the mistakes you made," I growled.

I wasn't angry with Grayson, but thinking about the fact that I thought I would always have time to rebuild that relationship and now that option had been taken away from me, made me upset. I was angry with my sister for letting so much time pass.

"She would have fixed it. She had a picture of the two of you on her bedside table. She didn't tell me what happened, and I never really pried, but I know she loved you," Aurora whispered from the back seat.

I took a deep breath. "I hope so, honey, I really hope so," I whispered back. That was all I could do, hope my sister realized she left me behind and would have changed it had she lived. That was the thing with death; it leaves you with unanswered questions that can haunt you for the rest of your life.

Chapter Fifteen
Home

Grayson didn't want to stop and spend another night away from his pack, so we pushed through the exhaustion and gorged on twenty-four ounce coffees at truck stops and convenience stores, where I also nabbed a gazillion different types of junk food and made everyone pull over every few hundred miles to pee. At one point Jackson took my coffee away while muttering under his breath.

I was fine without the coffee because I had my junk food. That's the rule; if you're on the road you eat whatever is available, in large quantities.

Stress eating you say?

Nope.

Once we crossed into Idaho I couldn't stop looking around. It was like untouched territory. Valleys hugged both sides of the land we traveled through, but it didn't feel confined like it had in some places. I had tried to stay in populated areas when I traveled, mostly because it was easier to find a job. This place was breathtaking.

"So how close are we to a town?" I asked, wondering if this was considered living off the-grid. Please say they have bathrooms. I wasn't sure if I could do out-houses.

I could tell that the closer we got to his territory his posture was becoming more and more relaxed. His entire frame seemed to settle in on itself. Being in charge of the care and safety to that many people had to come with exuberant stress and worry.

"Our land starts about 20 miles out of town, but we have over ten thousand acres," he explained.

"Ten thousand acres, that's a lot," I said with astonishment.

Grayson chuckled. "I guess it can seem that way, but we have several hundred pack members. And we do turn furry on occasion and need to run without the worry of getting buckshot in the ass.

"People shoot at you?" I asked, but I couldn't get my mouth to close.

Grayson nodded. "Yeah, our area is full of hunters of all kinds, and some specifically target wolves. Most packs have a healer or two depending on the size. Leroy will complain too many of the pack get shot. I know it seems like massive amounts of land, but we've bought land continuously over the last few hundred years. I will say it doesn't feel like much when you're running. There's lots of land that isn't ours but is unpopulated, so it makes our area even bigger," he announced with pride.

I smiled at him while he's talking about his family. It made me happy that he had such a large family. Sometimes I would imagine what it would feel like being part of a family.

I hope that while I'm here I can meld with the folks here.

As if Grayson was reading my mind, his fingers find mine. "Avery, don't worry. Wolves can be suspicious, but we are a tight pack. And if I say you're okay, most people will welcome you with open arms," Grayson said as he padded his hand on my thigh. He seemed so confident in that statement.

That word 'most' had me a little worried though.

One thing I like about Grayson was how soothing he was to be around. He makes me feel safe, something that Ryan had never done. Ryan makes me nervous, I'm always worried I might upset him, or not be good enough for him. I don't feel like that when I'm with Grayson. I feel calm, relaxed, and safe. I shook my whole body to try and stop the comparison of Grayson to Ryan. Ryan is my husband, and I should never compare the two. I was here because I couldn't go back to Asheville or Max might hurt me.

The town took my mind off my man problems with its genuine, old-school charm. Side streets were cobbled with baskets of vivid blue and yellow flowers running along the main street hanging from lamp posts.

"Please, tell me this is Main Street?" I asked.

"Yep," he answered as I tried to close my mouth. I wasn't expecting him to say that.

"Even though we have land away from town, the old saying rings true. In a small town, everyone knows everyone and everything. Remember that because not all of the people working in town are wolves. I will say though, that even the humans who live in this town know something isn't the same with us. They might even know we're wolf shifters, but they don't ever cause problems for us. I think it's their gut telling them we are predators, but because we've lived here for so many centuries they've grown to know that we protect them. Even though they aren't part of our pack, we still consider the town's people under our protection. It also helps that we own quite a few businesses in town, and we do charity functions for all sorts of things. We have a strong presence in this town. It's an unsaid rule that no one messes with us," he finished and pulled up in front of a bakery.

I had my window rolled down when the smell of sugar, butter and flour smacked me in the face.

"Are we going in the bakery?" I asked with excitement. I was hopping up and down in my seat when I realized that my seatbelt was still on.

"Do they have coffee too?" I asked as I flung my seat belt off. "Or pastries, I haven't had a pastry since we left Asheville. I might go into pastry withdrawal," I told Grayson, but kept my eyes glued to the bakery windows.

I was getting ready to ask something else when I felt a hand on the back of my neck, and I was pulled across the console of the jeep and right into Grayson's lap. Before I got a chance to ask him what the fuck he thought he was doing, I had the fullest, softest lips covering mine. It felt so good I couldn't stop myself, both my hands had found a home on his chest and they started to move all on their own. I swear I was not in control, but I didn't seem to care because my mind could only lift his shirt wanting to know what his chest and abs felt like. Grayson's tongue had already found its way into my mouth, with little resistance.

Was I in heaven? All my thoughts were focused on the kiss, and how it felt. I felt like I was on fire, literally.

"I really hate to interrupt, but I'm not asleep back here, and I don't want to watch the free porn show. Also, I can smell the sugar. I need some real food." Aurora snickered. 'This is why you need a four-door jeep," Aurora admonished.

That whipped my blank mind right into place, and it felt like cold water was dumped on my head. I opened my eyes and pulled away from the kiss. I wanted to keep my eyes closed, but when I looked into Grayson's eyes I saw no judgment. I think I saw his lip curl a little.

"I'm so...," I tried to apologize to him for letting myself get out of control.

Grayson's finger came up quick to cover my lips. "Nope, not one word," he said, and he plunked me back in the passenger seat and hopped out like nothing happened. He came around and opened my door to help me out. The jeep wasn't lifted, but it required a hop out because I had the biggest tires possible.

"That's why you need a four-door jeep," Aurora repeated herself as she had to crunch her young adult body down to squeeze out of the back seat. My passenger seat would normally come all the way up and allow anyone in the back seat to get out. At some point, the seat broke and I hadn't rushed to fix it. Sometimes procrastination catches up to you.

"Actually, I'm technically old enough to drive, so how about we work on getting me my own ride? Then you don't have to spend the money to fix the seat," Aurora threw over her shoulder as she was first through the bakery door.

"Goddess, dammit, that shit pisses me off," I let fly.

"She's a teenager. She hasn't learned you could piss off the wrong person and regret it. Give her a week with the pack, and I bet she learns to keep her mouth shut about what she can hear in people's heads," Grayson explained as he propelled me forward with his warm hand at the small of my back. "Let's get you some food to take the edge off." He laughed under his breath.

"Are you saying I'm grumpy when I'm hungry?" I frowned because with Grayson being happy all the time, I was starting to look like an asshole, which just pissed me off more.

"I'm just saying that it's been a long four days, and we both could use a sugar pick me up," he finished as he opened the door and kept his arm around my waist.

I wanted to pull away, but it felt natural to have him so close. I took a deep breath and his musky earthy scent raised goose bumps up and down my arms. My whole body did a shiver, which made his arm tighten around me.

He leaned in and whispered, "Are you cold?"

I looked up at him and popped out, "Nope." I really needed to stop having such a strong physical reaction to this man.

The glass cases which held the yum factor were lining the back of the bakery. I had never seen so many sweets. I think I got stuck in awe until Aurora grabbed my arm and gave it a squeeze.

She laughed and went back to pursuing the case of treats, which I needed to be doing too. As Grayson and I made our way to the glass display case the two people behind the counter both noticed Grayson and bowed their heads to the side. He gave them a head nod. Just as fast they went back to what they were doing, like it never happened. I looked around at the crowded bakery and not one person had noticed what happen.

Weird.

"The pack owns this bakery, so pick what you want. Just add two to everything you pick," he whispered into my ear.

I almost asked him if he wanted me to get him anything from the case.

He let go of my waist so I could start at one end of the case and really check out what they had. I could tell this was a place I would be frequenting. I could smell aromas of some cheesy kind, and I know I saw soup and sandwiches listed on the chalkboard that hung on the wall behind the display case. As I made my way to the least populated end of the case, I noticed one of the people behind the counter was tracking my movements. When I would stop and stare at a particular item, so would the kid, who looked too young to be working. I decided to ignore this and just get what I needed so all the customers that came in before me wouldn't feel shafted because I was getting waited on first.

"How about three chocolate éclairs, three brownies, three of the white chocolate chip macadamia nut cookies. I can't wait to try those. And how about—" I started to list all the deserts I couldn't resist getting.

"Listen, lady, we have all been waiting here and you just come in and pushed your way up front. The line is back behind me," a big dude yells as he steps out of line and walks closer to me. When he was right in from of me, I had to crane my neck all the way back to look at his face. I could smell a foul odor coming from his head and knew this guy was in desperate need of a breath mint. I reached down to my side to dig through my purse to see if I could help him out.

He stared at me while I continued to peruse my purse for about a second then he lost his patience and reached for me. I batted his big hand away from me and turned my head and said to the kid behind the counter who was still waiting for me to finish my order. "Please, add three cheese cakes and four of any of the different muffins you have." I looked up to notice the kid's eyes were bugged out, and was whipping between me and the dude that yelled at me.

"Thanks," I told the kid. His eyes snapped back to me, tilted his head to the side, and went about filling a box with delicious deserts. I noticed that they had espresso.

Yes!

"Can you add a twenty-ounce vanilla latte, too?" I asked the kid.

He looked up nodded but didn't say a word. I turned to see what Aurora was eyeballing when my face was level with a beer belly that smelled like a frat house.

Yuck.

Before I could say anything two large and clammy hands grabbed my arms and lifted me up. I was eye to eye with this large smelly man. I didn't even know someone could actually do that.

"Uh, hi," I said because really what do you say to someone that is bruising your arms and freaking you way the hell out.

"I told you to get behind me, and you didn't listen. It's rude to cut the line, and I don't like rude people," he spat. Yes, spit actually landed on my cheek. I was starting to get irritated, but I wasn't scared. For some reason I knew this lumberjack of a guy wouldn't hurt me.

I didn't know what to say to this giant so I scanned the bakery to see if Grayson was going to step in but he wasn't anywhere around.

"If you don't put me down, I'm going to sick my niece on you; she's meaner than I am," I said, hoping he thought he had made his point and would put me down.

He laughed which was a bad idea because his body shook me at the same time.

"Titus!" Grayson bellowed, and I swear to Goddess the windows might have rattled a little. “Put her down,” he said a little more calmly.

“But she cut the line,” he said ruefully.

“She is mine. Put her down,” he commanded.

The giant put me down, and Aurora came and stood next to me. “You could have taken him, Auntie, just kick him in the junk-mail next time,” Aurora told me then walked away with her jelly-filled donut dripping down her chin.

“I’ll have to remember that for next time.” I grinned at her back.

Grayson was by my side by the time I made it back down to the ground. He put his arm around my shoulder and introduced me.

“Nice to meet you, mate of Grayson,” Titus said with hunched shoulders, which looked awkward on such a giant of a man.

“I’m not—” I began to respond only to have Grayson interrupt me.

“Titus, you will treat Avery and her niece, Aurora, like you would treat me. Do you understand me?” Grayson scolded him.

“Yes, alpha, I understand. Sorry, Avery, but it’s not nice to cut the line,” he said and walked back to the line which had spread for him to give him back his place in line. I could tell on the terrified faces of the people in line they had no problem whatsoever to give Titus his spot back.

“That giant of a man is a wolf shifter? I’m afraid to see him turn furry. Can’t he kick your ass?” I asked Grayson.

He stiffened next to me then started to belly laugh. “I think you’re going to be great for our pack and my ego,” he said, but then I saw a serious look pass across his face.

“Fighting isn’t all about size, Avery. Knowing how to fight, knowing weaknesses, and being smart can sometimes be better than being giant,” Grayson said and then kissed my forehead. He walked away but came back with my coffee and a huge box of goodies I couldn't wait to dig into.

"I know you want to eat those, and you will, but let's get back on the road so we can get settled. This has been a long time for me to be away from the pack. Without the alpha, things can get tense and breakdowns start to happen. We'll come back down in a few days and tour the whole town," he promised as he guided me back outside to the jeep.

I could feel the stress of worry rolling off him in waves.

"Okay," I said and smiled.

I didn't want to be a burden, and I didn't want to be the cause of any breakdowns in the pack. That wouldn't help my integration into the pack (as brief as it was going to be), and I had a feeling two witches were going to ruffle some fur.

On the outskirts of town, I noticed a bigger building with tons of floor to ceiling windows. Several sets of men setting up the portable green houses I helped break down set back off the street. Then I noticed how large the parking lot was, and in my mind I was already deciding where to put my plants.

"Hey, that's Delphine's nursery, isn't it?" I asked Grayson, even though I knew the answer. I wanted to stop and supervise. My leg started to jump up and down, and I couldn't peel my eyes from the work going on.

"Yeah, I called ahead and had pack members on stand-by to help unload and get her situated," he explained.

"Did you ever met Delphine before all this happened?" I asked?

"No, but she's pack, and we all pitch in to help each other," he said.

"I get that, but she's been living in Asheville for many, many years.

Why would you decide to chip in now?" I wondered aloud.

"When you join our pack, mates are part of that too. We're all family, and if they choose to live away from the pack, they can. But if they ever need us and reach out, we will be there. It's not often this happens, but it does. Leroy came into our pack, our family, without his mate. We never met her, and we didn't pry, but when he asked for our help we jumped at the chance to help her move cross country, locate a building for her, and help get her business set up," he said as he navigated the windy roads.

I let that sit with me for a few minutes, but I had to ask, "So, what's in it for you?"

Grayson didn't answer for several minutes. "Does everyone in your world only take? Do you think every action has a price?" Grayson asked.

"Yes, it does. Every one of us is looking out for numero uno first and foremost," I said as I watched the beauty slide by. I know it sounded cynical and cold-hearted, but from my experiences in life there was always a price to pay.

"Avery," Grayson said, clearly wanting me to look at him, so I did. "You are absolutely right, but you're not at the same time. Does helping Delphine with her nursery benefit me? Yes, it does. Leroy has been half a soul since he joined us. Werewolves don't do well without their mates, and I'm not even sure of the ramifications of a fated mate. My point is the pack will benefit when they work on their relationship. We are as strong as our weakest member. My job is to make sure our weak spots are as strong as they can be. Have you ever studied wild wolf packs? The strongest are in the middle and back of the pack. They don't leave their weak behind and neither do I. It's taken me years to get Delphine back into our pack, and I will do whatever it takes to make her want to stay. Leroy was close to leaving our pack and be a nomad wolf again. I need him in my ranks, we all need him, and he needs us. Each of us brings something to the table that makes our pack stronger, happier, and most of all, healthier."

I kept quiet and decided to mull on what he said until we made it to the pack property. As we were turning onto a gravel road I noticed a no trespassing sign. The road wound for about two or three miles and opened up to a massive three-story modern cabin showcasing rows of windows and a wraparound porch. It was just about dusk and the glow from the windows enhanced its beauty. They had a rock fire pit off to the side of the porch with seating and cushions to match. This is what I had pictured when Ryan and I were looking at houses, maybe a little smaller, but rustic and homey were the words I used.

"Do you all live here?" I asked.

"Fuck no," he spat.

I jumped at the intensity of his words.

"Sorry, it's just that... Well, some of the pack members try my patience, and I can't imagine living with some of them. The main house is mine, and I live alone, mostly. It's the pack meeting house because of its size so it's never completely empty and the entire pack knows they're always welcome. My door is never locked. I'll show you around the grounds after we tour the house. Let's get you and Aurora's things settled and go from there," Grayson said as he parked and started unloading the jeep.

Jackson, who hasn't stopped at the bakery, was pulled up as close as he could and was already unloading the truck with a bunch of people helping.

Aurora was given the option of replacing the bed in her room with her old one, but once she saw her room she opted for donating it to someone else in the pack. Aurora and I were told they had a huge storage building a few miles up the road from the main house where anyone was welcome to store items.

I was surprised no one was waiting to greet us, but I'm glad because I was exhausted from traveling and just wanted to sleep on a mattress that didn't smell of sweat and dust. Grayson gave us the dime tour while I devoured way too many sweets. I glared at Grayson when he reached into my bag and took out a brownie. He winked at me and finished our tour.

Aurora and I picked rooms directly across from each other on the second floor which took way too long to decide. She wanted to be on the third floor, but I put my foot down and told her she is more than welcome to have a room on the third floor, but I refused to have to climb all those stairs. Aurora pouted for about a second until she walked into the room across from me and immediately changed her mind. There were ten bedrooms total, all with en suite bathrooms—four bedrooms on the second floor, four on the third floor, and the main floor had the master bedroom, also with an en suite bathroom with an additional bedroom and bathroom on the main level.

This house was huge; the biggest I had ever been in. I was so over stimulated I didn't really notice much of Aurora's room, but from her squealing I'm sure it was something she was happy with. I didn't really care what my room looked like; I just wanted a shower and bed, in that order. There was too much on my mind, but I couldn't seem to focus enough to think about one single thought.

"If this isn't to your liking there are plenty of others to choose from," Grayson said as he put my luggage on the bed. He had insisted on carrying my things and growled at me when I tried to wrestle it away from him.

"This is fine, really," I said.

The room looked inviting from all the natural light from the many windows to the queen size wrought iron bed with a beautiful geometric designed quilt that had different shades of green to the crisp white linens peeking out from under the pillows. A stone fireplace was nestled in the corner with an unfinished mantel displaying different sized candles and matching wood bedside tables with old style oil lamps perched on top. I noticed a dresser but not a TV.

This might be a problem.

The bathroom was what made the room. White tiles on the floor and gray granite counter tops. The sink was an oval piece that sat on top with the most interesting oil rubbed bronze faucet I had ever seen, both on the sink and in tub. It looked like an old fashioned pumping station from well water. The walls were a light gray, which highlighted the large claw-foot bathtub that sat beside a large window overlooking the forest. A bath to calm my nerves sounded heavenly.

Grayson was leaning against the bathroom doorjamb when I turned around. "Why don't you put your things away then take a bath. Come down to the main living room when you're done?" he insisted as he wiped powdered sugar from my cheek and walked away.

"Thank you!" I popped my head out of my door and yelled as I watched him saunter down the hall. I was wondering if coming here was the right choice.

My mom's voice popped into my head, "Your gut is never wrong. When you feel that feeling deep in your gut, when you think about how you feel in a situation, and that feeling is unease than something is wrong, but if it's peace then that's your answer."

I heard her like she was standing in front of me and telling me this. I started to stiffen with fear that I had just heard my mom and then I relaxed into the door jam and smiled.

I didn't feel unease when I thought about Aurora and I being here. I felt relaxed, at peace even. My mom had many one-liners that didn't always make sense at the time but are starting to now.

When I married Ryan, I had an uneasy feeling from the moment he asked me to marry him until the day we said I do. Once the wedding reception was over that feeling went away, but I wasn't at peace either.

I found some bath salts in a cupboard next to the tub and sat watching the squirrels fighting over food in the trees as the water filled in the tub. Must be nice to not have much to worry about much except where to store your nuts.

I had just settled in the extremely warm water when Aurora flew through the door.

"Oh, my Goddess, I love your bathroom. Mine has a tub, but it doesn't look like this one. Did you see my closet though? I could live in it. It has a window with a built-in bench seat," Aurora said as she sat on the toilet, content to hang out with me during my relaxing bath.

I put a steamed washcloth over my face hoping she might take the hint and either be quiet or leave me to some peace. It had been days since I'd been alone with my thoughts.

"Right." Aurora sighed. "I'll just leave you to your bath. I need to follow up with my friend at the coven anyway." She turned toward the door but swung back around and spouted quickly, "I'm glad we're here, Auntie" and then fled out the door.

I was finally starting to relax my whole body did a head to toe shiver.

I had fallen asleep in the tub, not surprising; it had been a very long trip. I wasn't sure how long I slept for and I didn't care except the water had turned cold. I got out and went in search of my luggage. I rifled through my stuff and found my favorite soft boyfriend-cut jeans and fuzzy pale blue v-neck sweater. I decided on thick cream-colored socks because who wears shoes in the house? I unpacked my toiletries in the bathroom and combed out my hair, not bothering to dry it and found my courage to face my new life. I wasn't stupid, but I had to push the thoughts of Ryan out of my head. I hadn't been able to come up with a solution to what was happening and how to bring him with me into this new path I was on so I left my room in search of Grayson.

It didn't take long to find Grayson; he was in the living room which was on the right at the bottom of the stairs. I didn't notice him right away when I entered the room, he was standing behind a wing back chair that was in the corner next to the gigantic stone fireplace and the room was packed with people. Two large couches sat across from each other, both filled with the pack members. Most people were standing facing the entry as I came through. Some I recognized, some I didn't.

Sensing my anxiety, Grayson waved me over. "Avery, come, sit."

I was tempted not to, but the fireplace was roaring, I was in the mountains, and it was chilly with my wet hair, so I sat in the chair he stood next to.

He smiled when I nodded at him.

"You doing okay?" He asked.

"Yeah, is this the whole pack?" I asked softly.

"No, not even close. We can't fit everyone in the house at the same time, but don't worry, gossip spreads faster than you can imagine." Looking at my arm, Grayson continues, concern clearly visible in his features, "How's your arm?"

I pulled up my sleeve and the faint white scare was barely noticeable. "I seem to be healing at a very fast pace. It's kind of freaky, but I guess I can't complain," I said with a smile.

Grayson looked like he wanted to say something to me but decided against it when he cleared his voice to get the attention of everyone in the room.

"Okay, let's get on with report. Leroy, why don't you start?"

Leroy started with, "Teri's labor will be starting at some point today we need to induce her. She's past her due date, so I won't be available for a while. But everyone knows where to reach me if it's an emergency."

"How is Teri holding up?" asked Grayson.

"Its twins, and she's probably in for a long few days. I have the clinic ready if I need to do surgery, but we're hopeful that she can push those cubs out on her own," Leroy told the room.

"Get Christian to cover the rest of the pack and assist you if necessary." Grayson looked to Jackson for more updates.

"The nursery is almost done being unloaded, and we should have set up and a go in about two days. Delphine seems to be settling in just find." Jackson pulled back like he didn't want to say the rest with his gaze locked on Leroy.

"She… uh… she also took the cabin at the back edge of our property," Jackson rushed his words, knowing Leroy's cabin was closest to the main house.

Leroy perched his lips at Jackson's words and looked to the side.

Grayson took over once again, explaining what had transpired at the summit, and how they had asked for his help. He explained he wasn't happy, but that this was important to their survival. Jackson would be in charge of the pack when Grayson started traveling for the council.

"I'd also like to introduce the newest two pack members, Avery and her niece, Aurora. They will be staying with me, and I hope you all make them feel welcome," Grayson finished with a little more force in the last few words of his proclamation.

New pack members?

Say what?

Aurora had been standing behind my chair and leaned down. "How cool is this? I'm not just a witch, but a witch who is now a member of a wolf pack," she whispered to me.

"And I'm the new mate to the alpha. Yippy," I sneered.

All at once the entire room expanded with something I couldn't explain. Every eye in the room was on me and some were glaring some with wonder but all with confusion.

"Ah… I forgot they can hear like dogs can," she smiled.

I decided to keep my mouth shut, and did not look for Grayson's eyes in that moment but in my head I yelled as loud as I could.

Shut up!

Geez, no self-preservation in this kid.

I for one knew when to keep my mouth shut. I had no defense, I couldn't turn into anything to protect myself, and I'm sure a child wolf could kill me in a second.

"Oh Auntie, you have the most powerful thing in this room," she kept whispering.

“Oh yeah, and what’s that?” I asked her.

“The alpha,” she smiled and walked away.

I took that moment to find Grayson’s eyes; the smoldering look he gave me sent me shooting up in my chair.

“Whelp, it’s time for this girl to take a nap. It was, ah, really ah nice to meet you all,” I said to no one and everyone. I waved my hand in a broad goodbye and flew out the door and up the stairs to my room. I had just woken up and nowhere near nap time, but I was running. It was what I had been doing most of my life.

Once I was settled in bed I could still hear murmured voices coming from the living room. I guess with so many people attending one pack meeting it probably lasted a while.

I was just drifting off to sleep sometime later when I heard my bedroom door click open. I was so tired I didn’t open my eyes, but I felt a soft kiss on my forehead and then the draft from the door closing.

Chapter Sixteen
Time to Face the Music

I woke feeling well rested, but I had a knot in the pit of my stomach. This wasn't a new feeling, but it had been awhile since it had reared its ugly head. The last time I had this feeling was when I was run out of town by the coven. Almost like when you know danger is near and your fight or flight response takes over. I wasn't sure why I had this feeling because it wasn't where I was at or why. I felt safe with Grayson ever since I had run into him. I giggled, thinking about it. I had literally run into him.

"Well, I guess I don't have to ask how you slept." Grayson asked as he pushed open my bedroom door.

I should be mad he didn't knock, or that he was even here, but all I could do was smile.

"Hi," I said quietly.

"Hi," he replied with a grin.

After a few seconds of silence, he pushed away from the door, went over to one of the windows, and pulled back the drapes.

"I wanted you to be able to rest and not jump into anything major immediately, but I'm afraid that's not going to happen," Grayson turned to me and crossed his arms.

"Is your phone still on?" Grayson asked me.

What a bizarre question.

"Uh yeah, my phone's on," I replied.

"Well, that explains it. You're going to have to get showered, dressed, and come down for breakfast," Grayson said as he made his way back to the door.

I was not getting a good feeling about his demeanor. The other thing that freaked me out is that I had slept all day until the next morning. I guess I was tired.

"What's wrong?" I asked him while I wrapped the blanket around my torso.

"Your husband is in town," he grunted and shut my door behind him.

"Oh shit," I said and flopped back down on the bed.

"Get up, Avery. I do not want him coming onto pack land," Grayson barked through the door.

I slammed my fists down beside me and cussed Grayson out in my head. If that alpha thought this was my fault he could kiss my ass.

After figuring out how to work the thousand sprayer heads in the shower, I got dressed and went downstairs to find coffee. If he thought he could get me to talk coherently in the morning without my coffee he was wasn't paying attention.

As soon as I walked into the kitchen and Grayson snapped, "Your coffee is on the island. Grab it and a donut and meet me in the living room."

He acted as if he has a right to be pissed at me.

I grabbed my coffee, made sure it had vanilla creamer in it, went to meet Grayson in the living room, and found we weren't alone. Aurora, Jackson, Tank, and a few unfamiliar faces watched me take a seat on one of the many couches. I just kept watching everyone in between sips of my coffee.

"Is that good coffee, Avery?" Jackson asked me while trying to hold back a chuckle.

"Why, yes, it is, Jackson. Do I have you to thank for making sure I had fuel before my morning turned into World War Three?" I asked him.

"Nope, coffee is all Grayson." He nodded to his fearless alpha.

"Thanks for the coffee," I smiled.

He nodded but didn't say anything.

"Okay, this is too much for—what time is it? Butt ass early. And just so we are clear, that means I'm not happy about being up. What the heck did I do to cause everyone to blame me for what's happening?" I asked Grayson, or frankly, anyone in the room.

"Oh, he's not mad at you, Avery. He's mad at himself that he didn't think about making you and Aurora turn off your phones. It's a rookie mistake. He normally gets to yell and stomp his feet at whoever made the mistake, but this time it was him and he's stewing about it," it was Jackson who answered my question.

"Okay, that's enough," Grayson stepped up. "I did fuck up, now we need to fix this. Avery, I'm taking you into town, and you're going to make him go away. I will drive you, but you're going to have to do this on your own. I can't be around you both. With my mating instincts riding me hard I might hurt him, and I know how that would hurt you. I want you to call him once we get to town and meet him at the bakery," Grayson said to me.

"And what exactly am I supposed to tell him? That I lied, and I'm not at my non-existent aunt's house. That I have this new tattoo on my hand, and because of that mark I'm the soul mate to an alpha of a wolf shifter clan? Let's not forget that I'm a witch who's been banished from North Carolina. Hmm, is that what you want me to say?" I asked while still trying to enjoy this first cup of coffee.

"Man, Auntie, you are doing really well when you haven't even finished your first cup," Aurora added. I glared at her before I turned my stare on Grayson, because really what did he expect me to do?

He took a deep breath.

"Everyone, give us the room," he ordered and then came to sit next to me. He also looked like he was enjoying his cup of coffee.

He took a deep breath and stated, "I don't know what to do. I don't think I've ever come across a problem I didn't have an answer to, some kind of solution. You're my one true mate, not my property. There is no other option for me. I can't ask you to leave your husband; I wouldn't want you to resent me later. I know you can't go back to Asheville, and I would like you to stay here so we can figure this out. I'm going to leave this up to you. If you trust him, he can stay here if you want. This is no one's fault, and it's definitely not your fault. So whatever you and he decide I will it make work."

I couldn't believe he was saying this to me. I didn't know what to think.

"You would do that? If I asked him to come stay here, you would let him? Isn't there some sort of secret code where we can't tell humans about yourselves? I know there is for witches. The only exception is your partner in life. I never told Ryan about my family because I was shunned, but I don't know if I feel comfortable exposing your pack, your family to outsiders," I said.

"I will do whatever makes you happy. Your happiness is my happiness. I will admit it would be difficult to see you with him, but I would try, for you." With that he got up, kissed my forehead, and walked out the door.

Whelp, guess my coffee time was over. Now what in the hell do I do with what he just said? I sat in the living room until my coffee was cold and it was time to face the music, or my husband.

Riding shotgun and watching the landscape coast by gave me an opportunity to mull around in my head what my situation really was. My sister is dead. Nope, not going to even think about that one. I haven't dealt with my sister's death yet. I have a wolf shifter who thinks were soul mates, and a husband in town looking for me. Shame started to sink into my psyche, but not because I have feelings for said wolf shifter. Nope, it's because I should have told my husband who I was and where I came from before we walked down the aisle. I think I remember reading in some gossip magazine all lasting marriages start with honesty. And what had I done? I married Ryan without being my true self, even if I was a dud witch with not a single drop of magic to spare or I was until I met Grayson.

Could I tell Ryan? Would he understand that I lied but for a very good reason?

"I'm going to drop you off at the edge of town and make my way to the bakery. I'll let them know not to let on that they know who you are." Grayson took a deep breath. "Every instinct I have right now is to destroy your cell phone and take you home," Grayson finished while I could tell he wanted to say more. His breathing had sped up, and I saw a few drops of sweat glisten on his brow.

"Even if my instincts match yours, which they do, I feel I need to see him and make this right. I'm not exactly sure how today is going to turn out—" I grabbed his hand in mine—"but I do know I have felt more cherished and cared for in these past days than I have my entire life. Thank you for being there for me and Aurora," I confessed.

I knew he wanted to keep me close, but I had to do this. As I exited his pickup, the knot in my gut was growing and pain had started to take over. I watched Grayson's truck drive by, and I was glad he didn't see me bend at the waist to catch my breath.

By the time I caught my breath and made it to the bakery, I had collected myself as best I could and the pain was more bearable. The bakery was rocking busy, but I noticed a table toward the back that was open, and I made my way in line to grab a Carmel Macchiato and something with chocolate to calm my nerves. Chocolate dipped chocolate chip cookie would do nicely. I even had them bag an extra for later. I called Ryan and told him where to meet me.

It took about thirty minutes before Ryan showed up which gave me the chance to enjoy my yummy chocolate chip cookie and make sure I didn't have chocolate smeared on my face which usually was the case when cookies were involved.

Ryan spotted me the minute he hit the door, and I recognized the look on his face immediately—rage, pure unadulterated rage. For a split second, I racked my brain to remember if I knew where the back exit was. I had never in my five years of being with him seen him direct this look at me.

I stood up and spoke before he could, “Hi Ryan, want to take a seat and I’ll grab you a coffee?”

He scowled at me and crossed he arms.

“Fuck no, I don’t want a fucking coffee, Avery. What I want to know is what the fuck is going on, and I want to know right now,” he spit between clenched teeth while glaring at me.

“Um, okay, well, um—” I started but didn’t get to finish.

“If you start that stuttering bullshit, I swear to god I’m going to…,” Ryan started to say.

“You’re going to what, motherfucker? You better sit your ass down before I rip your throat out. You will listen to your wife and keep your nasty attitude to yourself,” Grayson said right into Ryan’s ear.

Wow, where did he come from? I never even saw him anywhere near Ryan.

Ryan’s right hand flew up to his chest, covering a bright blue light that shining through his shirt.

I looked at Grayson, but he was staring across the table at me so he didn’t notice it. It looked like Ryan came to a decision after that glow appeared. Whatever rage he had turned to something else. A smile appeared on his face then he looked at me and his face was blank.

Ryan took his seat.

I nodded to Grayson, and he walked away, but I knew he wouldn’t go far.

“Ryan, I have to tell you something; I just don’t know how to say it,” I said softly.

“You’re a fucking cheater, is that what this is?” he asked through clenched teeth.

When I heard a growl I looked across the bakery at Grayson was leaning back against the wall with his arms crossed and eyes intent on Ryan's throat.

I looked back at Ryan.

"No, cheating is not what this is about. Something happened in Asheville; actually, something happened when I was born. No, that's not… See I… Shit, this is harder than I thought," I said while looking at the top of the table.

"Just spit it out. But do it fast because I have places I need to be," Ryan declared. It actually seemed like Ryan didn't want to be here anymore.

"Okay, see my mom and dad, well they are, or were… witches," I finished not having the courage to look up and into his eyes.

When I finally looked at Ryan he had a confused look on his face.

"I know it's hard to believe they are real, but they are. My family comes from a long line of well-known witches actually. I mean in the supernatural community, but anyway they're witches. I'm a witch, but I don't have powers so that's why I never told you," I said. The more I said the more I knew telling him was the wrong decision.

That mass in my gut turned into a swirling vortex, and it felt like it was going to consume me.

"You're not a witch. I know your parents passed away, you said as much while we dated, but I can tell you for sure you're not a witch. I would never have married a fucking witch. Jesus," Ryan hissed.

"I am a witch. And how would you know anyway?" I started to get upset because I was from a witch family. "I don't have any magic in my blood, but I am the daughter of Marsden and Amelia Sinclair. As a matter of fact, I had to have my blood tested when I was younger for a coven ceremony, and if I wasn't born a Sinclair I would have known at that time. Sheesh, I'm trying to do the right thing here, but you're being a butthead," I started ranting.

I stopped when I realized Grayson was chuckling like he was part of our conversation.

Shit, wolf hearing, I have to remember that.

Ryan took that moment to call someone.

"Are you calling someone, like right now? I think this is more important than a phone call," I barked.

"Mom, look up Marsden and Amelia Sinclair. Witches, Seattle. Yeah, I'll hold, but it's priority one," he said.

I screeched and slapped my hand down on the table.

"You called your mom! Are you shittin' me? This isn't any of that bitch's business." As soon as that left my lips, I slapped my hand over my mouth.

Oh, my Goddess. I have to get my shit together, I just called Ryan's mom a bitch, and let me tell you he is a Momma's boy if I ever met one.

He didn't do anything, but his eyes told me all I needed to know. He would not put up with me calling his mom a bitch again.

"Okay, thanks. Yeah, I'll be there asap. Call an emergency meeting. Yes, now," he said and hung up.

Ryan rose from his seat with a look of sadness on his face that only lasted a second and then a firm determined look replaced that sadness.

"I would run, change your name, don't ever contact anyone you ever knew again. Goodbye, Avery," Ryan whispered, turned around, and walked right out the door.

Before I could even be confused about what had just transpired I was hauled out of the chair and stumbled through the crowd until I was placed in Grayson's truck.

He was racing back toward pack land.

My mind was whirling with questions and basically complete confusion, but I had to say something.

"What in the actual fuck just happened?" I asked Grayson.

Jawed clenched tight, white knuckles on the steering wheel, and still no answer.

"First, he's enraged, and then he calls his mom. Who calls their mom when they are having a discussion with their wife? That woman hates me, always has. She isn't going to make anything better. She would probably tell him how to kill me and where to dump my body," I said exasperated.

"You're not far from the truth," Grayson whispered.

"What does that mean?" I asked.

"It means what it means. We're almost home, and I don't want to repeat myself so let's just wait until I have at least Jackson with me. And don't get upset that I want my brother in on discussions but this involves all supernaturals.

Grayson was texting as soon as we hit the front steps and within five minutes the main living room was packed.

"We just found our first source of the True Hunters," Grayson said. "We are on lockdown. I want patrols round the clock, check ins every five minutes with Tank on dispatch. I need an enforcer with me now. We're headed to town," Grayson told Jackson.

It was as though Jackson and Grayson were reading each other's minds. "You sure he didn't get a call out about us?" Jackson asked.

"Yep, sure. Had Tank grab him on his way to his rental car. Dismantled his phone and the GPS on his rental. He's in the storage in the back of the bakery," Grayson said matter-of-fact.

I stood up and all the wolves went on high alert. I thought I saw fur sprouting on a few.

"You kidnapped my husband? Are you serious? What happened to my happiness is your happiness. You're just as full of bullshit as Ryan and every other guy in this world," I flung at him. I was pissed and starting to see red.

Jackson could see I was ramping up ,and he tried to intervene by reaching out to put a reassuring hand on my shoulder but before his hand even touched me he was flung over the back of the couch.

I gasped and turned to Aurora who had made her way back toward the edge of the room.

She put her hands up, "It wasn't me." She smiled huge.

I watched Grayson slowly stand up and straighten his clothes and I should have felt bad that I had done that but I was so pissed I didn't. I pointed my finger at Grayson.

"You will tell me what the hell is going on, or I'm going to pack my shit and Aurora and I are out of here. I mean it, if you don't explain..." I tried to finish.

"Calm down, Avery, I will explain. I need my wolves to calm down, and they can't do that when you're riled up like this. I need you to try to stay calm when I tell you what's happening," Grayson said.

I decided to sit down and draw as many deep breathes as I could.

"I heard both sides of that conversation with his mother. I know he's somehow involved with the group that has been killing off supernaturals. I couldn't let him go or let anyone know where he was. I have my tech gal, Cora, looking through his phone. I need to interrogate him without you there," Grayson said to me.

"Interrogate him, as in torture him?" I asked but I really wasn't asking just wondering what the actual fuck was going on. "I'm going, end of story, and if you or anyone of your pack tries to stop me so help me Goddess I will lose my every loving mind," I said with as much muster as I could.

The room was quiet, no one seem to be looking at me. Everyone one in the room was staring at the carpet like there was something to see.

"Deep breath, Avery. They will listen to you. I don't want you there, but I know I can't stop you. Let's go," Grayson said to me.

"Everyone who has a job to do, go do it," Grayson thundered, and he held out his hand for me to grab.

"My bad ass Auntie. Making all those mutts almost take a knee," Aurora said as she went back to the kitchen.

"That will be the last time she calls my wolves mutts," Grayson said under his breath.

"Yeah, good luck with that one," I told him.

We drove to a warehouse set back behind Delphine's nursery. I noticed there weren't any low windows and the building seemed like it was only a few years old.

Grayson stopped us at a door on the side of the building. Another car had followed us and over walked a man I had seen at the pack meeting but hadn't met.

"Avery, this is Glen, he's one of my enforcers." Grayson nodded to the man that had come to stand in front of me.

"Ah, hay," I waved at him.

"Nice to meet you," he said as he tilted his head to the side. Were all wolves' necks so thick and did they all look like linebackers? He was handsome in a beach boy way but his eyes weren't as pretty as Grayson's. Glen's eyes were a silvery color. Intriguing but Grayson's were still my favorites.

"Let's do this. If we stay out here any longer I might chicken out," I said as I opened the door. I had to face this. It wasn't going to be pleasant, and I didn't know what was going to happen, but I was ready, or so I thought.

When I walked in I expected him to be tied to chair in the center of the warehouse. What I didn't expect was to smell wood, all kinds of different woods. I guess this was the place they kept the inventory for their construction business. The warehouse was massive. We walked almost to the back before entering what looked to be an office through a door partially hidden behind a pallet. As soon as I entered I saw Ryan tied and gagged, sitting on the floor with Tank standing right next to him with his arms crossed over his chest, one foot resting on the wall like he had better things to do than babysit this man.

My eyes flew to Ryan's pissed ones.

Oh boy.

"So are you going to take the gag out, or do you read minds?" I asked Grayson.

"Tank, get him in a chair and take his gag off," Grayson told Tank.

Glen went and grabbed a chair while Tank picked Ryan up by his arm with one hand and tossed him into it.

"I almost have his phone cracked," a woman said from behind me. I squeaked and flew around. Guess I was jumpy.

"Avery, this is Cora my tech gal. She is a wizard with technology.

I don't know what the pack would do without her," he said with pride. I took a good look at her, and she was tiny. She couldn't be more than five feet, but I wouldn't know that until she stood up. Sitting behind a computer screen typing away I wondered what her wolf would look like. One side of her head was shaved and the other was long and straight to her chin. She had a lip piercing that she was using her tongue to play with.

"Sorry I scared ya. I didn't think you missed me sitting here," Cora said to me as she went back to messing with her laptop that had Ryan's phone attached to it.

"Um, no worries, I am a little preoccupied," I said as I went back to starring at Ryan. I wasn't sure how I felt about the large black and blue bruise that I saw forming on the right side of his face.

"Tank, did you have to bruise his face?" I asked.

"Yep," was all Tank said, but I couldn't help but see a smirk crawl across his face before he locked it down and went back to stoic Tank.

Okay.

Grayson placed a chair backwards in front of Ryan and straddled it as if he and Ryan were buddies having a friendly chat.

"This is how it's going to go. You're going to tell me who you told that Avery was here, and then you're going to spill all about your gang of killers and where I can find them.

Before Ryan spoke a word he spit right into Grayson's face, I mean right on it.

How gross.

"Really, you think that spitting in my face is going to change how this goes?" Grayson said as he took his t-shirt and wiped the spit from his face.

"I will not be telling you anything, you piece of shit animal. Your kind will be erased from this earth before too long. Now that I know where your pack lives it's only a matter of time," Ryan told Grayson.

"You're a racist," I blurted out. I had no idea that Ryan was racist; this was something that was not adding up in my mind.

"Racist, I'm not racist. These dogs are not even human. These things are an abomination to the human race, they need to die, every last one." Ryan slide his eyes to me.

"You would hurt them? Kill them?" I asked astonished.

"Avery, I know you want to be here, but I need to get some information from him and you need to let me do this." Grayson turned his head back to Ryan. "You get one minute before I let Tank and Glen figure out who can punch the hardest, to give me the information I asked for."

"Wait!" I yelled.

"He found you from a tracker he placed in your phone. He's also been monitoring your calls and texts," Cora said from behind me.

I whirled around with my mouth hanging open.

I slowly turned back around to face Ryan. "You've been spying on me this whole time? So, even though I wasn't honest about who I was, you weren't honest either. Nobody needs to be tortured. Ryan, just tell them what they want to know. Did you tell anybody you were coming to find me or that you had found me? Did you tell your Mom?" I asked Ryan. My anxiety was rising because I was starting to see that this was not going to end well for anybody.

Ryan just stared at me but didn't say anything. And before I could ask him another question Tank and Glen had both punched him in the face. It happened so fast it was hard for me to be sure it even happened.

Looking at Ryan's face, I could tell that it had. His nose was bleeding and bent, and he had a split right under his eye that was bleeding.

I jumped back because Ryan was laughing through all this.

"Did you hit him too hard in the head? He seems to be cracking up," Glen asked Tank.

"Ryan, please, I don't want to see you hurt," I reached out to him, but he flew back like my hand was diseased.

"Don't touch me!" he hissed and spit blood at my feet. "You're a polluted whore witch who needs to die too." He closed his eyes as he said the last part.

I was quiet for a minute. Grayson kept his eyes on me, he was waiting for something.

"What?" I whispered. My whole body was shaking.

"I shouldn't have let my guard down when that foul niece of yours moved in. I did, and she slipped right past me," Ryan said to me.

"How can you know Grayson is a wolf but miss that my niece is a witch?" I asked.

Ryan was silent.

"I can help with that one." Grayson reached over and pulled Ryan's button-down shirt open halfway down his chest. Buttons flew everywhere, revealing a bright blue glowing stone necklace.

"This amulet right here. I noticed it in the mirror in the bakery when you were speaking to Ryan. I saw it glowing when I stood behind him and stopped glowing when I walked away. This must tell him when a super is near. And I'm guessing it glows a different color depending on what kind of supernatural he's around," Grayson explained.

"So why didn't it work on Aurora?" I asked.

Again, Ryan was silent.

“I bet he doesn’t wear it when he’s home around you. You would see it glow and ask questions,” he suggested as he ripped it right off his neck.

Grayson stood up and walked over to me. He tried to hand me the necklace.

I unconsciously backed up. “What? I don’t want that thing.” I waved him off.

“This was obviously made by a witch. Maybe between you, Aurora, and Delphine you can figure out who made it,” Grayson said.

“Oh, right,” I said. Goddess, I could be a real dummy sometimes. I grabbed the necklace, and it started to sputter light like a strobe before it just stopped glowing altogether.

That was strange.

“Why don’t you go back to the house. I’ll meet you there soon,” Grayson asked.

“Why do you want me to leave? What are you going to do with him?” I asked even though I was sure I knew the answer to that question.

“We do what we must to keep our pack safe.”

“You can’t kill him. That would make you just like them,” I pleaded.

“Do you think if I let him go that he won’t go straight back to where he came from and tell his people about us? And where to find us? We’d end up with many dead bodies on both sides. Humans have wars and so do we. If there is a group of humans killing off supernatural beings don’t we get to defend ourselves? We damn well will, even if that means killing off these fuckers,” he said to me.

I stared at him, trying hard to understand what he was saying. I knew little about the supernaturals and how they lived there lives, but one thing I understood was self-preservation. I understood what it meant to protect yourself from others. Could I stand here while they tortured my husband and then killed him?

"I'll leave, but I need a few minutes with him. Alone," I said while I scrutinize Ryan. Was this a man who could kill me and if so why?

"We'll step outside for a minute, but that's all you get," Grayson said as he nodded to the guys, and they all stepped outside the door.

"Ryan," I pleaded.

He just looked at me with a bored expression on his face.

"Would you really kill me? Your wife?" I asked him in disbelief.

"I would mourn you, but yes, you and your kind have no place on earth. You're an abomination in the eyes of God," Ryan said.

I felt a tear drop onto my shirt. I was crying and I hadn't realized it.

"So you don't love me?" I asked.

"Love?" Ryan laughed. "Love is not what we have. You can't love a mutation. I loved who I thought you were, but even then I barely tolerated you. My mother was hounding me about having children, and when I found you I thought I could get married, have some kids, and please her. Thank god you kept taking your birth control pills because it would suck to have to kill my own child. Know this though, I would kill a child we had together as easy as it would be to kill you. I warned you in the bakery, but you didn't run so now you will die," Ryan said just as his hands flew up and wrapped around my throat.

I pulled my arms up and broke his hold on my neck and punched him in the face as hard as I could. It felt like I broke something in my hand but at this point I didn't care.

Another person to throw me away.

"You lied to me. You left me for a dirty dog. You fucking whore," Ryan spit in my face and surged again at my neck, grabbing it and squeezing with all his strength.

I wasn't scared; I knew the energy on the other side of that door would not let me die, but the shock of what Ryan was doing to me kept me from gathering up much energy.

Before I blacked out, Ryan was ripped away from me and thrown across the room.

Grayson was next to me in a second. "Avery, are you all right? Fuck," he growled as he checked out my neck.

I sat down in the chair Grayson pulled up for me and took long choking breaths. That's when I realized that my husband had just attempted to kill me.

"I wouldn't have let him kill her. I was just getting up when you guys stormed in. You missed her punch. It was awesome, but I think she needed to see he would hurt her before she could walk away," Cora said from the desk behind me.

I had forgotten all about her.

"Jesus, Cora, why did you let him get his hands on her?" Grayson asked her.

"Well, because I cracked his phone, and if I had stopped I would have lost all his data. I knew he couldn't kill her that fast so I had time," she explained while still scanning the phone.

Wow, that was some compassion. I wasn't sure she would be in my girl squad.

"Was he able to get a message or a call out to anybody where we are?" Grayson asked her.

"No, he told someone that he was off-grid for a few days. He had disabled his own phone so no one would know where he was. I guess he liked to keep his private life private. I had a ton of stuff to sift through but from what I can see were safe for now." Cora stood up putting her laptop and Ryan's phone in a shoulder bag and started toward the door.

"Let me know as soon as all the data is organized," Grayson told her.

"Yes, Alpha," Cora tilted her head and left.

"Avery, let Glen take you home. You haven't eaten anything today and only sugar yesterday. You'll feel better with some food. Mom texted and said she was making dinner tonight, but help yourself in the kitchen and eat something. I'll see you there soon. See if you can have Leroy look at your hand too, okay?" he asked me.

"You're going to kill him, aren't you?" I kept my sight on the floor.

"Yes, I am. He can't live. He's a danger to the pack. He's a danger to you and Aurora," he told me as he helped me stand.

I turned back to Ryan who had pulled himself up to sit against the wall.

"I thought I loved you, but I'm starting to understand what love means. I'm sorry," I told Ryan.

"Fuck your apology," Ryan spewed.

"That apology was for myself for not seeing who you were sooner," I spat at him.

I walked out of the room and didn't give it another thought until I made it to my bedroom at Grayson's house. I cried for a long time before I fell into a deep sleep.

Chapter Seventeen
Prophecies Explode

I woke up hours later and smelled food. Food could always whip me out of bed, and I hadn't eaten anything since yesterday morning. I was assuming it was lunch time or maybe closer to dinner. I made my way downstairs toward the kitchen when I spotted a dozen people sitting around the dining room table.

"Avery, glad you're awake. Dinner is set and ready. Why don't you take a seat next to Grayson? I just have to get the rolls and we can start," Josie told me as she walked back into the kitchen.

Grayson stood up with a smile on his face and pulled out the chair next to him. I sat down and gave it my best effort to smile.

"It will be okay," he told me as he put his hand on my thigh. "How's your hand? Did you get a chance to see Leroy before you passed out?"

"No, but it feels fine," I told him surprised. I tested my hand by opening and closing it.

"Shifter healing," Grayson whispered to me.

I was too hungry to start a conversation about that right now.

"That's okay, Auntie, you don't have to talk. I can talk for everybody when I say the food smells delicious. Is there any dessert?" she asked.

"Dessert? We haven't even had dinner," Jackson laughed.

More people jumped into the conversation, and as I started eating I was lulled into a peaceful calm so strong I had at one point leaned my head on Grayson's shoulder and fell asleep.

I slept through the knock on the door, but I sat up quick when I heard squealing. "Show me where my Averill is. I got messages she needs to hear. You're wasting my time standing there like you're in charge. My little queen needs me, so step aside wolf man. Oh, and be a dear and find me some tuna. Thanks, doll," Rosie ordered as she swept through the house as if she had a standing invitation.

My head whipped around to see Rosie in all her colorful glory. I jumped out of my seat and fast walked to her, wrapping my arms around her as tight as I could. I didn't even care that her musky incense smell was strong.

"I missed you," I whispered into her ear.

Rosie patted my back and finally pulled me to her side, walking over to Grayson. "Introduce me to your King, sweetness," Rosie commanded.

Yes, she commanded.

Grayson rose and put his napkin on his plate as he smiled and extended his hand to Rosie. "Grayson Hayes, Alpha of the Sawtooth pack. It's a pleasure," he said.

"Rosie Guerrero, hedge witch and coven leader of the Gila Coven from Truth or Consequences, New Mexico," Rosie said.

Grayson chuckled along with most of the table.

"The town you're from is called Truth or Consequences?" I blurted out.

"Yes, it was meant to be a gag, but it stuck and we are all very proud of our town." She lifted her chin just begging anybody to say anything.

Just as you would expect from Rosie, something hissed from inside her purse, if you could call it that. That thing was more of an extra-large beach bag.

Grayson eyed her purse but stated, "Yes, well, any friend of Avery's is a friend of the pack. I welcome you in my home. We have plenty of rooms if you are staying overnight. I'll have Jackson grab your luggage and show you to your room. If you're hungry I can have a plate made up for you,"

Wow, this man had command of his self. I hadn't even gotten over the fact that Rosie was here. So much was happening so fast I hadn't had a chance to think about the fact that she had told me she would see me at the end of the week.

"Yes, I will be staying for the foreseeable future. My bags are in my car. Sebastian will help bring them in, he'll need a room too. Dinner would be appreciated. I'd like to see my room now so I can freshen up, and then I'll be down," Rosie declared.

"Oh, and this lovely monster is all for you. Mind her claws if you can," Rosie explained as she pulled out the prettiest fluffy gray kitty I had ever seen out of her enormous bag.

I love this coo-coo crazy lady.

Wait a minute.

"You brought me a kitten?" I asked, perplexed but absolutely in love. The kitten had dug into my chest with her claws (assuming she was a she) and was purring like a well-oiled engine.

"Every witch knows they need a conduit for their powers; at least any witch worth their salt. I had to leave poor Cat at home. She doesn't much like being around so many wolves. You understand," Rosie said while she looked at Grayson.

"You're staying here?" I asked her.

"Well, yes, how am I supposed to help you with the prophecy and what the spirits are telling me if I can't be around you?" she told me.

"We have a room on the ground floor if that would work better for you," Grayson told her.

She scrunched up her nose at him. "I am not some old silly mille who can't climb stairs," she hissed.

Grayson just grinned and nodded his head.

"Well, I'm going to go freshen up in my room you are having someone show me which will be on a floor that is upstairs," she said as she started walking toward the staircase near the front of the house.

Grayson looked back at the table and nodded to Glen, who flew out of his chair to catch up to Rosie. Jackson and Rosie's manservant, Sebastian, were coming in with a shit ton of luggage. More than a week's worth.

"Glen, put her and her companion on the second floor next to Avery," Grayson directed him.

Glen nodded his understanding.

I stood speechless, wondering how my life became so bizarre.

"Babe, this is nothing. Life is not quiet or calm here. You'll get used to it, and until then you have me to help you." He squeezed me in his arms.

"You have me too, Auntie, and I find all of this craziness wonderful,"

Aurora stated as she slid the chocolate cake toward her. "So who's cutting this cake?" she asks the room.

"I could eat some cake," I said with a smile because what else are you going to do when you're offered chocolate cake.

We had just finished cake with coffee when Rosie sashayed her way into the dining room with her man Sebastian on her tail. Sebastian pulled out her chair for her, took her napkin and laid it across her lap, kissed her cheek then proceeded to stand against the wall glaring at the entire room.

Grayson took his finger and closed my mouth, taking the opportunity to slide his finger across the corner of my mouth to snatch up some frosting that I had no idea was there and sucked it off his finger.

Yowza.

I shook myself out of my fascination with Grayson and turned my attention to Rosie, who was enjoying her dinner that had magically appeared without my notice.

I hadn't heard about Sebastian before, so I took this time to check him out and try to figure out how he plays a part in Rosie's life. Was he her manservant, hired help? There was a ton to take in, starting with his build. For a man that looked like he was in his late forties, or early fifties, he sure was a sight to behold. His hair was a coifed style he obviously used product in. He was wearing black slacks with a black button-down shirt. I admired the red paisley vest coupled with the black ascot to complete his outfit. His wingtips even shined. He didn't match the gypsy bohemian vibe Rosie pulled off, but it matched her attitude for sure.

"Rosie, did you happen to run into your soul mate?" I smirked.

"As a matter of fact I did. He's feeling a little uneasy being here today, so he's acting as bodyguard instead of my lover." She looked at me and winked.

Huh?

I shot my glance at Sebastian and noticed his mouth was set in a tight line.

I elbowed Grayson who was in a conversation with Jackson.

"Yeah?" he leaned over as asked.

"Why are we not feeding Sebastian?" I asked.

"Because he refused," he remarked and went back to his conversation with Jackson.

What? Why?

I got up without really knowing what I was doing but made my way over to Sebastian. I placed my hand on his bicep and started to pull him toward the table to sit next to Rosie.

"Glen, can you please go to the kitchen and make up a plate for Sebastian? Thank you," I said.

Sebastian pulled the chair out for himself and sat down but didn't seem happy about it. I patted his shoulder.

"Okay, I'm new to this whole supernatural business, but you're safe here Sebastian. Not one person here is going to hurt you." I flung my arm out motion to the people sitting at the table. I took my seat next to Grayson, and he just chuckled when I looked at him.

"Wolf shifters in other wolves territory tend to get a little anxious," Jackson leaned across Grayson to tell me.

Good to know.

After the food was served to Sebastian, and he started digging in, he seemed to relax a bit. Geez these people are so tense all the time, well except for Grayson. He seems to smile all the time.

I sat and kept deep breathing until I felt peace come back. Stroking this kitty was helping calm my nerves and my mind.

"You're getting better at that," Aurora says to me as she looks up from her phone.

"Better at what?" I asked.

"Calming down a room when it starts affecting you," Aurora says as she goes back to typing on her phone.

"Darling, it's part of your air control. Air witches have the potential to control emotions as well as controlling air," Rosie stated as she set her fork down.

"People seem to think I have powers, but I don't," I said, though once that came out of my mouth it didn't feel true anymore. I had a sneaking suspicion that my powers were coming in but admitting that was hard and I wasn't sure why.

"I've heard of late bloomers, but this is ridiculous. I'm thirty-one years old. How can my powers decide to show up now?" I asked her.

"I have an idea, but I don't know enough to answer all of it. I think it's because of your cross-linked mate. Well, not because of him, but because you found your mate. From what I could learn cross-linked mates are rare these days. Back in the day I think they were more common, but especially after the war supernaturals didn't associate with each other, because of that they stopped finding their one," Rosie told the table.

"And?" I asked because I still was having a hard time facing that my powers are manifesting, at least all the evidence is pointing to it and it was time I rose up to the present and quit living in the past. I physically shivered as I looked at Rosie and saw that knowing look in her eye.

"Souls my dear, souls," she smiled as she lifted her right palm and what I saw stopped my shivers in their tracks because I was looking at a similar yet different tattoo just like mine and Grayson's. That freaked me out if I was being deadly honest with myself.

"You found the other piece of your soul and when that was found so were your powers. You've been dreaming about Grayson and his wolves since you turned eighteen. I would say your soul was searching even then," Rosie said like that was supposed to explain everything.

I just sat there because what was I going to say to that? I barely knew about witchcraft, how could I refute anything she says? Like Grayson said, I am akin a new pup.

"But it could also have do to do with you being a Grand Witch cross-linked to a Hyper-Alpha, and the prophecy that surrounds you both," she threw out there. "I would love a piece of cake, Avery." Rosie smiled.

"Cake? You can't throw something like that out there into the universe and then ask for a piece of cake," I screeched at her. I noticed Sebastian had already grabbed the cake and was cutting his Rosie a slice.

"His Rosie, that's cute," Aurora said but was still typing away on her phone.

I growled loud and long.

Every single person snapped their heads up and looked at me.

Grayson stood up and pushed his chair away from the table and held his hand out to me. I frowned because I realized I wasn't getting a second slice of cake.

Grayson leaned over and whispered, "I'll save you a slice."

"You can read minds," I blinked at him.

"No, I can't, but the drool on your lip tells me you might hurt someone if there isn't a piece for you tomorrow." He laughed.

I, of course had to check. Nope, no drool. Huh

"I'm taking Avery to bed. Rosie, Sebastian, you are both welcome guests in my home and within the pack. Please, make yourselves comfortable and let me know if you need anything. It's been a long day and tomorrow will be here for talks about prophecies," Grayson commanded.

I looked over and noticed that Rosie was taking a deep breath to start on a rant about the dire prophecy.

Grayson grunted, "Tomorrow!"

"You go, Auntie, get yourself some," Aurora pumped her first in the air.

"What?"

Grayson cleared his throat and said, "I'll be helping Avery to her room, and then I'll be in my room, which is on the first floor at the back of the house if anyone needs anything," Grayson said to everyone but made eye contact with Jackson.

I couldn't help it, the last few days, hell the last few weeks, had been so fantastical and chaotic I bent over started laughing so hard that I started to cry, sobs tore through my whole body uncontrollably. The kitten didn't like being woke up and started clawing and hissing to make her displeasure known.

Grayson swung me up into his arms, and I tucked my face into his neck, trying to hide from everyone. I still had a hold of the hissing kitten clinging to my shirt.

I expected once Grayson got me back to my room he would have put me to bed but he flung the covers back, slid off his shoes and got into my bed while still holding me in his arms. I was glad he didn't let me go because I felt like if he did I would just float away.

While I continued to cry, I heard Jackson lightly knocked on the door and asked Grayson if he needed anything which made Grayson say the word kitten. Then kitten was pulled out of my embrace and passed off to Jackson, all of which I had not one care about. My body and mind decided it was time to shut down. All the events, all the emotions hurtled together too fast. I was worried I might crack up again if I didn't sleep. It was during those thoughts that I drifted off.

Morning came and before I even opened my eyes I felt refreshed and warm. Very, very warm.

I opened my eyes and my face was nestled in Grayson's neck. We were now more prone and entangled then we were last night. My left leg was thrown over his as well as my left arm was laid across his chest. My hand under his shirt was resting on his warm abs. I slide my hand around just get a lay of the land. Making me gasp aloud, Grayson snatched my hand and pulled it out of his shirt and laid it back on his chest.

"Good morning. How are you feeling today?" he asked me.

I keep my head in his neck and say quietly, "Good."

"No reason to be embarrassed about anything. You've had a fuck of it lately, and you were due a break down. Frankly, I was surprised it didn't happen earlier," he said while pulling his arm out from under the pillow to put it around my shoulders.

I stiffened.

"Now don't go getting all shy on me. I don't believe in hiding our feelings or feeling shame for having them. I want you to know I got you," he says.

"Okay." I say because really what can I say.

I lifted my head out of his neck and looked him square in the eye. "I still think you can read my mind."

He smiled.

"Also, I will say that if you expect to have any kind of conversation and don't want me to get shy on you, I need coffee," I stated.

"Got it, coffee before talking," he says and starts to maneuver out of bed, which made me stare at the way he moved his body with confidence, power, and grace.

"You slept here all night with me in your clothes?" I inquired to no one since Grayson had already left the bedroom.

"Yep," was all I heard from somewhere down the hall.

I flop back down on the bed and stare at the ceiling. I hate he probably slept like shit being in his clothes, but it feels nice he stayed with me all night. I slept so hard, I'm not as fog brained this morning as I normally am. I heard a scratching noise coming from the floor and peered over the side of the bed to see a gray kitten struggling to climb her way up into bed. It must have felt like she was climbing a mountain she was so small. I put her out of misery and plunked her off the blanket carefully detaching her little claws from the quilt and pulled her on to my chest. She immediately started to purr and kneed my shirt. It was quite relaxing having a purring kitten lay on me. Guess I needed to think of a name, I couldn't keep calling her kitty.

What felt like mere seconds later, Grayson comes in the room with a mug of coffee. He sets it on the bedside table and said, "You want cake you have to come to the kitchen." He beamed and walked out. Well at least he smiled before he left.

He sure smiles often.

"No crumbs in the bed guy, got it," I smiled.

That was the first cup of coffee anyone had ever brought me in bed. It felt wonderful. I sat in bed and drank a few sips while petting the kitten until I decided I was ready to face the day.

I put kitty down on the floor because I had a feeling she wouldn't care that the bed was too high and would try to jump down. When I set her on the floor she immediately started exploring the room. I decided to leave her to her exploration while I showered and changed into one of my typical outfits, a pair of my lucky jeans, long-sleeved cotton, red V-neck shirt, and my thick cashmere socks. I never have been much for makeup and my hair always seems to dry with a nice wave so I leave it. Now socks I splurged on. I always bought the softest socks. I still have my garnet studs in my ears, which I never take out. They were a gift from my grandfather, and I hadn't taken them off since he gave them to me for my tenth birthday. I didn't wear much jewelry, not because I didn't like it, but because I never had enough money to splurge on those things. I had my earrings and my wedding ring, which made me pause halfway down the stairs.

I hadn't taken my wedding ring off. I looked at it and realized I never really liked it. It was a plain band of yellow gold with a two carat round diamond sitting on top. I'm sure it wasn't cheap, but I thought it had no personality. I always believed colored gems and stones had more appeal to them anyway. I do remember my mom teaching Sam about stones and the power they held. I took it off and then realized I didn't know what to do with it. I put it in my front pocket and decided

I'd deal with it later.

Kitty followed me to the stairs and then sat beside my leg waiting.

"Okay, I guess that's a lot of stairs," I said to kitty as I scooped her up. As I walked down the stairs, I realized how small she was and carrying her around would be the norm for a while. I didn't want her out in the woods and alone.

I could smell bacon and followed my nose until I came into the kitchen. The dining room sat twenty people, so I kept walking to the heart of the kitchen and came across a sun room extended from the kitchen with a built-in circular bench seat with seating for another dozen. The room was huge with glass windows expanding the length of the kitchen, it was beautiful. You could see the valley of trees flowing down toward town. It reminded me of a castle sitting up on a hill. I tore my gaze away from the view and took in the kitchen. I don't think I could have dreamed up a better kitchen if I tried. The gray slab counter tops popped next to the white cupboards that lined the entire space up to the ceiling. You could have a massive group of people in this kitchen and it would still feel big.

I took my gaze away from the kitchen and noticed I wasn't the only one out of bed. Aurora sat next to Tyler and Trace. Jackson and Grayson were cooking together.

"Auntie, I think you should sell that ring and buy yourself something you want," Aurora piped up from scrolling through her phone.

I scowled at her as I sat down and realized my life was never going to be the same. The family I thought I was building wasn't real, but this one just might be. Grayson came over to the table, placed a mug of coffee with creamer on the table in front of me, grabbed kitty, and took her over to two bowls where there was food and water. Glad he thought of it because I hadn't.

"This is a much bigger and better family anyway," Aurora whispered.

I started to get angry but then Aurora looked up from her phone and all I could do was smile. "I think you might be right," I mumbled. "Let's take some time today and see if you can teach me some magic and let's start with how to block you." I glared with a smile at her as I sipped my coffee.

As I listen to Jackson quietly reporting to Grayson about some pack business my mind started to drift.

"I want an espresso machine," I blurted out loud.

All talk stopped, and I felt every eye in the room was trained on me waiting to figure out why I blurted something so random.

The many journeys I had taken since being kicked out of my coven had led me to traveling all over and with it many jobs, one being a barista. That job didn't pay well, but I loved making coffee and drinking it. When Ryan and I had finally moved in together I had told him I wanted to save my money and buy an espresso machine. The one I wanted was not cheap but I knew I could save for it. I hadn't been allowed to pay any bills, it wouldn't take long to save what I needed for the one. I had planned to buy it for myself during the after-Christmas sales during the first year Ryan and I were together. When we exchanged gifts on Christmas day, Ryan got me a regular coffee pot, explaining he didn't like espresso drinks so there was no need to have one. Regular coffee would do it for him, and if I wanted an espresso I could go into town for one. He didn't want the kitchen counters cluttered with nonsense stuff. I remember feeling bummed, but I enjoyed going to the local bakery and getting an espresso and a treat, so the sting of it didn't last long.

But now that I thought about it, I realized Ryan controlled all aspects of my life. From not wanting me to work full-time, not wanting me to have my own checking account, to deciding what I wanted in the ways of coffee. I hated doing things behind his back but I had no choice. Anything I wanted that he didn't want me to have I would manage to secretly do. He at one point wanted his name on my checking account so he could see how I was spending my money. I had agreed at first but had told Delphine about it, and she had flipped out, hollering about men for hours and hours. After about thirty minutes of her freak out, she grabbed my arm and marched me to her car where we drove to her bank, and I opened a checking account. She had set it up so that half of my pay would go into mine and Ryan's joint checking account and the other half would go into my own account that Delphine demanded I open,. She had another freak out on her accountant when her accountant tried to pitch a fit. All she said was, "Make it work or you're fired." I had always admired her ability to say exactly what was on her mind.

"Avery, you ok?" I heard Grayson call out to me.

The longer I sat in these thoughts the more pissed I got, and the more pissed I got the hotter I became until my coffee mug shattered right in my face at the same time a loud boom vibrated through the air and the window I was sitting next to exploded. I looked around the kitchen and noticed all the windows exploded.

"Holy fuck," Jackson yelled.

"Son of a bitch," Grayson bellowed.

I still hadn't said a word, as I didn't understand what was happening. Grayson and Jackson abandoned the breakfast they were making and came flying over to the table, checking everyone out for injuries. It was a good thing I was almost done with my coffee.

"No one's injured, Uncle Grayson," Trace assured him.

I was about to speak when Rosie and Sebastian came busting into the room. She had her arm wrapped about Sebastian elbow and her mouth was agape surveilling all the damage and checking each person with her eyes that we were ok. After a minute she tapped Sebastian's bicep and released her arm and walked over to the coffee station saying,

"Oh dear, I think your training needs to start now. That took some serious anger to blow out all the windows in the house. What, my dear, had you so upset?" Rosie asked while she sauntered into the kitchen to find a mug for coffee.

I still couldn't talk.

I did this?

No way.

"I think Auntie wants an espresso machine" Aurora said through laughter.

"You blew out all the windows because you want something. What are you? Five years old?" Tyler barked.

Aurora's finger flipped out so fast I couldn't stop her. I could feel her anger like it was my own. Tyler's mouth snapped shut and he couldn't talk.

"Now that was not very nice and you should learn to respect your elders. Apologize to my aunt, and I'll release your mouth," Aurora proclaimed. "Tsk, Tsk, again not nice thoughts. I guess you don't need your mouth today."

I looked to Jackson to see what he would think of my teenage niece keeping his son's mouth shut like that. He was grinning but trying hard not to at the same time.

"Aurora, I appreciate you sticking up for Avery, as I would have if you hadn't jumped in, but you can't just use your powers willy-nilly like that. You have to remember not to piss off the wolves," Grayson requested. I had a feeling Grayson wasn't going to be nice about her teenage behavior for much longer.

"No one can blame Avery. She doesn't know what she's doing. Every day she is getting stronger and stronger, if anyone is to blame it's me. I knew this would start happening, but I wanted to give her time to settle into her new life. It looks like we need to speed up your training, but it can at least wait until I've had one cup of coffee," Rosie said as she dusted off the bench seat and slid in next to me.

"Avery, you okay?" Grayson asked on a whisper.

I looked up at him and saw no blame, no anger.

"I'm so sorry. I didn't mean to do this. I will pay for it, whatever the cost. I can't believe I did that," I pleaded.

"What made you so angry?" Rosie asked as she turned to me.

I didn't even have to think, I just answered, "I've always wanted an espresso machine. Not the cheap ones. I wanted a professional one. I love making espresso drinks and experimenting with flavors. I realized as I was thinking about it that Ryan had controlled me so tightly I never got one simply because he didn't want me to have one," I explained.

"You can have whatever the fuck you want and not one person is going to stop you," Grayson belted out.

Rosie studied Grayson for a minute. "One thing you need to understand is that you and Avery are connected. On a soul level, a major amounts of energy connection. If you get fired up it will cause Avery to become angry again and since there are no more windows, well let's not find out what else she can blow up, shall we?" Rosie explained.

"I heard there's a green witch here. Between myself, Aurora, and this green witch I think training might go a little faster," Rosie stated.

"This green witch has a name," Delphine stated flatly.

It was easy to predict where this power struggle was going, and I was still whirling from blowing all the windows out, so I jumped in. "Rosie, let me introduce you to my boss and dear friend, Delphine. She has decided to help train me in plants and herbs," I said to Rosie.

"Yes, I apologize. Nice to make your acquaintance, Delphine. I believe we need to have a meeting. Between you, Aurora, and I, I think we have a great combined teaching circle, and we must not delay in training. I would hate to see Avery explode into a million little pieces," Rosie threw out to the room.

I looked to Aurora and then Grayson. I thought with Grayson's face turning red that he was going to blow.

"Now," Aurora spat loudly. "As I am closest to my Aunt and know what makes her tick, I think it would be best if we left out the part where she might explode. I know I've only heard rumors and nothing more, so stop freaking out the person who you're trying to keep calm," she said with venom dripping from every word.

"You can blow yourself up? That's a thing?" I asked the ladies. They all ignored me and continued to drink their coffees looking at anything but me.

Aurora seemed to take a deep breath and relax all her muscles. "After breakfast, because Auntie has a hangry problem, we'll go for a walk, explore the lay of the land, and slowly release information. If you all start spitting information at her… Well let's take this slow. We'll start with the most explos— um the most powerful items first and teach her how to control them. It's my opinion that we should start with the soul connection to Grayson. I think that's what is messing with her so much," Aurora explained.

"You mean she's hungry?" Delphine inserted.

"Nope, I mean she's got a hangry problem. When she's hungry, she can get really angry," Aurora told the group.

"I'm sitting right here. And I'm going to live in ignorant bliss about possibly blowing up because it's way too early for talk like that. And yes, I do need to eat," I told Aurora.

Everyone seemed to ignore me and the room grew silent.

"I think Aurora just put a lid on the dominance attack. Righteous," Trace said with a smile.

"Jackson is going to salvage breakfast. I want this room kept on calm topics until we get outside," Grayson told everyone as he leaned down and kissed my head.

"Man, I think it's cause she's a girl that she just got away with this," Trace grumbled.

Tyler punched him in the arm.

"Dude, don't be dumb," Tyler frowned at his brother.

When Tyler realized that Aurora had released is mouth and he could talk again he told me, "Sorry Avery."

I looked in his eyes and saw his true self and he was a beautiful kid inside. He was sincere in his apology and I needed to stop being so guarded in my relationships and let people in.

I smiled at him "Sometimes I can act like I'm five. "No worries," and he blushed.

I decide to just enjoy my coffee. I keep picturing the windows blowing out. I had thought it was just the kitchen, but I did that to the whole house. How many windows are in this house? Man, there goes my espresso machine. Replacing these windows is going to wipe out my savings.

"Do you think after what just happened Grayson isn't going to run out and make sure you have the espresso machine of your dreams? Windows for this house aren't going to be cheap but he would do anything for you," Aurora informed me.

Oh, hell no. I was not going to let another man buy me shit. I will buy my own damn espresso machine. God, are all men the same?

Grayson plopped a stack of French toast on my plate with four crispy bacon strips right in front of me. I looked around and realized I had been served first.

"You can buy your own espresso machine. I wouldn't know where to get one or what you might want. The windows won't cost much because of the pack's construction contacts and the pack will put the windows in. That's what family does for each other. We all chip in when it's pack business." Grayson stared at Aurora when he told me all this. Grayson seemed to communicate just fine with her.

"Yes, alpha," Aurora said while making eye contact.

That surprised me. Aurora seemed like she was deferring to Grayson.

"Grandma Josie and I had a talk, I can follow the rules. Geez," Aurora admonished.

I decided to stay silent and just eat my breakfast, ignoring the snide comment. I didn't even roll my eyes. I can be mature sometimes too.

Aurora laughed aloud. I looked at her, and she was looking at her phone. I again just kept my mouth shut. I think I had heard people say you should pick your battles with teenagers. This must be one of those moments.

I noticed that everyone else who came for breakfast had to dish themselves up. Guess I was the special one. Grayson sat down next to me and smiled while digging into his own pile of French toast.

Others had wandered in and devoured the rest of the food while visiting with everyone at the table.

Grayson stood up and grabbed my empty plate along with his to wash them but decided to pull rank at the same time.

"Before you ladies get into Avery's training, we need to have a pack meeting about this prophecy. You all have ten minutes and then we meet in the front room," he stated and walked away, but not before getting me a refill of coffee. I felt so pampered and I liked it.

"What fucking prophecy?" I heard Delphine say from across the table starring at Rosie.

"Rosie says—" I started to say but was interrupted.

"I know damn well who is spewing prophecy crap around here. Hedge witches tend to blow into your life and drop bombshells and then walk away, leaving you to wade through the ruins," Delphine spat.

"Oh, you're a Hedge witch, Rosie?" Aurora asked in wonder.

"Yes dear, and she is a Green witch," Rosie said while flinging her finger toward Delphine. "And you're an Elemental Air witch," Rosie Aurora. That must be why Aurora's binding spells are so strong.

"Yes, Auntie, that's right," Aurora beamed with pride.

"It's rude to read your Aunts mind, child," Delphine mumbled.

I glared at Aurora. "That is one of the things we are working on immediately." I put up my hand to Rosie because I knew that she was going to disagree.

"If everyone wants me to be calm and happy then learning to block a mind invasion is first on the list. Aurora has already helped me a little with that," I stated.

Delphine and Rosie both agreed, and we all got up to filter into the front room, which was the largest room in the house. I think it could hold fifty people in it comfortably; probably why it's the meeting room.

When we reached the room I was expecting there to be many pack members, but only a few were present, Grayson's mom, Josie, his dad, Grant, Jackson, Leroy, Delphine (who was on the opposite side of the room from Leroy), and Rosie who perched herself in a wing back chair that was centered so it looked like a throne. I took a seat on a loveseat next to Josie and waited, sipping my coffee. I decided to wonder what brand the coffee was instead of mentioning that the feeing in the room was gloomy. A thought popped into my head that I hadn't heard anything about Sasha since we were in North Carolina.

Grayson started a low grumble, which triggered Jackson and their dad Grant to join in.

Rosie took that as a sign to speak.

"Everyone needs to relax right this instant. What we have to talk about is extremely important and if you keep this up, we won't get to finish. I will remind everyone who doesn't know, Avery is an elemental air witch like Aurora, but not just an elemental witch, but all four elements and possibly all types of witches as well. This would make her a Grand Witch, an untrained Grand Witch which can be a ticking time bomb. We all need to keep our moods in mind so that they don't leek into Avery," Rosie told the room.

I laughed so hard coffee flew out my nose.

Well, that was attractive.

Josie pulled a handkerchief out of somewhere and handed it to me.

"Here, sweetie," Josie smiled.

"Thanks," I marveled. Who keeps handkerchiefs on their bodies these days?

When I had my face cleaned up, I lifted my chin and looked around the room. Jackson was smiling, Grayson looked like he wanted to scold me, and Rosie looked shocked. I couldn't help it I started laughing harder.

"I hardly find this funny, Avery. Do you have any idea the shit that is going to land on you if anybody finds out you're a Grand Witch? Your coven will be the first to attack. Fuck," Delphine exclaimed.

What she said had me stop in my tracks.

"We don't want them anywhere around me. I might kill one." I glared at no one in particular. I didn't really think I could kill anybody, but looking at what I did to the windows it might happen by accident.

"Could we hold all comments until we get all the information?" Grayson snapped.

"Yes, yes, the prophecy. There was a prophecy that came from a long-lived Hedge Witch out of a coven on the East Coast. I'm not positive, but I think she originally came from somewhere in the UK and had migrated over, but I digress. Word had traveled until it got to my coven, so I traveled to find out what she had to say. This was about twenty-eight years ago, give or take a few years. When I finally met with her, she told me a witch would be born a dud but would grow into power when she met her other half. She went on to say this witch with her mate would be the ones to unite all supernaturals and bring back the cross-linked mates. She did warn the future wasn't set in stone, that there was a threat out there that would try to stop her. That was all she said even though I stayed for a few days hoping I would get more information. The day I met you on the plane wasn't a coincidence, Avery; one of my spirit guides guided me to take that specific flight. She wouldn't shut up until I booked the flight to North Carolina and then to Seattle. Sometimes they can be pushy and annoying but obviously very helpful," she told me.

"Could we keep on track, please," Grayson grunted.

"Okay, alpha, keep your pants on. Geez, I hope this isn't what my lot in life will be," Rosie turned to Sebastian who was now standing by her side. Sebastian just stared down at her and smiled.

Wow, I didn't even see him come into the room.

"As I was saying, I didn't get anything else out of her while I was there, but I had asked around about this witch and everyone told me that she was never wrong with her visions. Through the wolf packs in New Mexico I have learned about the Grand Wolf history." Rosie looked to Grant. "Grant, you might have heard these stories."

"I was told stories while I was young about a Grand Wolf who at one time had led all wolves. It was many generations ago, but from the stories I heard as a child the Grand Wolf's mate was a Grand Vampire. I think that was why I didn't give it much thought because we all knew supernaturals kept to their own species. One thing that stood out to me when I heard these stores was how abundant each supernatural community was," Grant explained.

"So you think Grayson is a Grand Wolf? Why?" Jackson asked the room.

"From what I learned, the Grand Wolf cannot be beaten. The wolf packs across the world would hold a Grand Wolf challenge once a year. Well, unless there were no challengers, which would be the case once wolves realized he couldn't be beaten. I looked into you, Grayson, and heard you've never lost a challenge. You went through dozens of challenges to become alpha, and you were never close to losing," Rosie explained to the room.

"Why can't a woman be Grand Wolf, that's stupid," I heard Aurora pipe up from the edge of the room.

Everyone ignored her because at this moment it wasn't about that. I couldn't stop starring at Grayson. Grand Wolf, Grand Witch. What in the hell?

"Avery, take a deep breath. Blow it out slow. Now close your eyes and take another deep breath," Delphine said to me. I did what she told me, mostly because she had been teaching me meditating techniques since I had met her and they seemed to work. I had always wondered how she could teach me to calm down when she was the crankiest person I had ever met.

"That's because her soul hasn't been with its other half which means she's not getting any," Aurora singsonged to the group.

Delphine snapped her fingers and a vine came crawling up from the floor, wrapped around Aurora's body, and covered her mouth. A flower bloomed and it covered most of Aurora's face.

I shot out of my seat, ran over to Aurora, and started clawing at the vines.

"Jesus, Delphine, she can't breathe!" I yelled.

"She can breathe, but she needs to learn respect," Delphine said casually.

I looked over at Leroy, and he was glaring at Delphine who was ignoring his look.

"Okay lesson time for this group," Josie commanded. "There is no shifting in this house, which means no magic in this house. Once you step outside you can shift, grow things, whatever you will, but in this house you will respect the alpha and not use your powers. And if any of you break that rule I don't care how old you are, you will answer to me and believe me there will be consequences."

"Oh, and Avery, that rule does not apply to you," Josie said to me with a wink. I think Grayson's mom likes me.

Thank goodness for that. I wonder what my consequence would have been after blowing out all the windows?

As I thought about the windows, I noticed that all the windows in the room were boarded up. I didn't even notice it being done. Man, these wolves can move fast. I needed to start paying better attention to my surroundings.

"I understand your Aunt is still learning how to block you, but until she learns you need to keep your comments to yourself. If you can't control yourself, you won't be welcome in these meetings. Are we in agreement?" Grayson asked her.

"Yes, alpha," Aurora groaned as she was flinging the last of the vines from her body.

"This is your last warning," he added.

I checked Aurora over to make sure she was vine and flower free before I went to sit back down. "If this keeps up I'm definitely getting an espresso machine. I'm exhausted, and we haven't even started yet."

Jackson had left the room and brought back the pot of coffee and left it on the coffee table right in front of me.

I smiled at him and he winked.

"We also have to discuss Avery's husband and his connection to this group of killers," Jackson piped up.

"Can I just say I would rather not talk about him? Let's just all pretend he never existed," I said.

"I know you'd like that to be the case, but I was charged with contacting all the supernatural groups and finding out if they have been targeted like the wolves have. We know where Ryan's mother lives and that's a start," Grayson told me.

"He is… well, he was very close with his mother, and since he called her and asked about my family I can guarantee she will be looking for him when he doesn't call her," I told the room.

"I can answer that," Cora looked up from behind her laptop. She was sitting on the floor next to one of the boarded-up windows.

"He disconnected his tracker on his phone so the only thing they might get is a ping on the cell tower that's over 50 miles away. That's why our phones don't always work up on the mountain, but I digress. Basically, if they have an IT person who's worth their salt they'll know he was in Idaho but not the exact spot," she concluded before she lowered her head back to what she was working on.

"So we need to stay sharp when we go into town. Let's all be aware of strangers, and if you have to go into town for work or otherwise always go in pairs. Jackson, make sure that's understood."

Grayson looked around the room searching for something. "Anybody seen Sasha today? I haven't seen her for days. Jackson talk to…actually never mind. I'll stop on our trek and have a word with her. She can't keep her place as an enforcer if she doesn't attend the meetings. Actually I haven't thought about her punishment yet for attacking Avery. I ordered her not to leave her cabin until I contacted her." Grayson stated.

That got me thinking about what followed me in my life and how it had put all these people in danger. Guilt was something that reared its ugly head many times in my life. But at this moment my grandfather's voice floated into my head, 'Avery, guilt is like fear, it doesn't exist.

You need to let those feelings go.'

I remember when he told me that and him laughing at the look on my face. How can guilt and fear not exist? When something was causing me to feel guilty or be fearful, he would always distract me with gardening, teaching me all about plants. By the time a few hours passed, Grandpa Isaiah would turn to me and ask how I was feeling and with a smile on my face I would say great. He always knew how to soothe my heart when unwanted feelings would overtake my life. Grandpa Isaiah didn't like the coven, and he would spit on the ground anytime he would find out things they had said or things they did to me, always letting me know that what they think about me didn't matter but it was how I felt about myself that was most important. Thinking about Grandpa Isaiah put a huge smile on my face.

"What is that smile for, Avery?" Grayson inquired.

"So you really can't read minds, that's a relief," I rejoiced.

"Okay, before we wrap up this meeting I'm taking Avery for a tour of the land. Aurora, Rosie, and Delphine, meet back here at the main house in three hours. Then you can start your training," Grayson spoke.

"Three hours, we need to start her training now and we haven't discussed the prophecy fully yet," Rosie retorted.

"Avery needs time to adjust to her new life and part of that is regaining a sense of normalcy in her daily life. Since the moment I met her she's been living life in fear of what is happening. I need to show her the extended family she is living with, and frankly, I need some time with her without all of your influence. So, she will meet you here in roughly three hours," Grayson proclaimed then turned to me and held out his hand.

"Glad I got to decide what I get to do today," I retorted.

Grayson chuckled. “Avery, would you like to go for a ride, meet some people, and see the land that we live on?”

“Why yes, I would love to do all those things. Thank you for asking.” I smiled.

“Smartass,” Grayson added with a playful smack on my ass.

Everyone seemed to go off to do whatever it was they were going to do while Grayson walked to the coat rack that took up a portion of the entry way. He grabbed a women’s mossy green down jacket and held it open for me to put on.

“I have a jacket upstairs. I don’t want to take someone else’s jacket,” I explained.

“This is your jacket, Avery. I had someone get you a few things I noticed you didn’t have. This one is a warm jacket that can get dirty. Your red coat is beautiful and you look lovely in it, but sitting behind me on a four wheeler in a jacket that doesn’t move with your body will prohibit me from being able to feel your body wrapped around mine. Also, it might get muddy and I would hate to ruin it,” he said.

Of all the things he said, one stood out above the rest even though he said so many delicious things. He noticed I didn’t have something I needed.

“You had someone get me things?” I asked.

“Yes.”

As I slide my arm into the jacket, a whole body shiver happened. I finished putting the jacket on and realized I loved the color, and it helped that it fit me perfectly. It sat just at my hips and was so thin it was hard to tell I had a jacket on. Grayson put on his black down jacket and grabbed two beanies and two pairs of gloves, grabbed my hand and took me to the side of the house where the four-car garage was. The last garage door on the end was up and idling in the driveway was a black four runner. It as if he was a magic genie. He didn't even have to communicate to anyone and things just happened or appeared.

"I can talk to my wolves when I'm shifted and it doesn't have to be a full shift. I asked Glen to get the wheeler ready before the meeting started," Grayson explained while he put a beanie and then a helmet on my head. He handed me a pair of soft, tan leather gloves that were lined with fur.

"I might be the witch, but I think you have magic too," I said.

"I do, all supers have magic. It's what makes us different from millies," Grayson stated.

I kept my mouth shut because I knew that and if I opened my mouth nothing nice would have come out. I do remember my mom telling me if I didn't have anything nice to say, not to say anything at all.

Chapter Eighteen
What it means to be Pack

Grayson was sitting forward, holding out a hand to help me. I put my foot on the step and climbed up behind him on the ATV. I was surprised at how comfortable I was. I had wondered what it was like to ride one of these but was always too preoccupied with surviving I never found out. I placed my hands on Grayson's hip, and he immediately grabbed my hands and wound them around his stomach and patted my hands before taking off. I thought since I had never ridden on one of these beasts before he would start out slow. Nope. He took off like a bat out of hell.

We left from the main house and headed away from the gravel road we took to get here. The main house sat on the rocky bank of a massive lake I had yet to explore. I decided in that moment it was on my agenda in the near future. I had thought Grayson was going to stop so I could meet some of the pack, but he just kept on flying down the road. He was in complete control so I let go of my fear and enjoyed the scenery.

Many different kinds of pines and firs made up the forest on both sides but sparse enough that you could see through it. It gave me goose bumps to imagine all of the pack members having such a beautiful view. I couldn't have picked a better dream home for myself then Grayson's. I had one heebie-jeebies about the forest—spiders. Delphine had rolled her eyes so many times with me when we would move a section of the nursery and a spider would shoot out at me, sometimes crawling across my hand. I would scream, mostly startling Delphine but occasionally toppling over plants while freaking the fuck out. I would apologize and try to shore up my nerves so my response wouldn't piss her off. Grandpa Isaiah believed that every living creature had its purpose and not to harm them. He would never let me kill them and neither would Delphine. I told them both that once a spider makes its way into my house he has decided his own fate. So, I would not kill them in nature because who could purposely kill anything unless it was harming you. Just thinking about spiders made my body shiver so much so that Grayson pulled over turned around and asked, "You okay?"

I was so embarrassed I had made him pull over I scowled at him.

"I see on your face that you didn't need me to stop to ask that, but I'm not moving until you tell me what had you shivering so hard?" Grayson said softly.

"Spiders. I know that sounds strange, but your forests are so beautiful and that got me thinking about spiders. I hope you're not going to tell me I can't dispose of spiders in our house," I spoke.

Grayson had a blank look on his face.

"It's their legs, they have so many and they bend the wrong way!" I snapped.

Grayson burst out laughing, bending over to hold his stomach.

"It's not funny. Have you read the statistics on how many spiders people eat while sleeping? That shit is crazy. I once tried sleeping with a scarf wrapped around my head so I could keep myself out of those statistics," I admitted.

Grayson slowly stopped laughing. But I could tell that he was ready to laugh again. I smiled, the anger leaving my body.

"I noticed you don't sleep with a scarf around your face, so I take that to mean it didn't work?" Grayson asked with a smile.

I glared at him.

"No, it didn't work. It was suffocating and hot. I would wake up feeling like someone was trying to choke me," I said.

"Well, I will make sure no spiders bother us today, and you have my permission to 'dispose of' any spiders you find in the house," Grayson chuckled.

"Since we've stopped for a minute," I said while removing the goggles that went over the helmet. "Are we going someplace specific?" I asked.

"The property is spread out; it can take hours to get through it all. I didn't think Rosie and Delphine were going to allow us to be gone all day. I thought I would take you around to a few of the property boundaries, stop at a few of the pack's places, and just enjoy the day. Does that sound good?" Grayson asked.

"That sounds great." I beamed at him.

Grayson pulled my goggles down and adjusted them, turned around before grabbing my hands again and wrapped them around his middle. He arranged himself and we continued for another thirty minutes or so. The ride was so relaxing I almost fell asleep at one point, so I focused on the flowers that were popping up around the base of the trees. It was a mixture of what looked like Bachelor's Button, which is a beautiful blue color that reminded me of the sky on a sunny day, and Ghost flowers, so white they seemed to glow.

We had passed others on four wheelers and a few trucks and cars. The road was barely wide enough for two vehicles and each person we passed slowed down and waved as we went by. I noticed every person had a smile on their face.

We ended up stopping at a cabin about 200 feet from the shore of the lake. It was a small, A-frame cabin with a ton of windows that wrapped around the covered porch. By the front door were four white rocking chairs and a few tables spread between. Fresh flowers were on the table closest to the door, and in the chair next to the table sat an older woman with long, silver hair in two braids down both sides of her face. She did not have a smile on her face. Which made me wonder why we were stopping here.

Grayson helped me take off my equipment and store it in a compartment that was attached on the back. He grabbed my hand and linked our fingers together before pulling me up a few stairs onto the porch.

"Well, if it isn't the usurper," the older woman spat.

"Good morning to you too, Bran," Grayson chuckled.

Bran did a full body scan and sneered. "And what the hell have you brought to my doorstep?" Bran boomed, talking about me as though I was something the cat drug in.

For a second I almost looked down to see if I had mud on my clothes.

"I would like to introduce you to Averill Sinclair, she and her niece, Aurora, joined our pack recently, and I wanted to personally come and let you know the news," Grayson beamed.

"Can't count on that grandniece of mine to come and let me know what's happening. I blame your generation. Always relying on your electronics to pass on information. I haven't seen hide nor hair of that girl. Always chasing the tails of those boys and not mindin' the one she brought into this world. She dropped him off here days ago, and I haven't heard one word from her. You got her so busy she got no time for her boy? You doing that to this old wolf?" Bran patted her chest as if she was having a heart attack.

Grayson started to growl and the vibration of it traveled down his arm and up mine until I was growling as loud as he was. That made Grayson abruptly stop and turn to me with a wince.

"I'm sorry, Avery. I forgot," he apologized.

I shook off the feeling running through my body and smiled at him.

"It's okay. I think I'm finally coming to terms that I have powers, but it's like hard to react because I can't stop it from happening. I think this is why the girls didn't want me gone all day. I need to know how to control the power with my feelings so I can control my own body. Your power is so strong I can feel you when you're not even in my vicinity," I told him as I let go of his palm grabbed his and traced his tattoo that matched mine.

Grayson nodded, grabbing my right hand and traced my tattoo with his finger causing a full body shiver.

"Huh, you're a witch. Well all be! Not in my life time did I think I would see it finally happening," Bran wobbled and then smiled the biggest smile that changed her entire face.

Bran stood and came toward with her arms spread open. "It's a real pleasure, Averill."

Grayson just stood there dumbfounded.

"It's Avery," I explained as she got close, I let go of Grayson's hand and received her hug with one of my own. The feelings flowing through me were of relief and peace. A peace I had never ever felt in my entire life. Not even when I was happy, not even when my parents were still alive. Huge sobs tore out of my mouth. I sounded like a wounded animal.

This behavior did not make Grayson happy. He came unstuck and a growl slowly started to rumble out of his chest. Bran looked up at him and let me go from the embrace. She led me to the rocker next to hers. As soon as she physically quite touching me my emotions started to even out.

"Sit down, dear, and let me go inside a get you a throw and glass of ice tea. It's still nippy this time of year. Name's Branwen MacDuff, but everyone calls me Bran," she said to me as she walked toward her front door.

"Alpha, could you please help me with something in the house?" Bran asked Grayson as she slide into the cabin letting her storm door close with a tap.

Grayson looked at me with the second biggest smile I had ever seen. The smiles were starting to become contagious.

"She has never, not once in my life said the word 'please'. She has never deferred to me as alpha. She is the eldest wolf in our pack and many see her as the leader. Our behavior toward one another has caused so much strife it keeps me up at night. I think something has changed, and that change is because the other half of my soul showed up." Grayson beamed to me and followed Bran inside.

So many emotions had flown through my body in such a short time the only thing I could do was laugh, which was what I was doing when Bran and Grayson returned. They both stood there and waiting for my laughing fit to be over.

With my hand covering my mouth as I laughed I said, "Sorry, sorry, once it starts I just have to follow it til it's done."

Bran carried a tray with a pitcher of iced tea and two glassed and set it on the table between the two of us. After she set the drinks down, she took a soft, beautifully knit afghan with a braided pattern running up and down out of Grayson's hands. The colors were all different hues of blues bleeding into themselves. It was gorgeous."Us ladies are fine right here for a while. Could you please chop some wood in the back and bring it up to fill my storage chest?" Bran asked.

On the end of Bran's covered deck stood a massive box I assumed she kept her chopped wood in.

"My grandniece usually does that particular chore for me, but since I haven't seen her I've run out. With my great-grandnephew here it's hard to get everything done during the day, and I don't like leaving him in the house alone at night, he gets night terrors. Anyhow, I would be most appreciated if you could help me out, Alpha," Bran added.

"Yes, of course. It would be an honor to do that for you, Bran." Grayson nodded and then took off around the back of the cabin.

I was staring into my ice tea, lost in thought. I looked up and Bran was looking directly at me with the most intense happy smile. Her eyes were glistening with tears.

"I knew, I just knew you would show up one day. Everyone thought I was a silly girl, then a silly woman, and now they all think I'm the crazy old wolf. I can be cantankerous at times, but I just knew, my sweet girl, you were real," she said with obvious rejoice.

"I don't mean to be rude, but I don't think I am who you or anyone else thinks I am. It's why I was kicked out of my coven and exiled from my family. I might have some powers that have shown up here and there, but it just reaffirms I'm nothing of power in the supernatural community. I'm just Avery Sinclair, who had a murdering psychopath for a husband, a dead sister who left her sixteen-year-old practicing witch daughter in my care," I explained.

I did not want her thinking I was here to make anything better; not one thing about me helped anyone.

"Child, I see the doubt in your eyes. I dreamt about you when I was very young. I told the elders that our wolves would be saved. I didn't know when it would happen, only that one day a Grand Witch would show up and cross-link herself to a Hyper-Alpha. Once that day came all supers would prosper. Our wolves lost so much in the war. Everyone lost so much in that war. It's okay if you don't believe because I believe enough for all of us," Bran sang.

It seemed that Bran was finished with her hero speech and went back to rocking and sipping her tea. It wasn't terribly cold, but a breeze was blowing which had a slight chill to it. It made me glad for the blanket.

Bran seemed to keep her prolific ideas to herself for the moment. I asked her a few questions about herself. She told me she never met her mate and in turn had no children. She had a brother who lived in a pack down south. His daughter and son-law had passed away leaving a teenager behind. Her brother sent his granddaughter to live with Grayson's pack. She explained her niece was spoiled living with her granddad and in turn had become a teenager who wanted everything and damn the consequences.

Bran explained Sasha was a struggling single mother. She also explained Sasha had a crush on the Alpha and wouldn't let the idea go. I didn't say anything to Bran about her niece attacking me. She hadn't scowled once since I sat down, and I didn't want to set her off. She seemed so happy.

We talked about Teri and how she was doing giving birth to twin pups. She mentioned I would get a chance to meet all the wolves because every birth was a huge celebration, which hadn't happened for quite a while. We sat on the porch for about an hour, me mostly listening, but that was okay with me. What would come out of my mouth would sound like complaining, and this woman who didn't have much family left herself was emanating waves of energy that made me just sit and smile. I took the time to take in the forest surrounding the lake. It wasn't so dense you couldn't maneuver around, but thick enough the wolves who lived here had some resemblance of camouflage, which made them feel safe. Safe was a word that hadn't ever really been in my emotional vocabulary. In the few days I had been in these mountains with Grayson, I had come to understand what safe really felt like. Most people probably always felt that level of safety, but not me, not until this very moment.

"I see something important just ran through your mind," Bran said while watching me.

I squirmed in my seat. "Yeah, I feel safe," I admitted.

"I would say so child. That man there—" Bran she pointed to Grayson who was wheeling a barrel of chopped wood around the side of the house—"would give his life for you. He is the Alpha, but even if he wasn't, he would be strong enough to take care of you. You're his missing' piece of soul. The power of two souls combining creates miracles, and I have been waitin' so many years for this. The universe and I are going to have a long conversation tonight for making me wait so long."

I had seen Grayson come around the corner, and we made immediate eye contact. The smirk on his face made my nipples tingle. For a few seconds I couldn't feel the wet glass of iced tea in my hand. It felt like he was physically touching me. When that feeling happened my eyes got really big which made Grayson's smirk stronger.

I did hear a noise and broke my eye contact with Grayson to look at Bran. With a smile on her face, a lone tear slid down her cheek.

I must have had a concerned look on my face because she quickly wiped her face. "Don't be getting concerned for this old wolf. These are happy tears. Now, you both need to get gone. I have things to do and you being here interrupting me is putting me behind. I won't get my afternoon nap," Bran hissed.

I stood up and put my drink down. I folded the knit throw and handed it to Bran. She pushed my hands away and said, "That's for you, Avery. I had an itch last week to make it. Lords knows I don't need another one. Those aren't my colors, they're yours. I'll see you soon, and any of those wolves give you trouble just tell them they'll have to answer to Branwen; and they'll start acting right," she said as she kissed me on the check and hugged me.

Grayson had unloaded the wheelbarrow and made his way onto the porch.

"I'll send over one of the boys to stack and load the rest. I have to get Avery back to the witches to get her training started. I'll find Sasha and send her to pick up her son. Leroy took a sample of Spencer's blood and should have the result of who his father is soon. I want him living with both parents or at least in cabins next to each other," Grayson explained.

Bran didn't say anything, but she tilted her head to the side. Grayson bowed his.

"Bye, Bran, it was very nice to meet you. I love the blanket. Thank you." I smiled.

"You're welcome girl. We'll be seeing each other soon. Don't let those wolves push you around. I have a feeling you could kick some serious butt," she insisted.

Grayson guided me back to the four-wheeler took my blanket from me to store in the saddle bags and helped me put all my gear back on which I thought was super sweet.

"Everyone seemed so nice," I said as I was putting my gear back on again after several visits with pack members.

"The ones you've met are nice," he grinned.

"So, not all of them are nice?" I asked.

"Are all people nice?" he asked.

I stuck my tongue out at him and then climbed up behind him. "We have a wide variety of personality in our pack, as I'm sure there was at the coven. You have a lot to adjust to and I thought if I could show you the easiest part of our family you might not want run away," he said.

"I have a feeling you would come after me if I tried to run away." I smirked.

"You bet your ass I would, now hold on, I'm going to try to make good time back to the main house. I want to show you something before I lose my time with you," he said then patted my leg and off we shot.

The drive back felt like minutes when in reality it took longer than that. I was bummed out when I saw Grayson's house come into view.

Grayson drove around the house and past the garage and kept driving down toward the lake. At one point I might have squealed which made Grayson chuckle. He parked almost next to the shore and helped me off the ATV.

Once I took my gear off, I was in awe of the view. From our standpoint, we could see most of the cabins nestled in the woods around the lake. The water shimmered and so clear, you could see the rocky bottom. There was a dock to the left that went out about ten feet with a boat tide at the end. On the right was a place where stone stadium seating was ringed with a fire pit in the middle.

As I was enjoying the view and feeling content my mind was free of thought. I just stood soaking up the beauty. Grayson came up behind me and wrapped his arms around my middle and put his chin on the top of my head.

Geez he is a big guy.

We didn't talk the entire time, just stood and absorbed all of it together.

"As much as I would love to continue this, you have training and I have things that can't be ignored," he said as we walked back to the ATV.

When we arrived at the garage, Delphine, Aurora and Rosie were all waiting for us. Delphine looked annoyed, while Aurora and Rosie were in a discussion you could tell they were both enjoying. Grayson helped me out of my gear for the last time and walked me over to the group.

"She needs to eat before you start her training. I had packed lunch, but we didn't get a chance to eat it, so food before training," Grayson commanded.

Grayson turned me to him.

"And I'll see you at dinner," he said before he leaned down and softly kissed me. It was just a peck, but he lingered for a few seconds. I was so into I hadn't opened my eyes when he pulled back. When I finally opened them, he was walking away laughing.

I started to get upset when Aurora came bounding over to me clapping. "He is so sweet. You should have seen your face." I finally turned my brain back on and got a little embarrassed that I had done that in front of everyone.

"Don't be embarrassed. You two are soul mates. Soul mates are supposed to kiss," she explained.

"Do you need another lesson on privacy, girl?" Delphine spat.

I could see Aurora's teenage brain getting ready to start something with Delphine, and I was still on my energy high from today, and I wanted to keep it for a few more minutes.

"Okay, until I've had some food no one is allowed to say anything upsetting to me or anyone else. No one wants to see what happens when I get hangry. I need food like yesterday," I said and walked into the house.

"No need to worry, Sebastian has been working all morning on lunch. Just head to the dining room," Rosie announced.

As soon as I opened the door, a small ball hit my calf and climbed up my entire body all the way to my shoulder with claws digging in all the way.

"Ow, fuck that hurts," I said in pain as I dug kitty's claws out of the skin on my neck. I could see blood spots welling up on my skin and feel the burn of the claw marks on my legs, stomach, and chest.

I put her right in from on my face and scolded, "Not okay, kitty.

You either need me to cut your claws down or you need to learn to fly," I said with a smile. She decided to meow loudly in protest. I wasn't mad at her. She was so small she can't do much damage. Her purr got louder as I scratched her behind the ears. She kept rubbing her face all over mine. When I made it the dining room and sat down, I set her in my lap hoping she would behave so I could eat.

Delphine sat across from me and asked, "How was your day?"

"It was great. I got to meet several of the pack. They all seem to be a close family," I told her.

"Most supernatural groups are close. It was the only thing that kept them alive during the human wars," Rosie stated as she took her seat at the head of the table. Aurora decided sitting next to me was safer than sitting next to Delphine.

Sebastian brought out broccoli cheese soup followed by BLT's. I love broccoli and paired with cheese and put into a soup, well that just made it better. I was also glad for the warmth. When Sebastian had served everyone, he took his seat next to Rosie. The way they smiled at each other made me happy.

"So Sebastian, if you're a wolf and Rosie's a witch, where are you two going to live?" I asked while trying to figure out how to get that first bite from the sandwich. It was stacked so high. I decided that squishing it down might work.

They both looked at me with blank stares.

"What? You have thought about that, right?" I asked without looking at them. I picked up the sandwich and opened as big as I could and took a bite.

They both turned to each other and started to laugh. I decided not to ask anything else because my sandwich was so good I didn't want to stop eating to talk.

Rosie and Sebastian stopped laughing and they too dug into their food.

We all thanked Sebastian for lunch and us girls all headed back outside with kitty trailing behind us. I stopped to pick her up because she was so little I didn't want her to wander off and be eaten by something bigger then her. We walked for a bit until we came to a clearing that was surrounded by trees.

"I think we need to start with teaching Avery how to block her thoughts. I can imagine the rage she feels when Aurora pokes around in there," Delphine said while pulling a blanket out of her bag slung across her chest.

The blanket was big enough that we could all sit down comfortable and not be touching. I remembered the morning incident in the kitchen, and I didn't want anyone close to me if I were to lose control.

"All right, Avery, this is what I want you to do. Close your eyes and focus only on my voice. I want you to clear all your thoughts. Take slow deep breaths and try to feel your magic. Do you feel anything?" Rosie asked.

I peeked one eye open. "I feel something like a tingle," I said.

Rosie waved her hand at me. "Keep your eyes closed and keep a hold of that feeling. I want you to reach out, touch it, and bring it toward you. Now wrap that around yourself like you would a coat," Rosie instructed.

"Now what?" I asked while I stroked the kitty. She was so soft. I need to come up with a name for her. Can't keep calling her kitty.

"Now, I want you to think about something," Rosie said.

"I thought you wanted me to clear my mind," I asked.

"I did, for the first part. Now I want you to keep a hold of your energy coat, and I want you to think about something, anything really," Rosie said.

I took a deep breath and felt that energy, keeping it wrapped around myself as much as I could and then began to think of something. Nothing was coming to mind. All of the things I wanted to think about were things I didn't want to think about.

"Not all things that have happened have been bad. I get to be a part of your life, and you met your soul mate. Those are pretty important and cool things," Aurora beamed.

"Good, good, now I want you to imagine your coat or energy covering you; encompassing all of you not just what a coat would cover but your whole body. Once you've done that, think of something specific so we know it's working," Rosie said.

I imagined myself grabbing that energy which almost felt like a warm pulse and I imagined a blanket wrapping me completely from head to toe. I started to get sleepy. My sleepiness could have also been because I was a pig at lunch and ate everything, hoping for dessert that never came.

"Aurora, did you get anything?" Rosie asked.

With a smile, Aurora said, "Nope, not a thing. I can tell she's there, and I can feel her energy but I can't hear anything she's thinking. Glad that wasn't so hard."

"What do you feel?" Rosie asked me.

"It almost felt like someone was running a hand over the blanket," I said.

"That was Aurora trying to read your mind. We all learned how to use our magic to protect our minds at a young age so most of don't use the blanket technique. We learned to recognize that feeling and it became second nature, like breathing," Rosie explained.

"So I have to try and focus all the time to keep this blanket of energy around me? That seems almost impossible. Even talking right now I'm having a hard time keeping it there," I said.

"It's like any muscle in your body. You have to work it out and get it stronger. You might not be able to keep it up all the time, but the more you focus on it when you realize you're not, it will get easier and become stronger. Soon you won't even notice it, it just will always be in place," Delphine remarked.

That was good to know, but I hated working out, so I dreaded trying to work on this blanket of energy.

We were just getting ready to start more training when Sasha walked up to us. It surprised me because I hadn't seen Sasha since North Carolina, and the look on her face told me she wasn't happy to see me either.

"What can we help you with?" Rosie asked her. Sasha didn't even acknowledge Rosie's presence and looked straight at me.

"Grayson asked me to come get you," Sasha snapped.

"What is so important that it can't wait? We've just started her training. We need a few hours at least to even make a dent," Delphine said to Sasha.

"I just follow orders, and I need you to come with me now," Sasha barked.

The hairs on my body were standing on end. I turned my attention to my gut, it was starting to hurt again like it did a few days ago. My attention turned from my thoughts when Aurora started talking.

"I can't imagine the Alpha would send you to get Avery since the last time you saw her you tried to kill her," Aurora piped up.

Sasha swung her glaring look at Aurora.

"If I had tried to kill her she would be dead, now let's go. I don't want to get into trouble because of you." Sasha motioned with her hand for me to follow her. I couldn't imagine Grayson would send her to get me, but I felt safe here so I decided to go. We both had to live with each other so we might as well start to get along.

I stood up and looked down at the girls.

"I guess I'll be back," I told everyone.

"Leave the varmint here," Sasha told me.

I started to pick kitty up off my chest when she started to hiss and spit in protest. I guess she wanted to go with me.

"Kitty stays with me," I told Sasha.

"Fine, let's go," Sasha said. We walked down the road and a four-wheeler was sitting there. Sasha handed me a helmet. "Get on," she barked.

Wow, this chick really doesn't like me.

"Sasha, maybe I should just go back to the girls and you tell Grayson where to find me. I'm not getting a good feeling about this," I told her.

She took a deep breath, "Look, I know you know that I attacked you. I shouldn't have done that. I'm sorry ok. Grayson wants us to get along so I'm willing if you are?"

That feeling in my gut was still there but she seemed to mean what she said.

"Ok," I said hesitantly.

I put my helmet on and climbed on behind her, but not before I unzipped my jacket to place kitty inside. When Sasha took off, I had no choice but to hold on to her waist. If I wasn't mistaken, I could feel her venomous hate for me seeping out of her body.

This ride was different than the one Grayson had taken me on today. Sasha wasn't being careful and didn't care I had a kitten between us. I was beginning to think this wasn't a good idea and that I need to listen to my intuition.

The road we were on didn't look familiar; it seemed Sasha had taken a side road off the main trail that ran through the property. It looked like we were leaving the lake area and going deeper into the woods. I tried to ask Sasha where we were going but she ignored me or maybe she couldn't hear me.

Kitty was getting agitated, but I couldn't tell if it was because she was squished inside my jacket or she was sensitive to my feelings. I didn't have a good feeling about this. I was starting to regret my decision as Sasha started to slow down. She pulled up to a dilapidated cabin; one that didn't seem lived in if the roof was any indication. The A-frame roof sagged in the middle with thick moss covering ninety percent. The few windows were mostly broken out.

Why would Grayson want to meet me here?

Sasha turned off the four-wheeler and jumped down while taking off her gear as she went. I proceeded to do the same, but the feeling in gut tightened with pain. At one point after I got my helmet and goggles off, I had to lean my hand on the seat to steady myself because the pain was intensifying.

"I'm not feeling well. I need to go lie down. Can you just tell Grayson I'll talk to him later?" I said while studying the bike, seeing the keys still hanging from the ignition.

Sasha continued to walk toward the cabin door as I contemplated my next actions.

With a speed that surprised even me, I jumped onto the bike and took off down the trail. Kitty had dug her claws into my chest and started yowling like a dying animal. I couldn't stop to see if she was okay. I had to get away. That's all I knew. I just wished I had turned the bike around to go back the way we had come.

As soon as I jumped on the ATV, I heard Sasha yell something. I didn't hear what she said, but I did hear another four-wheeler start up and race after me. I turned around to see how close Sasha was and realized it was a man chasing me. I whipped back around before I crashed and wondered where I was going and how much fuel this four-wheeler had.

CHAPTER NINETEEN
GRAYSON

I was glad my study was at the back of the house next to the master bedroom. Most people looking for me gave up after checking the front of the house. It gave me some time to sit down and get back to work.

I had just hung up the phone when I heard Rosie, Delphine, and Aurora talking in the kitchen. I couldn't hear Avery's voice though. I walked into the kitchen and looked around.

"Did she ditch you already?" I chuckled.

All three of them whipped around so fast I became instantly hyper alert.

"Why the hell are you asking us where she is? You're the one who sent Sasha to come fetch her when we had just started her training," Delphine yapped.

I froze and my mind halted.

"Um, guys, I don't think that's true," Aurora murmured.

I whipped my phone out and dialed Jackson.

"Where's Sasha?"

I haven't seen her."

"Call Tank and find out when the last time he's seen her."

"Is everything okay?" Jackson asked me.

"No, everything is not okay. Sasha took Avery somewhere. We need to find her. I want everyone on this." I growled as he hung up the phone. The mate sign on my palm was starting to pulse. I reached over with my left hand and placed it on my palm.

"I suggest if you three witches can do a location spell you do it now," I demanded.

"Why don't you tell us what's going on. Is Avery in danger?" Rosie asked me.

"Aren't you the one with a spirit guide who told you Avery was in danger? Why the fuck aren't they letting you know now if she's in danger now?" I yelled.

"Let's stay calm so that we can stay focused," Rosie said as she put her hands up in a pleading gesture. "Spirit can't interfere like that and usually only repeats something I hadn't relayed. And I told Avery she was in danger. We can do a location spell and see if we can find her. I'm sure it's just a misunderstanding," Rosie said.

I just stared at them and couldn't believe this was happening. I looked at all three of them and wanted to blame them, but I knew this was on me. I hadn't dealt with Sasha yet. If she hurt Avery I'm not sure I could stop myself from hurting her.

My phone rang while the girls didn't look up from what they were doing on the island in the kitchen. They had pulled out herbs from the cupboard.

"Talk to me," I ordered. "Send him here right now," I ordered, and hung up.

"Do you ladies need anything from me?" I asked.

They all started to fidget. "Just spit it out. What do you need?" I bit out.

"We need your blood. You have a soul connection to Avery, and even though you two have not consummated the relationship I believe we should be able to track her with what herbs we have here and little blood from you," Rosie stated and Delphine nodded in agreement.

"Let me know when you're ready," I agreed.

While they were working on the location spell, I had stepped outside to shift into my half wolf form. I could have done it in the kitchen, but I didn't want to alarm the women. I needed them to concentrate on what they were doing. When an Alpha is in his wolf form, half or completely, he can communicate with every single one of his pack. The transition flowed easily despite my fear on the forefront of my mind. I did have to concentrate though because getting into the minds of every single pack member could be dangerous. It could be lethal if I took the attention away from a pack member who was doing something crucial.

I took a deep breath and spoke as calmly as I could. "Pack, you're needed. Please stop what you are doing and concentrate," I said.

I had to give my pack a few minutes to stop using any piece of equipment or being involved in something that needed their focus. There were a few in the pack who could handle my orders and keep doing what they were doing, but only the more powerful in the pack. If my focus was off or I used too much Alpha power, I could make any one of them submit in a moment, and if someone was driving I could cause them to crash.

"I need to find Avery. Not all of you have met her yet, but I will send a mental picture for those who haven't. We will find Avery when we find Sasha. Sasha has gone rogue. Avery is my number one priority. I need everyone at the main house. If anyone has direct information I need you to contact Jackson or myself before you take action. Stay sharp and be safe," I said as I slowly cut the connection. Sometimes if you broke the connection too quickly it could cause pain.

Through my link, I felt everyone accept my order and move to make it happen. I took another deep breath and tried to find Sasha's line. I closed my eyes and found her thread. It wasn't very strong which bothered me.

"Sasha, you will bring Avery to me at once. Unharmed," I commanded.

I felt resistance and knew it wouldn't work, but I had to try anyway. I might not like Sasha in the way she desired, but she was pack, family, and I was her alpha.

"Sasha, don't do this. You betray your Alpha and your pack if you harm Avery. You know the punishment if you betray your pack, but if you bring her back unharmed, I will forgive this and we can work toward your place in the pack again. If you want to leave the pack, I understand that too. I will grant you leave to find your happiness, but please don't take her away from me," I pleaded. I was showing weakness but there was no other choice for me. I would beg if I had to.

I could feel Sasha's indecision, but I couldn't get a grasp on her emotions. When I tried to reach out again she shut me out. I had never had this happen before, but I knew that when a pack member isn't aligned with themselves and those of the whole pack, their connection can sever itself or dim. It would make what I would have to do to Sasha easier, easier on myself anyway. Bran was not going to be happy about this.

My phone rang at that moment pulling me out of that thought.

"Talk," I grunted.

"It's Bran. What the hell has Sasha done now?" Bran hissed.

"I'm not sure yet. She took Avery somewhere on the property. The last time she approached Avery was in North Carolina, and she attacked her, ripping her arm open." I took a deep breath. "I know you have Spencer, and I don't expect you to come—," I tried to finish, but Bran cut in.

"I will leave immediately, and I'm bringing Spencer with me," Bran insisted and then hung up. I knew she would come. Every pack member had either a four-wheeler to get around or a vehicle of their own. Bran was old enough she didn't leave pack land, but she had her four-wheeler to get her around the community. It made me sigh with relief that Bran was coming. She might be the only one that could stop me from hurting her niece or be the only one that could get her to bring me Avery.

I went back inside to check on the witches and I didn't get far before Cora was right behind me.

"Alpha," I hear Cora's voice yell from besides me.

"I put trackers on all vehicles a while back. Sasha's four-wheeler is heading away from pack land toward our eastern property line. I tried her phone but she must have shut it off, knowing I could track her. I would start at old man Gus's cabin, which was where it stopped a few minutes ago and then took off east again," she rushed to tell me.

"Thank you, Cora." I grabbed her shoulder and squeezed. She tilted her head and walked off toward the den, probably to keep an eye on the vehicles location. Cora was quiet and kept to herself, but she believed in the pack and would do what she could to find Avery.

With determined strides, I went to the kitchen to find out if the witches had made any progress. I didn't want to jump on my quad and go off blindly in one direction.

"We sort of found her," Aurora explained.

"Explain quickly," I demanded.

"She's moving. We have a general area to search, but it looks like she might be on an ATV moving east," Delphine said.

It was in the same area Cora had said Sasha's ATV had stopped.

"I want you three to send backup once they get here. I'm heading in that direction." I showed them where on the map.

"It looks like she's heading towards the cliffs," I told them.

I walked over to a drawer in the kitchen and pulled out two walkie-talkies and a head set.

"Call me with updates," I told them as I tossed one to Aurora, grabbed my own while putting the headset on, and ran out of the house to jump on my ATV. I hadn't known true fear until this very second, finding the other half of my soul and then to lose her to a jealous wolf. This was all on me, I knew Sasha was getting out of hand but I ignored it. My whole body was shaking with adrenaline. I needed to get myself together so that we both made it back in one piece.

"Please, Goddess, don't let this end before it even begins," I prayed to the Goddess Moon, and I prayed hard.

Chapter Twenty
Ex's

Grayson had showed me a few of the controls on the ATV when we had stopped at one of the pack houses. He did ask me if I wanted to drive it, but I declined, saying I wanted to get home for lunch in one piece. I was thanking the Goddess for at least knowing the simple things on this machine, but I feared I wasn't experienced enough to out run whoever the hell was chasing me. I tried to look behind me a few times, but I was scared I'd run into something so I kept going.

I had decided to go off road, hoping to lose the person who was following me, but I feared I made a bad decision. The terrain was rough, and I had almost fallen off once; also the kitten was distracting. Even if I managed to lose the other ATV, I wouldn't be able to hide. Anyone within a mile could hear the cat. She sure has some lungs on her.

I had no idea where I was going and the ground was getting rocky, making me slow down which allowed the other ATV behind me to catch up. As I looked out ahead of me, it looked like the trees were thinning and I figured out why quickly.

I slammed on the brakes and skidded to a halt about half of a foot away from a ledge. I leaned over the ATV and looked down to a river about thirty feet down. Now what?

I had left my cell phone at the house, not wanting the electrical interference to mess with my training.

Maybe I have enough magic to tap into that would keep me alive until Grayson came, although I still wasn't positive I could do it. I just knew he was coming. I had felt warmth surrounding my palm while I was driving and was hoping it was the connection we had, telling me he was on his way. I just needed to distract the man following me until he got here.

I had just jumped off the ATV and was looking to see if I could climb down the ravine when the other quad stopped, blocking me in. I was surprised when I looked up and Ryan was smiling at me.

The Ryan that was supposed to be dead. The one I mourned a few nights ago. Ryan looked both pissed and pleased at the same time.

I was frozen, frozen from fear, and frozen from disbelief that Grayson didn't kill him. Did he lie to me? He looked like he had been worked over. His left eye was almost swollen shut, and he had multiple cuts on his face, including a split lip. I wanted to feel joy that he wasn't dead. I wasn't sure how I felt about killing people. From what exposure I did have with the coven, I was taught from a young age that all of nature is sacred and human life was included in that.

"I know exactly what you're thinking. I'm supposed to be dead. Good thing you pissed off your lover's girlfriend." Ryan laughed as he looked at his watch.

"It's almost time, and I need you to cooperate fully for me to get my satisfaction from all of this," Ryan said as he waved around at the wilderness.

"You're upset because you had to go into the woods?" I asked him. I was a little confused.

"I thought you were a bright bulb when I saw you working at that coffee shop. I should have listened to my mother when she told me you weren't worthy," he sneered.

Now that was a trigger to get me angry. "Your mother is a judgmental bitch who you have an unhealthy relationship with!" I hissed.

"Watch your mouth," he roared.

"We are so divorcing, immediately," I yelled. "I made a huge mistake when I married you. I take it back," I screamed. At this point, I don't think Ryan cares if I want a divorce so why was I wasting my energy.

"You won't need a divorce because I'll be a widower and you'll be in hell," he roared as he whipped out a knife and charged me.

I didn't even think when I wrapped the wind around him and he froze a few feet in front of me mid-run.

I took a deep breath. "You are a small-minded soul who needs to learn a few lessons. One, I am a witch, and you have no power over me. And two, haven't you ever heard that you shouldn't piss off a woman?" I asked. I waited a minute for a response before I realized that my holding spell was keeping his mouth shut, which made me grin.

"This is how this is going to go. I'm going to wait until Grayson gets here; who I'm sure is already on his way. Then I'm going to turn you over to him because I just can't seem to muster up the guts to kill you myself. You have to know that you and the group you conspire with are not doing 'God's work'. Do you honestly believe your God would want you to kill innocent people because they are different from you? Wouldn't your God want you to love everybody and embrace their differences? Isn't all life precious?" I asked him.

Again, no response, but I knew he couldn't talk which was fine by me. He did have a glare on his frozen face. As I studied his face I wondered if people could really change. Could we ever change Ryan's mind about supernaturals? We just wanted to live our lives as they live theirs.

I heard another ATV coming, and I was praying that it was Grayson and not Sasha. I kept my focus on Ryan because if I looked past him to see who was coming I was worried I'd lose my hold on him. The ATV parked next to Ryan's and Grayson jumped off with Sasha close behind. My fear whipped about so fast at seeing Sasha with Grayson I lost my focus and Ryan continued his momentum forward, grabbing me by the arm and whipping me around, placing the knife at my throat.

My eyes found Grayson's. "I knew you would come." I smiled.

"Always," he replied and then glared at Ryan.

"If you let her go I won't draw out your death," he fumed.

Ryan laughed and while laughing I felt a slight sting and then warmth run down my neck.

That's not good.

"It looks like I have the upper hand here, and I'm so glad you could join us. Your girlfriend was very eager to help me get to Avery," Ryan explained.

"I know all about Sasha's betrayal; she will be dealt with. Your only concern should be your own life and how much pain you want to be in before I snuff you out," Grayson calmly explained while slowly inching forward.

I turned my attention to Sasha. She had her head bowed and hadn't left the side of the ATV. I wondered what her punishment would be.

It looked like Grayson was going to say something when two men in black battle fatigues repelled from the sky on ropes, fitted with enough weapons to take out a village. They both trained their guns on Grayson. I looked up to find out where they came from and saw a silent helicopter hovering above us. How in the hell did I not hear that?

"You better hope they kill me before I can get to you," Grayson growled out.

"Oh, they aren't going to kill you. They're going to take you," Ryan explained.

Take him, why would they do that?

Before I could ask any questions, both men fired at Grayson. Two quick pop noises and I braced for blood but was surprised when Grayson reached up and pulled out two darts from his shirt.

"Those darts have enough sedative in them that even you won't be able to burn through it fast enough. We'll continue this conversation on my turf," Ryan spoke while he took some sort contraption from one of the men.

While Ryan was trying to put me in what looked like a harness, I was watching Grayson. He kept shaking his head, moving forward like his mind was foggy.

I snapped out of my fear and started to focus on my magic when Ryan flung a necklace around my neck.

"Try using magic, it won't work. This was made by a witch, it negates all witch power," he explained while he went back to strapping the harness on me.

True fear made me shudder as I watched Grayson falling to his knees. I looked to Sasha for help but wasn't holding my breath. It didn't help both the men in fatigues were now training their weapons on her. She looked scared and when she looked at me I couldn't help but shake my head at her. I didn't feel bad that she was scared. What did she think would happen?

"You said you just wanted Avery. You didn't say anything about my alpha," Sasha pleaded.

Ryan snapped his focus to her but not before nodding to the man on his right. And just like that Sasha had a tranquilizer dart in her leg as well.

"The only reason I'm not killing you right here is because you helped me, but make no mistake you will all die," Ryan said while he took one of the ropes that were attached to the men and clipped it onto my harness. I decided it was now or never. I pulled my fist back and punched Ryan in the face. I don't recommend ever doing that, it hurts like hell.

He wasn't ready for it and stumbled back a few steps. That felt so good, I might have broken something in my hand, but I realized I wouldn't be able to get another hit in when I was shot in the leg with a dart. I pulled it out and threw it as far as I could into the bushes off to my right. I couldn't think of anything to do at this very moment to help our situation, but maybe they could track us with that dart. I fell to my knees and started to fall forward when I remembered I have the kitten in my coat so I flung myself onto my side and my head bounced off the hard, rocky ground.

"You better hope I never get away from you… pie… pie," I slurred. I wanted to call him a piece of shit but I kept saying pie.

I lay here, watching them connect an unconscious Grayson to a harness, and hoisted him up into the air. I couldn't' move my head so I wasn't able to follow his progress into the sky. Ryan yanked on my cord, and I was being lifted up into the air too. At least I knew I was going in the same direction as Grayson.

My fear of heights should have reared its ugly head, but the chemical they shot into me was working fast. I didn't have control of my body. I felt hands grabbing me and unhooking the harness. They laid me down next to Grayson, and I wanted to cry. He looked so peaceful sleeping and brutally handsome. I knew what was going to come, and I couldn't stop it. Ryan and the two other men finally entered the helicopter.

"How did we not hearrr… hear… the helec…" I slurred out. I was fading fast.

Ryan squatted down and got in my face. "We learned to use the supernatural community for our own purposes. Just like the necklace you have on, we also have witches who can mute sound. We didn't start making headway with eradicating the scum until we realized we could use them against themselves," Ryan praised.

So, that was how we didn't hear it. Kidnapping witches to use them against each other. It was quite brilliant.

Our only hope was that between Rosie, Delphine, and Aurora they would be able to find us, and if they couldn't I didn't think our time on this planet would be much longer. That was the last thought before everything went dark.

"I lost her. She just disappeared," Aurora panicked.

"Grayson, can you hear us? We've lost our tracker on Avery,"

Rosie said into the two-way radio.

Delphine was ignoring both of them and walked out the French doors onto the patio. She continued walking until she stood on the grass and bent down digging her hands into the earth. She stayed that way for several minutes, then stood up and wiped her hands off as much as she could and then walked back into the kitchen.

"She's gone, both of them are. I feel energy at the location they stopped at but not either of their energies. We need to head out there," Delphine stated and then walked through the kitchen toward the front of the house.

Rosie and Aurora followed with worried thoughts.

When they made it to the main room it was packed with people. Delphine had moved through them going straight for Jackson.

"They're both gone. We have to go see the area they were at last. We might be able to see what happened and figure out where they went," Delphine told Jackson.

Several of the pack members heard and started to freak out.

"Everyone needs to stay calm. We will find our people but we need to stay calm and organized. Tank and I are going to drive Delphine, Rosie, and Aurora out where Cora said Grayson stopped, and find out what's going on. Gene you're in charge while I'm gone. I want everyone to gather here. No pack member is left out on their own. We don't know what danger we are facing. I want patrols stationed around the perimeter of the house. We check in every five minutes. Only contact me if necessary," Jackson explained.

"I'm coming with you." Bran pushed through the crowd and stood in front of Jackson.

"I know you're worried about Sasha, but I need you as an elder to stay here and keep everyone calm," Jackson told her.

"Yes, I'm an elder, and I want to go and get firsthand news of what is going on. Don't argue with me because you won't win. I'll be out front waiting for you," Bran commanded and stomped out the front door.

"I'm coming too," Sebastian told Jackson and then walked over to Rosie, held his elbow out to her, and escorted her outside.

"You all have your orders. Everyone who doesn't have something to do find something. Help in the kitchen or with the young," Jackson announced and then lifted his chin to Tank and they both made their way outside.

They took two SUV's and hauled ass east, hoping the witches were wrong and their Alpha and his mate were safe.

No one said anything on the trip, but you could feel the anxiety of what they were about to face.

It took about a little over forty-five minutes to reach where the three ATV's were parked. As soon as the trucks stopped everyone jumped out. Tank was the first to reach Sasha lying unconscious. He put his fingers on her neck, already knowing that she was alive. Shifter hearing.

"She's alive." Tank sighed.

Delphine walked around the area, Rosie and Aurora went to Sasha and tried to wake her up. Rosie put her hand on Sasha's head and closed her eyes. "She's okay, just in a deep sleep," Rosie announced.

"Where the hell did my aunt and Grayson go?" Aurora asked, looking around the area.

"That girl has a lot to explain for when she wakes up," Bran said to everyone.

Jackson followed Delphine as she walked the area around the ATV's. "Are you looking for something specific," Jackson asked her.

"The ground tells me things," she said as she squatted down and dug her hands into the ground. "They were here, I can see their residual energy," Delphine said with her eyes closed. "Wait, something's over there," Delphine pointed to a cluster of bushes.

Jackson walked over to the bushes and started to look through them. He bent down and picked up a dart.

"This must be how they subdued Grayson. I can't imagine anyone getting the drop on them without something like this." Jackson lifted it to his nose and sniffed. "Ketamine, bastards, this stuff is strong," Jackson grunted.

"Try not to touch it too much; we might be able to use that to track them," Delphine explained.

Jackson put it in his pocket and walked back over to Sasha.

"We need her awake, now," Jackson demanded.

"We can't do anything for her out here. If she's been drugged we need specific herbs for a remedy or we need a doctor who can give her something to reverse it," Rosie stood and told Jackson.

Jackson pulled out his phone and called Leroy to tell him what he could and that they would meet him at the main house.

"Tank, help me get her in the truck," Jackson commanded. Tank lifted Sasha into his arms with care, walked over, and placed in her the back seat of the first vehicle. "I'm driving Sasha back. Whoever is riding with me, we're leaving now," Tank stated then moved around the truck.

"Bran, why don't you ride with Tank. Sebastian, do you know how to ride one of these?" Jackson asked, pointing at the ATVs, and

Sebastian nodded. “Rosie, you drive the other vehicle with Delphine and Aurora.

“I can ride one of those,” Delphine piped up.

“Great, that takes care of all the vehicles, let’s move out,” Jackson commanded.

Everyone seemed overly calm, but the energy was swirling with buildup and ready to blow. Everyone knew something torrid had taken place and when they found out what it was, they would deal with it and get their alpha and his mate back. This was what family was about. This was what Avery had been looking for her whole life, and she wasn’t there to feel the love from her new family.

Chapter Twenty-One
Traitor

They all arrived in record time at the main house. The calls had gone out, and most of the pack gathered around the fire pit, and on the covered porch that wrapped around most of the house.

Jackson tried to help Tank carry Sasha inside, but he refused the help. Tank placed her gently on one of the large couches in the main living room. He had to growl at a few people to get them to get up, which they did with quickness. Tank wasn't much of a talker, but people didn't mess with him when he got that way. Leroy just seemed to appear right at Sasha's side as she was laid down.

"Can you wake her up? Grayson and Avery were taken, and we need to know by whom." Jackson walked up next to Leroy.

"It won't take but a few minutes. I'll need the witches on standby to make what I need," Leroy explained as he laid his hands over Sasha's body moving up and down.

After what seemed like hours but really was only a short few minutes Leroy stopped and looked up to the three witches that were anxiously waiting to hear what they needed. "I need—" Leroy started to say and Rosie handed him a pad of paper and pen.

"Write it down. We probably don't have everything here in this house, but I bet Delphine does at her cabin," Rosie said to Leroy.

Leroy wrote down everything he needed and handed it to Delphine who ran off to the kitchen with Rosie and Aurora quick on her heals.

"What do we now? We know she was hit with a ketamine dart. She was the only one at the scene. Did you smell anyone else there?" Leroy asked Jackson.

"That's the weird thing. I only smelled Grayson and Avery but saw many different footprints. There were at least three others. We know we took care of Ryan before he was able to tell anyone where we were, so I have no idea what is going on," Jackson sighed.

"Who was in charge of Ryan?" Leroy asked Jackson.

Jackson looked to Tank. "You helped Gene, right? I'd ask Gene but he's on patrol," Jackson said.

Tank didn't look up or say anything; he just continued to stare at Sasha.

"Tank?" Jackson inquired more forcefully.

Without looking at Jackson, Tank whispered, "I love her. I wanted to give her something she wanted. She told me she wanted to redeem herself to the pack. She just wants to belong."

After hearing Tank's words, Jackson started to realize what happened or at least he thought he knew what happened. Waking Sasha up was more important than ever.

Jackson put his hand on Tank's shoulder. "You can't change who she is, and you certainly can't buy her love. You need to prepare yourself for what she's going to say when she wakes up," Jackson admitted.

Tank turned at looked at Jackson, and his eyes were glowing which meant his wolf was right on the surface.

"Don't even think about fighting me right now," Jackson growled. "I will kick your ass all the way out the door. Finding our alpha and his queen is the most important thing right now. Whatever she tells us, and if it's what you and I both think it is, we need to move fast. Her part in all this will be dealt with later by Grayson. Understand?" Jackson squeezed Tank's shoulder.

Before Tank could respond, the witches rushed back in the room with a cup they took directly to Sasha. Aurora lifted her head while Delphine opened Sasha's mouth and poured the liquid inside. Once just a little bit of the brew reached her system you could tell, she started to wake up.

Once she started to stir, Delphine encouraged Sasha to drink some more. "That's it, just take small sips. Focus on your swallowing," Delphine stated.

While they waited for Sasha to wake up, Jackson gave orders to those who were hanging around waiting to find out the fate of their pack.

"We're going back to the kitchen to do a tracking spell on this dart. It might take a while, but I feel and my spirit guide is telling me that time is of the essence," Rosie told Jackson.

"Yes, do that. Thank you, Rosie," Jackson smiled but he was to worried about his brother and his mate to put feeling behind it.

"I didn't come all this way not to see it through," she smiled back.

Once the witches went back to the kitchen, Tank had taken over helping Sasha drink the brew. It didn't smell good, so Jackson was glad he didn't have to drink it.

"Enough. I've had enough. I'm awake," Sasha said as she opened her eyes.

"Great. Now tell us what the fuck you did," Jackson growled.

Tank turned his head and looked at Jackson.

"Don't even start with me, Tank. She is one hundred percent responsible for what has happened to Grayson and Avery. She will spill all of it now, or I'll have Gene extract the information," Jackson bellowed.

"I'll tell you everything. I…I really fucked up, and I'm so sorry," Sasha said as she started to cry.

Bran walked up to Sasha and smacked her upside the head. "Girl, stop crying and tell us everything."

"I just wanted—" Sasha started to stay.

"We don't care what you wanted. Tell us what happened. We know someone took Grayson and Avery," Jackson demanded.

"Shit, Jackson, she's just barely awake. Give her a minute," Tank yelled.

"Tank, if you can't be impartial go wait outside," Jackson boomed.

"Tank, it's okay," Sasha said and raised her hand to Tanks arm.

"I let Avery's husband go with the understanding he would kill Avery," Sasha admitted.

"You let him go, knowing he's part of an organization that would kill us all. What the fuck were you thinking?" Jackson boomed.

"He promised he wouldn't hurt anyone but Avery. Ever since Grayson met her he's been different. All he thinks about is her. He ignores me because of her," Sasha snapped.

"For fuck's sake, girl, she's his soul mate. If you'd get your head out of your ass you'd see yours sitting right beside you," Rosie snapped from the entrance of the room.

Sasha sucked in a huge breath and looked right at Tank.

"We do not have time for this shit right now. What phone did you let him use?" Jackson asked.

"Mine, but he took it," Sasha whispered.

"Fuck," Jackson belted.

"I got it, I got it," Aurora flew into the room chanting with a map billowing behind her.

"I knew you could do it," Rosie beamed.

"I helped," Delphine chimed.

Aurora laid the map out on the coffee table, and Jackson bent down to see what the witches had found. A line from our property to what looked like Boise.

"That's not where I expected them to be. Why aren't they farther away?" Jackson asked.

Sebastian stepped up. "If I may, from what I've heard from Rosie this group is after supernaturals. If he hasn't traveled far from here then it probably means he's going to kill your alpha and his queen and then come here." Sebastian waited for Jackson to confirm and he nodded. "If their goal is to kill supernaturals then I'm sure they are torturing them to get information about your pack. I would suggest that whoever isn't part of the rescuing party leave this land," Sebastian said.

"Leave? We can't leave," someone piped up from the crowd of people who had gathered in the main living room.

"He's right. They know where we are, and we have no information about them. We don't know how many they are and they seem to have magic on their side. To be able to fly a helicopter onto our property and no one heard a thing. We need to relocate," Jackson stated.

People started to wine while some were angry.

"It's only temporary. We would rather be safe, and when we get Grayson back we will figure this out," Jackson told the room. Gene had slid up next to Jackson.

"Let's call Clay. He would take us in, and I know he has the room in his territory," Gene whispered to Jackson.

Jackson nodded. "That's good, call him and arrange it. I want you in charge of the move. Have everyone take only what they can fit in their cars. Make sure if anyone has camping gear that they bring that as well. I want this done in two hours. Everyone on the road in three," Jackson commanded.

That command cleared out the room quick. Jackson turned to his parents. "Could you pack for Grayson and Avery? Tyler and Trace will pack for me," Jackson asked his mom and dad.

"Of course, son, but what about Grayson and Avery? Who's going after them?" Grant asked his son.

"Myself, Tank, Sebastian, and the witches. Once we scout the place where they're being held, we'll assess then if we need reinforcements. I want every able person to make packing a priority," Jackson said.

"Um, I probably should tell you that I called Kalen. I thought you might need his help since he can read minds," Aurora muttered.

Jackson just stared and then smiled.

"Vampires are fierce warriors, and Kalon is one of the best. I'm glad you called him. How long did he say it would take him to get here?" Jackson asked Aurora.

"He should be here within the hour. I'm glad you're not mad. I would have asked, but with so much going on I just did it," Aurora admitted.

Jackson smiled. "You're showing yourself as one of the pack."

Aurora beamed at Jackson "Thanks."

Rosie stepped forward. "What about Grayson's office. Are there any documents that would help this group find other supernaturals?"

Jackson just stared at Rosie for a moment. "Yes, let's get someone to pack up Grayson's office too. Good thinking." Jackson didn't smile this time because he should have thought about that. He needed to get his head in the game.

Everyone had their orders and moved out. Jackson, Tank, Sebastian, and the witches all piled into the SUV's and took off with the map to find and rescue their alpha and his queen.

Chapter Twenty-Two
Real power

My head was pounding so hard I couldn't open my eyes. My thoughts jumbled, and I couldn't orient myself. I concentrated on my breathing as best I could and kept trying to feel the rest of my body. I started with my toes because the pain was too harsh to start with my head. I felt my toes, wiggled them and then moved on to my feet. I moved onto my legs and then the rest of my body, noting that my arms were secured behind my back. I was sitting in a chair with my arms and legs secured. My chin was resting on my chest. I took another deep breath to orient myself. My skin was cool from the drafts that were blowing from my left side, which meant that someone had taken my coat off. Why did I have a coat on?

My body locked tight when the memory of why I was tied to this chair came back to me. My husband had kidnapped us with intent to murder Grayson and myself. Who marries someone that turns around and decides she needs to be taken off this earth. I did. I made a mistake, but I wasn't going to blame myself. Ryan was obviously mentally ill and hid his secret life well.

I needed to figure out how to save us, because it hit me with clarity that my journey had finally lead me to my soul mate. That truth rocked me so hard I shivered.

"It's nice to feel your soul," Grayson quietly told me.

Hearing his voice filled me with warmth that drowned out the chill that had settled on my arms.

"I can be a little stubborn sometimes," I opened my eye and smiled.

"You don't say?" Grayson grinned.

Sitting about ten feet in front of me on a metal chair with his arms tied behind his back and each leg strapped to the chair legs with chains was Grayson. It looked like they might have worked him over as well. Blood was smeared across his face, around his nose, with a few cuts on the temple. Had someone hit him with rings on their fingers?

Bastards.

"Let's get you fully awake before we get angry. Anger is going to make you act without thought. We're outnumbered and will probably only get one shot at escaping. Just keep focusing on your breathing and try to get the fuzziness out of your body," Grayson whispered.

Right, don't talk loud and let your captures know you're awake, got it.

I took another deep breath and closed my eyes. I could tell the sedative they gave me was still coursing through my body. My mind wasn't working as fast as I knew it could.

A thought occurred to me. What would happen if I could wrap my shield around my body? Would it push the medicine out? I decided to try instead of having a conversation in my mind about it. I looked with my mind's eye and found the my magic how I had earlier when I was training with the girls. I found it with ease. Once I gave it attention it seemed to bloom brighter, and it felt like it was happy to see me, like a puppy when you come home after you being gone all day. I decided to go with those feelings and immerse myself in them, or at least that was what I was imagining. As soon as that happy cloud clicked into place around me, my mind completely cleared of any lingering fuzziness. I was so focused on the feeling I didn't hear when Ryan walked into the room from a door that was behind and off to the left of Grayson.

My eyes flew to meet Ryan's, and what I saw in his eyes scared me. It wasn't helping that he was wearing some creepy black robe with a hood pulled so low I had a hard time meeting his eyes.

Grayson whispered without moving his lips, "Breath, stay calm."

I noticed I heard him like he was whispering in my ear. I quickly looked to Grayson who winked at me. Did he just speak to me in my head? That was a weird feeling.

Why didn't he tell me he could talk to me like this?"We keep are most valued gifts a secret. I can't talk to my wolves like this unless I'm transformed, but I think with us it's because of our soul link. Once you fully excepted it with love you were able to hear me," Grayson said inside my head.

I moved my eyes back to Ryan, not wanting to draw attention to Grayson, and I didn't want to give anything away either.

"I wasn't surprised when this mongrel woke up as fast as he did, but you are a surprise," Ryan sneered.

"Why is that a surprise? You not ready to torture your wife?" I fumed.

"That's not staying calm," Grayson thought but also growled low and deep out loud, which just made Ryan smile.

I looked at Grayson briefly, and then realized Ryan might notice something so I quickly averted my gaze.

"Your life was spared. Why can't you do the same for us?" I asked, trying to buy time. I could feel my magic blanket, but it didn't want to do anything else for me.

"You can try to use your magic, but it won't work and will only drain you of energy faster. You never did listen very well," Ryan added as he went over to a table that was against the wall by the door. The only light in the room was coming from a single bulb hanging from the ceiling. I took a deep breath and smelled forest, moss, dirt, and animal. I realized I didn't have the kitten with me.

Goddess, I prayed Ryan didn't hurt her.

"I had a feeling the alpha wouldn't give me what I want, but I knew you being here might motivate him to give up what I need." Ryan smirked while he went through tools I could barely see laid out on the table.

I swept the room quickly to see what I could see. It looked like we were in some sort of cabin. The room had one door and no windows, which meant we had one escape route leading into the unknown.

How many men did Ryan have with him? Did they have weapons? If they're using witches there could be a perimeter spell trapping us inside the cabin. There was a table along one of the walls with things I couldn't make out laying on top, and a fire burning in a barrel next to that.

Ryan had picked something up from the table and walked over to stand in front of me. He had a pair of scissors in his right hand.

"Are we giving haircuts to each other, 'cause I would like for you to go first. If you untie me I'll give you the best hair cut ever." I smiled at him.

"Funny," Ryan snarled and then gripped my long sleeve shirt from the bottom and cut all the way to my neckline. He did it so fast I flung my head to the side so he didn't poke me in the face.

"Didn't your mom ever teach you scissor safety? Geez," I snapped.

"Let's not provoke him," Grayson thoughts flew into my consciousness, calming be a bit.

Ryan was going to do what he was going to do regardless if I gave him lip or not, so why not have a little fun. If you are going to cause me pain then it was loose lips for me. At least to distract me from what he was going to do.

After Ryan cut my shirt, he walked back over to the table and grabbed two items.

"This can stop any time you want, Grayson. Just answer my questions." Ryan looked at me but was talking to Grayson.

Shit.

I can take it I thought to myself.

I couldn't bring myself to look at what he brought over to me. I closed my eyes and chanted in my head, 'Don't scream, don't scream.' I kept repeating that.

"I want your eyes open, Avery, and if you refuse, I'll just start on your eyes," Ryan whispered. I could feel his breath on my face.

My eyes popped open, and I started into his plain brown eyes.

Ryan took the knife and ran the tip from my belly to the underside of my bra and sliced upwards cutting my bra in half.

"Please, don't do this. Ask your questions, there isn't a reason for this," I pleaded. I wasn't a coward, but I didn't like pain.

Ryan turned around to face Grayson. “How many wolves are in your pack,” Ryan demanded.

“Why don’t you come over here and ask me those questions,” Grayson growled.

“Nope, tried that already. I’m going to hurt your bitch here.” Ryan pointed to me. “So unless you want to hear her screams of pain, and believe me I know how to make her scream,” Ryan beamed.

Ryan turned to me and held up a black handled knife.

“Have you screamed for that dog yet? Does he know that you like a little bit of pain and pleasure at the same time?” Ryan asked while taking his knife and sliding it over the swell of my left breast.. The blade was cold. I felt a sting, looked down, and saw the blood well up and run down my stomach.

That’s when I noticed the necklace Ryan had thrown on me before we left Grayson’s land. A thought occurred to me. This necklace as made by witches so it only seems logical that a witch can use or at least make it powerless. I blocked out the stinging pain and tried to dive into the blue stone that lay on my chest. I wished I had had a little bit of training because I didn’t know what I was doing.

Then I remembered the words that Delphine had said to me. Center yourself, deep breaths slow and easy. I saw in my mind’s eye a glowing spec of magic and tried to draw on it but wasn’t getting anywhere. The magic felt familiar somehow.

“You’re a fucking coward to torture a woman. Let me out of these chains, and we can have some real fun,” Grayson bellowed while struggling to break the chains that held him down.

I could hear Grayson trying to break free, but I knew if they had the amulet to stop me from using magic then Grayson would never get out of his restraints.

"Enough. If you don't want to answer questions, fine." Ryan smirked.

He took the knife and cut me from the top of my shoulder down to my breast. I screamed. The pain was like nothing I had ever felt before. I started retching because my stomach couldn't handle the pain.

"Stop! I'll tell you whatever you want to know. Please, just stop," Grayson shouted.

"Tell me how many wolves are in your pack?" Ryan asked again.

"No," I stammered. "He's going to kill both of us anyway," I mumbled through the pain. I could feel blood running down my chest and pooling under my butt. I wonder how long it takes someone to bleed out.

"Eighty-four, we have eighty-four in our pack. Stop hurting her. I'll tell you whatever you want to know," Grayson begged.

I hated hearing him beg; it broke my heart.

I opened my eyes just as Ryan plunged a white-hot rod against my wound, searing it. The pain was too much, and I blacked out but not before I screamed, "Fuck you."

I don't know how long I was out before I woke spitting water out of my mouth. I opened my eyes to Ryan standing before me with an empty bucket.

"No time for sleeping. We have wolves to kill, and I'm not done having fun yet." Ryan smirked.

"It's all going to be okay, my light, just focus on my voice," Grayson thought to me.

Hearing Grayson in my head dulled some of the pain from the wounds Ryan had inflicted. I wanted to keep my eyes closed and just bask in the feeling of love.

I snapped my eyes open noticed the pain on Grayson's face. He was taking the pain away from me.

"No," I barked.

"Oh yes, we are just getting started," Ryan said. He assumed I was talking to him. I held Grayson's eyes and shook my head. He just smiled at me while trying to make be believe he wasn't in pain.

"If you tell me everything I want to know your death will be quick, but if you make me work for it I'll have to get creative, and believe me, I've been waiting to use some of these," Ryan explained as he waved his hand over the items on the table.

"What do you want to know?" Grayson hissed.

"How many wolf packs are there in total? Where are they located? How many in each pack? Then we'll move onto the other groups, but we'll start with your wolves for now. How many can fight? What kind of weapons do you have?" Ryan turned and asked Grayson.

While Ryan was focused on Grayson, I took another stab at the necklace around my neck. I wasn't going to let him take my pain if I could help it. I found my magic quickly, just hovering there, waiting for me to acknowledge it. I grabbed it and focused on the blue stone once more. I was able to see the magic cords coming out of the stone and wrapped around my body like rope. I focused my attention on one strand, and I was surprised when it touched me it felt like it knew me.

I realized that no magic is bad, which I always assumed since I had no teachers. I had always thought that bad witches did black magic, but this necklace holding me in place wasn't bad or dark magic, it was just magic. Once I understood that I knew I could manipulate it, make it do what I wanted because I had magic too. I took all those strings and imagined myself winding them up and shoving them back into the necklace. As soon as that was done my blanket of magic welled up and around me giving me strength, the pain lessoned a bit, but it was enough for me to have hope.

"If you let Avery go I'll tell you everything you want to know," Grayson stated.

I opened my eyes and had to blink several times because I could see how everything was connected in the room. It was like I could see all the energy flowing through everything in my sight. I had to close my eyes for a few seconds because it was so overwhelming I thought I might throw up. I took a few deep breaths and blew them out as slowly as I could before I opened my eyes again. Things didn't seem as severe as they did a moment ago, but what I did focus on was the chains that held Grayson. I could almost taste the magic. I tried to focus on it but nothing seemed to happen.

"I know you'll tell me everything," I heard Ryan tell Grayson. I wanted to listen, but I needed to get us out of here. I had a feeling Ryan was enjoying what he was doing to me and wanted to inflict more pain.

I opened my eyes and saw Ryan was back at the table filled with torture tools. I shook my head because fear would get in the way of my focus, and I really didn't want to know what other ideas he had for me.

I took a deep breath and concentrated on Grayson's chains once more. The color of the spell that was wrapped around the metal was mossy green mixed with some yellow. I did what had worked with the necklace; I reached for the stings with my own magic and pulled them to myself. The first string I grabbed gave a bit of resistance and then it was like it popped like a balloon and they all flowed from the chains and raced toward me. I got scared at the last minute that I didn't know what to do with the magic once it arrived so I threw it into the necklace.

I closed my eyes and took a deep breath of relief when I heard Grayson yelling, "I said I would tell you, don't do this."

I opened my eyes and Ryan was walking toward me with some iron contraption that must have been sitting in the fire because it was glowing red. It was v-shaped with a horseshoes on either end that were pointed. I couldn't figure out what he was going to do.

"You're wondering what this little gem is? Well, let me tell you. This wonderful device is called the breast ripper. It was used on witches back in the day, and I thought since we have a witch here why not try it out." Ryan smiled.

I closed my eyes and thought to Grayson, "I think I took the magic out of your chains. Kill him." As I got that last thought out, I felt excruciating pain radiating around my breasts. I opened my eyes and saw that Ryan had punctured those red-hot horseshoe pieces under each breast. I felt like I was dying.

I heard Grayson scream, and I forced my eyes open because if Grayson was going to kill Ryan I wanted to watch. I had never been someone who believed in killing people, or even hurting anyone, but Ryan was a sick bastard who needed to die. I saw Grayson bust out of his chains with ease, pieces flying all around. He jumped up and was already partially shifted. Hair had sprouted up all over his body and large fangs sat outside his mouth. Claws ripped out of his hands and feet. The partial shift made him seem like a terrifying beast, but I knew he would never hurt me.

"Never," Grayson thought into my mind. I smiled at him.

Ryan had been startled when Grayson broke out of his chains but didn't get a chance to call for help when Grayson picked Ryan up by his neck, his claws digging into his neck, blood spurting out and running down Grayson's hand.

He spoke with a guttural voice I hadn't heard before. "I wish I had the chance to make your death long and drawn out, but I don't have the time. Know that I will find your entire group of sick fucks and kill them all." I heard the crunch of his snapped neck.

He tossed Ryan toward the torture table and rushed over to me. "This is going to hurt. I'm sorry, but I have to pull it out," Grayson said. "I need you to stay awake for me. If you pass out I don't think I can get us out of here. I don't know how many people he has with him,"

"Do it, quick," I told him. I decided to focus on his animal features. I wanted to reach up and touch him, but I knew that wasn't possible.

"It's okay to scream because whoever is on the other side of that door is expecting it." Grayson opened the tongs and pulled it out of either side of my breasts. I couldn't scream even if I wanted to. I felt myself start to lose consciousness because the pain was so intense so I pulled my magic around me to numb the pain. It worked to keep me awake, but I couldn't say anything for a few minutes. I heard Grayson set the torture device on the floor, and when I opened my eyes I didn't look at it, knowing it would have my flesh and blood on it.

I didn't care that my body was mangled. All I cared about is that Grayson was right there with me.

Grayson untied me, trying not to hurt me with is claws. "I really don't want anything of him touching you but it's all we have." He had taken Ryan's hooded cloak and wrapped it around me then gently pulled me into his arms being careful not to hurt me. I couldn't wrap my arms around him because of the pain, but I rested my forehead on his cheek. He stood there holding me while silent tears slide down my face.

"Those tears better not be for that fucktard," Grayson said gravelly.

I shook my head and whispered back, "Never."

"What can you do with your magic? I might have to put you down to take out whoever's on the other side of this door," Grayson said.

"No, don't leave me. I think I can manage to wrap my magic around both of us. Just don't leave me," I begged him.

"Never." Grayson cupped my cheek with hand.

In all of this violence, hate, and betrayal on both sides I had never felt so loved and secure. This man would die for me and never harm me. He came with a family so large and loyal it made my black heart just fall away. I realized it was what I was missing and what I wanted for all my life. The feeling was so strong I started to wail with tears.

Grayson squeezed me closer to him. "Shhh… It's all okay. We're okay. We're going to be fine. I want to comfort you, but I need you to focus for me. We are stepping into a room we have no information about. I need you to be able to react in an instant. Do you understand?" Grayson whispered into my ear.

I froze and realized I had forgotten we were still in danger. I wiped my eyes on his chest. "Sorry", I groaned.

Grayson didn't say anything, just gave me that panty-dropping smile. The smile that said he found me funny and cute at the same time.

"I think I might be able to tell you how many people are in the room and where. I found the way to see energy lines. Not that I know what that means," I whispered.

"Do it," Grayson snapped.

I frowned at him. "Hey, you're making my happy vibe not so happy."

"Avery, I don't know how long we have before someone checks up on him," Grayson whispered gently.

"Okay," I pursed my lips and closed my eyes. I took a deep breath, reached for my magic blanket, and wrapped it around both of us. It took a minute but once I knew we were protected I opened my eyes and looked at the door. I could see the energy running through the door and around the perimeter of the next room. It moved like a flowing river. All the wood seemed to have its own frequency, which made making out the five people in the next room easy to see with the change in flow. Each person seemed to represent fire.

"I bet this is what seeing through night vision goggles is like," I said aloud.

"Avery, focus," Grayson said.

"Okay, okay. It looks like there are five people in the next room. Three of them are on the left, and I think they're sitting down, maybe at a table. One is right outside this door." I tried to lift my hand, but I winced it pain. I took a deep breath. "The last one is standing over against the far wall.

"What can your magic do for us?" Grayson asked.

"I have no idea. I can manipulate my protective bubble wrapping around us both, but I don't know if it will stop bullets. And if you put me down you won't be protected," I said with a wobbly voice.

"We can do this. I'm going to start with the first person by the door and work my way around the room. If I have to put you down, just keep yourself protected. I'm stronger than you think," Grayson said with a husky voice, which went with his animalistic face. I wanted to reach up and pet his nose. It's width and shape was more wolf, but I could still see Grayson in his eyes.

"Ready?" Grayson frowned.

I could only nod, but I did give him a tentative smile hoping he couldn't hear my thoughts.

Grayson kept one of his arms around my middle, keeping me steady. I was glad he was supporting me because I wasn't sure I could stand on my own.

Grayson threw open the door and swept me with him through it with lightning speed. With his deadly claws, he sliced through the first guys throat with ease; blood flying through the air splattering all over us. I tightened my grip around Grayson's middle despite the pain.

I noticed three people sitting at table on the left with big guns strapped across their chests. I didn't want to test my possible bulletproof bubble I had just learned about in the past twenty-four hours.

Grayson whipped us around passing me to his other arm like jarring me and making me gasp in pain. The guy by the window didn't get a chance to lift is weapon before Grayson sliced through the air right through his neck. I couldn't hold onto Grayson's arm anymore, my strength was spent. I slid to the ground as Grayson moved forward holding the guy by the throat grabbed the gun with the other hand.

I moved my eyes back to the three guys standing around the table pointing their military guns at us, and I screamed in a high-pitched voice, "No." Even as I continued to scream, I watched all three men crumble to the ground.

I looked over at Grayson, and he had one of their guns up and had obviously shot all three of those guys.

"You've got a set of pipes on you. I think I might be deaf," Grayson joked.

"I didn't even hear a gun go off." I looked at him dumbfounded.

"Yeah, like I said, you have got a set of pipes on you," Grayson said and rubbed his ear at the same time. He walked over to me and squatted down to look at me while he changed back to his fully human self. He cupped my cheek. “We did it. We’re okay,” he whispered.

“And all without coffee,” I jested.

Grayson threw his head back and laughed. Goddess, he has a great laugh.

I was so exhausted from the day’s events, my magic wasn’t blanketed around me when I noticed someone standing behind Grayson with a gun touching the back of his head.

“If you move a muscle I will pull the trigger,” an orotund voice said from behind Grayson.

“Put your hands behind your head real slow,” a man dressed in military garbed said.

I didn’t even think as I gathered my magic blanket and tried to throw it around Grayson. I had just gathered the bulk of my magic when a gun went off.

Grayson looked at me and smiled.

“Please, no,” I whispered to him, and I used every bit of strength I could to reach out to him. He grabbed my arms and pulled me into his arms and sat on the floor.

I buried my face in his neck and cried, “We didn’t get a chance to begin and you’re gone,” I belted.

Grayson snuggled me and was rubbing my back when he said, “It wasn’t me.”

I stopped sobbing into his neck and pulled back and looked into his very alive eyes, “What?” I looked around Grayson and saw Jackson was bent over with his hands on his knees taking deep breaths hunched over the guy a very dead bad guy. The front of his face was unrecognizable.

I had to look away. I looked up at Jackson.

"Thank goddess Sebastian was a sniper in the military or this might have gone differently," Jackson strangled out through a labored breath.

"Brother, it's good to see you," Grayson chimed in.

"Good to see you too." Jackson walked around and put his hand on his brother's shoulder. "And you too, sister."

"Can we never do this again, please," I begged.

That comment had both Grayson and Jackson frowning.

"Okay, I can see from your looks that that won't happen, but can we at least get a shower, coffee, and food? That'd be nice. I'm starving," I retorted.

Both men threw their heads back and laughed. Geez these guys were too good looking for normal mortal women.

Grayson stood up with me in his arms, and we started to head out of the cabin and down the stairs.

"Wait, kitty. I haven't seen her since we were taken?." I said frantically to Grayson.

"I'll go in and look for her. I'm sure she hid somewhere," Jackson reassured me. "Head in that direction." Jackson pointed toward the west. "About a mile that way you'll come across the witches and first aid."

"When you're done looking, burn everything," Grayson grunted out.

"Yes, Alpha." Jackson bowed and went past us into the cabin. I was glad he was going to look because I didn't think my stomach could handle all that gore.

Chapter Twenty-Three
Family

Grayson and I didn't talk while he quickly walked through the sparse forest which gave me time to process what just happened. I made such a grave mistake with marrying Ryan. I had wanted so bad to have someone love me I didn't see what he was. How could I have missed that?

"Let's not dwell on what was. It happened, and I'm damn glad it did. If none of this shit had gone down, I would never have found my queen, my other half. The only thing I would change is what he did to you." Grayson looked down at me, meeting my eyes.

Grayson was leaning down to kiss me when we heard, "No time for that, your wee kitty has found something," Rosie yelled.

"Later," Grayson thought and pecked me quick on the mouth.

"Later," I sighed.

Grayson picked up his pace and made his way toward Rosie who had Aurora, Delphine, and Sebastian standing over a circular iron lid in the ground. My kitty was sitting on top of it, yowling loud.

Aurora scooped up kitty and handed her to me. “We can’t get her to stop screaming, maybe you can,” Aurora whined.

I tried to reach for her but the pain radiating through me prevented any movement.

“Just set her on Avery’s lap. She’s hurt pretty badly. Avery needs some first aid,” Grayson barked as he laid me on the ground.

“I beg your pardon, Alpha, but we need to open this lid and retrieve what’s down there,” Rosie spoke up.

“I agree,” Delphine said as she squatted and plunged her hands into the dirt. “I feel witch magic.”

“What if more of those men are hiding down there?” I asked as my kitty was rubbing her body on my hands. I couldn’t lift my arm to pet her, but I moved my fingers and stroked her. She started to purr which was better than the howling.

“Then they’ve breathed their last breath on this earth,” Sebastian grunted.

“Sebastian, you take Tank and find out what’s down there. You three—” Grayson pointed to Rosie, Delphine, and Aurora—“take a look at Avery’s wounds,” Grayson commanded.

“Yes, Alpha.” Sebastian bowed and then nodded to Tank who had appeared next to us.

“You all move like ninjas,” I stated because I hadn’t noticed Tank move.

Everyone just looked at me; I guess no one found their quick movements as awesome as I did. The girls swarmed me and started to go through their supplies to clean and wrap my chest. A few times I thought I heard Rosie curse, which was funny to hear coming from her mouth. They all reassured me that I wasn't dying when I would curse at them from the pain of all their menstruations. Each of them voiced their frustrations at not having everything they needed to speed up the healing. Delphine chimed in that she had contacts in Boise who could give us what we needed.

Sebastian and Tank together turned the wheel that was on top of the metal hatch, which reminded me of a submarine lid.

They got the lid open and started to descend.

"Wait," I yelled. "Don't you guys need flashlights?" I asked.

They both rolled their eyes and ignored me as they descended down a ladder attached on one side.

"Avery, first, and most importantly, let's not yell and let who's ever down there know were coming and second, we're shifters we can see in the dark better than most nocturnal animals," Grayson murmured.

"Right, that makes sense," I smiled.

"You feeling okay?" Grayson asked me.

Before I could respond Sebastian poked his head up through the hole and asked, "We need a witch down here, one that can break magical chains."

"Oh, I can," I chirped. I was feeling a little too happy. It must have been in some of the tonics the girls made me swallow.

"Not you," Grayson snapped. It was my turn to roll my eyes at him.

"I'll go," Delphine said.

Sebastian helped Delphine down the ladder and we all waited to see who was chained down in the dark hole.

Jackson had joined our group, explaining there wasn't anything to save in the cabin, and that he wouldn't start the fire until we were on our way. Which I guess made sense. Though, sitting by a fire sounded

good right about now. I was starting to get cold.

"Kalon is by the vehicles waiting and keeping watch. He says he's going to stay with us for a while. Speaking of staying with us. I evacuated the pack to Clay's territory. I just got word before we arrived that everyone has left for Washington," Jackson told Grayson.

"Good. It's what I would have done. They know where we are, we aren't going to be able to go back until this is done," Grayson replied.

"We need help," Tank barked from down the hole.

Jackson jogged over to the hole, reached down, and pulled up a woman.

"Momma!" Aurora screamed and ran over to help Jackson pull her the rest of the way out of the hole and laid her on the ground. Not that Jackson needed help.

Samantha was barely conscious and very beat up and dirty, but alive.

"Sam," I breathed.

My sister was alive, lying on the ground with Aurora holding her while sobbing.

"Baby, I never thought I would see you again," Sam wobbled out, stroking Aurora's face.

Tank and Sebastian both climbed out of the ground dusting themselves off.

"I know this is supposed to be a family reunion, but we need to get the fuck out of here. Who knows when more of these freaks are going to show up," Tank belted.

"Let's roll," Jackson ran over to the cabin to light it on fire and jogged back to us so we could make our way down the road toward the vehicles.

Sebastian took the initiative and picked up my sister. As we walked, my thoughts were scattered and overwhelming. My sister wasn't dead. She had been captured by these religious fanatics who wanted to wipe out all supernaturals. They had used her to do Goddess knows what. I'm thankful she's alive, but what torturous things did they do to her?

We arrived and all piled in the vehicles. Sebastian climbed into the third row, and Grayson the second. Aurora started to complain that she wanted to be with her mom when Grayson snapped, "We don't have time for seating arrangements. We have a long drive and time is not on our side."

"Right, okay." Aurora sulked her way to the second vehicle.

"You need to be more sensitive, Grayson. She thought her mom was dead," I whispered.

"Now is not the time for feelings. Keeping everyone safe is my first priority. She'll have time when we get to the Tala pack," Grayson reassured me.

"Right, okay. I'm just going to shut up now," I mumbled.

"No, I don't want my queen to shut up. I think it's been a trying few days, if not few weeks, and you're injured, which we still have to deal with. But I always want to hear what you have to say," Grayson chimed.

"Sleep sweetheart. We have a long journey," Grayson murmured to me in my ear.

I wanted to talk to Sam and find out what happened, but I didn't even have the energy to lift my head.

Grayson pulled the cloak over my head and closer around my body, and I enjoyed the warmth of his wolf..

"Alpha, I hate to bring this up because I know the importance of us getting out of this area, but the smell of blood is overwhelming my senses, and I know it's not from the woman I'm holding. Have Avery's wounds been treated?" Sebastian asked.

"The best that can be done right now, but we're stopping in Boise to get more supplies and feed everyone. Sorry, you're just gonna have to suck up the smell," Grayson stated.

Sebastian went quiet and I wondered if he had a hard time taking command from an alpha that isn't his.

Chapter Twenty-Four
New Home

I woke up for about thirty minutes to eat some scrambled eggs, French toast, and hash browns which were hand fed to me by Grayson in a house belonging to one of Delphine's friends, Bluebell, another solitaire witch. She corrected everyone when she was introduced and told us to call her Blue. She seemed like a sweet girl, probably mid-twenties, rocking an azure blue inverted bob.

She turned out to be a healing witch and could do more than my friends, which started a brew ha-ha. Grayson had to put a kibosh on the girls wanting to stay longer. They all had things they wanted to ask Blue and have her show them, but it would have to wait until later. Numbers were exchanged with reassurances that they would be in touch. Grayson was eager to get back on the road, and I didn't blame him.

Blue had given me a tea to drink that had taken a majority of the pain away as well as making me feel like I was floating. She had done a spell and laid her hands on me. She explained I would be left with some scars, and she felt terrible about that. She went on to tell me that I would be sore for a few days but could do all range of motion with time, but to take it easy and go slow.

With all the commotion and activity, I was fading fast from exhaustion. Being able to breathe deep and know that no one was going to show up and try to hurt someone in my family made me feel safe. Sleep was coming, and I didn't think I could stop it. This pack of wolves with a few witches thrown in was my family, and I cared a great deal if anything happened to any of them. I wrapped my hand around her wrist and told her that she had my deepest gratitude.

When my skin touched hers, a light shot up toward the ceiling.

"Well, that's not unusual," Blue said to me as we both just stared at the light. I slowly took my hand off her arm, and then we both looked at an eight-pointed geometric flower the size of quarter on her arm where my hand had been. Blue reached for my right hand and turned it over and there was an identical symbol on my wrist.

Grayson started to growl and the whole house went alert. Everyone gathered around trying to see who the enemy was.

"Alpha, if I may. This is part of the prophecy. You both will bring into your lives the strongest of all our different kinds of beings. They will all be accentual in helping you defeat the enemy," Rosie stated.

"I'm a healer not a fighter. I devote myself to help others," Blue said with a strangled voice.

"There is a war coming, child, and we all need each other to defeat them," Rosie entered the conversation. "That doesn't mean you'll be a soldier. You will be exactly what you were meant to be. A healer. Probably the most powerful one in the world. I have seen many healers, but what you did and how easily it flowed from you I've never seen before. You don't even seem tired, and I've known healers that would pass out for days from healing the types of wounds Avery had. Those matching symbols mean you are important to Avery, therefore you are important to all of us," Rosie told Blue and everyone in the room.

"Jackson, help Blue pack up her car with whatever she needs. Make sure all her affairs are in order. I have no idea how long until she'll be back," Grayson ordered.

"As for the rest of you, let's get packed up and on the road," Grayson barked.

I nudged Blue with my arm, and she looked at me with terrified eyes.

"His bark is bigger than his bite. It's going to be okay. I know it seems strange, but with this symbol showing up I have to think that you need to come with us," I whispered.

Grayson must have heard me because he snapped his teeth at me and then smiled.

Blue took a deep breath and blew it out before saying, "I knew something huge was going to happen to me. I've had a weird feeling in my gut for months. The other weird thing is my job laid me off a few days ago unexpectedly. I don't much care because I was tired of cleaning up vomit and other bodily fluids that people would leave in their hotel rooms. I trust the mother goddess, and if she's giving me a symbol tattooed on my arm then I better listen." Blue giggled.

At least someone found all this funny.

"Grayson, while you supervise the packing I'm going over to talk to my sister," I mumbled.

"You need to rest," he said quietly.

"I will, but I want to see Sam first, then I'll sleep. I promise," I told him. He nodded at me and kissed my forehead, before he went barking orders at people.

Sam had been taken to the back of the house where she and Aurora could have some privacy. I felt somewhat bad for interrupting, but I couldn't help it. I had to see her.

I walked into the room to see Aurora cuddling on the couch with her Mom. You could tell Aurora had been crying, but they both had smiles on their faces.

Sam noticed my presence, looked up, and said softly, "Thank you for keeping my baby safe."

"Of course," I whispered back and smiled.

I went and sat on a foot stool that was close to the couch they were sitting on.

"Sam, I am… I don't… I am so fucking sorry," I cried.

"Sorry? For what?" Sam asked perplexed.

"Ryan had no idea you were a witch. He couldn't have known about Mom. This had nothing to do with you. You just happened to be married to one of the lieutenants," Aurora said. "Bad luck."

I didn't believe in luck, I believe things happened they way they should. At least that's what I was starting to believe.

I hung my head because even though Aurora was right I still somehow felt responsible.

My sister leaned forward to put her hand on my cheek. "Oh, Avee, if anyone is owed an apology it's you. I owe you the biggest I'm sorry ever. I was your sister, I should have protected you. Especially after Mom and Dad died. I let my ego take control of my soul, and for that I'm so sorry. I remember the day you left, and I still feel that stabbing pain of regret that I let you go. That I let those old hags tear our family apart. Can you ever forgive me?"

"I forgave you as soon as I walked away," I said through tears.

Sam grabbed me, pulled me onto the couch, and hugged me so tight I started to feel some pain. "You're my sister, and I've missed you so much, but I might have to punch you in the face if you don't loosen your grip. Blue did a bang-up job of healing me, but I'm still sore," I hissed.

Sam loosened her grip and we both started laughing.

"You know I can still kick your ass," Sam insisted.

"Maybe," I said with a wink.

"Yeah, Mom, there are things you don't know about Auntie. She's not a dud anymore," Aurora beamed.

"I knew she wasn't a dud." Sam smiled.

We all jumped and squeaked when we heard, "Hey, enough of the reunion. We need to head out. Now," Grayson bellowed and walked away.

"He seems like a peach," Sam remarked.

"Actually, he's normally super sweet, but we've had a shitty few days, and his patience has run out. Once we're on his friend's land he'll feel more secure and mellow out. We're like targets out here with no back up," I told her.

"Let's not piss him off more," Sam said and slowly got up from the couch.

"Ride with Bell and see if she can do some healing on you. You seem like you're sore too," I told her.

"Aye, Aye, Captain," Sam saluted me, and we all went off to get loaded up.

I had missed my sister's attitude and was excited I had the opportunity to fix our bond that had once been so strong.

While we were driving out of town, I noticed a sign that said free horses. It took forever for my begging to take effect with Grayson, but he pulled off and called about the free horses. The people said they couldn't afford to take care of the horses anymore and they would even give us the trailers if we could take all four horses.

"So we have now almost two hundred people, one dog, and you want to add four horses to that, with no home?" Grayson asked me.

"There important to us, I just have a gut feeling. You have to trust me," I told him.

"Home is wherever we are together," I proclaimed.

So we showed up at Clay's house with four cars, a shit ton of people, and four horses I couldn't wait to get to ride.

On the way to Clay's, Grayson had explained that most packs owned many acres to house the number of wolves. Wolves could feel claustrophobic if they didn't get to roam when they wanted to. Clay's property was in Snohomish County at the base of the Cascade Mountains. He also explained this would be our new home for the foreseeable future. We couldn't go back to Idaho until this threat was eliminated.

It was a cluster fuck when we arrived. Bella came running out of Clay's house hell-bent on seeing Aurora. Aurora cried and told Bella she would never leave her again.

Clay didn't seem surprised that we had two horse trailers with us. He simply told Grayson he had stables for them on his property. See, I knew taking those horses was the right move.

I was surprised and charmed by Clay's house. It was a small

artisan's home with a wraparound porch. His house wasn't the size of Grayson's so we couldn't all convene inside, but he said he had a pack lodge where we could all sit down, eat, and talk about the future.

The lodge was a short walk away. Clay explained that his pack was much smaller than Grayson's, but when he was building this lodge he had an uncontrollable urge to build it bigger than necessary at the time. "It all makes sense now. Most of my pack thought I was crazy to build it this big, but I ignored them and did was I was feeling. Fate's a fickle fucker," Clay told Grayson and I as we sat.

Jackson had called Clay so he knew when we'd show up, and food and drink were waiting. The sandwiches were divine and there was even chocolate cake. I had counted the cakes on our way in and realized that I might have to fight to get my slice.

"You never have to fight to get your chocolate," Grayson whispered in my ear.

"Is that a promise?" I asked back.

Grayson didn't answer, just laughed. He decided to cut me a slice of cake first and handed it to me. I take that as a yes.

When everyone was done eating, Grayson stood up and spoke to his family. "We made it, whole and with extra family to add to our pack. Life will be different for a while, but I promise you we will make it work. Our pack has always lived frugally and because of that we have enough to last years and be comfortable, so I don't want anyone worrying. And any of you who have concerns please bring them to me, and we'll work it out together. I want everyone to welcome Bluebell—" Grayson looked to Blue for her last name.

"Frost. My name is Blue Frost," Blue wheezed out. She seemed very overwhelmed.

"Blue is now part of our pack, and I want everyone to welcome her. She also is a healer so keep that in mind. We also have a vampire named Kalon who will be spending time with us for the foreseeable future as well as Rosie and her mate, Sebastian. Others will show up, and we will welcome them as well. I don't know how long this threat will last, but we will defeat them and return to our homes in Idaho. Once everyone is done, I want you to wait around for housing assignments and other instructions that will come." Grayson raised his glass and sat back down.

"Where is everyone going to live," I asked Grayson.

"We have a dozen cabins empty and land enough to build what we'll need." Clay answered my question. "It looks like most people brought tents and the like so it won't be too bad. Plus, we have this lodge people can sleep in too if the weather gets bad." He turns to Grayson, his face solemn. "I talked to Alistair. He's on his way here. I filled him in on what's been happening."

"Why don't I show Grayson and Avery to their cabin so they can get comfortable?" Claire asked.

"Right, yes, thank you," Clay told his beta.

I almost looked around for Aurora, but realized I wasn't her guardian anymore. There was a small feeling of sadness but also happiness that she had what I could never give her, her mom back. I didn't have a teenager to look after anymore, but I did have a kitten who was curled up asleep in my inside pocket of my parka.

We climbed into one of the SUV's while Claire rode in the back, guiding Grayson to the location. It was several miles from the lodge and deep in the woods. The woods were thicker here with more evergreens and ferns. we pulled up to a small cabin with a two-car carport next to it. We exited the car and followed her inside, which blew my mind. We walked into a living room with a smaller couch and chair facing a stone fireplace and huge wood mantel; the space was small but homely. The kitchen was open to the rest of the house and had wooden butcher-block counter tops with black appliances. It was small but more than I had anticipated.

"There's a powder room and office down on this floor. The master is upstairs with a full bathroom as well as an extra bedroom. We stocked the fridge so you should be all good. We have landlines in all the cabins. Next to the phone is a list of all the cabin numbers on the property and phone numbers to go with them. Let me know if you need anything," Claire said as she moved toward the front door.

"I do need some supplies for my kitten," I told her.

She nodded. "Right. I'll get someone to take care of that. Shouldn't be too long."

"Just leave it on the porch," Grayson said as he carefully took off my jacket which held the sleeping kitten. He laid the jacket on the sofa, being careful, knowing kitty was in my pocket.

"Now what?" I asked as I watched Claire walk out and shut the door.

"Now, I get to worship you," Grayson said as he advanced on me.

I tried backing up, but he was on me too quick. He flung me over his shoulder and he ran up the stairs, taking them two at a time, not even breathing hard.

"Grayson," I laughed. It was hard to talk with all the air being bounced out of my stomach.

Once at the top of the stairs he entered the room on the left. This must be the master because it had an en suite bathroom. He threw me on the bed, and before I could finish the bounce he was on me.

"Glad I had a healer get to me before you did. Geez," I wheezed. Grayson was a big man; he wasn't squishing me, but he was definitely heavy.

"Shit, Avery, I forgot you were hurt for a minute." Grayson started to get off me. "Maybe we should give you a few more days before we do this."

"Wait." I grabbed his arms and pulled him back down.

"Before we do what?" I asked with a husky voice.

"Well, first I'm going to take off these clothes." Grayson sat up to straddle my waist, pushing my shirt up as he went. Once he got my shirt off, he started to unwrap my bandages.

I put my hand on his to stop him. I had never been shy about my body, but I had watched while Blue had tended to my wounds; they weren't pretty. On each side of my breasts were huge, ugly puncture marks, not including the scar that ran from my shoulder down to one of my nipples.

"You haven't been around wolves long enough to know we don't treat nakedness like others do. We have to be naked to shift, and we go on runs together several times a month. We also view scars as a sign of strength. These scars—" he said as he took his finger and lightly traced them all—"show that you survived. You were brave, my little queen. Don't think I didn't notice when you took back your power, and I wasn't able to help with the pain anymore. Don't ever do that again," Grayson commanded.

"Don't tell me what to do Gray, it was my pain to take back. If you think I was going to sit by and watch you hurt when I could stop it, think again," I hissed at him.

"So angry, let's see if we can change that attitude," Grayson said as he leaned down and sucked one of my nipples in his mouth.

I could feel it all the way to my pussy.

"Oh, goddess, don't stop," I begged.

"Never," Grayson murmured as he switched nipples. I wrapped my arms around his back and dug my nails into him, needing more.

Grayson started grinding against me, and I could feel his cock rubbing on my entrance. I felt ready to come and I still had my pants on.

Grayson must have heard me because he scooted down, and while watching me he unbuttoned my jeans and slide them down my legs. He realized he had to get my boots off first so he stood up and took each boot and sock off, dropping them to the ground. He finished taking the rest of my clothes off. I was completely naked and exposed, and I loved it.

Still keeping eye contact with me, Grayson slowly unbuttoned his own jeans and slid them down his legs, tossing them to the side. It gave me a great view of his cock, but I was a little scared it wouldn't fit.

"It'll fit," he smiled and climbed back on the bed, grabbing my knees and pushing them open to make room for himself.

"See I told you, you can read minds," I told him while I explored his smooth defined chest with my hands.

"Only you, and only because our souls are linked together," Grayson whispered into my ear and then started to kiss and bite his way down my neck. I never knew the curve of my neck was such an erogenous zone.

The fire was building in my body, and I felt ready to explode. His hands were stroking my ribs and down my hips. I lifted my hips up to ask for more. Grayson's hand made its way down to my leg, which caused goose bumps to appear over my entire body.

I noticed some scars on his chest I wanted to ask him about, but every time my mind would start to wander, he would bring me right back to where we were and what we were doing.

I tried reaching for his cock to line it up, but I was thwarted when he grabbed both my wrists and brought them up over my head.

"Patience, little witch," Grayson grunted while staring at me with a look I had never seen from him.

"Little witch? I thought I was your little queen?" I giggled.

Grayson face lit up with a huge smile. "I love to see you laugh."

He came down and took my mouth with a fierceness that made me forget about anything but him and what he was doing. Our tongues were exploring each other, and I could feel the love radiating from both of us, our souls were linked.

He pulled away from my mouth but not before he grabbed my bottom lip and sucked. "Our souls are connected and after today they will be forever."

Grayson released my wrists and brought his hands down, slowly exploring my breasts and tugging on each nipple with enough pressure it was almost painful, but as soon as I thought this he went on to explore my stomach, and down further until he reached my pussy.

"I think I need a taste first," was all Grayson said before he moved down and went at me like he was a starving man and I was his lifeline. I knew I was wet before he started. He sucked my clit into his mouth, causing me to nearly buck him off the bed. "No more, I can't take anymore," I exclaimed.

Grayson gave it one last lick before he moved back up and kissed me again. I could taste myself and I liked it, it turned me on to know what I tasted like.

When I thought the sensations were going to overwhelm me so much that I couldn't breathe, he lined up and pushed in slow and steady.

"Yes," I wheezed and grabbed his back with all I had.

When he was fully seated inside of me, he took one hand and rang his thumb across my face.

"Do you feel it?" he asked me.

"Are you not paying attention?" I breathed. I almost said something else, but Grayson started moving and with each thrust I felt like my soul was leaving my body with a tugging sensation.

Before I could ask him to pick up speed, he did. Our bodies seemed to dance together. It didn't take long before I came so hard and fast I screamed his name.

"Open your eyes," he demanded while an orgasm more powerful than anything I've ever felt before flowed through my body.

I did, I opened my eyes, and I was in awe of what I was looking at. Streams of colors where intertwining with each other all around us. The glare was so bright it was hard to keep my eyes open, but I didn't want to close them and miss something.

I had a huge desire to look into Grayson's eyes, so I did, and it was as if his eyes were a mirror. I could see the rainbow of colors playing together in his eyes.

"Are my eyes doing the same thing?" I asked him.

"Yeah, and it's beautiful just like you," Grayson grunted right before he peppered me with soft tender kisses as he came inside me.

I thought we might be done when Grayson picked me up and carried me to the bathroom. He sat me on the cold counter top and walked over to the claw foot tub and started running a bath. Once started, he came over, pushed between my legs, and kissed me long and hard.

"I dreamt about you," I blurted. As soon as it came out of my mouth, I regretted it. It sounded so corny.

Grayson leaned back from me with a blank expression.

"Yeah? And what did you dream?" he asked straight-faced.

"We were usually running in wolf form. Sometimes I was a wolf and sometimes I was just me," I whispered.

"I don't ever remember my dreams, but I bet if I did they would be similar. These marks on our hands mean we were fated to be together." Grayson leaned in and continued on a whisper, "I like that you dreamt about me."

Once the bath was full, he picked me up and stepped into the bath with me in his arms. He took care to wash all of me including my hair.

When he was done washing my hair, I was about to stand up but he had other ideas. He turned me so my back was to him and proceeded to penetrate me. The water kept splashing over the edge but I didn't care. At one point I grabbed onto the edge of the tub so I could get more leverage. I could feel my orgasm building when Grayson reached around with his hand and played with my clit to push me over the edge, coming so hard I bit my tongue. We collapsed back against the tub, catching our breaths and just soaking in the feelings we were both having.

After cleaning ourselves up and drying off, we crawled back into bed and cuddled for a while until he ran downstairs to get us some food. I tried to get out of bed and help, but he shook his head and commenced bringing us food.

The level of intimacy that had been happening had never happened to me in my adult life, and it was so fucking awesome I embraced it. We lay in bed, munched on food, and just enjoyed being with each other.

It felt like a few hours of us cuddling when I heard a howl from hell.

“Oh, my Goddess. Is that how she’s going to communicate with us? I will go to the ends of the earth to find a spell to keep her quiet,” I snarled.

I looked at Grayson because he hadn’t said anything, and I wondered if he’d make her sleep outside. He smiled so big I could make out the lines around his shimmering blue eyes.

“What? How are you going to feel when she does that in the middle of the night?” I exclaimed.

“She’s a baby. All babies need extra attention for a while. I can see I’ll be dealing with the cubs at night,” Grayson declared.

I frowned and then froze.

“Cubs?” I said in a high-pitched voice.

The smile died from Grayson’s face, and for a brief moment I couldn’t read his expression.

Grayson sprung up, went over to his bag, and pulled out some athletic pants. I didn’t want him to put pants on because I enjoyed watching his backside. His muscle definition on his thighs and his round behind were yummy. He slid them up his legs commando. He came back over to the bed, pulled the covers up and around me, bent down and kissed me quick but soft.

“We’re new so we’ll not talk about pups just yet. Okay?” Grayson asked while holding my gaze.

“Yeah, okay,” I whispered.

"I'll go see if they brought supplies for kitty and get her squared away. Hungry? I could bring us another snack," Grayson asked.

"Sure." I smirked as Grayson left the room, but not before looking over his shoulder and winking at me.

I listened to Grayson make his way downstairs while cooing at Kitty. I really needed to come up with a good, solid name for her, something that would sound nice when I yelled at her. I wonder if Grayson understood she would be sleeping in our bed every night. I might have to go out and get a pillow for her.

"No pillow," Grayson yelled from downstairs.

I ignored his comment because it wasn't as if anybody would stop me from buying her a pillow. If I thought she needed her own bed I would buy her a bed because my life was my own again. I had a mate that only wanted me to be happy. That he loved me for everything I was and would ever be. The coming war didn't bring good feelings, but I decided I would focus on this present moment, and right now I felt wonderful.

This is Not the end of Avery and Grayson's story. The battle is just beginning. The next book in the series is Sam and Iric's story with appearances from all the family. I hope you enjoyed this as much as I do. I would love it if you could leave a review. Reviews help new authors get noticed and move up in the millions of books.

Rushell Ann is the author of the Cross Linked series, an ongoing paranormal romance saga full of spicy and a bit of sassy. When Rushell's not writing she can be found soaring through the clouds on her magic carpet, reading her favorite author's new releases. When her head isn't in the clouds, she's cooking up smashing dishes with the help of her live-in fairy sprite who doesn't enjoy doing dishes. Wrangling her slipper away from the new puppy or just binge watching Netflix with her family keep her happy along with planning out new and exciting stories that float through her head on a daily basis.

Rushellann@outlook.com

https://facebook.com/rushellann

https://instagram.com/rushell_ann

Made in the USA
Middletown, DE
13 May 2022